Her Protector

D. E. Bartley

Copyright © 2022 D. E. Bartley

All rights reserved.

The characters and events portrayed in this book are fictitious. Any similarity to real persons, living or dead, is coincidental and not intended by the author. No part of this book may be reproduced, or stored in a retrieval system, or transmitted in any form or by any means, electronic, mechanical, photocopying, recording, or otherwise, without express written permission of the publisher.

ISBN: 9798843129088

Cover design by: Roni London

DEDICATION

To all the amazing readers that have made my dream come true!

To my amazing friend Karen, you know who you are, and I hope you know how much I appreciate everything you do. x

Also by, D. E. Bartley

BLOOD MOON SERIES

ROGUE

HER PROTECTOR

CORNISH LIFESAVERS SERIES

BENEATH THE SURFACE

Her Protector

D. E. Bartley

Prologue

What the fuck was I thinking? Why did I think trying to scare Daisy by pretending to be Jackson would be a good idea? Never in a million years did I expect her to head back to Exeter. I was sure she'd run back to her family in Cornwall.

I should have known the whole plan would go wrong. Everything I've ever done to protect that girl has gone to pot. At least, it seems that she's gotten away, for now. He might be a moron, but Michael should have found her by now and will keep her reasonably safe. At least she's not here with me tied to a chair in the middle of a room, beaten and starved.

I have no idea how long I've been here. There are no clocks or windows to see whether it's day or night. I'm sure I'd be dead by now if I were human. My brother has made it abundantly clear that I'll stay here until I agree to work for him. He doesn't realise I've been conjuring some plans of my own. He's mistaken if he thinks I'll let him hurt her again.

"Have you come to your senses yet?" I turn slowly to my brother's monotonous voice as he strolls into the room.

"I give up. You win." I whisper as I force a cough from my dry throat. Time to play the role of the pathetic weak brother, who has barely a brain cell in his thick skull. It's an act I've played for years, hoping to hide the truth from him.

"I'll do whatever you want. Just untie me from this fucking chair, and please, give me something to eat and drink." I whine. My brother turns to face me with that evil look he gets in his eyes when he thinks he has broken somebody. I've always hated that look. He would get it after each beating he issued to Daisy when he held her captive. I was too scared and weak to help her then, but I now know how to beat him at his games. I've become stronger for this moment.

"Have you finally come to your senses, little brother? I have to give it to you; you took longer to break than I thought you would." Jackson squats in front of me so he can look me in the eye. "But why should I believe you've finally seen sense? How do I know you won't just disappear as soon as I release you?"

"Tell me what you want me to do, and I'll do it. I don't have the energy to fight you anymore; you win. Like you always do." I answer, trying to appear as submissive as possible.

"Of course, I always win. Because I never give up on what I want."

"Answer me one thing. Why her? Why has it got to be Daisy?" I ask; Jackson looks at me and frowns.

"Does it matter?"

"Of course, it matters. Why go through all this trouble for one girl?"

"Because I know how powerful she can be. With her by my side, I would never lose. My pack would be unbeatable. Her magic makes her the most powerful luna in this sad, pathetic world. Together we could achieve amazing things." Jackson states, grinning.

"How do you plan on getting her to leave the mate?" I ask, digging for information.

"That won't be hard. The mate bond isn't as strong as they make out it is. If it were, I wouldn't have been able to kill mine so easily." Jackson shrugs. Maybe he's right, and the bond isn't that strong.

"Seems ironic that it had to be Adams your luna would be mated to." I point out. I watch that evil grin spread over his face again.

"The fates have had their fun with this one." Jackson chuckles before turning to face me. "You never told me, little brother. Why do *you* want the girl so bad? Since I picked her up, you've made it your mission to stay close to her. You hid her from me and followed her around like the lost sheep you are."

I look up at my brother and sigh whilst letting my head drop.

"Mother once told me I would meet someone I would fall in love with, but another would want her. She said I would have to fight for her, that love wouldn't be enough to keep her." I take a deep breath before looking up at my brother. "I guess she was right because even when I was right there in front of Daisy giving her everything she wanted, she didn't even look at me that way. I was always in the 'friend zone', as they call it these days. Even the fucking fire demon got closer to her than I did. You win. I give up."

Jackson walks over to me and places his hand on my bruised shoulder.

"Welcome to the world of women, little brother, even those fated to love you don't. Look at my mate, she was beautiful and strong, but she already belonged to another. She had the nerve to reject me for someone else." Jackson growls.

"So you made sure that if you couldn't have her, then neither could he," I whisper, knowing this story like the back of my hand; I've listened to it so many times in the last few years. Jackson winks at me as he smirks. It takes all my effort not to roll my eyes at him. I feel him untying my hands at the back of the chair. I know there are cameras in here, so I have to appear as the obedient little brother he loves to push around.

"So how do I know you won't try and double-cross me? What can you give me to ensure that you stay on my side and don't run off with Daisy once I have her?" Jackson asks.

"I'll perform a blood oath to stay by your side and do as you ask until you get Daisy back. I'll stay until you have her safely in your den and hidden from Adams." I answer as I run my now released aching hands through my dark brown hair, which has been irritating my eyes for ages.

"I'll agree to that," Jackson says as he pulls an army knife out of his pocket and flips it open, he cuts his palm and then holds the knife out to me.

"Last chance to back out, Brother. Will you help me get Daisy back, no matter how difficult it is?" I look at the knife in his hand and nod as I take it to slice open my own. I hold my bleeding hand out to him, and he takes it in his as we shake to seal the deal.

"I swear it."

Chapter One

Michael

"Hey Mikey, you getting close?" Carl calls through the car hands-free. I hear music in the background and know he'll be sitting in his usual place by the bar in "The Crow", which he owns with his fated mate Richard.

"Yeah, I'll be five minutes tops. Does Daisy know I'm on my way yet?"

"Nope, she's still oblivious. I'm warning you, though; she's been on the gin again tonight." Carl chuckles.

"I never dreamt she'd stay away from it." I laugh.

"That's okay then; give the door a knock when you get here, and I'll let you in. We've been keeping it locked and 'members only'." What he means is pack wolves only, with the exemption of one fire demon they employ to work the bar, who also happens to be Daisy's best friend, Tony Simons.

"Thanks, Carl, I owe you. See you in a few." I reply, smiling as I end the call.

It's been the longest three days away from Daisy, my mate. I hate it when we're apart. I feel like I'm missing part of my soul. I wouldn't have left her if it wasn't essential.

Almost two weeks ago, Daisy had fled back to her old home in Exeter in the middle of the night. She feared somebody from her past had tracked her down and threatened her new life here in North Wales. She had no plans to return when she ran, so she'd taken all her belongings. Once in Exeter, she'd ditched everything, including her car and travelled to a safe house where her family live, down in Cornwall. That was where I tracked her down and made her realise that Jackson, the guy she was running from, had not found her, that it was someone pretending to be him.

That someone had been Kellan Cole. A guy from Daisy's university class. It seems Kellan intended to scare her away from me so he'd have her to himself. We can only guess that was his overall plan, as he's been missing since. He has to resurface at some point, and I'll kill him when he does.

I'm on my way back from Exeter, where I went with my team of werewolf protectors to collect Daisy's things. We looked around for signs of Jackson, the male who kidnapped, tortured, raped, and turned Daisy into a werewolf without her consent. We think he initially paid Kellan to keep an eye on her for him.

Whilst in Exeter, my alpha contacted a few shifter packs to update them on the situation and ask them to report any sightings of either Jackson or Kellan to the Supernatural Council or us directly, hoping we can free Daisy from her painful past. But so far, there has been nothing.

I pull up outside the bar and push all thoughts of Exeter out of my mind. Inside is the most beautiful woman ever to walk this earth, and she's all mine. All I can think about is getting her home and burying myself deep inside her, making up for the time apart. I jump out of the car, head straight to the front door, and quickly knock. Carl opens it, grinning.

"Hey Mikey, how you doing?"

I squeeze his shoulder as I walk past him into the bar. "I'll be better in about ten seconds," I reply as I look straight to the one place I know my mate will be.

There she is on the dancefloor, her hips swaying in time to the music, her long golden bronze hair cascading down her back, stopping halfway between her shoulders and her perfectly grabbable arse.

"I swear you get more beautiful every day." I send down our unique bond, which allows us to communicate telepathically. Daisy spins around and stares at me. The world stops for a second, and all I can see and hear is her. Daisy screams and launches herself towards me. I take three long strides meeting her half way before she jumps into my arms and wraps her legs around my waist as I hold her tightly against me.

I hear her sob as she places her head between my neck and shoulder. I lean into her so I can inhale her sweet floral scent.

"I've missed you so much, Darling," I whisper down the

bond.

"Not as much as I've missed you, Handsome." She whispers back.

I chuckle as I lean back to see Daisy's face properly. Before getting a good look at her, she threads her fingers into my hair and crushes her lips into mine. I don't care who's around and watching; I kiss her like I've been starved of her because I have. The last three days have been torture without her.

"For fuck's sake, Daisy. Let the man breathe." I hear Tony moan as he walks past us. Daisy pulls away and winks at me before jumping down from my arms.

"You're just jealous as you aren't getting any." She replies as she turns in my arms to face her friend with her back against my chest as I hold her close.

"Please bitch, I can get what I want when I want, and you know it." He looks at the two of us, smirking. "But I'm always open to making this a threesome; you know you would love it." He winks at me before wiggling his eyebrows at Daisy.

Daisy walks out of my arms and towards Tony, patting him on the chest as she passes.

"Sweetie, you couldn't handle us." She looks over her shoulder at me and winks. "Plus, I don't share."

"I'm never sharing you, Baby," I reply as I rush up to her and grab her around the waist, pulling her back into my arms as my lips meet hers.

"Uhh, get a room." Tony groans as he walks past us; I look into Daisy's eyes as I reply, smiling.

"I plan on it. Go get your stuff and get in the car, so I can get you home and inside you within the next half hour." I whisper, nibbling on her earlobe. Daisy rushes out of my arms, squealing as I slap her ass. I watch her run up the stairs and into the apartment where she's been staying. As soon as she's out of sight, I lean against the bar where Tony and Carl are sitting on stools and take the bourbon drink Richard hands me.

"You look like you need that." He says as I take a sip.

"You have no idea," I reply, holding the glass up as thanks.

"How did it go?" Tony asks. I put my glass down on the bar and check Daisy's still upstairs.

"Someone has been through all her stuff in the car. They've also broken into the house. I called her uncle Nigel, and we decided to board the house up for now. The guys and I did it today; it's why we stayed the extra day." I explain quietly.

"Any sign of the arseholes?" Tony asks. I shake my head and take another sip of my drink.

"No, but there were signs of a fight, but only one scent, so we think one of them was Kellan since it seems he can hide his scent. It could have been him and Jackson, but as none of us knows Jackson's scent, it's hard to say for sure."

"Do you think Kellan's gone for good?" Richard asks. I down the rest of my drink and shrug.

"Who knows. He could be anywhere, but so could Jackson. We all felt like we were being watched the whole time. I was glad to get away if I'm honest. It was exhausting being on edge all the time. The Alpha seems to have made some progress with the packs around there. It turns out they've all been working against each other rather than together, and that's why so much has been missed. There's still a lot of work to do with them, but the Alpha has it under control." I take a deep breath and look at Carl, "he asked me to ask you something, and I'm not sure how you will take it."

He holds up his hand to stop me. "Don't bother; the answer's yes." He says as he looks at his partner. Richard reaches over and takes Carl's hand, giving it a reassuring squeeze.

"Are you sure? I know you wanted away from that life." I ask, checking.

"I left the team as I wanted to protect Richard after that mission followed us home. But I know you're stretched, and I'm here to help. Even if it's to watch Daisy for you. I'm at your disposal."

"Thank you, Carl. You have no idea how grateful I am." He looks at me and nods once.

"I promised to protect the pack like the rest of you. I stand by that promise." Just as I'm about to respond, a bang comes from upstairs, and we all turn to see Daisy rushing down the steps with her bag in hand. I smile when I see the grin on her face.

I hold one arm out for her as she rushes straight to my side, dropping the bag by our feet.

"You ready to go, darling?" I whisper as I kiss the top of her head.

"Yep, take me home, handsome." She replies as she walks out of my arms and hugs Richard and Carl simultaneously. "Thank you for keeping me sane whilst he was away."

They both chuckle, "Thank you for not drinking us out of house and home." Richard says, winking at her as she pulls away.

"Do I even want to know how much that bar tab will cost me?" I ask as I shake Richard's hand, as he shakes his head.

"I'll send you the bill. Just make sure you're sitting down when you open it." He jokes.

"Hey! I'm not that bad!" Daisy protests next to me; I put my arm over her shoulder and laugh,

"Oh, darling, you are so much worse, now get in the car; I want to get you home to bed."

Chapter Two

Daisy

It's been the longest two nights and three days whilst Michael's been away. I'm so glad he's finally home. I glance at him as he drives home, one hand on the steering wheel, the other holding mine.

"Is that it now? Will you have to go back to Exeter?" I ask as I watch Michael's expression change.

"I can't promise anything, darling, as the Alpha may need to sort out the other packs further. He wants Marcus and me to go with him as security." He lifts my hand and kisses the back of it. "I hate it when I have to leave you, especially with everything going on." I squeeze his hand.

"I know you do, Mikey, but it'll be over soon enough. With Kellan not making himself known, I think we're over the worst of it." I say optimistically.

"Darling, I wish it was that simple. But I want to know where Kellan is hiding as I'm worried about his overall plan." I bite my bottom lip, realising there's no way Michael will agree to my next request.

"So not being babysat whenever you have to work or go on a mission isn't an option anytime soon?" I ask carefully.

Michael glances at me, and I can see the pain in his eyes before he turns back to the road. "Darling, I know you hate it, but I don't know what else to do here."

"You promised to let me fight my own battles, Mikey. You promised to stand beside me, not in front of me, protecting me." I can feel the tension in the air as this is something that has been building for the last week or so.

Since we came back from Cornwall, Michael's ensured I'm never alone. I get that he panicked, especially as he admitted he's worried Jackson saw me when I was in Exeter. But I'm not scared of him, not like I was.

When I ran two weeks ago, I didn't care if Jackson had found me or not; I was more worried about what he would do to everyone here. I wanted to lead him away from them. But since seeing how well Michael and the guys can look after themselves, I'm no longer worried. I turn and look at Michael and see he's fighting with his wolf.

The problem with wolves is we mate for life. When we find our fated mate, nothing or no one else matters. For a male, it's down to the primal need to protect what's theirs. For Michael, it's more complicated as he's also an alpha who's fighting the urge to protect his mate and his pack, even if he isn't the pack's Alpha yet.

I know how hard it is for him, as I've felt it myself the last few days. Knowing that Michael may be facing danger and I wasn't there was hard. All I want to do is protect him, our family, and our friends.

I've been so lost in my thoughts that I don't realise we're home until the car stops. I look across to Michael and smile, hoping to lighten the mood.

"Home, sweet home."

Michael turns to me and smiles, nodding, before leaving the car. As I climb out, I spot my car parked on the driveway.

"You brought her back!" I yell excitedly.

"I told you I would. Marcus drove her; I figured you wouldn't want to risk her in Jon's hands." Michael calls from the trunk of his car as he grabs our bags.

I laugh as I make my way to my car. I peer inside and realise there seems to be more space in the back than when I left it in Exeter. I turn to Michael frowning.

"Has someone moved some of my stuff? It's not all here." I can see the change in Michael's face as he nods.

"Come inside, darling; I'll explain everything over a glass of wine. I think you'll need it."

I follow Michael into the house and watch as he places our bags at the bottom of the stairs before heading into the kitchen. When I join him, he's in the fridge, pulling out a beer bottle and a bottle of wine. I watch as Michael pours me a glass of wine before opening his bottle. Now he's finally home and can relax; I can see how exhausted and worried he is.

I walk up to him and wrap my arms around his waist. He

sighs and relaxes further as he holds me close.

"What's the matter?" I ask. I feel his lips rest on the top of my head.

"I'm sorry, darling. I've not been honest with you; I'd planned to tell you everything tomorrow. I promise. I just wanted you to have one last night of peace." Michael says into my hair.

"Mikey, please, stop trying to protect me." As he takes a deep breath, I feel him kiss the top of my head one more time.

"We think Jackson has always known where you were and that Kellan is working for him."

It takes a second for his words to sink in. I let my arms drop from around him and step away. Michael goes to step toward me, but I hold up my hands.

"How?" I ask. Michael closes his eyes before answering.

"Kellan's house in town was owned by someone who owns property in Exeter and St Austell. He's also been receiving substantial payments from the same name." I clutch my stomach as a knot forms, and my chest tightens.

"When did you find this out?" I ask as Michael looks down at his hands resting on the breakfast bar in the middle of our kitchen.

"The night before our blessing." He replies quietly.

"A week? You've known for seven days and didn't think to tell me? Were you actually going to tell me tomorrow, or are you just saying that now I'm asking questions?" I demand as I take a step back from him, my voice rising with my temper.

"I was going to tell you, I promise, but things kept coming up, and I just didn't want to scare you." I turn as I throw my hands up in the air and storm out of the kitchen. I can hear Michael cursing as he starts to follow me. I spin around and hold my hands up in front of me again.

"Give me space, Michael." I walk up the stairs and into our room, closing the door behind me.

I look around, instantly regretting my decision to hide in here. There's still very little of mine in this house, as I've only been living here for ten days, and my stuff was in Exeter. I remember the stuff in the car and feel my temper rise further.

I storm downstairs and find Michael in the lounge with his head in his hands and a bourbon on the coffee table.

"Why is some of my stuff missing? You never got to that bit." Michael looks up at me, and I know I'm not going to like what he has to say,

"When we got to your old house, we found somebody had been inside and in the car; they had gone through all your stuff. We weren't sure anything was missing, but now you've confirmed it." He explains.

"Do you think it was Kellan or Jackson?" I ask.

"We don't know Jackson's scent, and Kellan doesn't seem to have one," Michael says, shrugging. Well, there's one way to find out. I walk out of the lounge and head to the bowl we always put our keys in by the door. My car key has been put in there, probably by Marcus. I take the key and head to the car. I know Michael's behind me, but I don't acknowledge him.

As soon as I reach the car I realise this may be a bad idea. I have no idea how Jackson's scent is going to affect me. I haven't smelt it since the night I escaped him three years ago. I grip the back door handle and press the unlock button. I take a deep breath to settle my nerves and open the door. Marcus's scent is the first thing I pick up, quickly followed by Will's. They travelled back together in the car. Without turning to Michael, I start asking questions.

"Other than Will and Marcus, who's been in this car."

"Stuart and me." He answers.

I sniff and pick up on Michael and Stuart's scents. I let out a sigh of relief when I don't smell Jackson.

"There are two scents I don't know, both wolves. Are you sure none are from the Exeter packs?" I hear Michael mumble that he's sure. I look through what I can see from where I'm standing.

"If they've gone through all this, they will have my dorm address and course details." I point out as I stand up straight and close the door before locking it. Fuck. I can't believe I was so stupid to leave all this stuff in Exeter. When I ditched it, I believed Jackson had already found me, So there was no point hiding everything.

"I figured they'd been looking for something like that, so I was loud when discussing your new living arrangement. I know we were being watched, so the word should have gotten back that you no longer live in the dorm. Your friends and Tony will be safe." Michael explains. I nod and head back to the house.

I walk into the kitchen and grab my glass of wine. I'm going to need the bottle to deal with this shit. I have my back to the kitchen door, but I can feel Michael watching my every move.

"Darling, talk to me, please. Everything I've done was to protect you. Do you think I wanted to hide this all from you? The last week has been a complete whirlwind of emotions, with the blessing and the intense mating bond. Plus, I've had to return to work, and you've been trying to keep up with all the assignments that you have due. It kept being brushed under the carpet until later, but later never came." I spin around, look at Michael and see he's waiting for me to explode.

"Oh, he should be prepared. I'm going to kick his ass; I don't care if he's fucking sorry." My wolf growls, and I agree. I want to scream at him, but I know it'll solve nothing.

I turn around and grab a bottle of gin, a bottle of mixer from the fridge, and a glass from the cupboard.

"I'm going upstairs, don't follow me; I can't even look at you right now." I storm past Michael heading straight to our bedroom. As soon as I'm in there, I walk into the bathroom and start running the bath. The only thing that might calm me is a few drinks in a deep bubble bath.

Chapter Three

Michael

Fuck, I messed up. I should have handled this better. I should have told her the truth the morning after the blessing, but I kept finding reasons to put it off. I hated the idea of her feeling scared or threatened. I had promised her she would never be scared again; I'd then break that promise by giving her the news she dreaded hearing. If she's mad now, she'll be furious when she finds out she's the last to know.

I consider calling around and asking everyone to act ignorant, but that's the coward's way of dealing with it. I push myself away from the breakfast bar I'm leaning against and walk back into the lounge, where my drink's sitting on the coffee table. I can hear the bath running in our bathroom above me and know that she'll be in there for a while. It's her go-to when she wants to relax. I don't think the bath has ever been used as much as it has in the last two weeks.

I sit on the sofa and pick up my glass before leaning back to rest my head on the back. It's times like this; that I'm reminded of how little I know about relationships, as I have no idea what to do to make this better. I can't believe I'm going to do this, but I pick up my phone and turn on the TV, so Daisy can't hear me before dialling my brother's number.

"Yo, what you doing calling? Why aren't you balls deep in hot sex?" Jon laughs down the line.

"I knew I'd regret calling you." I groan into the phone.

"Oh shit, that doesn't sound good. What's happened?"

"I told Daisy about Kellan possibly working for Jackson." I hear Jon hiss through his teeth.

"Oh shit, how did that go?"

"I'm on the phone to you rather than being balls deep in hot sex," I reply.

"Good point. So it's not gone well, then. Hang on; I have a text." I roll my eyes as I hear Jon messing with his phone; he mumbles something to Stuart before coming back on the line.

"Mikey, you might want to take the gin off her."

"Why?" I ask as I stand up. My phone beeps and I see I have a message from Tony. Jon starts to speak, but I interrupt him telling him to wait.

Tony: Thanks for the heads up that you were telling her; I let it slip; we all knew. I'm now public enemy number two, you being number one. Take the gin off her, and fix this, Adams!

Fuck, I start walking towards the stairs.

"I take it she texted you too," I whisper down the phone.

"Bro, you need to get the gin off her and give her space tonight. She's not good. Stuart's on the phone with her now, trying to calm her down. Sleep in my room." I walk up the stairs and realise I can hear Daisy on the phone with Stuart; she sounds furious.

"I'm not attempting to take the bottle off her. There's a chance she'll bottle me with it," I whisper as her voice gets louder. My phone beeps again, and I reluctantly look at it.

Marcus: Do you need reinforcements? Remove the gin.

I sigh as I lean against the wall.

"Well, that's you, Tony, Stu and Marcus. She's messaged or called. Only Will left." I inform Jon, I half expect him to start laughing, but even he isn't making a joke out of this.

"What do you expect, Mikey? We all told you to tell her. I don't understand why you thought hiding it was a good idea. She hates not being in control or in the know." My phone beeps and I moan, knowing who it will be.

Will: Sofa here, if you need it. Seriously, take the gin off her before she can turn it into a weapon.

"Nope, there's Will. Every single one of you has told me to remove the gin." I tell Jon. I hear him saying something to

Stuart and then moaning.

"She's asked Stuart to pick her up and take her to Tony's."

"Tell him, no, I will speak to her." I hear Jon speaking to Stuart again.

"Stuart says good luck. You'll need it."

"No words of advice from you?" I ask, hoping he will have something.

"Nope, other than grovel and admit you fucked up. Because you did." I shake my head as I step away from the wall.

"Thanks, I'd have never figured that out." I hang up before Jon replies. I take a deep breath and turn the handle on the bedroom door, only for it not to move.

"Darling, have you locked the door?" I ask carefully

"Yep." She snaps at me through the door.

"How? There isn't a lock on this door," I call back, frowning.

"I'm a witch, dumbass!" Daisy calls back. Well, that's me told.

"Can I come in so we can talk? Please, darling."

"No, leave me alone, Michael." I can hear the anger in her voice, but I can also hear that she's close to tears.

"Please, baby, I want to fix this. I know I fucked up, but I want to make it better," I whisper as I lean against the door. Daisy doesn't respond, and I'm unsure if that's a good thing. "Darling?"

"You lied to me. You said you would never lie to me," Daisy replies. I hear her voice break as a sob leaves her.

"I didn't lie," I reply. Instantly knowing it was the wrong thing to say.

"You hid things from me. That's just as bad." She yells. I step back from the door and hear the pain in her voice. I did that. I hurt her after promising I never would.

"If you want Stuart to pick you up, tell him to." I sigh, defeated, as I walk back down the stairs. I don't even make it to the bottom before my phone rings.

"Tell Stuart it's fine, Jon. If she wants to leave, I can't stop her." I sigh.

"You sure that's a wise move?" Jon asks. I head into the

kitchen and grab my bottle of bourbon.

"She wants to get away from me, Jon. Can you blame her?" I hear the sound of a car door and a car engine start on the phone.

"We're on our way; Stuart will take Daisy where she wants to go, and I'll stay with you."

"I don't need babysitting, Jon." I sigh as I pour myself a large drink, not even bothering with the ice.

"No, but you need your brother." Jon answers. I take a sip of my drink as I sit back on the sofa. He's not wrong. I need to talk to my brother as much as I need Daisy to talk to me right now.

Chapter Four

Daisy

I look at my phone as it starts ringing.

"I'm not talking to you, Tony." I sigh as I answer it.

"But yet you still answered your phone." He sighs down the line.

I sip my drink and lean against the bath. The water's not even that hot. I don't know why I'm still lying in here.

"What do you want?" I snap at my best friend.

"For you to lose the attitude for one." He snaps back.

"Fuck off, Tony. I'm pissed off with the lot of you! You all hid this from me! You should have told me! Michael should have told me!" I yell, trying not to cry again.

"Have you spoken to him?" Tony asks.

"Nope."

"Are you going to?"

"Nope," I reply again as I sip my drink.

"Real mature Daisy." Tony sighs. I'm just about to respond when I hear a knock at the door.

"Go away, Michael," I call out.

"It's Stuart."

I roll my eyes before removing the locking spell I'd placed on the door.

"It's open, but stay in the bedroom. I'm in the bath." I hear the door open and close. I listen out for Michael's footsteps. I wouldn't put it past him to sneak in with Stuart.

"Oh, you're pissed with Michael and me, but Stuart's fine?" Tony groans down the line.

"I'm pissed at Stuart, but he's the only one who's not had a drink, so he's driving me to yours." I point out.

"Why are you coming here?" Tony demands.

"Yeah, why are you going there if you are pissed off with him?" Stuart adds. I should have known he'd hear Tony even through the door. I roll my eyes and put my phone on loudspeaker so that Tony can hear everything, too, as I place the phone on the floor.

"I'm coming to yours, Tony, as I have nowhere else to go." I point out. Since I moved out of our shared dormitory at the university to live with Michael, Tony has got his own place closer to The Crow. Richard and Carl gave him the references he needed and a pay rise.

"You always have mine. It's only Jon staying at the moment." Stuart calls from the bedroom.

"But you both go running back to your pack, brother," I reply as I stand up and grab my towel to dry myself off.

"I'm just as loyal to you as I am to him," Stuart calls back, making me laugh aloud.

"If that were true, you'd have told me what you knew." I snap as I step out of the bath and pick up my phone.

"Look, Dais, I get you're angry, and you have every right to be, but think about it logically. Michael found out the night before your blessing. He wanted the day to be perfect for you, which it was. Yes, he should've told you the next day, but from what you told me, you were in a loved-up daze that day. Being in bed with Michael was all you could think about. Are you telling me he didn't feel the same? Cause babes, he did, if not more because he's male." Tony explains, trying to be logical, which isn't what I want to hear right now.

"Stop making excuses for him, Tony." I snap

"He's not; he's right," Stuart adds as I walk into the bedroom. Grabbing my yoga pants and top. Stuart's sitting in the chair by the far wall brushing his shoulder-length blonde hair with my brush, which I snatch from him as I walk past and start brushing my own.

"The day after that, you were called to the Alpha's office and told about the university refusing Michael's resignation and request to move. Straight from that meeting, Michael held the team meeting, and you spent the day painting the mural on the Luna's nursery wall. Class that as two days because Michael went to work, and you went back to finish it before I picked you up, and you came here to study." Stuart points out as he pulls his hair into a top bun and secures it with a hairband from his wrist.

"He could have told me that evening," I answer as I plait my wet hair.

"You were knackered and horny—your words, not mine. Plus, you were sulking over Michael having to go to Exeter. That leaves the three days he was actually in Exeter." Tony adds. I grab my stuff and signal Stuart to turn around, which he does as I pull on my clothes.

"It's all well and good you standing up for Michael, but what about you guys? Or Jonny, Will, or Marcus. Any of you could have told me." I reply as I get dressed.

"We could have, but Will, Jon and Marcus have been at work and not seen you, and it's not our place to tell you. You would have wanted Michael to." Tony says calmly through the phone, which is on the bed.

"He's right," Stuart adds, still facing away.

"So we're back to Michael being in the wrong," I reply as I sit on the bed, looking at Stuart holding the phone between us. "So, your argument is mute."

"Okay, yes, Michael should've told you. But look at it from his perspective, every time he's had a chance, you've tried to jump him, or one of you has been knackered. Neither of you has had a break in the last week. It's been non-stop. You've been working flat out at the bar the last three days on essays whilst he's been in Exeter trying to find a way to protect *you* and keep *you* safe. As well as run his team and do anything else his alpha asked." Tony points out. I flop back onto the bed and moan as I know he's right.

"I'll always have your back, babes; you know that. But you need to cut Michael and the rest of us some slack with this one." Tony says, calm but firmly. I look up at the ceiling as a tear runs down my face.

"This isn't just about no one telling you, is it?" Stuart asks as he moves to the bed and lies next to me. I feel another tear escape my eye as I refuse to look at him.

"I never escaped Jackson. I thought I was free of him." I whisper. I feel Stuart take my hand and gently squeeze it.

"But he doesn't control you now, babes," Tony answers softly.

"Doesn't he?" I sigh deeply, "I couldn't go back to my parent's graves in case he saw me. I can't speak to most of my family and friends in case they find out where I am. We were doing everything in the hope of keeping me safe, and the kicker is I could have done all that as he knew where I was the whole time. He knows where I am now. I'll never be free of him." Stuart puts his arm under my head and pulls me, so I'm lying against him, resting my head on his chest as the tears come.

"You might not be yet. But believe me when I say Michael is working on it. I've never seen him so determined. All he's thinking about is finding Jackson and eliminating the threat he poses to you. Your safety is the most important thing to Mikey and us." Stuart says softly.

"Dais, Michael loves you more than anything in this world. There's nothing he won't do to protect you," Tony adds from his end.

"I know," I whisper in response.

"Don't hate me when I say you're not going to Tony's tonight. You're staying here to face this head-on. You're going to talk to Mikey." Stuart says before kissing me on the top of the head.

"Without the gin," Tony demands. I roll my eyes.

"Definitely without the gin," Stuart adds, chuckling.

"I can't just forgive him, not yet. I'm still mad at him." I sigh.

"Of course you are. We aren't saying he shouldn't have told you. We're just saying we can see how it never came about." Tony answers. I lean up and kiss Stuart on the cheek.

"You two are the best friends a girl could ask for. Even when you drive me up the fucking wall." I sigh as I lie back down.

"Right back at ya, baby girl. Now can I go to bed? I've had a mental three days, and I'm exhausted." Stuart chuckles into my hair.

"Same here. That late-night study session last night was too much," Tony calls through the phone.

"And it's nothing to do with you drinking in the pub with

me since three." I chuckle as I sit up out of Stuart's arms.

"That may have something to do with it. Now, could you leave me alone; I need to sleep? Stuart deserves a break, so let the poor guy go home." Tony chuckles.

"Go to sleep, Tony. I love you, dickhead." I call.

"Love ya too, bitch face." He calls as he hangs up. I pick up my phone and place it on the nightstand to charge. Stuart is now sitting on the edge of the bed.

"I'm going home too. Want me to tell Mikey the coast is clear?" He asks as he stands up.

I shake my head, "tell him to give me at least five minutes. I still need to clear my head." Stuart smiles at me, nodding as he walks over and pulls me into a hug.

"Give him a chance to explain. He had a shit time in Exeter, and it was all for you and the Alpha. He's worn out, Dais."

"I know," I admit quietly. Stuart kisses the top of my head and walks away towards the door. He looks down at the floor and smiles before picking up the almost empty gin bottle.

"I'm taking this with me as well. You and the guys will all thank me tomorrow." He says as he rushes out the door to avoid the pillow I throw at him.

Michael

"What's taking Stuart so long? You don't think she's hurt herself, do you?" I ask as I walk around the lounge for the hundredth time since they arrived.

"If she were hurt, he'd have called you up. He's probably just trying to get her to calm down. He's good with her." Jon says from his spot on the sofa. I know he's right. Stuart seems to have taken the role of big brother and best friend with Daisy. I know it shouldn't bother me, but it does. I don't like how he looks at her at times or constantly messages her. It seems different with him somehow. My phone vibrates, and I see a message come through.

Tony: You owe me and Stuart a beer or six after tonight, Adams. We've talked the crazy bitch down from her high horse. Don't make us look like dicks now!

"Do you think she will forgive me?" I ask Jon as I pick up my drink.

"Of course, she will. It's Daisy; she worships you." My brother replies, frowning.

"She hates me at the moment." I stop pacing as I hear somebody walking down the stairs. Stuart places the now almost empty gin bottle on the coffee table.

"I've confiscated that. She agreed not to have anymore."

"Is she okay?" I ask; Stuart looks at me and smiles softly, nodding.

"She will be. She's still mad, but Tony and I talked to her. There's more to it than you not telling her, though. It's the realisation she was never as free of Jackson as she thought. She gave up everything to escape him, but he knew where she was the whole time. That's got to her more than she's willing to admit." Stuart explains.

"So when are you taking her to Tonys?" Jon asks from the couch.

"I'm not. We've told her to sort her shit out and face Michael rather than hideaway." Stuart turns to look at me again.

"She wants five minutes before you go up there again. I'd give her longer than that. But we've told her straight that you'd never meant to hurt her and that you love her more than anything."

"Thank you, Stu," I reply as I look at the youngest member of my team.

"Don't thank me yet. Wait and see if you survive the night." Stuart answers as he looks at Jon. "Are you coming home? Or staying here tonight?" Jon gets up off the sofa and stretches.

"I'm coming. These two will be loud tonight, whether from shouting or sexy time." He winks at me as I flip my middle finger at him.

"Fuck off, Jonny," I mutter and head towards the front door. Jon walks past me and pats me on the shoulder.

"Everything will be fine." He says as he walks out and towards Stuart's car. Stuart stops next to me.

"He's right. She's already calmed down a lot. She's still mad at us, but give her time, and she'll come around." He says, giving me half a smile.

"I know. I'll see you in the week."

Stuart turns and walks to his car, where Jon's already in the passenger seat. I wave one last time and close the door behind me before leaning back against it and letting out a deep sigh. I push myself away and look toward the stairs. I want to rush up there, pull Daisy into my arms and hold her whilst begging her to forgive me. But I know Stuart's right; I have to give her space. Instead, I enter the lounge, turn everything off, and finish my drink before getting two glasses of water from the kitchen. With the glasses in hand, I stand at the bottom of the stairs and give myself a moment to work up the courage to head up. When I do, I stop outside of our bedroom door. Do I knock, or do I just walk in? *"walk-in. It's our room too."* My wolf pipes up for the first time all night. I decide to ignore him and knock on the door.

"It's open," Daisy announces quietly. I take a deep breath and enter the room. I look around and see that Daisy has moved the chair so she can sit on it and look out the window at the night sky. She is sitting with her knees up, one arm around her legs, hugging them against her chest, whilst playing with the necklace I gave her on the day of our blessing.

"I brought up some water for you, darling," I whisper whilst putting the glass on the bedside cabinet, her side of the bed.

"Thanks." She replies, not turning to look at me. I stand there for a moment and realise she needs more time.

"I'm going to sleep in Jon's room tonight to give you some space. I know you don't want to be around me right now." Daisy doesn't reply. She looks out the window as I turn and walk out of the bedroom. Before closing it, I look at Daisy, unmoved in the chair, one last time.

"I'm so sorry, darling. I love you," I whisper as I close the door and head into my brother's room.

Half an hour later, I'm lying in Jon's bed, with my arms behind my head. My mind is working in overdrive. There's no way I'll sleep tonight, not when Daisy is on the other side of the landing in our bed. It feels wrong being in the same house as my mate but sleeping in different rooms.

I hear our bedroom door open, followed by Daisy's footsteps. I look up as she walks into the bedroom in the shorts and T-shirt she wears for bed.

"Darling?" I whisper as Daisy climbs into bed but turns her back to me.

"I haven't forgiven you, Mikey. My wolf won't settle, and I don't want to spend another night away from you." I lie back down and stare at the ceiling until I slowly drift off to sleep with Daisy breathing lightly next to me.

Chapter Five

Daisy

I wake up to Michael's arms tightening around my shoulders, my head resting against his smooth muscular chest. I must've rolled over and taken my usual place in his arms at some point in the night. No wonder I slept better than I thought I would. My wolf's also settled for the first time in four days. As much as I want to get up and walk away from him, I can't bring myself to do it. I love him more than I dislike what he did right now.

Talking to Stuart and Tony helped put things into perspective last night, and I understand why Michael didn't tell me everything that's come to light. When I think back, there were times he tried to talk to me, and I cut him off by kissing him, which led to other things until we passed out wrapped in each other arms, sweaty and gasping for breath.

I feel him move and groan slightly underneath me, his arms tightening around me protectively as they always do as he starts waking up. I think about how I felt when he walked out of our room last night to sleep in here, and I tighten my hold on his chest as I come close to tears again.

I feel Michael's head move, so his face is in my hair. He takes a deep breath and kisses me on the top of the head before slowly releasing his breath.

We lie in silence for a while, neither of us wanting to burst the bubble we're in, knowing the moment one of us speaks, we have to acknowledge the elephant in the room, the reason we're in Jon's bed and not our own. I feel Michael reach up and stroke the top of my hair and know the bubble of ignorance is about to burst.

"Tell me what to do to make this right, darling. I'll do anything you ask. I hate this." Michael whispers into my hair.

"There's nothing else left for you to do," I answer honestly because there's not.

"I'm so sorry." Michael sighs as his voice breaks a little.

"I know," I reply as a single tear escapes. I know he feels it. I hear him gasp as the tear touches his skin. I also know how much he'll hurt, knowing that he's the reason I'm crying. I take a deep breath before continuing.

"I know why you didn't tell me; I know there were probably times you tried, and I distracted you. I'm not saying you shouldn't have tried harder because you should have, but I get it." I take a deep breath and remove myself from Michael's arms. I don't turn to face him, knowing I'll cry if I do.

"I need a shower. Don't forget we promised Mama we would go for lunch. I don't want to let her down." I walk out of Jon's room and into ours to get ready. Leaving Michael lying in Jon's bed alone.

)) ● ((

Michael pulls up outside his mum's house two hours later and sighs deeply. We've hardly spoken since this morning. We aren't arguing or ignoring each other; we just don't know what to say. Michael looks over at me and takes my hand, and I can feel his relief when I don't pull it from him.

"If you want to leave at any point, say the word, and we're gone. Mum will know something's wrong and will understand." Michael says softly. I nod, as I know he's right. Barbara picks up on everything when it comes to her children.

Michael kisses the back of my hand before getting out of the car. I take a deep breath and try to calm my racing heart.

We don't even make it to the front door before it opens, and I see Michael's mum looking out at us, her arms crossed and a look that makes us both stop in our tracks.

"Daisy dear, can you go inside for a moment, please? I want a word with my son." I look from Michael to his mum Barbara and back again. Michael looks at me and nods quickly.

"Go on in." He says as he walks me closer to the door before stopping in front of his mum. As I reach Barbara, she takes my hand, her face softening.

"The kettles on, dear, make yourself a coffee; we won't be long." She says, smiling at me. I nod and walk past her into the house.

"What the hell is wrong with you?!" I hear Barbara hiss at her son.

"Mum, I fucked up; I know it. By the Goddess, I'm paying for it. You can't make me feel any worse than I already do." I hear Michael exclaim as I walk into the kitchen. I don't want to hear anymore. I head straight over to the little radio Barbara has in the kitchen and turn it on in the hope of drowning out the bollocking Michael's getting. Sometimes werewolf hearing sucks.

I busy myself making the three of us drinks. I'm just putting the milk back in the fridge when I hear the front door closing. Barbara walks in and doesn't stop until she's in front of me. She pulls me into her arms and holds me tight. I hug her back but know that if I allow myself to melt into her arms, the tears will start, and I'm worried they'll never stop.

"Where's Mikey?" I ask as I look up behind her. Barbara pulls away from me and places a motherly hand on my cheek.

"Giving us a minute. I want to speak to you without him being here." I turn and walk over to the mugs on the side. I pick up Barbara's favourite and hand it to her.

"I'm okay," I say as I turn to pick up my own.

"Daisy, I'm not blind; I can see neither of you are okay. Mikey's brought it on himself, and I have no sympathy for him. You, however, deserve better." I take a sip of my drink and shake my head.

"Honestly, Mama, it'll be fine. It's not completely his fault. It's not like we've had much time together since the blessing."

"That's no excuse, and you know it. If you honestly believed that you wouldn't look like you haven't had a wink of sleep, and Jon and Stuart wouldn't have had to go round last night to see the two of you." I should've known that Jon would tell their mum everything.

"Mama, please," I whisper as the burning returns to my eyes and throat. All I've done is hold in the tears since Michael told me last night. Barbara steps toward me, but Michael appears in the kitchen as she does. The sight of him makes it harder to keep it together.

Michael looks defeated. His usually bright blue eyes have

lost their spark—the evidence of his poor night's sleep under his eyes.

"I told you to stay out there." Barbara snaps at her son without turning to face him.

"Mum, all due respect, when I hear my mate on the verge of tears, I'm *not* staying away." Michael snaps at her as he walks straight to me. "Darling, I never wanted to cause you this amount of pain, or any pain. I hate myself for what I've done to you." I open my mouth to reply, but Michael's phone starts ringing; it's the Alpha's ringtone. I can see the determination on his face.

"I'm not answering; he can fuck off. You're more important." Before I can say a word, the phone stops ringing and instantly starts again.

"Answer it," I whisper, taking a step back. I can see Michael's internal fight to come after me or obey his alpha. "Answer it," I say again. He curses as he pulls his phone out of his pocket and answers it.

"What?" he snaps, unable to keep the anger out of his voice.

"Lose the attitude Michael and get the team together. We have an incident." The Alpha barks down the line.

"So do I. The others will have to do. I need to stay here." I can feel my eyes widen with shock. I can't believe Michael is addressing our alpha in such a manner and choosing me over the protection of his pack and team.

"That wasn't a request, Adams. Whatever domestic you have going on can be put on hold. Get your fucking arse to HQ in the next twenty minutes, or me and you are going to be having more than words. Is that understood?" The Alpha yells down the phone. My wolf stands to attention.

"Yes Alpha," Michael answers through gritted teeth as he hangs up. He looks at me, and his whole face softens. "Do you want to stay here or go home? I'll leave you the car or get Carl to pick you up."

"I don't want to go home," I admit. I can't face sitting in that house on my own at the moment.

"Daisy can stay here; I'll make up your room for her if you

end up out all day," Barbara says behind him. Michael looks at me, and I nod to show that I'm okay with it. Michael lets out a sigh and takes a step forward. He cups my cheek in his hand as he looks into my eyes.

"I'll be back as quickly as I can. I want to make this right." He leans down and kisses me on the head before facing his mum.

"Thanks, Mum. Any issues, call Carl." Barbara nods and kisses him on the cheek before he starts walking out of the kitchen. The second the front door closes, the realisation hits me where he's going and that he could get hurt or worse, I can't breathe.

"Mikey!" I call as I rush past his mum, through the lounge and to the front door, I throw it open and see him on the phone by the front gate. "Mikey!" I call again. He spins around and looks at me as I rush out and throw my arms around his neck. He catches me with ease and lifts me off my feet as he buries his face into my neck. He holds me tight before placing me back on the ground. I reluctantly loosen my hold on his neck and move slightly, so his arm is still around my waist as I look up at him.

"Please be careful. Please come home to me." I sob as all the emotions I have bottled up rush to the surface. Michael leans down and places a soft kiss on my lips.

"Nothing will ever stop me from coming home to you. No matter how much you hate me, you are stuck with me," he whispers.

"I don't hate you." I protest, slapping his hard chest. Michael smiles at me softly.

"I know you don't, but you don't like me very much right now, either." He jokes although I can see that part of him believes it.

"I love you, you fucking idiot. More than anything in this world!" I declare.

"I love you too." Michael looks down at his phone as it starts ringing. "I have to go, baby, but I'll be back," Michael whispers as he kisses me before stepping back.

"Look after her," he says, looking over my head. I turn and

see his mum standing at the front door; she smiles and nods.

"Of course, you and the lads look after each other." She replies. Michael nods back, then looks down at me one last time before turning and walking out of the gate towards his car. I stay there until I see Michael pull away from the curb and drive out of view, obviously talking on his hands-free.

The floodgates open as soon as Michael's gone, and the tears flow freely. I hate the idea of Michael being on a mission. It's the first time he has been called on one since we moved in together, he's only been on guard duty in Exeter. I hate the idea of anything happening to him, especially as we've hardly spoken to each other, and I've been horrible to him. I feel Barbara take hold of my shoulders as she steps beside me.

"Come on, Daisy dear, let's get you inside. I think we deserve something stronger than coffee now." I nod as I sob, letting Barbara guide me into the house.

Chapter Six

Michael

I step up to my mum's front door and listen to the silence within. It's past midnight, and I've been out for over eleven hours. I can't remember the last time I came back here after a mission; I usually go to Marcus's if I can't go home. I pull out my keys and slowly unlock the door to let myself in. I stand in the entrance hall for a moment and listen. Both Mum and Daisy are breathing gently as if asleep upstairs. I sigh with relief as I need to sort my injuries before they see me.

I sneak up the stairs and head straight for the bathroom. As soon as I turn on the light, I smile. Mum's left the first aid kit out for me. She always left it out when Jon and I lived here. Just in case we'd gotten injured. I don't know why she bothered, though, because as soon as she heard us coming in, she'd be up and checking us over herself.

I try to be as quiet as possible as I close the bathroom door before filling the sink with warm water and pulling the flannel out of the box. I look in the mirror and curse. Gods, my face is worse than I thought. I take stock of my injuries, a cut eyebrow, scratches on my cheek, a black eye and a split lip. Shit, I know the guys kept telling me to get cleaned up, but I didn't realise I was this bad. I dip the corner of the flannel into the water and press it to the split lip.

"Fuck." I hiss as the pain shoots through it. Why do split lips sting like a bitch?

"Mikey?" I turn to find Daisy standing behind me in one of my old t-shirts that falls to just above her knees. She looks at my face, and her eyes instantly fill with tears, which she quickly tries to blink away.

"It's not as bad as it looks, darling. You should see the other guy." I wink at her, instantly regret it as it's my black eye I try to wink with. Daisy rolls her eyes and points toward the toilet.

"Your jokes are as bad as your face. Sit down, and I'll clean you up," She orders. I do as I'm told without question. As soon as I sit down, Daisy stands between my legs, looking down at me. I place my hands on her hips and wait to see if she pushes me away. I thank the goddess when she doesn't, as I don't think I can handle the rejection right now.

"This might sting a bit but stay still." She whispers as she starts dabbing at my eyebrow. I flinch away, which earns me a raised eyebrow. "If you're going to be a baby about it, you shouldn't put your face in the way of people's fists." She sighs, shaking her head, as I shrug.

"I think that one was a foot." One side of my mouth lifts as I smile playfully.

"Yeah, because that's so much better." Daisy chuckles, and I squeeze her hips gently.

"Hey, be nice. I'm injured." I pout, which stings because of my lip. Daisy giggles, smiling at me softly.

"You're right. I'm sorry, baby." She leans down and kisses the side of my mouth that isn't injured gently, "Is that better?" she asks. I look into her eyes and nod slightly.

"A little," I whisper. Daisy leans over and kisses my swollen eye, cheek, and eyebrow. The whole time my eyes are closed as I savour her touch, be it ever so fleeting.

Daisy stands straight and starts cleaning me up again. This time I don't take my eyes off her the whole time.

"What was the mission?" Daisy whispers as she rinses the cloth and starts on my cheek.

"The Alpha told us there had been reports of five rogues camping on the outskirts of the territory. When we got there, they instantly started to put up a fight, even though all we wanted to do was talk to them. As we were distracted by them, five more arrived. It got messy quickly." I explain as Daisy continues to clean me up. I keep my hands on her hips, slowly moving my thumbs across her hip bones. Needing any contact I can get.

"How bad are the others?" Daisy asks as she rinses the flannel again.

"We all look the same. Stuart's the worst as his arm was broken." Daisy freezes and stares at me. I quickly give her hips a reassuring squeeze. "He's fine, I promise. Edward already set it. It will be healed by the morning. It'll just ache for a few days." I feel Daisy relax before she goes back to my black eye.

"It's a good job you're all fit then." She says, smiling down at me. "I take it the rogues are all in the cells or dead?" I nod, looking at the floor. "Did you find out what they were up to?" She asks. I shake my head.

"No, it's strange. Every time they got close to telling us anything, they became unable to speak, and two died. It's like their tongues swelled up. We've never encountered anything like it before."

Daisy looks down at me, frowning. "It's a gagging curse. A person casts the curse and dictates what can't be said or discussed. Every time the person who has been gagged tries to discuss what they've been forbidden, their tongue swells if they keep thinking about talking about it, they end up dying." She looks to the side and smiles. "Clare put one on me once when I caught her sleeping with a boyfriend in her parent's bed."

"Why doesn't that surprise me. How did you manage to stop it?" I ask. Daisy laughs and presses the flannel to the cuts on my cheek. The flannel feels warm to the touch.

"Alex came in and heard me and her arguing about it. He realised what she'd done and made her remove it straight away. She didn't talk to me for a week." Daisy moves the flannel to the cut on my lip, and the warming sensation starts again.

"Is there a way we could remove the curse? Or work around it?" I ask. Daisy shrugs.

"I don't know; I'll have to ask Alex. He made Clare remove it herself, but I'm not sure that was part of her punishment or because she had to."

"Are there any other spells you two used to try and cast on each other to stay out of trouble?" I ask as Daisy starts holding the flannel, now cold, over my swollen eye, the aching quickly feeling better than it has since I noticed it. She looks deep in thought for a moment, so I just sit admiring her as she goes onto her own little world. After a few moments, she pulls the flannel away and looks at me, smiling slightly.

"Only the one I just used." She leans over and kisses me before stepping back and smiling. "All healed and back to being handsome." She declares. I frown at her as I stand up and look in the mirror. I'm amazed to see no sign of injury left on my face. Not even a scar.

"That's amazing," I exclaim. I look at Daisy and see how tired she's looking, "did healing me take it out of you?" I ask. Daisy smiles weakly.

"It's worth it." She whispers before turning and leaning against the doorframe to steady herself. I scoop her up into my arms and carry her into the bedroom as she leans her head against my chest. I place her on the bed and whisper that I'll be back.

A week ago, I learned that when Daisy uses her magic, it can take it out of her and cause dizziness, headaches, migraines, and exhaustion. It happened when she attempted to cast a protection spell on the house. It had taken her an entire night to recover. I'd been so worried about her.

I walk out of the bedroom and head back to the bathroom. I quickly put the first aid box away and get the painkillers and some water. I head back into the room and find Daisy almost asleep. I place an arm behind her head shoulder and help her sit up.

"Come on, darling, take these painkillers," I whisper. Daisy takes the tablets without argument. I tuck her into my old bed and get undressed. Daisy instantly cuddles into me as I climb in next to her and wrap my arms around her.

"As much as I appreciate you healing me, darling, please don't do it if it will drain you," I whisper into her hair. Daisy lazily draws circles on my chest with her finger.

"It shouldn't have drained me; it never used to." She whispers. Daisy's magic hasn't been the same since Jackson turned her, and no one knows why. Now and again, just doing a simple spell will drain her more than usual. Daisy blames her wolf, but her auntie and uncle think it may be something else.

"Sleep, baby; you'll feel better for it," I whisper. Daisy nods as she closes her eyes.

"I've hated the last two days," she murmurs as she starts to drift off. I tighten my hold on her.

"So have I, darling. I'll never be able to tell you how sorry I am."

"You don't need to, I know." She whispers. "I love you, Mikey." I feel her fall asleep in my arms as I press my lips to her hair and close my own eyes.

"Not as much as I love you, darling."

Chapter Seven

Michael

In nothing but a pair of old sweatpants, I walk into Mum's kitchen, following the smell of coffee and bacon, to find the team already around the table. Mum, as always, is standing over the oven cooking. I walk over and plant a kiss on her cheek.

"Morning Mikey, where's Daisy?" She asks as I step around her.

"Still sleeping," I answer as I steal a piece of toast from the board. I turn and look at the rest of my team.

"What happened to your face?" Jon asks from his seat; I look at him, frowning.

"What?"

"It's completely healed, not even a bruise." He exclaims. I look at the rest of the team and realise they still have various bruising and almost healed cuts on their faces.

"Daisy healed them when I got in," I explain as I walk over to the coffee machine and fill my mug.

"How was she afterwards?" Marcus asks. He'd seen first-hand how drained Daisy was after performing the protection spell the other day. I look up at him shaking my head.

"Not great. She had a migraine in the night and was sick twice. She says her magic's getting weaker, which is upsetting her." Marcus looks at me, and I can see the concern in his eyes.

"You shouldn't have let her heal you," Stuart says, not daring to look at me. I stare at him for a moment, deciding whether to beat the shit out of him or not.

"Not that I have to justify anything to you, Stuart. But I didn't even know she was doing it until she'd finished. I thought she was just cleaning the wounds with a flannel." Stuart looks down at the table and mumbles 'sorry'. I bite my tongue to stop myself from saying more. Instead, I turn back to my second.

"Any news from the security guards?" I ask.

"Nothing new. The rogues slept all night. No one else has died, so that's a bonus." Marcus sighs

"I'm going to head down there in a bit. I'll get one of them to talk by the end of the morning." I hear Jon declare. I look at my brother as I take a sip of my coffee.

"It won't work. You might as well leave them for now."

"Why, what do you know?" Marcus asks, looking at me.

"I spoke to Daisy when I got back last night. She says it's something called a gagging curse. They can't tell us anything without their tongue swelling. The more we push, the quicker they'll die. I'll call her godfather, Alex Rogers, in a bit and see how the curse can be undone." I explain.

"So if it can be undone, how do we do it? Would Daisy be up for it?" Jon asks as he leans back in his seat. I shake my head, picking up a clean mug to fill with coffee.

"I wouldn't let her even try. As I said, her magic is draining her more than usual. It's not worth the risk of what it could do to her." I answer.

"So, what do we do then?" Will asks before taking a bite of his bacon sandwich.

"I don't know. I'll speak to Alex, hear his thoughts, and take it from there."

"Well, before you do that, you can take this up to Daisy with that coffee. With how much she was being sick in the night, the poor girl's stomach must think her throats been cut." Mum says as she hands me a plate of bacon and toast.

"It's okay. I'm here." We all turn as Daisy walks into the kitchen, still wearing my old t-shirts with her leggings. She walks straight to me as I quickly put the plate on the side and hold out my arm. She wraps her arms around my waist as I tuck her against my side before planting a kiss on her lips.

"How are you feeling now?" Marcus asks. She takes the coffee out of my hand and heads to her usual seat, with me following behind with her food.

"I'm alright, just exhausted. I'll be fine after I have something to eat." Daisy looks up at Mum and smiles. "Thank you for breakfast Mama." My mum smiles back at her.

"Anything for you, darling girl." I see Jon looking at me as he crosses his arms over his chest whilst leaning back into his chair.

"Do you remember when she used to love us like that, Mikey?" I can't help but laugh.

"What was it, she would say? 'I could never have a

favourite'?" I ask.

"Don't forget 'I love you all equally'," Jon adds before yelping as Mum slaps him around the back of the head. I hear Daisy giggle beside me. After her being so ill last night, it's like music to my ears.

"I could never have a favourite," Mum says before turning to Daisy, "until Mikey brought Daisy home. Now it's easy to favour her," she adds, winking at Daisy, whose whole face lights up.

"Mikey, do you hear this?!" Jon exclaims.

"Yep, we should have seen it coming, she'll be changing the locks next, and we'll be orphans. Only Daisy will be allowed in." I say dramatically, placing a hand on my heart. Daisy turns to me and smiles as her eyes shine.

"You'll be okay. I'd miss you if you were gone for too long." She looks at Jon, "you, not so much."

"Bitch please, only yesterday you would have changed the locks and kicked him out yourself." I watch as Daisy's face drops and tears spring up in her eyes, causing me to lose my temper. No one upsets my mate. I jump to my feet, sending my chair flying. Marcus instantly jumps up beside me with a hand on my shoulder to restrain me, if he needs to.

"Jonathan!" Mum exclaims next to him as Daisy gasps.

"Low blow, Jonathan," I growl, my hands on either side of me in tight fists as my temper rises further.

"It was. I'm sorry, I didn't think," Jon exclaims, holding his hands up in defence, not rising from his chair. He looks at Daisy. "I'm sorry, it was a poorly timed joke." I look down at Daisy. She looks sick but tries to force a smile.

"It's fine, Jonny. Don't worry about it." She whispers. I squat down beside her and take her hand.

"Look at me," I whisper through the bond. Daisy turns to face me. *"If he upsets you, tell him. Or tell me, and I'll kick his fucking ass for you."* Daisy reaches out and places a hand on my cheek.

"I'm fine, honest, just feeling sick again." Daisy turns from me and looks across the table.

"Mama, do you mind if I get my head down for a bit,

please? I'm still tired." Mum looks at her and smiles softly.

"Of course, go on up. I'll get Mikey to bring your breakfast up." Daisy nods and stands; as she does, she sways as her eyes roll to the back of her head. I only just catch her. As she looks up at me, the colour drains from her face. I scoop her into my arms and carry her out of the room. I hear the others scrambling to their feet behind us.

"Mikey, what's happening?" I can hear the panic in Mums voice.

"She's still drained from using her magic. I'll get her settled upstairs. Can we have some more painkillers, please, Mum?" Mum rushes off as I carry Daisy upstairs. As soon as we're back in my old room, I place her on the bed. I watch as she starts shivering.

"Darling, you're freezing. What's happening? What can I do?" I ask as I pull the duvet tight around her, followed by a blanket from the bottom of the bed.

"I don't understand. It's magic exhaustion. I need a tea and to recharge." Daisy whispers as she pulls the covers around her tighter. I dig my phone out of my pocket and quickly pull up a number.

"Nigel, it's Michael."

))●((

Twenty minutes later, Daisy's asleep in bed. Her auntie had given Mum the recipe for the tea she needed, which she made up, having all the herbs and plants thankfully in her garden. As soon as Daisy drank it, she stopped shivering and fell into a deep sleep. I'm now sitting on the bed, my back against the headboard, legs stretched out in front of me as Daisy rests her head on my lap. I watch her as I play with her hair, and she sleeps peacefully.

I'm just pulling up her uncle's number to call them with an update when there's a knock on the door.

"Yeah?" I call out as quietly as possible, hoping not to wake her. Marcus opens the door and slides in.

"How's she doing?" he whispers as he looks down at Daisy.

"Better. I'm going to make sure she's settled; then Mum

will sit with her whilst we go to the cells," I whisper, glancing down at Daisy as she murmurs in her sleep.

"That's what I came up to say. You might as well stay here and look after her yourself. There's no point coming to the cells now. There was an incident whilst you were dealing with Daisy." Marcus explains as he rubs the back of his neck.

"What kind of incident?" I ask as I look up at my second.

"They're all dead," he says stone-faced.

"What?!" I almost jump off the bed but remember Daisy's leaning on me at the last second. She murmurs in her sleep again but luckily doesn't wake up.

"The guards called you, but you were engaged, so they called me. They said all the lights and power went off in the building, they didn't even have a chance to start up the generator when everything came back on, but all those in the cells were dead." Marcus explains. I curse under my breath.

"How did they die?" I demand.

"That's what I'm going down to find out now. There's no sign of a struggle. It's like they all just dropped dead where they stood." I curse again as Marcus nods in agreement.

"How is that even possible?" I ask. Marcus shrugs.

"I don't know. Edward's on his way to examine them. How long will you be here for?" I look down at Daisy sleeping. Her uncle told me she would probably be out for the best part of eight hours.

"I'm coming with you. Mum can sit with Daisy as we planned. I need to see this with my own eyes." Marcus nods and opens the door.

"We leave in five, then. I'll send Mama B up." Marcus starts to walk out of the door and stops. "Oh, and Jon wants a word. Play nice." He adds as he gives me a look.

"It's not me who needs to play nice, Marcus; he was out of order." I point out.

"I know, and so does he. He has been beating himself up over it, especially with Daisy being ill. Plus, Mama B gave him hell. She was furious with him." I nod at Marcus and look back down at Daisy. I haven't thought much about what Jon had said. With Daisy becoming so weak, I'd almost forgotten about it.

I hear Marcus close the door, and I carefully get up from the bed to not wake Daisy and walk over to my old desk. I'm always surprised by how much of my stuff is still as I left it in this room. I know Jon's is the same, but he stays here more than I ever do. I grab a pen and paper and jot down a quick note to Daisy, letting her know where I am and that I won't be long. I ask her to make contact via the bond when she's awake, and I'll come straight back. The sooner I can get her home, the better.

"Don't give Jon a hard time." I turn to find Daisy looking at me from the bed.

"Why aren't you asleep?" I ask as I grab a jumper and pull it over my t-shirt.

"I'll sleep now. Just don't give Jon hell. It would have been funny any other time," she says quietly.

"Fine, if you say so. Now, please rest." I answer as I grab my keys from the bedside cabinet.

"Be careful," Daisy whispers as she closes her eyes.

"I will, darling," I reply, watching as Daisy drifts back to sleep. I walk over to the bed to kiss her temple, noticing that she's no longer ice cold to the touch.

I walk out of the bedroom and down the stairs to where everyone is gathered by the front door. As soon as I get halfway to them, Jon stands at the bottom of the stairs looking up at me.

"Mikey, I'm sorry." He begins, but I hold up my hand to stop him.

"Leave it, Jonny, no harm done. Daisy even said she'd have found it funny if she wasn't ill, so let's just forget it. I want to get this done quickly and get Daisy home." Jon nods and joins the others as they pile out of the door. I walk up to Mum and kiss her on the cheek.

"If there are any issues, call her uncle first. I wrote his number down upstairs. He can help her more than I can with this."

"She'll be okay, Mikey. I spoke to Mary, and she said Daisy just needs to relax and sleep for the rest of the day. All will be fine. Now go. The sooner you get there, the sooner you can get back to her."

"Thank you, Mama." I kiss her cheek one last time and rush out after the team.

Chapter Eight

Michael

We've been at it for hours, and we're still no closer to finding out what happened to these guys. Edward's completely stumped; the only explanation is a magical one. I've spoken to Nigel; he explained that to cause four deaths simultaneously, there has to be some powerful magic involved. He doesn't think it is the work of just one witch or sorcerer. I've added it to the ever-growing list of unanswered questions that keep popping up.

Nigel and I also had the chance to discuss Daisy and her magic. He wants me to take her down to see them because she shouldn't have felt so ill after using her magic last night, and she certainly shouldn't have gotten worse this morning when she wasn't using her magic. I've asked if our bond, which must use some form of witch or wolf magic, could make her worse, but Nigel doesn't think it's connected.

We're both concerned with how weak it's making her at the moment. So we've arranged for Daisy and I to go down in five days for the weekend. Will and Jon are coming down with us to look around the house we think is also owned by Jackson and work with the pack down there to see how they're getting on with the new training schedule I sent them.

I want to keep that pack sweet as they check in with Nigel and Mary regularly and are on standby for any issues that arise while we're far away. The number of favours I'm calling in regarding the Jackson situation is ridiculous, but it'll be worth it when Daisy and her family are finally free of him.

Daisy surprisingly woke up two hours ago; I asked Stuart to take her home. His arm is still healing after yesterday, so he's no use to us as we dispose of the bodies. He messaged to say she was curled up in the garden with a book. Her auntie suggested that being surrounded by nature would help her recharge more quickly. We're hoping the full moon tonight will help too. We're all planning on running together in the forest where I took Daisy in the early days of our relationship.

It's hard to believe we've only spent two full moons together. I've gotten her to change twice a week, even if we just run in the woods behind our house. It's helped her ability to shift so much, and she's no longer feeling any pain.

I pull up outside our home and climb out of the car; the rest of the team's making their own way here. I'd dropped them all off at Mum's half an hour ago, where they'd left their cars.

I hear Daisy laughing loudly from the back garden. It's the first time I've heard her laugh properly since I collected her from the pub two nights ago. I've missed that sound. I head straight to the back garden, where I see Daisy lying on a blanket in shorts and a bikini top with a book in her hands. Stuart is sitting next to her with his sketchbook.

"Well, someone's looking better," I call as I close the gate behind me; Daisy's head shoots up to look at me. She jumps to her feet before rushing over. I lift her so she can wrap her legs around my waist and arms around my neck. I chuckle, holding her tight to me, all the worry about how she would be dissolving.

"Why didn't you say you were on your way home?" Daisy asks as she loosens her grip on my neck and leans back. I place a hand on her head and pull her to me until our lips finally meet and I can kiss her properly for the first time in days.

"I wanted to surprise you. Plus, I thought you'd be sleeping." I reply as my lips brush against hers.

"I'm feeling fully charged." She smiles at me, causing my heart to swell.

"I can tell, but you should still be resting." I point out. Daisy grins at me before leaning to whisper in my ear.

"Take me to bed then, handsome." After being deprived of her for the last five days, every nerve in my body comes alive with those six words. I'm about to take her to our room when we hear a car pull up. I moan with frustration whilst Daisy giggles. "I guess it'll have to wait until later then." She winks at me as she presses her lips to mine again.

"Looks like Daisy's back to her usual self," Will calls as he walks through the back door, quickly followed by Marcus and Jon.

"Thank the Goddess for that; you scared the shit out of us earlier," Marcus adds as he walks over to the patio furniture and sits down. I kiss Daisy again before placing her back on her feet. She looks over at Jon, standing by the doorway, looking anxious. She walks out of my arms, heads straight to him without missing a beat, and wraps her arms around his waist. Jon lets out a sigh of relief and hugs her back. I can see him whispering in her ear, but it's too quiet to pick up. Daisy looks at him and shakes her head before whispering back. I leave them to it as I head into the house.

I pull my phone out of my pocket to check my emails. I haven't checked them all day, and I'm expecting some from my third-year students. I flick through the received emails, calculating how many I could get through before our run when I see a username that jumps out.

Jackson273

Cautiously, I open the email containing a short message and three attachments.

To: M.G.Adams
From: Jackson273
Subject: I have eyes everywhere.

Your security doesn't live up to my expectations.

I open the attachments and freeze. All three are photos of Daisy and Carl in various locations.

"Fucking bastard," I growl out loud before I can stop myself.

"Mikey? What's going on?" I turn to see Marcus standing in the kitchen doorway. I hold up one finger and grab two beer bottles from the fridge before nodding to the stairs. Marcus follows me up to the office and closes the door behind us.

"Alright, spill, what's happened?" he asks as I hand him a bottle, followed shortly by my phone. I sip my beer as I watch Marcus flicking through the photos. "Who?" Marcus growls through gritted teeth.

"Check the sender's name." His eyes widen, and his lips curl back over his teeth.

"Are you fucking kidding me?! When were these taken?" he asks. I shake my head whilst taking my phone back from him.

"I'm guessing whilst we were in Exeter. I'm going to confirm if they are real now." I answer as I call Carl's number. He answers on the third ring.

"Alright, Mikey, what's up?" He calls cheerfully. I take a deep breath.

"Carl, where did you go when Daisy was with you?" I ask.

"Umm, we spent most of the time here. But we popped into the library for an hour as Daisy needed more textbooks. Then we meet up with Beth and Tony at the Café at the university because Daisy was anxious about you being away. Why? What's up?" Carl asks, the worry evident in his tone. I silently count to ten in my head to try and stay calm. Marcus looks at me before addressing Carl himself.

"Carl, it's Marcus. It looks like you were followed, pal." The line goes silent for a moment. I know Carl will be trying to process it.

"There's no way, Marc. I did all checks myself. I didn't relax the whole time we were out. There's no way we were followed." I can hear how confident Carl is. I feel bad for proving him wrong.

"I've received pictures of the two of you, Carl. One in the library, one in the cafe with Tony and Beth and one from the bar, through the same window as Kellan took them." I hear Carl use several different profanities.

"Mikey, I was so careful. She didn't leave my sight, and I didn't let my guard down for a moment."

"I believe you, Carl. You can see you are on high alert. I have no idea who took the pictures and how they took them, but it couldn't have been Kellan. You would have seen him." I sigh as I know Carl would never relax when on guard duty. He was one of my best guys at one point. I hear Richard asking what's wrong in the background, and Carl quickly fills him in.

"How did they know she'd be there?" I ask Marcus, who shrugs.

"Process of elimination? They knew you wouldn't leave her alone; she hadn't gone to Tony's, so they tried the bar next? But I'm only guessing." Marcus speculates, pinching the bridge of his nose.

"What's Daisy said?" Carl asks.

"I haven't told her yet. I wanted to speak to you first, I just found the email." I admit. "I wasn't sure if the photos were authentic. But now I know I'm going to have to tell her. Especially as she hated me the other day for hiding things from her." I sigh again.

"Yeah, she messaged us as well as everyone else. If I were you, I would tell her now; it saves her from thinking the worse again." I know he's right; it feels like something happens every time things are good between us and causes issues.

"Will do. You still coming to the run?" I ask as I take a sip of my beer.

"If you'll still have us. I'm sorry for letting you down, Michael. You have no idea how bad I feel."

"You didn't let me down, Carl. It's fine, well, it's not fine, but I don't think there was anything you could have done to prevent it. I guess we have another person to watch for now; I just have no idea who." I say goodbye to Carl and end the call before turning to my second.

"Are we going to catch a break any time soon? Seriously what the fuck is going to happen next?" I lean back into the chair. "Don't answer that I don't want to know," I add quickly. I look at Marcus and see the sympathy written all over his face.

"I thought things were simple when you met your mate. I thought everything was meant to just click into place, and you live happily ever after. But all we seem to get is one drama after another." I moan and run my hands over my face, feeling the two days' worth of extra stubble.

"That's not fair, Mikey, and you know it. Daisy never asked for any of this." Marcus says with a raised eyebrow.

"I didn't mean it like that, Marc. I would deal with all this shit and more for the rest of my life if it meant keeping her in it. I'm just tired. It's been a shit five days." Marcus nods; I know he gets it.

"You need to tell her about this. She may kill you if you hide anything else from her." He points out. I close my eyes as I take a deep breath.

"When I pulled up outside today, she was laughing in the garden, and I realised I hadn't heard her laugh in days." I shake my head before taking a long drink from my bottle.

"I know, Mikey, but you can't keep her in the dark." Marcus points out. I sigh and stand up.

"Let's do it then. I'll tell her in the lounge if you can tell the others outside. We all must be on the lookout tonight when we're running." I down the rest of my bottle before Marcus and I leave the office.

We are about to head downstairs when Daisy bounces into the hallway, smiling.

"There you are. Where have you two been hiding?" She asks as her smile grows at the sight of us. Marcus reaches over and takes my empty bottle from my hand before heading down the stairs, leaving me at the top. I wave to Daisy to come up. I watch as the spark leaves her face; and the large grin. A pit forms in my stomach. Daisy frowns at Marcus as he stands next to her at the bottom of the stairs.

"What's happened?" she asks, looking between us, worried.

"We'll be back in a bit," I say to Marcus as Daisy climbs the stairs.

"Take your time. We don't have to leave for at least three hours," Marcus says, giving us a weary smile. I nod and put a hand on Daisy's back before leading her into the bedroom.

"Mikey, what's happened? You're scaring me." She whispers as we walk into our room, and I sit on the bed, pulling her down onto my lap.

"I've just opened my emails and found one we think is from Jackson. There are three pictures of you attached. All taken whilst I was in Exeter." Daisy looks at me, frowning.

"But Carl was so careful when we went out, even I was looking around for Kellan," Daisy exclaims. I tighten my hold on her as she leans into me, tucking herself under my chin.

"I know, darling, I spoke to Carl, and he said the same thing. We don't know who took the pictures, but there are ones of the two of you in the library, the cafe, and the bar." I can feel Daisy starting to shake in my arms, and I kiss her on the top of the head in the hope of calming her. "Speak to me, darling."

"I'm fine, just ... What if it was him?" she whispers.

"Do you think you would know if he was near?" I ask. I've heard that some wolves can sense the ones who changed them when they are close.

"Yes," Daisy replies as I feel her body shudder. I study her face as she glances at the bedroom window. "I don't think it was Jackson who took the pictures," she adds.

"I don't either," I answer honestly. Daisy instantly seems to relax in my arms. "I think he's trying to scare us," I add as I run a hand over her thigh.

"So, what do we do?" Daisy asks as she places a hand on my chest. I place a hand over hers, holding it in place.

"I want to keep someone with you at all times. Us hiding out here whilst I'm still working at the uni will be useful as we can't go anywhere anyway. But when you're there, I want someone else with you or close by."

"As in Tony or one of the guys?" she asks, looking up at me.

"Can Tony fight?" I ask. Daisy nods.

"Kind of. We used to spar in our dorm when others weren't around."

"You sparred?" I ask, a little shocked. Daisy nods again.

"Alex taught Clare and me after I was taken. He wanted to be sure we were never left defenceless again. Clare didn't take it seriously, but I did." She pulls away from me slightly so she can look at me properly. "I'd like to learn more and train against another wolf. Would you train me?" I look at her and smile.

"Of course. The guys and I usually train at least twice a week. You're more than welcome to come with us. We have our own gym in the middle of nowhere. You can use it whenever you want. We're going tomorrow, so I was going to take you along anyway. I'm sure someone will spar with you."

"No, absolutely not. She could get hurt!" My wolf growls. I smile down at Daisy before continuing. "I may not be the best person to teach you, though. It's too embedded in me to protect you. My wolf is already fighting me on the idea." I add.

"Too right, it's a stupid idea. We protect our mates, not fight them!" I quickly tell him to shut up. "I will try my best, though," I promise her.

"So when I'm in uni, I don't need to have one of the guys following me, right?" I tilt my head as I look at her.

"I would feel better if one of them was on site. Just until I know how well Tony can protect you." I reach up and brush some hair off her face. "I know you probably think I'm being paranoid, but I can't risk anything happening to you, darling. I promised to let you fight your battles, but we don't know who or what we're dealing with here, so please meet me halfway. We do this together, but one of the guys will be with you when I can't be." I watch as Daisy closes her eyes and takes a deep breath before slowly nodding. I smile at her as I lean in and softly kiss her lips.

"Thank you, darling," I whisper as I gently kiss her.

Daisy moves to straddle my lap, her fingers thread into my hair, and deepens the kiss. I place one hand on her back, another on the back of her head so I can pull her harder against me. I feel her tongue slide against my lips and welcome it gladly. Daisy's hands leave my hair and thread around my waist, her hands wandering until she finds the bottom of my t-shirt. I pull my lips from hers and grin.

"The guys are only downstairs, baby." The look I receive from Daisy tells me she doesn't give a damn. She leans back and tugs my t-shirt off completely before forcing me to lie back on the bed. She leans over me and plants a soft kiss on my lips.

"You'd better be quiet then because they've seen more of you this week than I have, and I plan on making up for that." I close my eyes and moan as she kisses me on the lips one last time before moving her kisses along my jaw and finding my neck. She continues to kiss me down my neck until she reaches my collarbone. Using her teeth, she nips her way along it. Suddenly I feel her reach the mark she left on me the night we mated.

"Mine." She growls quietly. My whole-body contracts as the feeling of her tongue on my mark sends shock waves through every nerve in my body. I feel her shudder on top of me and wonder if she felt it.

"Yours." I gasp as she does it again. Shit, if she carries on, I'll cum in my pants like a teenager. From the look on Daisy's face, she knows it too. She looks at me, smirking before directing her kisses across my chest, then painfully slowly down my stomach whilst she repositions herself from straddling my lap to kneeling on the floor between my legs.

As she reaches my jeans, she looks up at me with those sexy green eyes as she undoes the buttons and pulls the fabric down as I lift my hips, releasing me from the constraint of my jeans and boxers. The second I'm free, she takes me in her hand and strokes me once, twice, three times before kneeling up and running her tongue from my balls right up to the tip. I hiss through my teeth as she licks the tip of my enlarged dick before taking me in her mouth. Each time she takes my cock into her mouth, she takes me deeper until she's swallowing me deep into her throat.

"Fuck, baby." I groan and grab the covers to my side as she nearly sends me over the edge. I don't think I will ever get used to how this woman makes me feel when she takes me in her mouth. It takes every ounce of self-control not to shoot my load down her throat instantly.

I feel her slowly move back up my shaft before sliding down again. She does it over and over again. Each time she reaches the tip, she starts swirling her tongue around it again before taking me back down her throat. I can only stand it for a few minutes before I grab her under the arms and sit up as I force her to stand. She giggles playfully as she stands in front of me as I undo her shorts, quickly pulling them and her thong down before falling to my knees and pulling her plush, shaven pussy lips to my mouth so I can devour her as she has me.

With my hands on her hips, I keep her pressed against me

as I guide my tongue between her lips and up towards her ultra-sensitive clit. The second my tongue swipes against it, I feel her knees buckle ever so slightly as she moans out loud; I look up without removing my mouth as she places her hands on my shoulders for support, her head tipped back as she moans again.

"Shit, babe." She hisses as I circle her clit with my tongue again, I know how to make her climax in minutes like this, but sometimes I like to take my time and tease her until she begs me to take her. I try desperately to savour every second I am here on my knees before this remarkable woman as I worship her repeatedly with my tongue. The closer she gets to climaxing, the weaker her legs are. I love the effect I have on her body. I hear her call my name as her hand's fist into my hair and her sweet nectar flood my mouth.

Daisy's legs go from underneath her. I grab her before turning with her to lower her onto the bed. Slowly I move, lying over her, my lips kissing her neck and moving to her mark. I place the softest kiss on it and feel her body shudder as mine had. As she shudders, I feel the pleasure flood me. I look at her and smile.

"Mine," I whisper as I look at her. She looks at me, half-closed eyes, still coming down from her orgasm.

"Yours." She replies before lifting herself to kiss me. "I need you, Mikey." She whispers as she kisses me again. I move, making sure our lips never leave each other, as she lies on her back, with me, between her legs. I position myself, so I'm just at her entrance. I always look at her for permission,

"Please, Mikey." She begs. That's all I need to thrust into her causing her to moan loudly. I kiss her to muffle her gasps as I move in and out of her. This is my second favourite place to be. The first being on my knees worshipping her from the outside, the second inside her as we fit perfectly together.

I take her hands in mine and pull them up over her head; with our fingers entwined together, we move, in perfect sync, both trying desperately to be quiet, knowing four wolves below us have advanced hearing, but the longer we go, the harder it is to hold back. Before long, neither of us care how loud we are. All we care about is losing ourselves to each other for the first time in days.

As Daisy gasps and starts calling my name, I feel her contracting around me as the first waves of her orgasm start, pushing me over the edge. In seconds, we growl each other's name as we cum together, her orgasm milking me of my own. I fall to the side, pulling her with me as I wrap my arms around her and hold her close to me as we both struggle to catch our breath and come down from our incredible high.

Chapter Nine

Daisy

"How long until the shift do you reckon?" I ask Stuart as we all head into the forest. This is the first time I've run with anyone other than Michael and Jon; I'm not feeling as nervous as I thought I would be. Even with Carl and Richard joining us as Tony watches the bar.

Carl has been apologising non-stop since he arrived. I've had to threaten him with his life if he apologises again. Like Michael said, how can he look for a threat if he doesn't know what it looks like? The person taking the photos could have been anyone. Kellan always said he lived here for years, so he could ask anyone to keep an eye on me for him. There's no way of knowing who.

"About fifteen minutes. How did you judge it when you were on your own?" Stuart asks.

"I didn't. I'd head out at about nine and hide until it happened." I admit shrugging.

My first two years as a wolf were very different to how it is now. Before Michael, I hated my wolf, I blamed her for what Jackson had taken from me, and I wanted nothing to do with her. I fought her constantly, even during our forced monthly shifts. Since being with Michael, my wolf and I have a much better relationship, and I now listen to her most of the time.

"I honestly don't know how you managed only to shift once a month. You must have been in so much pain. My wolf gets antsy if I only shift once a week." Will says next to us,

"I didn't manage it. I'd have lost control if Michael hadn't stepped in when he did." I look ahead of me, where Michael's walking with Marcus and Jon, the three of them deep in conversation. "He saved me," I add, smiling as I remember our first run and how it changed everything for me, not just with my wolf, but for us as a couple as well. It was the night I realised what I felt for Michael was more than a schoolgirl crush on my teacher. He was where I felt the safest, the most complete. I remember looking at him in his beautiful brown wolf form for the first time and feeling like I was home.

"You saved yourself. I just got to watch you grow," Michael says as he turns to look at me, smiling before going back to talking to the others.

"Smooth, Mikey." Will chuckles as he grins at me.

"And he knows it." Stuart laughs.

"Careful, Stu. Michael's looking to let off some steam tonight. You don't want to be his target, not with your arm still healing." Richard laughs at him.

"I think Daisy helped him release some of that steam earlier," Will says as he winks at me. I flip him off, trying to hide the smile on my face, and failing.

"You're just jealous. How long's it been now, Will?" Michael calls as he waits for us to catch up. He throws his arm over my shoulder as soon as we reach him, pulling me closer to him.

"Too fucking right; I'm jealous. That sounded like some hot sex." Will laughs. I hide my face in Michael's chest as he laughs into my hair.

"That's because it was."

"Michael!" I exclaim, slapping his chest. Michael laughs harder, tightening his hold on me.

"What would you prefer I say? That I was faking it?" he asks, grinning at me.

"Can men even do that?" I ask, shocked.

"Hell yeah," I hear about four different voices answer in unison. I look around wide-eyed.

"Well fuck me."

"Okay," Michael answers quickly as he takes my legs out from underneath me and lowers us to the floor.

"I don't mean now!" I squeal, pushing against his chest.

"You spoil all my fun, baby." He pouts as he rolls off me and jumps to his feet before pulling me up onto mine as our friends stand around laughing at us. I pull my hand out of his to dust myself off.

"I need more female friends," I mutter as I walk away from them, purposely swaying my hips as I go, knowing what it does to Michael. I can hear him laughing behind me with the rest of the gang.

"You know you love us, Daisy," Will calls as I walk off to where Jon's leaning against a tree; I hold my hand up and flip him off as I go. I hear them all roar laughing as I reach Jon.

"What's up with you?" I ask as I get closer; Jon shakes his head as he lifts his shoulders in a half shrug.

"Nothing, just watching you lot." I turn and look at our large group of friends and family. All are laughing and joking, all the stress from the last week forgotten for a short time as we enjoy each other's company.

"They are a group of misfits, aren't they" I laugh as Michael and Marcus both turn and take Will and Stuart out with a rugby tackle whilst Carl and Richard jump out of the way laughing.

"It's not been like this since Michelle died," Jon says quietly as he watches his brother and friends. "Yeah, we've had a laugh, but Mikey's been shut off for a long time." Jon turns and looks at me. "That all changed after he met you. You might have walked into Mikey's life as his mate, but you've affected all of us. We're all happier and more relaxed around each other than we've been in years." I look from Jon back to the guys and swallow the lump that's formed in my throat.

"I've brought a lot of stress to the group, Jon. Don't think I don't know it because I do." Jon looks at me and smiles sympathetically.

"We would all rather deal with that stress than lose you, you're not only our pack sister, but you're also our friend, our family, and we love you." I step closer to Jon and throw my arms around his neck; he chuckles before hugging me back.

"I love you all too," I whisper. As I pull away from Jon, I can sense Michael through the bond.

"Everything okay?" I turn and look at him. I can't miss the concern on his face. I stick my tongue out, making him laugh out loud. *"I'll take that as a yes then."* Just as I close the bond, I start to feel the start of the shift. I look around and notice everyone's starting to strip. Michael quickly rushes over to me.

"Want to find somewhere private?" he asks as he takes my hand. I know the pack's females all strip in front of the males;

it's part of being a wolf. All modesty goes out the window.

I look up at Michael, smiling.

"No, I'm fine." He nods as he holds out our bag for my clothes before quickly adding his and putting the bag up into a nearby tree.

"You ready for this?" he asks. I lean upon my tiptoes, hyper-aware that I'm completely naked in front of everyone and kiss him on the lips as I feel the shift start.

"Last one to shift is getting thrown in the pond!" I call out as I drop to my hands, landing as my beautiful light brown wolf.

Chapter Ten

Daisy

"Come on. You can do better than that. Hit me!" I put my fists up and look at Michael as he lowers his own.

"Darling, I'm going as hard on you as I can. It goes against every wolf instinct I have to even be in the ring with you." I look around the team's makeshift gym and sigh. I know he's right; it was a stupid idea. How can I expect my mate to train me in defense when his wolf's primary focus is to protect me? I slump onto the floor and start unwrapping my hands. Michael squats down in front of me, places a finger under my chin and lifts my head so I'm looking at him.

"I'm sorry, darling. I did say I may not be the right person to train you." I lift myself slightly and press my lips to his.

"I know, handsome. I'll ask one of the guys to train with me again." Michael leans over and kisses me once more. This time with a little more passion.

"You know, you look amazing when you're sparring. I'm not sure I like another male making you hot and sweaty. If anyone's going to leave you breathless, it should be me." I squeal, laughing as Michael crashes into me, knocking me onto my back. I wrap my arms around his neck as he kisses me, positioning himself between my legs. I feel his hands slide from my hips onto the bare skin of my waist.

"These sports bras leave very little to the imagination, baby. Every time I look at you, I want to rip it off with my teeth." I tip my head back as he lowers his mouth to my stomach and kisses it. Whilst his hands move up to my breasts. I feel my back arch into his touch as my fingers entwine themselves into his hair.

"This is highly inappropriate behaviour for a leader to be displaying. Any team member could walk in." I murmur as Michael pinches my nipple. He glances up at me from my stomach and smirks.

"You're right. I guess I should stop." He starts to lift himself away from me. But I stop him by wrapping my legs around his waist and using the momentum to roll him onto his back.

"Not a chance, Adams. You're finishing what you started." I lower myself down so I can kiss him again.

"Well, in that case." Michael quickly flips us again with ease as he lands back on top. "If I remember rightly, you were on top last night." He leans down and kisses me again as he pushes his hips into mine, as I feel how turned on he is.

"Oh fuck." I moan as he rubs against me in just the right spot.

"It works better with your clothes off." Both our heads snap to the sound of Marcus's voice. Marcus, Will, and Stuart are all standing at the gym entrance.

"What the hell, Boss? That's just wrong on so many levels." Stuart exclaims, shielding his eyes. Marcus leans against the wall shaking his head whilst Will looks fit to burst. Michael jumps up and pulls me to my feet.

"Sorry guys, we got carried away," I call across the room, blushing with embarrassment. Michael looks at me, grinning.

"I'm not sorry."

I roll my eyes at him. "Won't happen again." I quickly add, smiling back at him.

"No promises from me." Michael winks at me before slapping my ass and climbing out of the ring to speak to Marcus. Will claps him on the back as he passes before reaching me.

"Hey Dais, you looking forward to your trip home later?" Will asks as he jumps up on the other side of the ropes and plants a kiss on my cheek. I look over at him, smiling.

"Yep. I can't wait to see my auntie and uncle. It's been a long three weeks."

"Did you ask your auntie to make any of those famous cookies you don't shut up about? It's all I've been thinking about since Michael said I'm coming with you." Will laughs as I hold the ropes of the boxing ring open for him to climb in. I roll my eyes as I punch his arm playfully.

"Do me a favour, and I'll make sure some are waiting for us."

"Why do I have a feeling I'm not going to like this." Will sighs, looking worried.

"Go a quick round with me? Mikey's being pathetic again." I hear Michael clearing his throat from across the room. We both turn to face him. He has his arms crossed over his bare chest as he stands next to Marcus, who's leaning against the wall, grinning.

"I wasn't being pathetic; I just didn't want to hurt you." He calls out with a raised eyebrow. I lean on the ropes, smirking at him playfully.

"Oh, handsome, It's cute that you think you can." I hear Michael growl at me as his team starts laughing. I turn back to Will smiling; I watch as he looks from me to Michael and back at me again.

"Mikey will have my ass if I hurt you. I'm not sure I'm up for the risk." He states as he holds his hands up.

"Chicken shit," I mumble as I turn to find Stuart. "What about you?" I ask, but Stuart shakes his head.

"Not after the other day, the boss nearly killed me when you didn't block that blow to the head." I spot Michael glaring at him.

"That's because she had turned away from you." He says sternly.

"I was trying to teach her to always be prepared," Stuart answers defensively.

"You were showing off," Michael exclaims. Stuart mutters a 'whatever' and heads off to the weights area of the gym. I turn to Marcus, grinning. He sighs as he pushes himself away from the wall.

"Fine. But I'm not sparring with you. It'll be all pad work." He sighs as he looks at Michael, who nods his approval.

"Fine by me," I reply, grinning. I quickly re-wrap my hands as he heads to the padded mat area. I climb out of the ring and start walking over to him. Michael steps in front of me and places a finger under my chin to tilt my head to look at him.

"Be careful. I don't want your uncle asking me why I'm taking you back to him damaged." I tap him on the cheek, smiling.

"Don't worry; I'll make sure to blame you for not training me yourself." Michael walks away, muttering to himself about me being a handful. "That's why you love me so much," I call after him. He turns back around as he responds through the bond.

"You're lucky you are so damn hot. It makes the stress worthwhile."

"The fact we're amazing in bed helps as well," I reply quickly, sending an image of us entwined in each other last night. Michael spins around and looks at me, his eyes black with desire. I wink before turning around to find Marcus, watching us with arched brows.

"Any chance of you focusing now?" Michael's second asks.

"Yep, let's do this," I reply, lifting my hands into the guarding position as Marcus holds up the pads.

)) ● ((

Forty minutes later, I'm lying flat on my back, soaked in sweat, and gasping for breath.

"Mikey, I think I killed her," Marcus calls as he grins over me.

"I'm not dead, just resting," I call back. When Michael doesn't respond, I roll onto my front and look over to the boxing ring where I last saw him.

There he is, topless, sweat glistening from his torso as he fights Will. The two of them are giving it their all. Michael moves like the predator he is, his eyes never leaving Will, his stance constantly on the defence, but the second he has a chance, he switches to the attack. The punches fly between them, very few connecting as they block them, but those that do are perfect. I'm mesmerised by their dance that I almost miss the punch Michael lands, which knocks Will onto the floor. Michael's on him in a flash and has him pinned. Will tries to throw him off, but there's no chance.

"I'm done," Will calls as he taps against Michael's arm. Michael climbs off his pack brother and gives him a hand up. With a quick one-armed man hug, they both climb out of the ring laughing.

I watch from the floor, checking out my hot mate. Michael looks over at me and winks. I take stock of his injuries, split lip, cut eyebrow and a bleeding nose. All that work I did on his injuries the other night was for nothing.

"And you were worried about explaining me being damaged to my uncle. How are you going to explain all that?" I ask as Michael walks over and sits on the padded mats next to me.

"I'll say you lost your temper, baby. They won't question it." I reach up to push him over. But he jumps out of my way, laughing.

"I'd punch you if I had the energy," I add, rolling onto my back. Michael chuckles as he leans over and plants a sweaty kiss on my lips. This man does something to me when he smells of sweat and his muscles are ripped from his workout. What I would give to pull him down to the floor right now and help him get sweaty in a completely different way.

"Not up for a run with us then?" Michael asks, shattering my fantasy. I groan in response. Running requires effort, which I don't have. I used to run daily, but now I'm lucky if I manage once a week. Michael chuckles as he kisses me again, "I'll stay here with you then." A pang of guilt hits as I know he likes to end a workout with a run.

"She'll be safe here, Mikey. It's secure," Marcus calls.

"See, Marcus says I'm safe. You go with the guys." I add, also secretly looking forward to some time on my own. Michael looks at Marcus, who nods. Michael glances down at me and sighs. I can see the internal battle he is fighting.

"Fine. But I'm locking you in. We won't be long." Michael says as he stands up. I can see the worry in his eyes, but I smile up at him and nod.

"Keep the doors locked, and don't open them for anybody. We'll be back in half an hour. Shout if you need us." Michael adds, tapping his temple to show he means through our bond.

"I'd roll my eyes if they didn't hurt so much," I mumble, closing my eyes as I feel something fall over me. I pull it off my face to find it's a towel.

"Shower whilst we're out. You stink." Will laughs as he

follows everyone out of the building. I hear the door close behind them and the key twist in the lock.

I'm surprised Michael agreed to leave me here without a fight. He must know it's a secure building. It's my first time left alone in nearly four weeks. It's nice to have a couple of moments to myself for a change.

I go to get up from the floor and groan as my body aches from training with Marcus. I should have gone for a run with the guys to loosen up, but I'm too knackered. I grudgingly pull myself onto my feet and make my way to the back where the shower room is. Knowing the guys will be gone for a while, I put my phone in Michael's docking station and turn on my music app. With a mix of Ed Sheeran and Sam Ryder set up, I head into the shower and turn it on as I strip out of my sweaty training gear. Will's right, I stink.

I'm humming along washing my hair when suddenly every hair on my body stands up on end. I spin around, expecting to find Michael behind me, but I'm still alone. Figuring it must be a draft from an open window somewhere. I go back to washing my hair, but I can't relax completely.

As I finish in the shower, I feel like I'm being watched again. I look around, but I'm still alone.

"Guys, if you are trying to scare me, I will kick your asses. I'm not in the mood." I call out, but I'm met with silence. I pulled the towel off the peg and quickly wrapped it around myself. The whole time feeling like somebody's right there watching me. My heart starts racing as my other senses heighten.

"Guys, you're not funny. Pack it in now," I call out sternly. But I hear nothing but the sound of my music in return. Suddenly a loud bang comes from the gym. I rush in, hoping to catch somebody out. But it's empty. I try to tell myself that I'm just paranoid; the doors are locked, after all. But something feels off. I don't like it. It's then everything switches off. Leaving me in pitch black whilst my eyes adjust to the lack of light. There are only three tiny windows in this place, all in a tiny area, leaving the rest without any natural light.

"Darling, are you okay? It feels like you're panicking." I

hear Michael ask down through the bond.

"I don't think I'm alone." I hear him curse before telling me he's on his way. I keep the bond open as he talks me through what to do.

Michael tells me to try and get out of the fire door, but it's blocked or locked when I get there.

I rush to the back of the warehouse where Michael's office is situated. I get to the door and throw myself inside, slamming it shut and locking it.

"Darling, we're nearly there. Speak to me, please." I hear Michael's panicked voice in my head.

"I'm in your office. I've locked the door." I tell him as I back away from the door and feel myself bump into something tall. A scream escapes me before I can stop it.

"Daisy!" Michael shouts down the bond. I feel behind me and realise it's just the filing cabinet.

"I'm okay." I gasp. Kicking myself for being so jumpy.

"I'm coming in now!" I hear the main doors being thrown open, all four guys' voices raised as they rush into the building. Michael has gone into full protector mode, barking out orders.

"Why are the fucking lights off? Who opened that goddamn window? I want the full place search from top to bottom, now!" The office door flies open, and Michael barrels into the room. I rush straight to him as a sob leaves my throat. He wraps his arms around me as I press my face into his sweat-soaked chest.

"I'm here, darling. I've got you." He lifts me into his arms and carries me bridal style out of the office. I can feel myself shaking violently as he walks through the building and out to his car. He opens the passenger door and places me on the seat before checking me over, looking for injuries.

"Darling, your hair is dripping wet." He starts rubbing my shoulders and arms with a towel he grabs from the back seat. He then grabs his hoodie and pulls it over my head, helping me pull my arms through.

"What happened?" he asks as he tries to pull my wet hair from inside the hoodie.

"I was in the shower with the music on. Everything was

fine, but then I felt like I was being watched. I thought you guys were just messing with me, but then there was a bang from the gym, and the power went off. I panicked." I admit, as I start thinking, I overreacted a bit.

Michael pulls me to him and holds me close, trying to reassure me. I hear the gravel crunch under someone's feet and jump to find Marcus approaching the car with my clothes.

"I thought you might want these." He says, handing the clothes to Michael.

"Anything?" Michael snaps. Marcus shakes his head; I lean into Michael, sighing.

"So I was just being an idiot?"

"No!" Marcus and Michael both protest at the same time.

"Daisy, the main power switch was down. It could have been switched off or blown." Marcus attempts to reassure me. "With everything that's happened, I'm glad you reacted the way you did. It shows you understand how serious this is." I find myself nodding my head as I know he's right.

"I'm going to take Daisy home. Can I trust you will thoroughly search the area to ease her mind?" Michael snaps as he stands next to Marcus, who nods at him. I notice Marcus is looking a little sheepish; it's a look I haven't seen on him before.

"Of course. I'll meet you at yours before you all head down to Cornwall." Marcus adds. Michael nods as he steps away. Marcus squats down in front of me.

"Don't think you overreacted; you did the right thing." He leans over and kisses me on the head as a big brother would. "You reacted perfectly for someone unable to face the threat head-on. I'm proud of you." I glance at him and smile weakly.

"Thanks, Marcus." I watch as he winks at me before standing up; he holds on to the door as I pull my legs into the car before he closes it.

Marcus goes to join Michael in the front of the car. I can tell Michael is furious as he turns to face his second.

"I thought you said she'd be safe here! So much for it being fucking secure! What the fuck, Marcus?" Michael hisses at his second. He's trying not to shout.

"Do you think I would knowingly put Daisy in danger? Michael, ninety per cent of the pack, doesn't even know where this gym is. Why in the world would I expect someone to find her here?" Marcus replies, pointing at the building.

"Well, someone did as Daisy felt like she was being watched! I want this whole area searched, and then you report everything you find to me." Michael snaps, not giving Marcus time to reply before turning and storming away to the car door.

Michael climbs into the driver's seat, glances over at me, and places a hand on my cheek, visibly relaxing when he sees I'm okay.

"Ready to go home, darling?" I nod as I lean into his touch before Michael removes his hand and starts the engine taking us home.

)) ● ((

As we pull onto the drive, I feel myself relax for the first time since being in the shower. Michael's been quiet since we left the gym. I can't help wondering if he's annoyed with me for overreacting. Michael jumps out and rushes to my side as soon as the car's parked. He has my door open before I even have my seat belt off.

"Put your arms around my neck, baby." He instructs as he leans down.

"I can walk," I answer. Michael looks at me with his eyebrows arched.

"You have nothing on your feet." He points out. I look down and realise he's right. I quietly turn and place my arms around his neck as he puts his arm under my knees and lifts me whilst giving me the keys to hold. He bumps the car door closed with his hip before walking down the path. Once we get to the front door, I unlock it. Michael places me on my feet as soon as I'm safely inside. I thank him quietly before heading straight for our room, pulling off his hoodie as I go. I need to get dressed. I feel vulnerable, and I don't like it. My anxiety is racing through me, and I need to get it under control.

I'm rummaging around looking for a matching underwear

set when I feel Michael standing behind me. Why does it feel like there's tension in the air? I don't know if it's because of everything that's happened or if I'm feeling paranoid, but I find myself snapping at Michael before I can stop myself.

"If you have something to say, Michael, just say it." I snap, not turning around to face him.

"I'm so sorry, baby," I hear him whisper. I spin around to look at him. He's standing in the doorway, his shoulders hunched over, his head lowered as he looks at the floor.

"Sorry?" I ask, confused. Michael nods as he looks up at me. "Why are you sorry?"

"I promised to protect you and then left you on your own, locked in a building with no way of escape when you needed to. I should have known better." I stare at him, speechless. I thought he was annoyed at me, but he's annoyed with himself.

"You didn't know I would freak out over a blackout. It's not your fault. I shouldn't have been pathetic." I point out as my heart races.

Michael looks at me. I can see his jaw clenching.

"Do you think you were being pathetic? Darling, you felt unsafe. Of course, you weren't pathetic. You reacted how anybody who has been through something as traumatic as you would have." Michael says as he pushes himself away from the doorframe he had been leaning against.

"You aren't mad at me?" I ask, suddenly on the verge of tears. Michael's in front of me before I notice he's taken a step and pulls me into his arms, holding me tightly against his chest.

"Darling, why would I be mad at you? I failed you. You did nothing wrong." Michael whispers into my hair.

"You didn't fail me. You can't be with me every second of the day." I sob as I wrap my arms around his waist. I always feel the safest here in Michael's arms.

"If I can't be with you, then somebody else should be. I put that rule in place for a reason and then completely discarded it myself, and you nearly got hurt because of it." He states as he runs his hand over my head.

"I was fine," I reply, trying to reassure him.

"What if you weren't? What if somebody was in there? I

shouldn't have left you alone." I can hear the guilt in his voice.

"Mikey, I'm a grown woman. I can't be babysat twenty-four hours a day." I watch as Michael opens his mouth to argue with me, but I just give him what the guys have started calling 'the look', and I can't miss the slight smirk on his face.

"Let's just agree that things didn't go to plan for either of us. Lesson learned. Next time I have to get off my lazy ass and run with you." I sigh as I lean back into his chest.

"Darling, you're not going anywhere near that gym again. Not until I know you're safe there."

"I am safe there. I'm with you and the guys, so stop being overprotective and overbearing and let me get dressed as I've been in this wet towel for too long, and I'm cold." I joke as I step back from Michael, who pulls the towel from around me and throws it across the room as I giggle.

"I can think of a few ways to warm you up," Michael growls. He picks me up and throws me onto the bed; I laugh as I bounce before pushing myself into the seated position in the middle of the bed.

"I'm at a disadvantage here, Adams, as you're fully dressed still," I smirk at him playfully.

"That can be rectified." Michael grins as he pulls his training gear off until he's completely naked in front of me. His impressive member is already standing to attention. Michael crawls onto the bed until he's lying over me. I open my legs to allow him to lie between them.

"How about we finish what we started in the ring?" Michael whispers as he kisses me softly on the lips. Slowly he moves down the bed as he kisses his way down my neck.

"Where was I when we were so rudely interrupted," he whispers as his lips reach in between my breasts. I close my eyes as I feel his hand running up my thigh and resting on my hip as his lips move across my breast until he has my nipple in his mouth. As he teases my nipple with his teeth, he squeezes my hip before running his hand up to my other breast and squeezing it. My back arches into his touch as a moan escapes me. Michael lifts his mouth away from my breast.

"Feeling warmer yet, baby?"

"Not warm enough." I gasp as he pinches my nipple with one hand as his other slides down to my hip again. His lips find my skin as he painfully slowly kisses his way down my stomach. As one hand teases my nipple, the other lightly strokes up and down my leg until he moves it to the inside of my thigh. Slowly his lips move to my left hip as his fingers brush up between my swollen pussy lips.

"I love how easy it is to make you wet," Michael whispers as his fingers spread me wide open and his tongue slowly licks me in the right spot.

"Ah fuck." I curse as his magical, wonderful tongue flicks me in just the right spot. Michael continues to lick and tease me for a couple of minutes before I feel myself getting close. As I feel myself about to climax, Michael lifts himself, leaving me begging him not to stop. He chuckles as he positions himself at my entrance, his hands on my hips.

"Please, Mikey," I beg. It's all he needs to hear as he rams into me; I scream his name as I orgasm instantly. He holds himself still in me, his face taut with pleasure.

"I love the feel of you cumming around me." Michael moans before he starts moving in and out of me, slowly at first, until I wrap my legs around him and pull him in close, he starts to pick up speed, and before long, we are both a hot, sweaty mess, and we move in perfect time to one another.

"Michael," I gasp as I feel myself heading towards another climax. I can feel he's getting closer too.

"Fuck, baby." Michael gasps as he reaches his climax, as I hit mine. Michael collapses on me as I wrap my arms around him, holding him close as we both try to catch our breath.

Chapter Eleven

Michael

I'm walking down the stairs, showered and dressed when the front door opens and Marcus and Will walk in.

"Michael, we need to talk." Marcus declares as soon as he sees me. I nod towards the kitchen. Daisy's upstairs getting dressed, and as much as I want to forget what happened today. I can't.

"Why have I got a feeling I'm not going to like this," I reply as I head straight for the fridge. I open it and pull out three beers. I place two on the breakfast bar and open the third for myself. Will looks at Marcus before pulling something out of his pocket. I know it's a Polaroid picture, like the ones Daisy was sent a few weeks back. I take a deep breath and hold out my hand for it. Marcus takes it from Will and hands it to me. I take one look at it and lose my shit.

"Fucking prick!" I roar as I throw the beer bottle across the room, narrowly missing Marcus and Will.

"Michael?!" I hear Daisy call from upstairs, quickly followed by the sound of her rushing down the stairs and into the Kitchen. Marcus grabs her before she can step on the broken glass.

"What the hell happened?!" She demands, looking at me. I realise I still have the photo in my hand and quickly attempt to hide it in my pocket.

"Oh no, you don't. Give me that picture right now, Adams," Daisy demands as she holds her hand out.

"It's nothing, darling." Daisy looks at me with one raised brow and her arms crossed against her chest. Fuck, it's 'the look'.

"I call bullshit. Evidence A being the smashed bottle. Bring me that photo before I walk over this glass and get it myself." I reluctantly walk over to Daisy and hand her the picture. My hands are shaking; I'm so furious. I watch as she looks at the picture and curses.

"So, I wasn't being paranoid then? Somebody was in the shower room with me." She states calmly. I look at her, shocked.

"How are you not losing your shit right now? I'm about to fucking kill somebody." I demand. Daisy looks at me frowning.

"What's the point? Am I pissed off? I'm fucking furious, but was it you, Marcus, or Will who violated my privacy? No! What's the point in losing my shit at you guys?" She states as she looks at me.

"Well, I can't stay calm. I want to know why this keeps happening? How whoever took this got into a locked building and out again without being seen? I want to know where you found that fucking picture of my mate naked in the shower?" I know I'm shouting, and I don't give a shit.

"We found it on the ground where you'd been parked. We think it was on your car, but you hadn't noticed as you were so focused on Daisy." Marcus explains. Daisy steps towards me, but Will and Marcus put an arm out to stop her again before she steps on the broken glass. She rolls her eyes and steps back.

"For the love of the Goddess, Mikey, get out of there so we can all move into the lounge and talk about this rationally." Daisy snaps as she steps back and holds out her arm to signal everyone to move. Will and Marcus both head into the lounge. I walk out of the kitchen and pulled Daisy to me.

"I'm going to kill whoever keeps doing this," I growl as I look down at her. Daisy places a hand on my chest and pats it gently.

"I'm sure you are, but right now, you need to calm down. Having a mood on will not get us answers any quicker." She says with a soft smile.

I roll my eyes and sigh. "Fuck, I hate it when you're right."

"No, you don't. You hate it when I'm the reasonable one. There's a difference," Daisy teases me smirking. I growl as I lean down and kiss her before taking her hand and walking into the front room.

"You okay, Mikey?" Marcus asks as we walk in.

"Far from it, I want to know everything you found, no

matter how small." I start pacing in front of the fire, Daisy taking a seat on the sofa as Marcus starts talking.

"There's no signs of forced entry. The window latch was broken, but it's old damage from the looks of it. It could have been broken for months, and we never noticed it before."

"The window is big enough for someone fairly small to climb through," Will says. "But it wouldn't be easy to climb back out." He adds.

"What about the fire exit? The doors wouldn't open when Daisy tried them." I ask. Marcus nods.

"The dumpster had been moved to block it. I know for a fact none of us put it there. We always check that fire exit is accessible in case of fire." I know he's right.

"What's the CCTV showing?" Daisy asks from the sofa.

"Nothing from the showers for obvious reasons. There's nothing from the gym or outside. But I'm not ruling out them being tampered with. I'll need to analyse the footage to be sure," Marcus explains.

"I think we need to accept it's Kellan, and whatever power he has helps him access a closed building," Will says from his spot. It would explain how he managed to get in and out of her dorm to take photos of her in bed when she was living there.

"Have there been any sightings of him at his place?" I ask. Both Marcus and Will shake their heads.

"He'll know you are casing the joint." Daisy answers. We all turn to stare at her.

"Casing the joint? Really?" Will asks, his eyebrows raised. Daisy looks at us all and shrugs.

"Sounds cooler than 'spying' or 'sitting in your car watching an empty building'!" Daisy replies. Marcus laughs as Will shakes his head, grinning.

"You're banned from watching any more crime documentaries," I add from my spot by the fire. Daisy looks at me and sticks out her tongue, making me laugh aloud. She always knows how to make me smile when I'm on edge.

"Just because I sound cooler than you, handsome." I watch Daisy as she gets up off the sofa and walks over to me. I instantly open my arms and pull her against me holding her tight as I inhale her scent to help calm myself.

"If it's Kellan taking these pictures, he's not physically hurting anyone. Maybe the worse he'll do is keep pushing your buttons until he gets bored." She whispers as she looks up at me.

"Yet. He's not hurting anyone *yet*; by anyone, I mean you. I'm not willing to wait until he does. I'm not risking your safety." I point out as I look into her green eyes.

"Mikey, you're doing everything you can. We've been over this. He'll slip up or get bored soon enough, and then you'll catch him." Daisy sighs. I breathe in with my nose pressed against her head again, trying to remind myself that at this moment in time, she is safe and unharmed.

"And what about Jackson?" I ask. Daisy shrugs.

"We don't know how much he knows, do we? He hasn't got this address, so we know I'm safe here. Kellan and him may have parted ways for all we know. Kellan isn't the type to be pushed around, even by someone like Jackson. We can't live our lives walking on eggshells over maybes and could bes. We deserve better." She says as she reaches up and kisses me on the cheek.

"Daisy's right. We're exhausting all our resources in trying to find him. He has to slip up sooner or later." Will says from his spot on the sofa. I know they're right. But I hate that I didn't protect her today, that Kellan or someone got as close as they did because I dropped my guard. I should have never left her in that gym alone. I should have followed my gut.

I place a finger under Daisy's chin and lift her head so I can kiss her lips.

"Why don't you go and finish packing? Jon will be here in a bit for us to head off." I say as she looks at me, frowning.

"I know you want to discuss stuff without me around. I'm not an idiot." Will starts coughing from the sofa, attempting to hide his laughter. I look at him with an arched eyebrow before looking back at Daisy.

"I know you're not, and that's not what I'm doing. I don't hide anything important from you anymore." Daisy leans up and kisses me quickly.

"It's cute you don't think I know you're lying to me. But I'll play along. Marcus tells me everything anyway." I turn and look at Marcus, who holds his hands up. I can feel my temper rising again.

"I don't tell her shit, Mikey, and you know I wouldn't." He protests.

"He tells me jack shit, but he just proved you hide stuff. Pack it in, Adams. I'll play along, but you and I will have a long chat in the car when you have over six hours and nowhere to hide. So be warned." Daisy taps my cheek as she struts out of the room. All three of us watch her go.

"I've changed my mind. I'm driving myself down to Cornwall. I'm sure Jon will keep me company." Will states from his spot, looking in the direction Daisy just left.

"You're coming with me. There's nothing she doesn't know, so don't be a wimp," I growl as I run my fingers through my hair. I look up at my second and see he's waiting for instructions.

"Keep an eye and ear on everything, I don't know how Kellan got so far into pack territory without being seen, but I want answers. Can you check in on Mum as well? She's trying to hide it, but I know this is all getting to her. She had locked the front door the other day." I sigh.

"Mama B never locks her door," Will growls. I nod in agreement. I can't remember the last time she had done it, either.

"Maybe we should suggest she goes and stays with your auntie for a bit, just until this is sorted," Marcus suggests.

"The three of us tried. She isn't having any of it. Maybe see if you can make her see sense." Mum always listens to Marcus more than Jon and me as she says he fusses less. He doesn't; he just has a way of making it seem like he isn't pushing her into anything.

I glance at the coffee table and pick up the picture of Daisy today. I look at it one last time before handing it to Marcus.

"Put that with the rest of them. I don't want to see it lying around." Marcus nods and slides it into his pocket without even glancing at it.

"We'll get them, Mikey. We'll end this for her." He says, looking up at the ceiling where we can hear Daisy walking around packing for our weekend away.

"I hope you're right, Marcus."

Chapter Twelve

Michael

"Daisy, if you don't stop wiggling around in that seat, I swear I'll reach over, open that door and throw you out while the car is still moving." Will hisses through his teeth from the back seat.

"Mikey, Will's threatening me." Daisy whines from her seat next to me.

"It's not a threat; it's a promise. The chair keeps knocking on my shin." Will adds. I look in the rear-view mirror and smile at him.

"In all fairness, darling, you haven't stopped moving for the last half an hour." I point out as Daisy wiggles in her seat again.

"But I need to pee." Daisy whines. I roll my eyes and look at the sat-nav.

"Well, you shouldn't have had that extra-large coffee during our last stop." Will points out as he knocks the back of her seat.

"Hey, that's not helping, arsehole." Daisy moans as she reaches round to hit him.

"Will you two pack it in!" I groan, sighing. I hear Jon chuckle behind me,

"Mikey, you do realise this is just a hint of what life will be like travelling down here with kids. If I were you, I would persuade Daisy's aunt and uncle to move closer before you have any." I look at my brother in the rear-view mirror and roll my eyes.

"Trust me; I've already thought of that," I reply as Jon laughs.

"We're a long way from having kids, Adams! So stop it, the pair of you." My brother and I share a look through the mirror, chuckling. "And don't be mentioning kids around my aunt and uncle; they'd freak." Daisy groans before wiggling in her chair again, causing Will to curse at her. I let out a sigh of relief as we pull into the village where Daisy's family lives. The moment we pull up outside their house, Daisy's out of the car and rushing towards the door. We all laugh as her aunt opens the door and steps back, letting Daisy rush past her. I climb out the driver's side, still chuckling as her aunt and uncle come to greet us on the driveway.

"Large coffee at the last stop?" Nigel asks, grinning as he holds out his hand to me. I shake it whilst nodding.

"How'd you guess?" I let go of his hand and leaned down to hug Mary before kissing her on the cheek.

"Because she does the same thing every time." Mary chuckles as she steps away from me. "Michael, what happened to your face?" Mary gasps as she stares at me. I chuckle as I point to Will, who's grinning proudly, standing behind me with Jon.

"We went a little hard on each other whilst training," I answer, laughing with Will, who has a black eye, a swollen nose and bruising on his cheek.

"I can see that; look at the pair of you. I'll heal you both before you see the local pack." Nigel chuckles as he heads towards Jon.

"This is my brother, Jonathan," I say, holding my hand out to Jon, who's shaking Nigel's hand,

"I'm the eldest," Jon says, winking at me.

"By three months, Jonny." I sigh, rolling my eyes. I can see the look of confusion on Nigel and Mary's faces. "My parents adopted Jon when he was four after his mum died. She was Mum's best friend." I explain quickly.

"And this is my pack brother, Will." Will steps forward and shakes Nigel and Mary's hands.

"Thank you for letting us crash in your summer house," Will says as he steps back from Mary.

"You're sleeping in the garage." Daisy calls as she walks back out of the house.

"Daisy!" Mary gasps, turning to look at her niece.

"What?! He threatened to throw me out of the car!" Daisy exclaims as she walks to her uncle and wraps her arms around his waist. "He was mean to me, Uncle Nigel." She pouts; Nigel looks at me and raises an eyebrow as he places an arm over Daisy's shoulders.

"What did you do to annoy him?" he asks, looking at Daisy.

"Nothing!" Daisy protests; Nigel looks at Will, who's smirking.

"She kept wiggling in her chair, which was hitting my legs," Will explains. Nigel laughs and plants a kiss on his niece's head.

"I'd have threatened to throw you out too. Make sure you sit in the front on the way back, Will."

"Hey! You're meant to always be on my side." Daisy protests as she steps away from her uncle and towards her auntie. "Auntie Mary will side with me." She says as she plants a kiss on Mary's cheek, hugging her arm.

"Auntie Mary will not. I agree; you should sit in the back on the way home." Daisy throws her hands up and stomps towards the front door. Muttering to herself about being unloved. I laugh and head towards the car's trunk to get our things. Mary tells the guys to follow her to the summer house. It's where Daisy used to spend her time during the full moon.

I tell the guys to meet me back in the house in twenty minutes, and we'll work out the schedule for the next couple of days as I follow Nigel into the house.

"No rest for the wicked?" Nigel asks as we enter the hallway. I turn, shaking my head.

"I've forgotten what rest is." I laugh, trying to hide how exhausted I am.

"Well, try not to push yourself too hard. I know you're doing everything you can to keep Daisy safe, and trust me when I say we could not be more grateful. But you're no good to her or anyone else if you burn out." Nigel says as he squeezes my shoulder for emphasis. I look down at Nigel and realise that his hair is greyer than it was three weeks ago, and his dark blue eyes look tired. I've spoken to him a few times recently and know how worried he is about Daisy.

"I know, but something else happens every time I relax, just a little." I sigh.

"Try and relax for a bit while you're here. Daisy's safe, and we'll get to the bottom of what's happening with her magic,"

Nigel says. I know he sympathises; he's been here for three long years.

"I hope you can because it's draining her more frequently now. She scared me the other morning. Is there any chance she's using her magic without realising?" I ask, but Nigel shakes his head.

"No, if she were just coming into her powers, I'd say it's a possibility, but she's an experienced witch; she knows what she's doing." I run my fingers through my hair and look towards Daisy's bedroom.

"Well, whatever's going on, I hope you can work it out, as I hate what it's doing to her. She's so proud of her witch heritage, and the thought of not being able to use her magic is upsetting her more than she's willing to admit." I say quietly, so she doesn't hear me. I can see from Nigel's face that he knows how hard this is for Daisy. I take a deep breath and plaster on a smile.

"Anyway, I'm going to unpack and see what trouble she's getting into before chatting with the guys. Do you mind if I set up my laptop somewhere?" I ask, holding my laptop bag up.

"The office is all yours this weekend. If I need my computer for anything, I'll use it when you're busy elsewhere." Nigel says, nodding to his office behind him, with a smile.

"Thank you, Nigel. I appreciate it."

"No thanks needed. Go get yourself sorted; I'm sure Daisy will come looking for you if you take much longer." Nigel smirks.

"Yes, she will, as she wants her phone charger." Daisy calls from upstairs, making us both groan.

"Coming, darling," I call up the stairs. Nigel chuckles as he walks away.

"Mary did warn you about spoiling her," he calls over his shoulder.

"And yet I didn't listen. Lesson well and truly learnt." I call back as I walk up the stairs and into Daisy's room, leaving her uncle laughing to himself.

I walk into the room and find Daisy lying on her bed with her legs kicking in the air as she flicks through her phone. She looks so relaxed and at ease. I close the door behind me and lie down next to her. She instantly rolls onto her back, resting her head on my chest. We lie in silence for a few minutes, just enjoying a few moments just the two of us.

Her uncle's right; I can relax a little this weekend. There's no way Jackson knows where we are, and even if he finds out, we'll probably be home by the time he gets down here. For once, I can enjoy being here with Daisy. Even though I need to do things, I can take tonight off, and we can relax and have some fun. It's something we haven't managed to do other than during the full moon five nights ago.

"When are you heading over to the other pack?" Daisy asks. I look down at her and realise she's put her phone down.

"In about an hour probably, we won't be there long as it's late. Do you want me to leave Jon or Will here with you?" I ask; as expected, Daisy shakes her head.

"No, I'll be fine here. Unlike me, Uncle Nigel and Auntie Mary don't have to worry about using their magic." She sighs.

"I'm sure your uncle will work out what's going on with you. He seems confident that he can anyway." I say as I twist a section of her long silky hair around my finger.

"He's just being optimistic." Daisy sighs. I lean down to kiss the top of her head.

"You don't know that. I'm sure they'll work out what's going on." I feel Daisy shrug in my arms, but as I go to argue, she rolls onto her stomach, kisses me on the cheek and climbs off the bed.

"Come on, we better head down before someone comes looking for us." She says as she heads out of the room. I climb off the bed and stretch before reluctantly heading down after her wishing we could have stayed where we were for a few minutes longer.

)) ● ((

"You got everything done you needed to?" Nigel asks as the guys, and I walk back into the house four hours later. I nod as I stretch my back, aching from the training session, driving for six hours and then working with the other pack. I can hear

Daisy and her auntie singing together in the kitchen, which instantly lifts my mood.

"Yeah, we're going back for the training session in the morning, and then we're done, for now, I hope," I reply.

"Good, we'll use that time tomorrow to work on Daisy's magic. She's been enjoying some time with Mary this evening." Nigel explains, smiling.

"And she still has no idea?" I ask. Nigel looks at me and shakes his head. I'm just about to say something to Jon when I sense Daisy. I look up and see her grinning at me from the kitchen doorway. I can't hide the grin that spreads across my face as I look at her.

"Excuse me a moment," I whisper as I walk away from the three males and head straight to my beautiful mate.

I pull Daisy into my arms and kiss her without saying a word. When I pull away, she gasps for air smiling up at me as she places a hand on my chest.

"How do you fancy a night out? Just you and me, no pack brothers, no hiding, just us." I whisper into her ear as she looks up at me, shocked.

"Really?" she asks. I smile back, nodding.

"I've cleared it with your auntie and uncle. The guys will drive us and pick us up so we can have a few drinks." I pull her tighter against me. "We don't need to hide here, and we don't have to worry as Jackson can't possibly know where we are. We can just be a couple enjoying each other's company." I lean down and press my lips to hers gently.

"Let's have tonight, darling, as we don't know when we'll get another for a while," I whisper before Daisy squeals excitedly, throwing her arms around my neck and holding me tightly.

"Can I take that as a yes?" I ask, chuckling.

"Yes!" Daisy squeals as she jumps out of my arms. "Oh, dear goddess, I need to get changed."

"Well, you have until I get out of the shower, so hurry up. I don't want to waste a moment we could spend out." I laugh as I walk toward the stairs. Daisy rushes passed me and takes the stairs two at a time. I can hear everyone laughing behind me as I watch her go squealing excitedly.

Chapter Thirteen

Michael

This is precisely what Daisy and I needed. A night out with nothing to worry about other than where to go and what we'll drink. In the three months that we've been an actual couple, the closest thing we've had to a date was the day spent in the forest, and the last time we were down here when Daisy took me shopping. We've never had an evening meal in a restaurant or a couple of drinks in a bar. We've never been able to be an average couple, which is pathetic.

Daisy and I are sitting in a beer garden, as I look across the table at her I can't help but smile. Daisy's sipping her drink and singing along quietly to the music. She looks so carefree, her face glowing from the effects of the alcohol and fairy lights strung up above us. Her head bops along to the tune, showing her inability not to dance whenever she hears music. She catches me watching, and a huge smile spreads across her face.

"What?" she asks, chuckling shyly; I smile as I pick up my drink.

"Nothing, just looking," I reply.

"At what?" Daisy asks, blushing.

"At the most beautiful woman I've ever seen," I reply, winking, earning myself an eye roll.

"Cheese ball." She mutters, smiling. I take her hand and kiss her knuckles.

"But whose cheese ball am I?" I whisper as our eyes lock. Daisy leans across the table, grinning.

"All mine." She growls under her breath as she grabs my shirt collar and pulls me to her until our lips meet, and she kisses me passionately. I place my hand on the back of her head to deepen the kiss, loving the feeling of being able to kiss her out in the open and not worrying about who sees us. Daisy's the one to break the kiss; she grins at me before sitting back on the other side of the table. I look down and see that we've both finished our drinks.

"Take a walk with me?" I ask, standing up and holding out my hand. Daisy smiles at me before pulling her legs from under the table and placing her hand in mine. I pull her up to her feet quickly, making her squeal laughing. I plant another quick kiss on her lips before leading her out of the beer garden and towards Charlestown Harbour. My arm draped across her shoulders, Daisy's arm around my waist. She slips her hand into my back pocket and squeezes; I look down at her, smirking.

"Don't look at me like that, Adams. If you don't want to be grabbed, you shouldn't have such a hot ass." Pulling her hand out of my pocket, I spin her around and press her back against a wall, enclosing her with my arms.

"Is that all I am to you? A piece of hot ass?" I ask, smirking as she smiles at me whilst pretending to think about it.

"I guess you have other uses." She whispers, looking up at me with those beautiful green eyes as she toys with me. I lean down further and press my lips to the slight dip in her collarbone.

"And what would those uses be, baby?" I ask as I brush my lips against her soft, smooth skin, causing her to moan.

"Take me to bed, and I'll show you." Daisy groans as I kiss her on the neck again. I notice that it's low tide, meaning we'll have access to the cove Daisy showed me the first time we came down here a month ago.

As if reading my mind, as she always does, Daisy grabs my hand and starts tugging me down to the small beach with her.

The sun's setting, but there's still plenty of light for our wolf eyes to see. Before long, we're giggling like teenagers as we navigate over the rocks and head out of view of the harbour and everyone else enjoying their evening. As soon as the harbour is hidden from our view, I turn Daisy to face me and lift her so she can wrap her legs around my waist.

"Do we have to go much further to that cove? I need to feel myself in you now." I growl through the bond as I kiss her deeply, her fingers thread into my hair, causing my cock to harden and my trousers to be restricting.

"It's just around the corner." She replies as she tugs on my hair, causing me to moan into her mouth. I pick up the pace and rush around the corner, to be met by the sight of a group of teenagers sitting around a small bonfire with bags of cans and bottles.

"Ah fuck." Daisy moans as I lower her to her feet.

"Well, there goes my first time on the beach," I whisper in her ear, chuckling. Daisy looks at me and rolls her eyes as she starts sulking back the way we came. I let her get a few steps ahead, so we are out of sight of the teens before grabbing her hand and pulling her back to me.

"Mikey, what are you doing? We can't!" she laughs as I hold her against me. I place a finger under her chin and lift her face to look into her eyes.

"Can't what? Just enjoy each other's company? Because I think you'll find we can." I kiss her gently on the lips. "Close your eyes, darling," I whisper. Daisy frowns at me but still does as she's told. I let my lips brush against her ear.

"What can you hear?" I whisper as quietly as I can. Daisy is silent for a moment before answering.

"The sea." She replies just as quietly. I press my lips to her cheek softly.

"What else?" I ask,

"Music," Daisy adds. I smile as I place an arm around her waist and take her left hand in my right, lifting it slightly.

"Dance with me?" I ask as I start swaying our bodies slowly in time to the music. I watch as a smile spreads across Daisy's face and her right arm rises until it's resting on my shoulder, her fingers finding the hair at the top of my neck.

"I thought you'd never ask." She whispers as she opens her eyes and looks straight into mine.

"I've wanted to ask you to dance with me since the night of your birthday. I sat at that table in The Crows watching you on the dancefloor, and all I wanted to do was walk onto that floor, take you into my arms and dance with you for the rest of the night." I whisper into her hair.

Daisy leans her cheek against my chest and sighs. "Back when things were simpler."

I tighten my arm around her. "The simplest thing in the world was falling in love with you," I reply. Daisy lifts her head and looks at me, smiling.

"Will you ever stop being the biggest cheese ball?" she asks. I look at her, smirking.

"Tell me to stop, and I will," Daisy places her head back against my chest, and I feel her fingers play with my hair at the top of my neck.

"Don't ever stop; it's one of the reasons I fell so hard for you." She whispers. I kiss her head as we stay there dancing together on the small beach, as the moon and stars shine above us. The world could stop existing, and I would die the happiest man on earth as I have the most amazing, strong, beautiful woman in my arms.

We stay this way, dancing together until the song ends and the music becomes more upbeat. We walk to the rocks at the top of the beach. I sit down and pull Daisy down so she is in between my legs with her back to me so I can wrap my arms around her and hold her close. Here we sit and talk about everything, our plans for the future, and all that we hope to achieve. She tells me more stories of what Clare and her got up to as kids. I tell her some of the trouble me and the lads caused—neither of us mentioning everything that's happening with Kellan and Jackson. The only thing that matters at this moment is that we're together.

"We'll need to head back soon, darling. Will and I need to be at the training grounds for six." I whisper to Daisy an hour later.

"I never want tonight to end," Daisy sighs as she holds onto my arms, still wrapped around her. I lean to the side and kiss her cheek.

"I don't either. But I promise we'll be able to do this every night if you want soon. I'm not willing to hide for much longer. I hate hiding our relationship. I want to take you out for dinner, go to the bar, and not worry about who sees. I want to give you the world, and I can't do that in the confines of our little home." I kiss her cheek again as she leans against me.

"I love our time in our home. I'm not complaining about

anything we have, as it's ours. However, I won't miss hiding and being babysat. I want everything to be over with so we can start living properly." Daisy sighs.

"I'm working on it, darling." Daisy turns in my arms and kneels before me, placing a hand on my cheek.

"Mikey, you couldn't be doing more if you tried. I didn't mean to suggest you aren't trying to take care of everything because I know you are. You're amazing, and I couldn't love you more for all you do for me and us." I lean forward and press my lips to hers gently.

"I love you, darling."

"I love you too. Now call Jonny, and let's get back. I know the best way to end such an amazing night." Daisy says, wiggling her eyebrows at me before jumping to her feet. I leap to my own and grab her as she squeals. I pull her to me and kiss her deeply, knowing precisely what I want to do to her when I get her to bed, if she can stay quiet long enough.

Chapter Fourteen

Michael

I wake with a jump as Daisy screams and glass shatters across the room. I dive over the top of her as more glass flies over us.

"Stay down," I whisper to her as I shield her from harm. I need to get her out of here; I grab her from the bed and rush out of the room, not caring about the glass cutting into my feet. I'm focusing purely on getting Daisy out of harm's way. I place her on her feet on the landing and quickly check her over.

"Are you hurt?" I ask. Daisy shakes her head, but when she looks up at me, I see the fear in her eyes, which pulls my wolf to the surface.

"Stay here," I growl as I feel my wolf taking control. I'm just reaching the top of the stairs when her auntie and uncle rush onto the landing. "Stay with her and inside the house. I'll send Will." I call as I jump down the stairs in one leap, landing in the hallway before racing to the back door.

I see a guy at the back of the garden, in the shadows of the trees. I advance toward him, my shoulders back and my hands balled into fists as I let out a deep warning growl. He turns and runs into the woods like a coward. I race past the summer house as Jon and Will rush out.

"Jon with me. Will, the house now!" Both immediately follow orders.

As we run into the woods, I fill Jon in.

"See if you can pick up a scent. Some prick smashed Daisy's windows." We both stop and start sniffing the air. All I can smell is the grass cuttings and herb garden. I head further into the trees; I'm about to shift when Jon appears.

"Nothing this way. I'll see if they backtracked. Any chance it's Kellan?" He asks as I shake my head.

"The guy I saw was the wrong build, far too big for Kellan." Jon nods and rushes out of view. I strip and shift as my sense of smell is stronger in this form. I run around the woods, sniffing continuously but to no avail.

After five minutes, I head back to the pile of clothes and shift before pulling on my pyjama bottoms; the guy is long gone.

I'm about to head to the house when I hear Will whistle. I sprint to the back of the house as Jon comes from the front.

"What's happened?" I ask as I get to Will.

"Daisy found a note attached to one of the bricks thrown through the window." I run back into the house, ordering Jon to keep looking.

"We're in here," Mary calls from the lounge. I rush in and drop to Daisy's feet. She's sitting on the sofa in her uncle's arms, a panic attack starting. As soon as Daisy sees me, she throws her arms around my neck. Her uncle moves so I can sit down with Daisy on my lap as I hold her tight. We sit for a moment as I hush and hold her, talking her through some breathing exercises we've been working on for her anxiety.

I hear Will ask Nigel if he can check out Daisy's room. I know I can trust Will to be thorough, leaving me to focus on Daisy.

As Daisy relaxes, I pull away to look at her face.

"What happened, darling?" I ask quietly. Daisy looks up at me, and it takes all my control not to haul back out there and find the son of a bitch who's caused her this much pain.

"I went back into the room to see what had smashed the windows and found two bricks. One had a note attached to it." A sob catches in her throat, which cuts her off. I fold my arms around her again, holding her tight, resting my chin on the top of her head.

"Here it is," Nigel says. I look up at him as he holds out a piece of paper; I take it from him and read it quickly.

I gave you time to enjoy yourself as I built our pack, but it's time to come home now and fulfil your responsibilities as my luna.

Tell Adams that if he knows what's good for him, he'll leave by the morning and never return. If I ever see him around you again, I will kill him. Look at your little date in

Charlestown tonight as one last night together.
Don't fight me on this, sweetheart; you know it will only make life harder on you as I always get what I want.

Your true Alpha,
Jackson

Before I can stop it, a growl rips through me: my jaw clenching, my heart racing with rage. No one threatens my mate. I don't care about his threat to me, that's just laughable, but to threaten Daisy, that's a whole new level of bullshit. I close my eyes and nestle into her hair, inhaling her sweet floral scent. It may be the only thing that calms me right now.

I sit holding Daisy as she slowly settles; I don't let her go until she finally falls back to sleep, exhausted after the adrenaline rush. Mary has already set up the spare room for us. I carry Daisy upstairs and place her in the bed. I stay with her, sitting on the floor, stroking her hair and whispering to her until she falls asleep. Slowly, I sneak out of the room and close the door behind me. I take a deep breath to calm my aching heart and that angry pit in my stomach. So much for him not finding us here.

I turn around to find Mary and Nigel outside their room.

"Are you both okay?" I ask. Mary's crying as Nigel comforts her. But they both nod.

"We've replaced the wards around the house; I don't know how he got past them last time. But there's no way he'll get through them again tonight." Nigel says.

"I'm going to let Daisy get a couple of hours sleep whilst I investigate a bit, but then I'm taking her home," I explain. Nigel and Mary nod agreeing that it's for the best. Nigel looks at Mary and kisses her cheek.

"Get some rest, love. I'll wake you before they leave, I promise." He whispers. Mary nods and turns to enter their room; before she does, she glances to the room Daisy is now in.

"Why don't you sleep in with her?" I suggest knowing that Mary may sleep better being close to her niece. Mary nods and walks towards the door. She stops as she reaches me and places a hand on my cheek before giving me the slightest smile.

"I'm glad our Daisy found you. You're a good man, Michael Adams." Mary leans as I lower myself slightly so she can kiss my cheek. Before I can reply, she walks into the room with Daisy and closes the door. Within seconds I can feel the tell-tale tingle of magic in the air.

"She's putting a protection spell on the room. It'll take a little pressure off us as we put things into place." Nigel explains. I hear footsteps on the stairs and turn to see Will looking at us.

"Jon needs to speak to you, Mikey. He found something." I start to head toward the stairs. I turn to Nigel as I walk past him.

"Could you join us? I'd appreciate your input on a few things." I ask. Nigel nods and places a hand on my shoulder.

"Of course, Son, I'll do anything to help." Together we head downstairs, where we find Jon pacing around the kitchen. Nigel motions for us to go into his study.

As I close the door, I feel magic in the air again. I look at Nigel frowning.

"A spell to stop the ladies from hearing anything that's discussed. Let's give them some peace tonight." I nod in agreement. I see Jon sitting on the sofa with his head in his hands. When he looks up, I stop dead. He looks like hell. His face is as white as a sheet, his hands shaking like he's on the verge of falling apart. I drop to my knees in front of him.

"What's happened?" I ask my brother as I place a hand on his shoulder, he looks into my eyes, and everything in me freezes. I've never seen him so panicked.

"Jonny, you're freaking me out now. What did you find?" I demand, every possibility running through my head.

"There ... There was a bag on the floor by the back door. In the rush to find the guy, we must have missed it. But it was on the step." I watch as he takes a deep breath and looks up at the ceiling as if blinking back tears.

"What was in the bag, Jonathan?" I demand. He looks at me as his eyes fill with tears.

"It shouldn't have been here. It shouldn't have been this far from home. I just..." He opens his mouth to say more but stops and shakes his head; he looks like he is struggling to stay in control of his wolf. Jon turns to Will and nods his head towards me. I watch as Will holds out a carrier bag. I take it from him, looking between him and Jon; I'm sure I see a tear roll down his cheek. I stand up and look at Will again, he doesn't look much better, but he's watching me. I open the bag and peer inside. The scent hits me first before I realise what I'm looking at.

"No." My breath catches in my throat. Will grabs me as my knees buckle. He lowers me into a chair Nigel pushes behind me. The room's spinning as my mind attempts to process what I'm looking at; it isn't possible; there's no way.

"What is it, Michael?" I hear Nigel ask behind me; his hand is on my shoulder. As my whole body shakes, I take a deep breath and try to clear my head again, but that scent, or combination of the three scents in that bag, hits me again.

It's been four years. Four years since I smelt that scent outside of my childhood home and since I started searching for the wolf of the second scent. I never found it until tonight. Tonight, the wolf found me. They not only found me but stuck a knife in my heart and twisted the hole back open. The hole they created when they killed my sister.

Chapter Fifteen

Michael

I don't know how long it takes me to clear my head. I can feel Nigel beside me the whole time, the worry rolling from him; the atmosphere is so thick in this room you could cut through it with a knife.

"Can you open a window, please?" I ask, not aiming it at anyone in particular. I hear Nigel walking to the other side of the room before the sound of a window opening. I close my eyes and inhale the cold night air to calm my racing heart and mind. I allow myself one more deep breath before I stand up and walk over to where Jonny's still sitting on the sofa, looking like he has become lost in the ocean of grief that consumes us. It never fades, never disappears; we just learnt how to handle it and live with it. I hold out my hand to him. He looks up as he takes it. I pull him to his feet and embrace him. As we pull apart, I place a hand on the back of his head and hold it against my forehead, my other hand still grasping his in between our chests.

"I need you, Jonny. I need you to help me end this. Four years ago, he took our sister and won't take from us again. We do what we do best. We hunt him down and make him pay. We protect those we love. Can I count on you?" I ask. I watch Jonathan stand up to his full height, push his shoulders back, and proudly hold his head high.

"I'm here. I'll die before he takes another sister from me. Together we protect Daisy and avenge Michelle." I nod my thanks to him and turn to Will, also standing tall.

"I'm willing to do *anything* to protect your mate and avenge Michelle. I'm at your disposal, Mikey." I nod my thanks to him before turning to Nigel.

"I think I need to fill you in on a few things." Nigel nods and heads to a cabinet. He pulls out a decanter of amber liquid and four glasses.

"I have a feeling we'll all need one of these." I have never been so grateful for the offer of a drink in my life.

We all sit in that office, and I tell Nigel about Michelle and how she was taken from us. I explain how he'd stripped her naked; and how we never found Michelle's clothes until tonight. Tonight, they were left for Daisy or me. They still hold my sister's scent and that of her killer and my mate.

Nigel sits in silence for a few minutes, his head in his hands, before he finally speaks.

"Shit. It had to be Jackson, then. There's no other explanation. I knew he was a twisted son of a bitch, but by the Goddess, give me strength. I'm so sorry, Michael, and Jonathan."

"Our priority is to protect Daisy and ensure he doesn't get near her." I click into leader mode and look at Will. "We need to work out where he was before Michelle; how they met? How the hell did he then manage to escape to Exeter and find Daisy?"

"Do we tell Daisy about the connection? Do you think he knows? Or is it just a coincidence?" Nigel asks. I think about it for a moment.

"I don't believe in coincidences; however, I can't see how he'd know to turn my mate two years before I knew she existed. We need to ask Daisy to confirm it is, in fact, Jackson's scent on the clothes and ask how her scent ended up on them." I rub the bridge of my nose and try to fight the tiredness that is starting to take over. The adrenaline from the chase and the shock of the clothes is wearing off, and I'm now feeling completely drained. But I need to devise a plan and get Daisy to safety.

"The most important thing now is to take Daisy home; I need to get her as far away from him as possible. But I know she'll not leave if she thinks there is any chance you and Mary are in danger; I'm also not leaving you unprotected. Can you think of anything you or someone from the coven can do to ensure you are safe?" I ask, turning to Nigel. He nods and leans forward in his chair as he places his hands together on the desk in front of him.

"Mary and I discussed this between us whilst you settled

Daisy into bed. We're going home to Exeter. There's no point hiding here anymore, not now he knows where we are and, most importantly, where Daisy is. We need to be in the heart of our coven, not hidden hundreds of miles away." I look at Nigel and nod as I agree, even though I know Daisy won't when she hears.

"I want to know how he found her tonight. Or how he knew you had been on a date and where? We checked that property ourselves, and it's been empty for quite some time. There has to be a way he can track her." Jon says from his seat. I've been thinking the same thing; we've kept us coming here quiet for this reason.

"What if someone from the local pack is working for him?" I hear Will ask from his spot by the wall.

"Fuck." Jon curses. "That'd make sense. They'd know there would be a high chance Daisy was here because you were. They could easily follow you. They know the area better than any of us. It's the most logical explanation." He continues. I stand up from my seat and walk over to the window. Jon's right, it's the simplest explanation. They've known for a few days we were coming, so they could have easily given Jackson a heads up. He could have been down here before us. But then, something else comes to mind.

"But how did they find Daisy this morning at the gym? They shouldn't have been able to find her there. Very few people know of its existence. Most of the pack doesn't know about it. Plus, we moved the scheduled session from last night last minute." I ask before turning to Nigel. "Could Daisy be tracked by magic?"

"Usually, I'd say yes; however, we haven't been able to track her since she was taken," Nigel sighs.

"Of course, it would have been the first thing you tried when you noticed she was gone." Will chimes in. Nigel looks at him and nods.

"It was, but it was like something was blocking it. It's been like that ever since. I try it now and again to check, but it's always the same."

"Can you track me? Is it the wolf gene that's stopping it?"

I ask Nigel, who looks at me.

"I've tried it on you. I'm able to track you when you are on your own. But when you are with Daisy, I can't." I curse as I look back out at the window.

"Will, can you guys go and do a sweep of the grounds, please? Then pack up everything. I'll do the same here." I look up at the clock and realise it's coming up to one in the morning.

"I want to be on the road for two." Jon and Will agree and head out the door, leaving Nigel and me alone. I turn and look at the man who is as good as my father-in-law and wish I could do more to help him and his wife.

"You don't have to go back to Exeter, you know. You could just come to ours. We have spare rooms. Or I could get you in one of the spare pack houses until we find you something more suitable. There are empty ones available." I offer, but Nigel shakes his head,

"No, you and Daisy need to concentrate on keeping her safe and not worrying about us too. Mary and I have been discussing this for a few days now. I've already made the call, and we will be gone by the morning. But you have to promise you won't let Daisy come to visit us. She can't risk coming to Exeter. No matter what happens." Nigel sighs.

"I can promise you I'll never let Daisy step foot in that area. He could find her in minutes. I know she'll hate me for it, but I can't risk her safety." I reply, dreading what this will do to Daisy.

"Thank you, Michael," Nigel says, looking at me, trying to smile, even though his hearts not in it.

I bow my head. The pain in his eyes is hard to miss, but behind the pain is sheer determination. Determination to protect the two women in his life.

I look at the clock as I throw back the last bit of liquor in my glass before placing it on the table.

"How do you plan on asking Daisy about the connection to your sister?" Nigel asks. I lean forward,

"We need to be careful; She'll be delicate after tonight; she will also fight me every step of the way when I say we are leaving you here for a couple of hours alone."

I hear Nigel chuckle. "Welcome to the world of the Smith girls. She gets her stubbornness from her mother and auntie. Just be glad you never met her grandmother. She was as stubborn as they come; she made mine and David's life hell." I can't help but smile. I lean back to the chair and place my right ankle on my left knee.

"I'll just keep her supplied with coffee in the morning and gin in the evening. Hopefully, that will be enough to keep her sweet." I hear Nigel laugh a little harder this time.

"You're a fast learner, son; you'll be just fine."

I smile and take a deep breath. "Being a fast learner is the only option when it comes to that woman. Now to decide how to handle her when I wake her up." Nigel nods and takes a sip of his drink. I get up to pack up our things before waking Daisy. I'm just reaching the door when I hear Nigel clear his throat.

"Michael?" Nigel calls quietly from his desk.

"Yeah?" I turn to face him and see the sadness on his face.

"Protect our girl, give her the life she deserves, love her enough for all of us until we can all be together again," Nigel asks as he looks at me.

"I give you my word," I promise.

"Thank you." Nigel takes another sip from his glass. "David would have approved of you, you know. He'd have still been forcing whiskey down our necks calling us lightweights, but he would have accepted you as his son-in-law and known you'd look after his munchkin." I smile and mutter another thank you as I head out of the door to pack mine and Daisy's things.

Chapter Sixteen

Daisy

"Darling, wake up." I open my eyes to see Michael squatting by the bed, his hand resting on my head as he strokes my face with his thumb.

"What's going on?" I ask as I look around, trying to get my eyes focused. I'm not in my bed. Suddenly everything from last night rushes back, and I jump up from the bed in a panic.

"Hush, darling, you're okay. I know you're tired, but I need you to wake up for a little bit. You can sleep some more in the car." Michael whispers. I nod and rub my eyes. When I open them again, I look at Michael and my stomach drops.

"What's happened, Mikey? You look pale." I whisper as I place a hand on his cheek. Michael closes his eyes and leans into my hand as he places his over it. He looks exhausted, not just physically but also emotionally. His eyes are almost grey instead of their usual bright blue.

"Something's come to light, and we think you'll be the only one who can explain it." He says quietly as he looks at me. There's something in his voice that I can't place; it's something I haven't heard before, and it scares me.

"Okay," I respond wearily. "What is it?" I ask. Instead of explaining, Michael stands up and holds his hand out for me.

"I'll explain everything downstairs, I promise."

I place my hand in his and let him guide me out of the spare room. I look at my bedroom door as we pass it and find it closed. As we reach the bottom of the stairs, I notice our bags by the front door.

"We're leaving already?" I ask; Michael nods.

"I'll explain more in here." He says quietly as he places a protective arm around my shoulders and walks with me to the lounge.

As soon as we enter, everyone turns to face us. My uncle is standing next to Auntie Mary, sitting in her usual chair. He has his hand on her shoulder, and I can see Auntie Mary has been crying. Jon's standing by the fireplace, and Will's next to the window, obviously watching for more trouble. The feeling of unease becomes stronger as I look at my family, all pale, upset and visibly on edge.

"Can somebody please tell me what's going on? You're all freaking me out." I protest, stopping Michael from taking me any further into the room. I look up at him and watch his face soften.

"Darling, please sit down, and I promise I'll tell you everything." He answers; I humour him and I do as he asks.

Michael guides me over to a seat, and I sit down. I can feel my hands starting to shake as I know whatever he has to say can't be good.

Michael kneels in front of me, takes my hands, and inhales deeply with his eyes closed before opening them and looking straight at me.

"When I put you to bed, Jonny found a package left by the back door. I need to ask you about what was in it. I need you to be as honest as possible, darling, no matter how much you think it'll upset me or anyone else here. It will help us to know a little more about Jackson."

I look around the room; all eyes are on me and only me, as if they are all waiting for me to break.

"Okay," I answer quietly as I look at Michael.

"Can I show you what was in there? I need to know that it's what I think it is." Michael asks. I nod, the air feeling heavy in my lungs. My anxiety rises as Michael looks to Will, who steps forward and passes him a plastic bag. Michael takes it and looks at me.

"I need to know what you know about these items, darling," Michael takes another deep breath before opening the bag. I look into it and instantly jump back, the panic crushing my chest.

"No! Get them away. Get them away, please!" I scream, trying to distance myself from the bag and the items inside. Michael chucks it to Will and grabs hold of me, and I scramble to get away from him.

"Darling, they've gone. You'll never see them again, I

promise." Michael swears as he pulls me into his arms. I'm shaking and feel like I'm going to be sick. I notice I'm not the only one shaking, so is Michael.

"I'm sorry, darling, but I need you to tell me about them. I need to know whose they are and whose scents are on them?" Michael whispers into my hair.

"Does it matter?" I ask as I bury my face into his chest; I hear his heart beating quicker than usual. I don't like that something has upset him this much. It's not right; Michael is the strong one out of the two of us.

"I'm sorry, baby, but it does. I'll explain everything once you tell me what you know about the items in the bag." He whispers as he runs a hand up and down my back.

"It's a red t-shirt and a denim skirt. Jackson made me wear them when he first took me. He thought they'd help us to become mates." I explain as I sit back and start fidgeting with my hands. Michael places his hands on the top of mine to stop me.

"Why did he think they would help you to become mates?" Michael asks slowly. I look up at him and see a mixture of emotions in his eyes.

"Because he took them from his mate when he killed her," I whisper as I watch Michael's face drop.

"Fucking prick!"

I jump to the sound of Jon's voice from across the room.

"Jonny, not now," Michael growls, not taking his eyes off me. Michael's eyes are black, his wolf so close to the surface. I look up at Jon and see his eyes are just as black. I've never seen Jon so close to losing control before.

"I'm going to fucking kill him!" Jon roars as he storms out of the room. I start shaking harder as, for the first time since I met him, I am afraid of Jon and what he is about to do.

"Will," Michael says, not taking his eyes off me.

"On it," Will answers as he rushes out after Jon. I look at Michael and notice there are tears in his eyes.

"What's wrong?" I ask. There's more to this than they're telling me. Jon and Michael know what Jackson did to me. They know he raped me continuously for the time I was with him.

So why have they reacted so badly now?

"We know who the clothes originally belonged to," Michael says as he looks at me. I frown at him, confused, until something clicks into my mind, a memory combined with something Michael told me.

"My twin sister was murdered. We think her mate killed her when she rejected him. They had stripped her to her underwear and left her for us to find in the pack running grounds." I feel my eyes widen as I look up at Michael and shake my head. Michael looks at me and nods, realising I've connected the dots.

"They're the clothes Michelle was last seen in," Michael whispers as a tear slides down his cheek.

I jump to my feet and push Michael out of the way with my hand on my mouth. I just make it out of the lounge as the vomit flows from my mouth and through my fingers. I throw up until there's nothing left in me. At some point, Michael holds a bucket for me to be sick into as he rubs my back.

The sick son of a bitch had raped me whilst I wore my mate's dead twin's clothes. Every time I think of it, I retch again.

"I didn't know." I gasp as the tears stream down my face, my throat sore from being sick. "I had no idea it was her." I sob as Michael rubs my back; I look up at him and see the tears still rolling down his face.

"I swear I didn't know. You do believe me, don't you? If I had any idea, I would have told you, I swear." I beg as I cling to Michael's top. Michael looks at me wide-eyed and pulls me into his arms.

"Of course, I believe you. I know you would have told me if you'd realised." Michael whispers as he tries to reassure me. I wrap my arms around him, and he holds me tightly against his chest.

"Jonny..." I try to speak, but a sob tears through me as the thought of the guy I have come to love as a big brother might hate me. What if he can never forgive me?

"Jonny's upset as can be expected, but not at you, darling. Never at you. You're not to blame for anything that prick did before or after meeting you. Do you understand? You're not at fault here." Michael whispers as he runs a hand over my head.

He pulls away from me and stands, pulling me onto my feet. He uses his thumb to wipe away the tear from my cheek before bending down to lift the bucket. I see a hand reach for it at the same time.

"I'll take that, Michael." I turn to see my auntie; Michael looks at her and shakes his head.

"It's fine. I've got it. Can you take Daisy to sit down? Nigel wants to talk to her." Michael says as he kisses my head. "I'll be right back, I promise." He whispers as he pulls away from me. I feel my auntie place an arm around my shoulder before leading me away from Michael. I turn my head to look at him. I don't want to face this without him, but he gives me a reassuring smile as he carries the bucket, now full of sick, into the downstairs toilet.

"Why does Uncle Nigel need to speak to me?" I ask Auntie Mary as we enter the lounge. My uncle is standing with a box, placing the photo frames from the fireplace into it. I realise how empty the lounge looks, so different from how it was this afternoon.

"Because we've decided to go back to Exeter. Lawrence and Alex are already on their way to help us move." My uncle Nigel says as he puts the box down.

"What?! But it's not safe!" I yell as I freeze to the spot. My aunties arms tighten around my shoulders as she forces me to move and sit in a chair.

"Neither is here, Daisy. Jackson has found us now; there's no reason for us not to return." My auntie says as she sits on the arm of the chair, keeping her arm around my shoulder.

"If we return to Exeter, we're closer to the coven. Should we need them, they can be there in minutes rather than hours." My uncle explains as he comes to sit on the other side of me and places an arm around my shoulders. "You know it makes sense, Daisy. We left to protect you, but now you have Michael, we can go home." He adds as he plants a kiss on the top of my head. I wipe the tears from my face as I nod.

"It'll be difficult to visit you," I whisper as I look at my family, Mary and Nigel share a look, and I know what my uncle's about to say.

"You won't be visiting us for a while, Daisy. We've made Michael promise to keep you away."

"It's for the best, darling." I look up to find Michael leaning against the doorway with his arms crossed over his chest.

"Well, this weekend isn't going the way I thought." I sigh before the tears start falling again, and I am engulfed in a hug by my uncle.

Chapter Seventeen

Michael

It's ten in the morning when we finally get home. Daisy had begged me to put off leaving until Alex and Clare's boyfriend, Lawrence, had arrived. I reluctantly agreed as I was as worried about Mary and Nigel as she was. But as soon as they arrived, we left.

I look over at Daisy to find her fast asleep. Jon opens the front door for me as I carry her into the house. I tell him and Will to wait for me in the lounge whilst I get Daisy upstairs.

Once in our room, I gently place Daisy on the bed before covering her with a blanket. I'm closing the curtains when I hear Daisy whisper.

"Mikey?" I turn around to find her looking at me through heavy eyelids.

"Shh, darling, we're home. Go back to sleep." I whisper as I run my knuckles over her cheek. She's exhausted after such an emotional night. At one point on the way home, I'd turned to check on her and noticed her left arm hanging between the chair and the door; I was about to ask if she was stuck when I saw Will was sitting sideways in his seat directly behind her, his arm out towards her, holding her hand giving her the support she needed.

It was such a contrast to how they interacted on the journey down. But as I've seen many times in the last few months, when Daisy needs someone, our pack brothers always step up when I can't. I hope it's something I can pay them back for one day when they find their own mates.

I plant a soft kiss on Daisy's temple before standing back up.

"Thank you." She whispers.

"For what, darling?"

"Everything." She mumbles. I lean over and place my lips against her head again.

"I would fight the world for you," I promise her as she falls back asleep.

I find Will and Jon downstairs in the lounge; there's already a mug of coffee on the table waiting for me. I pick it up and take a large sip.

"Marcus and Stuart are on their way," Will says from his seat. I look at Jon, who's by the fireplace, looking at a photo of Michelle and us. Since Jon's initial reaction to Daisy's recount of events, he hasn't stopped. He packed our car before helping Daisy and her family pack their belongings. He smiled and tried to cheer Daisy up. Anyone watching from the outside would think there was nothing wrong with him. But I know better; finally knowing who killed our sister has broken him a little. I know because it has broken me too.

"There's something I want to ask you both before they arrive," I say as I look between the two males in front of me. I take a deep breath and steady my racing heart.

"Other than the four of us in this house, I don't want anyone to know the connection between Jackson, Daisy and Michelle yet. Not even Marcus." Will looks at me, confused, but Jon looks at me with pain in his eyes.

"You want to tell Mum first?" he asks. I nod,

"I think it's only right," I reply; Jon nods and sips his orange juice. I look at Will and can see the realisation in his eyes; he nods and sits back on the sofa. As I sip my coffee, I hear Marcus's car pull up outside, followed by Stuart's. I take a deep breath and look up at the ceiling, where I know Daisy's still asleep. We hear the front door opening, followed by Stuart calling out. The three of us quickly silence him; he walks into the lounge, looking confused.

"Why am I being shushed?" he asks as he takes his usual seat on the sofa next to Will.

"Daisy's sleeping upstairs," Will replies as he hands Stuart a mug from the coffee table. Stuart looks at the mug and then around the room at us, frowning. I look at my second and frown.

"Didn't you fill him in on anything?" I ask. Marcus shakes his head.

"Fill me in on what? I haven't been reachable because I

went home to see my parents. You know I get no signal there." Stuart explains and looks around at us again. "What's happened? I wasn't expecting you back until tomorrow."

"Jackson or one of his guys made his presence known early this morning," Jon says from his spot by the fireplace.

"What? Here?" Stuart asks; his eyes widen in surprise. Jon shakes his head before answering.

"No. They smashed two windows at Daisy's family home and left her a note, threatening to take her and kill Mikey." Jon's glass of orange juice explodes in his hands. "Shit," he curses as he storms out of the room. I jump to my feet as everyone else does.

"Can one of you sort that, please?" I ask, pointing to the mess. All three nod as I walk out of the room and follow my brother's scent up the stairs. I find him in the bathroom, running his hand under the tap.

"Well, this seems familiar." I sigh as I stand beside him and take his hand. I'd done the same thing whilst on the team Christmas night out. Jon had cleaned me up then. I pull a piece of glass out of his hand and examine the wound.

"It's not as good a job as you did," Jon mutters as he pulls his hand out of mine and runs it under the tap. I pull the first aid box out from the cabinet under the sink. I give it another quick once over for any glass left in the wounds before wrapping it in a bandage.

"He won't get to either of you, Mikey. I won't let him." I look up at my brother and can see the determination on his face. I finish wrapping his hand before stepping back, so I have Jon's full attention.

"Jonny, I need to ask you to do something for me. You aren't going to like it, but I need your word." Jon looks up at me, and I see he knows what I'm going to ask.

"Mikey please?" I place a hand on his shoulder and look him in the eye.

"Jonny, he can't get her; I won't let her go through all that again; it will kill her this time. It will kill me." I look over my shoulder and towards our room, where Daisy's sleeping. "If you ever have to choose, protect her, not me." I turn and look at my brother; I can see the tears in his eyes.

"I can protect you both." He whispers; I lean forward and rest my forehead against his. My hand still on his shoulder.

"And you would die trying; I know you would. That's why I need you to protect Daisy at all costs. If that means you grab her and run, you do it. You leave me and protect her. Please, Jonny, I can command the guys downstairs to do it, but not you. I need to know you'll do this for me. Promise me, Jonny." I beg.

"I can't." Jon whispers, "You're my brother, my best friend. I've already lost a sister; I can't lose you too."

"I would do it for you," I whisper, and he stops. Because he knows that I would, he can't argue it. "Promise me, Jonny, please."

"I promise I'll protect Daisy even if it means leaving you behind," Jon whispers reluctantly. I pull him into a hug and hold him.

"Thank you, Jonny," I whisper before pulling away from him. "I'll be telling the others the same now. I just needed a moment with you first." Jon nods. I know he understands why I need to ask this of him, and as much as I hope he's never in that position, I know he'll follow through.

"Let's go and see if Will has filled them in on anything," I say as I turn from Jon, who grabs my arm to stop me.

"Mikey, I wanted to run an idea past you. Something that I think might help you relax when you are here so you can get some real rest."

Daisy

Michael woke me up at half eleven and asked if I wanted to go with him to tell his mum about Michelle? Or stay at home with Stuart? I told him I wanted to be there when they told her.

Jon's meeting us there, as he's gone home first to grab a few bits. He's moving in with us for a while. With everything going on, Jon knows that Michael won't sleep if it's just him and me, so Jon will help by being alert at night, giving Michael a real chance to relax. They asked me how I feel about it, but

I'm willing to agree to just about anything that will take some pressure off Michael. I'm worried he'll burn himself out.

Pulling up outside Barbara's house, I feel the new constant knot in my stomach tighten even further. I look around and see that Jon's car isn't here yet. Michael turns to me and takes my hand.

"Darling, you don't have to come with us to do this; Mum will understand. I can drop you off with one of the lads and come back." Michael offers, but I shake my head as I squeeze his hand.

"I need to do this. I owe it to your mum." I answer. Michael grips my hand in both of his.

"Darling, you owe our family nothing. I've told you, none of it's your fault. Neither you nor Michelle asked for anything that coward did. Mum won't think less of you because of this; none of us ever will." I feel my eyes welling up and try desperately to blink the tears back. I take a deep breath and hold it for a second before slowly letting it out in an attempt to calm my racing heart. I don't want Barbara to know that something's wrong.

I spot Jon's car pulling onto the road behind us as I open my eyes. I'm trying so hard not to focus on my pain. He lost his twin and searched for her murderer for four years. I can't begin to imagine how Michael and Jon feel now that they know who killed their sister and why. They are trying to hide their pain from me but are failing terribly.

I place a hand on Michael's cheek before kissing his lips softly.

"I wish I could take all this pain from you," I whisper. Michael closes his eyes and leans into my hand as I move my lips away from his.

"You have no idea how much you help," Michael replies as he turns his head and presses his lips to my palm. I kiss his lips again before letting him go and opening my door.

As soon as we step out of the car, we're greeted by Jonathan, who is instantly by his brother's side. When we hear the front door open, we all turn to see Barbara Adams standing in the doorway, beaming at her kids. I hate that we're about to break her heart, and I consider running away for a moment. But when I look at my mate, his brother, and their mum, I know they deserve so much more than me being a coward like Jackson. I need to be their strength.

I walk around to Michael and take his hand in mine.

"Come on, handsome," I whisper. Michael looks down at our hands and gives mine a quick squeeze before heading towards Barbara, who has already picked up on the tension we are bringing.

"What's happened?" Barbara asks as soon as we get to the front door, her eyes full of panic.

"Let's go inside, Mama," Jon says as he leans down and kisses his mum's cheek. Barbara looks from her sons to me.

"Are you all okay?" she asks; we all nod.

"We're all okay, but we need to talk to you," Michael says. His mum realises this won't be said on the doorstep and walks into the house. As soon as we're in the lounge, Barbara stares at us with her hands on her hips.

"Enough; I want to know what's going on now!" She demands, staring at her sons. Jon turns and looks at Michael, who has said he wants to be the one to tell their mum. I can see he's struggling, so I tighten my hold on his hand, offering what little support I can. I watch as he lifts his head and looks at his mum.

"We know who killed Michelle," Michael says as he squeezes my hand back; I can feel him shaking beside me. Barbara gasps as she hears the words she's been waiting four years for. She sits down on the chair behind her, not taking her eyes off her remaining twin.

"Who?" she asks as her voice shakes. Michael opens his mouth to answer but shuts it again, he turns to Jon, but he's just staring at his mum, silent tears running down his face. "Who killed my daughter?" Barbara demands louder, looking between us all. Michael wanted to tell her, but as I look at him now, I realise he's frozen by his pain and grief.

"It was Jackson," I answer, stepping forward and taking over and helping him. Barbara stares at me, shocked.

"The guy who changed you?" she asks; I nod. "How do you

know it was him?" I take a deep breath and look at the floor, unable to look her in the eye as I break her heart.

"He left a package at my auntie and uncle's early hours of this morning. It was some clothes he would force me to wear. He told me he had killed his mate when she'd told him she loved someone else and rejected him. He told me he'd stripped her and kept her clothes, hoping the mixed scents would help a new mate bond form." I swallow and take a deep breath before looking at Barbara, who shows every emotion as she stares back at me.

"I'm so sorry, Mama. I never put the two together sooner." I gasp as the tears come closer to the front. Barbara looks at me, and her facial expression changes to something that looks unnatural on her soft round face. It's enough to make my breath catch in my throat.

"You're sorry?!" she exclaims loudly as she jumps to her feet. Michael pulls me behind him instinctively.

"Michael Graham Adams, you better step away from her now." His mum demands. But Michael presses me to his back protectively. I pat his back and quickly tell him it's okay through the bond before stepping around him. I come face to face with a furious Barbara.

"I'll never be able to tell you how sorry I am that I didn't make the connection earlier. Whatever you want to throw at me, do it. Just know I'm so sorry." I wait for her to hit me or scream, but I feel her hands grab my arms and drag me into hers as she steps forward.

"Don't you *dare* apologise for what he did to you and my Michelle. You did nothing wrong, and I won't let you feel guilty for one second for what he made you do." Barbara releases me and holds me at arm's length; the second I look into her eyes which have softened, I can't hold back the tears anymore, and they fall down my cheeks as I see the pain on this remarkable woman's face. Barbara pulls me back into her arms again, and we hold each other as we cry. I force myself to step away from her and excuse myself. Michael tries to stop me, but I shake my head and place a hand on his chest.

"Your mum needs you more," I whisper as I leave the

Adams boys with their mama to share their grief for their lost sister.

Chapter Eighteen

Daisy

I take a deep breath and knock on Michael's work office door.

"Come in."

Well, here goes nothing. I open the door and stick my head in; Michael's sitting at his desk, and Steph, another lecturer, is in the chair opposite him.

"Sorry, you're busy. We'll come back later." I say quickly as I back out of the room to close the door.

"Wait, it's okay, Daisy; I'm just leaving," Steph calls out. I nod and look at the two of them.

"We'll wait outside for you to finish," I reply, smiling as I close the door quickly. I lean against the wall and let out a deep breath. I open my eyes to find Tony smirking at me.

"Shut up," I mouth at him. Tony shrugs as he leans against the wall opposite me with his arms crossed over his chest.

"I don't know why you don't just tell him your 'special' way. Would save an argument," Tony says, tapping his head as I shake mine.

"Nope, I've learnt some arguments are better made face to face. It's easier to win him around then." I wink at Tony, who just groans. "Anyway, he agreed to me spending time at yours to study, so he needs to accept it includes overnight," I add quietly. With only eight weeks left until the end of the uni year, we're all working hard on the end-of-year exam prep work and presentations.

"We'll see," Tony replies with arched eyebrows. I'm flipping him the bird when Steph walks out and sees us.

"Do you two do anything apart?" she asks. Tony and I shrug at the same time. "Well, I think you both need to stop with the flirting and just start dating already." She adds. I stare at her open-mouthed as I hear Michael laughing from behind her.

"Not a chance in hell!" Tony blurts out, smiling broadly.

"Eugh, that would be like dating my brother!" I add, screwing up my face in disgust. Steph shrugs and starts walking off,

"Well, you'll have plenty of time to work it out for yourself now you're living together and working on your group project with Beth, Ellis and Ruth. Enjoy your study group sleepover tonight." Steph calls as she walks out of view. I feel my stomach drop as I realise what Michael would have just heard. I see Tony flinch out of the corner of my eye and know Michael will be staring at me when I turn around. Shit.

"It seems I'm free now." I hear Michael say. I turn slowly and look at him. His face is a perfect image of calm and collected, but his eyes have gone dark, and I know his wolf has come to the surface.

"I think I'll sit this one out," Tony says as he attempts to walk away.

"Get in, Tony," Michael says through gritted teeth. I hear Tony curse as he turns and walks into the office.

"Won't let me join in the sex but drags me into the drama." He mutters as he takes a seat in front of the desk. I walk behind him and try not to look at Michael as I sit next to Tony. I hear him closing the door; before he walks to the front of his desk and leans against it with his legs stretched out in front of him, placing his hands behind him for support.

"I take it that's why you needed to come and see me?" Michael asks me with a raised eyebrow. Ah, fuck it. I look up at him through my lashes and smile sweetly.

"Actually, yes. I came to let you know that I'll be staying at Tony's tonight as we have to work on this final group project and as everyone thinks I'm living with him, the others all insisted on studying at 'our house'. I can't *not* be there, can I?" I watch as Michael runs his fingers through his hair like he always does when stressed and wait for the argument.

"Okay." He sighs. I look at him and blink a few times.

"Okay?" Tony and I say together, both sitting forward in our seats. Michael looks at us and shakes his head, grinning.

"Yes, okay. You're right. You need to be there if we're to continue this shit story you live there." Michael says, smiling at us.

"Well, that was easy," Tony says, sitting back in his chair. I look up at Michael frowning.

"Too easy. What plan have you got in place, Adams?"

Michael smiles at me. "Nothing for you to worry about, darling. You have a good time, and please keep in touch."

"You know she can't go a full hour without texting you or communicating through that weird link," Tony says, groaning. I stand and step up to Michael, who opens his legs for me to slide in between them. He slides his fingers into the belt loops on my jeans and tugs me forward, so I am pressed against him.

"I don't know what you're up to, but I will let it go this time," I warn as I drape my arms over his shoulders.

"Maybe I just want a break from your cranky ass," Michael smirks at me as I slap his chest. He laughs, grabs my ass and pulls me tighter against him as I wrap my arms around his neck and kiss him.

"I would say get a room, but it doesn't make a difference to you two." Tony moans behind us. I pull back from Michael slightly and smile.

"Promise me you'll be careful tonight. I know you hate being told what to do, but please don't go out into town or take any unnecessary risks. We don't know if Kellan has been communicating with anyone, so be careful what you say." Michael says as he looks into my eyes.

"I hadn't thought of that; he was close to Ellis," Tony whispers behind me. Michael looks over my shoulder at him and nods.

"Both of you keep your wits about you." Michael turns back to me. "I'll get Stuart to pick up a few bits for you and take them to Tony's. Give him your keys when you meet him." I pout slightly as my lips curl up to one side.

"I hate asking him to do things for me; it makes me feel like I'm taking the piss." I sigh. Michael leans forward and kisses me softly on the lips.

"He wants to do it; he's bored since he lost his job," Michael says.

When his boss decided to retire, Stuart was made

redundant from his carpenter job. He now 'watches' me full time when Michael is busy. He sometimes helps the Alpha out if he needs anything doing. I know Stuart is bored, but it's still not easy asking him to do things for me.

"Tony, can you give us a minute, please?" Michael asks over my shoulder. I hear Tony mumble as he gets up.

"Sure, I'll wait outside and stop anyone from interrupting. Just don't get loud, and don't take too long." He adds. I turn around and hold up two fingers; Tony returns the gesture with a wink as he walks out the door.

"What's up?" I ask as soon as Tony is out of the room. Michael looks me in the eye, and I can see his wolf is there in the forefront again.

"Please be careful tonight. I know Tony will have your back, but as I said, we don't know if Kellan is still in contact with Ellis. I wouldn't put it past him to keep an eye on things that way." I lean forward and kiss Michael gently as his grip tightens on my hips.

"I promise I'll pay attention. I'm not taking any gin, just a single bottle of wine. I'm also going to lock my door when I'm in my bedroom." I lean back a little and look Michael in the eye. "Who'll be watching the house?"

Michael smirks. "I knew you'd figure it out. Not me, so don't worry, I've got a ton of marking to do, so I'll do it whilst I don't have the distraction of you at home."

"Don't act like you don't love it," I reply with a wink. Michael tugs me closer again.

"You're my favourite type of distraction, baby." He replies before kissing me in that way that makes me feel it deep in my core. I pull away from him before I jump him right here on his desk. I lean into his shoulder. As much as I'm looking forward to a night with Tony, and the others, I never relax fully when I'm not with Michael. The only time we've been apart recently was when he went to Exeter and if he's had to go on a mission, which has become more frequent the last couple of weeks since the disastrous trip to Cornwall. As if reading my mind, I feel Michael kiss the top of my head.

"I'll miss you." He whispers.

"I'll miss you more," I whisper back. I kiss him before reluctantly stepping out of his arms. "I better go and meet Stuart; he will be worrying where I am," I say, smiling at Michael. I turn to head towards to door.

"While you're away tonight, feel free to send some dirty texts when you get to bed." Michael chuckles. I quickly send an image of him and me in the shower this morning through the bond. Before I get to the door, Michael stands in front of me, growling in a deep tone, making my toes curl and my wolf pay attention.

"If you want to go tonight, you need to stop with that little trick, baby," Michael growls as his lips crash into mine. I kiss him back quickly before pushing him away, smiling.

"I'll see you in class. Try not to miss me too much tonight, handsome." I kiss him gently one last time and then leave the room.

I let out a deep sigh as soon as the door is closed between us.

"Miss you already, darling. I love you." Michael whispers down the bond. I smile and look at the closed door.

"Love you too, Cheese ball," I whisper back before walking down the corridor with Tony by my side.

Tony throws his arm over my shoulder and smiles at me as I text Stuart,

"Do you think you're going to manage a whole night away from matey boy? Or am I going to be sneaking you out in the early hours of the morning?" I shrug his arm off before hitting him as I roll my eyes at him.

"I'll be fine. But you may not survive if you carry on trying to wind me up, arsehole." Tony chuckles as he nudges me with his shoulder.

"Oh, come on, you know you would freak out if I was always nice to you." I side-eye him but can't help smiling as he's right.

We walk in silence the rest of the way to the café, where I've told Stuart to meet us. As soon as I walk in, I spot him sitting at the usual table with his sketchbook and three full mugs.

"He's so well trained. Can I have him when you are finished with him?" Tony whispers into my ear. I turn around and punch his arm.

"Shut up, prick," I hiss through my teeth as we approach the table. Stuart looks up from his sketchbook and smirks at Tony, who's rubbing his arm, pouting.

"What have you done now?" Stuart asks him whilst pushing a mug of coffee towards me. Tony mutters "nothing" under his breath and takes the cup Stuart passes him. Stuart looks at me with a raised eyebrow, and I shake my head.

"Just Tony being Tony. What you been up to?" I ask as I sit in the chair next to him. Stuart shrugs.

"Ran a few errands for the Alpha and then been sitting here pretending to be a student. Same shit, different day." He takes a sip of his drink. "Please say you have something for me to do, the coffee girl has been trying to flirt with me all day, and I don't know how to tell her that I'm not interested without her making my life hell." Stuart moans as Tony laughs across the table; Stuart chucks a balled-up napkin at him, calling him a prick.

"Mikey has asked if you can go to ours for me and pick up a few bits as I'm staying at Tony's tonight," I whisper. Stuart turns and looks at me, frowning.

"Is that a good idea?" I have to stop myself from rolling my eyes in frustration.

"We have a study group, and everyone has argued it's best to meet there as they think I live there too. I can't exactly not be there; they'd all start asking questions." I point out. Stuart nods in agreement. He rips a page from his sketchbook and hands it to me with a pencil.

"Write down what you need, and I'll sort it for you. Do you want me to drop it off at Tony's place so you don't have to explain why you have a bag with you?" Stuart asks.

"Would you mind? I hate asking you to do all this shit, Stu." I reply as I start making a list.

"Hey, I don't mind. It makes me feel useful; I'm so fucking bored right now." Stuart protests.

"Well, if Mikey ever takes the piss, make sure you tell

him," I reply as I finish the list and where to find them. I hand him the paper and my keys, quickly showing him which are for Tony's place. "Any issues, ring me. I only have one more class, and it's Mikey's, so he will let me answer." Stuart nods and puts the paper in his pocket.

"No problem, I'll sort it and tell you when it's all at Tony's. Is yours still the back room?" Stu asks. I nod as I take a drink of my coffee. I watch Stuart gather up his stuff and stand.

"Well, have fun; I'll message the boss now and let him know I'm leaving. If you think of anything else, just text, okay." Stu says as he pulls his car keys out of his pocket and pulls his shoulder bag over his head.

"Will do. Thanks again, Stu." I smile at him as he winks and walks off.

"Well, for once, you don't have a wolf escort. What do you fancy doing?" Tony asks as I finish off my coffee. I look up to answer but find him frowning as he looks out of the window. I turn to look in the direction he's looking, but I can't see anything other than the car park.

"What's up with you?" I ask.

Tony shakes his head and looks at me. "Nothing thought I saw someone, that's all." I watch Tony as he drinks the rest of his coffee, but he keeps glancing at the window and doesn't seem to shake off whatever is bothering him.

"Come on, let's go and find the others." I sigh as I stand up and pull Tony to his feet, hoping to distract him.

))●((

Stuart messages me as I'm leaving Michael's class to let me know everything has been left at Tony's. My keys are apparently with some bits that Michael had asked him to pick up for me. As soon as we get to Tony's, I make my excuses and head to "my room" to get changed and contact Michael. I walk into the room and head to the wardrobe; I open it up to see Stuart's hung my clothes up and made it look like I live here. He's put the bedding I had asked him to get from the spare room at home on the bed and made it look slept in. There's also a bottle of wine and a box of chocolates with my keys on the chest of drawers. I know these are the extras Michael asked him to pick up for me. He always buys me sweets or chocolates when I'm studying.

I check my watch and know that Michael will be finishing work soon. I quickly open our bond to speak to him.

"Hey, handsome, I'm here, and all is well. Thank you for the treats." I can feel him there before he responds.

"You're welcome, darling. If you need anything, shout, and Stu will hear you. Call me through this or on the phone if it's not an emergency. I'll be at work for a bit longer anyway doing this marking." I can hear Michael is on edge, and I know it's because I'm here, but as much as I'm missing him, I do miss spending time with my friends too.

"Okay, handsome, don't work too hard," I reply cheerfully.

"I'll try. Have fun, darling." Michael replies

I'm just about to shut the bond down when I remember something,

"Oh, Mikey, I stole the last cereal bar out of the car earlier, sorry. You'll need to put a new box in for your breakfast in the morning." I hear Michael chuckle down the bond.

"I'll pick some up when I do the shopping later. Now go and have some fun with your friends." I close the bond smiling as I put the cereal bar on the side, ready for the morning. I grab my wine and head back downstairs to where everyone else sits in the lounge, looking forward to the night ahead.

Chapter Nineteen

Daisy

"Daisy, get your arse out of bed. Michael will kill you if you're late." Tony hisses through the door. I try to open my eyes, but the light hurts; everything hurts. I use what little magic I have to unlock the bedroom door.

"Come in," I whisper. I hear the door unlock to the sound of Tony cursing as Beth gasps.

"Don't tell me you're fucking ill. He'll kick my ass." Tony moans as he walks over to the side of the bed. I feel something touch my forehead.

"Daisy, you're on fire. How do you feel?" Beth asks.

"Like I have the flu." I moan before clenching my head. "It's come on so quick. I was okay half an hour ago. I thought I was just hungover." I moan.

"I'm going to have to call him Dais." I hear Tony say. I slowly shake my head, regretting it as the pain shoots through it.

"I'll do it as soon as you guys leave with the others. He can't do anything until they've gone anyway. He'll probably call Stuart to sit with me or take me home." I can hear Tony cursing to himself.

"I'll tell the others you're ill and get them out as quickly as possible," Beth says as she leans over and kisses my cheek. "Let me know later how you are." She whispers before leaving the room, as I promise I'll text her.

"You had to fall ill on my watch, didn't you?! Michael's going to stop you from ever coming round again." Tony sighs as he stands over me. I start to laugh but cringe in pain. My head and throat hurt so bad.

"Go help Beth get those two out of here so I can get this conversation over and done with," I mumble. I feel Tony kiss the top of my head.

"Rest up and message me later, babes." He whispers before leaving my room and closing the door behind him.

I hear Ruth asking Tony how I am as they leave the house. As soon as I hear the door close, I open up the bond.

"Morning, beautiful." Michael's voice fills my head, and it's too much for once.

"Mikey," I whisper.

"Darling? what's wrong?" I can hear the worry in his voice.

"I'm not going to make it to class. I'm ill."

"Ill? As in hungover?" Michael chuckles as I feel him relax.

"No. As in flu." I explain as I clutch my head and hiss as the pain worsens.

"Darling, wolves don't get flu. Where's Tony? Are you in pain?" Michael demands as the worry returns to his voice.

"He's taken the others to breakfast so I could contact you. I'm really ill, Mikey. I feel like I'm being stabbed in the head, and I have a fever."

"I'm on my way." I hear Michael say.

I leave the bond open but can't concentrate on what Michael's saying. I hear someone come into the room and curse. I start to panic, thinking someone has come back.

"Daisy, can you hear me?" I open my eyes to find Stuart looking at me.

"How?" I ask before my eyes start to close. I can hear Stuart talking, but I can't seem to open my eyes again or respond.

"Edward, it's Stuart Harvey. Daisy, Michael's mate, has a fever and is unresponsive." I'm about to point out that it's just flu, but I can't speak or move. As I feel myself slipping into a deep sleep, I hear somebody else running up the stairs and pray that it's Michael.

Michael

I race into Daisy's bedroom and find Stuart already on the phone. Daisy's lying in bed asleep, and her skin is flushed. I go to put a hand on her head but can feel the heat coming from her. There's no mistaking her temperature is dangerously high.

"Shit. Baby, open your eyes." I beg as I drop to my knees beside her. Daisy makes the slightest sound, and that's it. I look up at Stuart, who's on the phone.

"Tony ran to the car as soon as Beth got the others out. He said he had just found her ill in bed. He's in a panic, saying she'd been fine all night." Stuart stops talking and listens to whatever Edward is saying on the phone. "We need to get her to Edward ASAP. Where's halfway between the two? Yours?" Stuart asks. I nod and take the phone from him.

"Edward, I'm taking her home; meet us there. What can I do for now?" I ask, trying to stay in control.

"Keep hold of her, Michael. The mating bond will help. You'll also need cool packs or flannels; place one on the back of her neck and one behind each knee." I pass the phone back to Stuart and rush into the bathroom. There are no flannels, so I settle for a small towel. As I get back to Daisy, I find Stuart's off the phone and chucking her stuff in a bag. I throw my keys to him.

"Let's go. I'll get Tony to pack up what's left." I say as I scoop Daisy up from the bed. She instantly starts to moan in pain. "Shh, darling, I've got you. I'm taking you home." I whisper to her as I carry her out of the bedroom and through the house. I turn to Stuart.

"Grab a bowl or something in case she's sick." Stuart nods before rushing into the kitchen. In less than a minute, he comes out with a washing-up bowl and a bag of frozen peas. "Good thinking, thanks," I say as I turn so he can take the wet towel from behind Daisy's neck.

"I'll give it back once you're in the car. Let's get going." Stuart says as he holds the door open for me.

We rush out to my car, Stuart opens the back door, and I climb in with Daisy on my knee. Once we're in, Stuart passes me the towel and peas before closing the door. He jumps into the driver's seat and starts the engine.

As soon as he pulls away from the curb, I ask him to connect a call to Jon through the car hands-free.

"Hey, Mikey," Jon answers on the third ring.

"Jon, Daisy's ill. Edward's on his way to mine; we're just leaving Tony's." I explain quickly.

"What do you mean by ill?" I hear Jon ask.

"She's unconscious with a fever. I'm sweating just from holding her." I answer.

"Shit." Jon curses down the line. I can hear a voice in the background. "I'm at Mum's; we're on our way. Want me to call the guys as I know Marcus was going to the uni to see you?"

"Yeah, please, Jon. Tell Marcus he's in charge; I need to focus on Daisy. Stuart's here with me." I say as Daisy starts to moan in my arms, her eyes scrunched up as if she's in pain.

"No problem, Bro; see you in half an hour." The line goes dead as he hangs up.

"How's she doing?" Stuart asks from the front of the car; I look down at Daisy and realise she's gone pale. I hold her to me and kiss her gently on the head.

"Not good, Stuart. What the fuck happened?" I look up and see Stuart looking at me through the rear-view mirror.

"I don't know. I spoke to her last night on the phone, and she was fine. I've never seen anything like it with a wolf." I can hear the concern in his voice.

As I try and think of something that causes this kind of reaction in wolves, Daisy starts to convulse. I hear it before it happens and manage to get the bowl under her mouth as she starts throwing up. I hear Stuart curse as he swerves to the side of the road and stops the car.

"What are you doing? Keep driving!" I shout as he undoes his seatbelt. Daisy stops convulsing, and the sickness seems to have stopped. Stuart turns in his seat, grabs the bowl of sick and sniffs it.

"Fuck! Shit!" He curses aloud as he hands me back the bowl and brings up Edward's number. I know to keep my mouth shut as Stuart starts driving again, this time faster than before.

"Edward, it's wolfsbane!" Stuart shouts as soon as Edward answers the phone. Edward and I both curse together.

"Are you sure?" Edward asks as I tighten my hold on Daisy as my heart starts racing. Wolfsbane can kill a wolf if the antidote is not given quickly. I can't lose her, not like this.

"Yes, I can smell it in her vomit." I don't question him, as Stuart has a better sense of smell than any wolf I know. Once he has smelt a scent, he remembers it and will know it again instantly.

"I have the antidote with me; I brought it just in case. I'll be at Michaels in less than ten minutes. How far are you?" Edward asks; I can hear the sound of his engine getting louder as he speeds up too.

"Half that," Stuart tells him.

"What can I do when we get back?" I ask from my seat in the back.

"Get her on the bed and put ice packs where I said before. Has she regained consciousness at all?" Edward asks.

"No," I answer as I look down at Daisy, unconscious in my arms.

"Okay, make her as comfortable as possible and lie down with her if she becomes agitated." Edward takes a deep breath, "Michael, if she stops breathing, start CPR."

"What? Is that likely?" I ask, terrified of the answer, Stuart and I share a look through the rear-view mirror, both as terrified as the other.

"I really don't know." Edward says as he hangs up. Stuart ends the call as I feel my world slip from underneath me. I reach through the bond and try to speak to her, but she doesn't respond.

"She'll be okay, Mikey; she's strong and stubborn," Stuart says from the front. I nod, not trusting myself to speak, as I think I'll be sick if I open my mouth. I look down at Daisy in my arms, and the thought I might lose her terrifies me. I push it to the back of my mind, refusing to acknowledge it is a possibility.

I feel the car stop before I realise where we are. Stuart opens the car door, and I climb out with Daisy. We rush to the house; Stuart opens the front door, and I take Daisy to our room. She moans as soon as I place her on the bed, and she's out of my arms.

"Tell me what you need, and I'll get it," Stuart says as I shrug off my suit jacket and undo the cuffs of my shirt.

"There are bags of frozen veg in the freezer, all nearly empty, so get me them as well as four wet tea towels and a cold glass of water." I dictate as I roll up my sleeves.

As Stuart rushes down the stairs, I hear the front door open.

"Where are they?" Marcus shouts.

"Bedroom," Stuart replies as I hear Marcus running up the stairs. He rushes into the bedroom and stops in his tracks when he sees Daisy.

"Dear Mother Earth, what the fuck is going on?" he demands. I look at him shaking my head as I finish rolling up my shirt sleeves.

"Wolfsbane. Edward's on the way. I want Tony's house searched, and I want to know how the fuck she was poisoned." I demand. Suddenly the most excruciating pain I have ever felt explodes in my head. I drop to my knees and scream, unable to stop myself. I grasp my head as it feels like it's going to explode. I can hear Marcus in the distance yelling at me, asking me what's happening. It sounds like he's in another room, but he's right there when I manage to open my eyes a little—Stuart's holding Daisy down as she screams, clutching her head. I realise it's the bond; I'm feeling her pain.

I start crawling toward her, unable to risk standing. As soon as I take hold of her hand, I can feel her panic ease the tiniest of amounts.

"Mikey, what's happening?" She sobs down the bond,

"I don't know. We have to try and close it; I can't help you whilst we're like this," I reply, leaning my head to her side. I hear Marcus and Stuart shouting for one of us to talk to them. Stuart is now on the other side of the bed, holding Daisy back to stop her from rolling off completely. I can feel Marcus gripping my shoulders.

"I'm trying to close it. I can't." Daisy sobs. I close my eyes and try to close it myself. Suddenly the bond snaps closed, and I feel myself fall to the floor as the pressure in my head disappears.

My ears are ringing. I can't hear or feel anything. Very slowly, I can hear a commotion in the background. Somebody grabs me and pulls me across the floor. It's as if someone flips a switch, and I suddenly hear and feel everything.

"Get her on the floor now!" Marcus roars as someone

grabs hold of me and shakes my shoulders.

"He's breathing. Concentrate on her." Marcus barks by me. I lift myself into a seated position and look around, dazed.

Daisy's lying on the floor, Marcus and Stuart leaning over her.

"Daisy, don't you dare give up on me now, girl!" Marcus growls. I feel for the bond to tell her to wake up, but I can't find it. The panic starts building in me; it's not there. Where is it?

"You need to rebuild the bond." My wolf shouts at me. *"Her wolf is fighting the wolfsbane, and it's killing Daisy; rebuild the bond so I can help her now!"* I throw myself at Daisy, pushing Stuart out of the way and then Marcus.

"What are you doing? We're losing her!" Marcus shouts. He tries to pull me from her, but I push him away.

"Trust me!" I snarl at him as I pull her t-shirt away from her shoulder, where her mark has almost faded.

"Shit!" Marcus curses behind me as he sees it. I don't stop to think. I put my mouth against the mark, and I bite her. The second my teeth break the skin, Daisy inhales a lungful of air and throws her arms around me as she starts gasping for breath. I remove my mouth and see that the mark's back. I wrap my arms around her and hold her tightly against me. I can feel my wolf soothing hers as I soothe Daisy.

"I've got you, darling. I've got you." I repeatedly whisper into her ear as I bury my face in her hair. I don't hear Edward arrive until I feel someone touch my shoulder. I look up, and the healer is looking at me.

"I need you to put her back on the bed, Michael. I need to help her." I quickly stand with her in my arms. Stuart's there in a heartbeat helping me. As I lower Daisy onto the bed, she moans in her sleep. I instantly look for the bond, and it's there just as it was before.

"I'm here, darling; I'm not going anywhere," I promise as I take a step back to give Edward access.

"Mikey?" She whispers as soon as I let go of her hand. I can hear the pain and fear in her voice.

"I'm right here, I promise. Stay strong, darling." I reply. I watch Edward giving her an injection; I know it is the wolfsbane

antidote. Edward turns and looks at me.

"Can you still communicate with her?" he asks; I nod before answering.

"I can now that I re-marked her," I whisper as Edward's eyes widen.

"What made you do that?" Edward asks, shaking his head in dismay.

"My wolf told me to do it. He said he could then help hers." I explain as I look from Daisy to Edward before continuing, "I can't explain it, but I can feel him helping Daisy's wolf to fight." I look back to Daisy, who now has ice packs under her knees and neck. Stuart's holding one to her head. I can see he's been crying. I walk over to him and hold out my hand for the ice pack.

"I'll do that. Go and see what Marcus needs doing." Stuart looks at me and then at Daisy before handing over the ice pack. It's obvious he doesn't want to leave her, but Daisy is *my* mate, and I'll be the one to care for her. I sit on the edge of the bed and gently brush some hair off her forehead before placing the ice pack against it.

"Michael, I need you to see if you can find out how she's feeling. I need to know if she's still in pain and if anything burns." I close my eyes and nod before opening the bond carefully, scared of what I will find.

"Darling, can you hear Edward and me?" I ask nervously.

"Yes, my stomach and head hurt." She whispers back, *"I'm so cold."* I let Edward know, and he gives her some pain relief and tells me to put a light blanket over her, so her body doesn't cool down too quickly.

"Mikey?" I lean over and kiss her gently on the cheek.

"Yes, baby?"

"I'm scared." Daisy's voice shudders as if she's cold.

"I know, darling, but you're going to be okay. I promise." I turn to Edward,

"What do we do now?" I ask as he looks between Daisy and me. He places a hand on my shoulder before answering.

"We wait and pray that we got the antidote in her in time."

Chapter Twenty

Michael

I sit on the bed facing Daisy, holding her hand as she sleeps. I can hear Mum and Jon speaking to Marcus and Edward downstairs. Will and Stuart have gone to meet Tony at his house to see if they can find out how Daisy was poisoned.

I still don't understand how it happened. I sat outside that house until six this morning until Stuart took over so I could come home to shower and change. There was no way I could have come home and slept knowing that Jackson and Kellan could have found Daisy at any point, and I wasn't there to protect her. But they still found a way to get to her anyway.

It just doesn't make sense. The only supernaturals there were Tony and Daisy. No one else should have known that wolfsbane was a poison and what it could do to Daisy. I told Marcus to ask Tony about how Ellis acted last night and this morning. Has Kellan been in touch with him? Was he acting on Kellan's behalf? I'll add it to the never-ending list of questions.

I look down at Daisy as she finally sleeps peacefully. I haven't heard her in a while; I'm hoping it's because she's sleeping the effects of the wolfsbane off. She feels so far away, and I don't like it. I can't shake the feeling I had when I lost her for those brief moments. It's a feeling I never want to experience again.

Thankfully a knock at the door gives me the distraction I need.

"It's open, Mum," I say quietly. Mum walks into the room, followed closely by Jon. They both look at Daisy, and I can see their worry. The bond between these two and my mate is more than I could have ever dreamt it could be. Daisy has fitted into our little family perfectly.

My mum slowly walks over to the bed and places a hand on Daisy's head; she's much cooler now. Edward and I have decided we aren't going to replace the ice packs when they warm up and see what happens. We're hoping the fever has broken.

"How's she doing?" Jon asks as he stands beside me and places a hand on my shoulder as he looks down at Daisy.

"Improving, we think, but we won't know for sure until she either wakes up or communicates with me." I feel Jon squeeze my shoulder; I can't bring myself to tear my eyes away from her in case I miss something.

"That link of yours can come in useful, that's for sure," Jon whispers as he steps away.

"You have no idea. I'd have lost her without it. The extra link between our wolves was what saved her." I can feel a lump forming in my throat. I take a deep breath and try to control myself, but it doesn't work; when I look at my mum, I feel myself crumble.

"Her heart stopped, Mama." Mum throws her arms around me as I sob into her shoulder. This was why I tried to hide from her. Very few people see my vulnerable side, but my mum sees it more than most.

"She's going to be okay, Mikey. Her temp has gone down quickly; I promise that's a good sign." Mum says as she hugs me.

"Then why doesn't she wake up?" I ask as I sit back up and wipe my face as I hear footsteps on the stairs.

"Her body has been through an ordeal; it needs time to heal." Mum sighs as she looks back down at Daisy. I know she's right, but I need to hear Daisy's voice, even if just through the bond. I need to know she's no longer in pain; I hate not being able to help her.

I look up as Edward walks into the room and heads over to check on Daisy. Mum moves out of the way to give him room.

"What time scale are we looking at for her to wake up?" Jon asks him. Edward carries on, checking Daisy over before answering.

"She won't wake up until tomorrow morning at the earliest. Her body needs rest to recover. All signs show that we got her the antidote in time. She should make a full recovery." I let out a sigh of relief and feel my brother's hand grasp my shoulder in a show of support.

"You can breathe now, Mikey. She's going to be back driving us mad in no time." He whispers next to me. I nod as I retake Daisy's hand and kiss her knuckles. As I sit up, there's a knock at the bedroom door. Marcus sticks his head around.

"They're back, and they found something."

)) ● ((

Five minutes later, I'm standing in the dining room with the entire team, plus Tony. Carl and Richard are also here as they brought lunch for us all and wanted to check on Daisy. Mum's staying upstairs with Daisy and Edward. I don't want Daisy on her own for a moment, so Mum promised to call me if there was the slightest change in her condition.

"Mikey, you don't need to be down here; we can fill you in on everything," Marcus says from his chair; I shake my head and walk over to the head of the table so I can sit down.

"It's fine." I look over at Stuart and Will. "What did you find?" I ask. Will looks at me and pushes over a bamboo container. I recognise it straight away as Daisy's lunchbox.

"This was in Daisy's room by the bed. It has been injected with wolfsbane by the looks of it." Will explains,

"It's not something that I took over there. I don't recognise it." Stuart looks at Tony, who clears his throat.

"It's not one of mine either. I don't buy them," Tony adds, not looking at me. He's been avoiding me since I walked into the room.

"You're not to blame, Tony. The last thing any of us expected was for someone to try and kill Daisy; it doesn't make sense." I sigh, sitting forward in my chair and pulling the tub towards me.

"Especially when Jackson claims to want Daisy to join him, why kill her?" Marcus points out; I nod and tap the top of the box, not ready to face what's inside, knowing it's what nearly took my mate from me.

"Maybe he's bored of trying and has decided if he can't have her, then no one can?" Jon pipes in. "Seems to be his M.O.", he adds quietly. I look at my brother and see from his face that he didn't mean to say that last bit out loud.

"What do you know?" Carl asks; Jon and Will look at me, and I know it's time to tell the truth. Up to now, we've only informed Marcus, Stuart and the Alpha.

"As you know, when we were down in Cornwall a few weeks ago, there was the broken window incident. You don't know that a bag of clothes was left at the scene. The clothes contained three scents: Jackson's, Daisy's," I look down at the table before adding, "and Michelle's."

You could have heard a pin drop. It's as if everybody in the room stopped breathing. Those who knew are hanging their heads whilst those who didn't stare at me, unable to process what they heard. It's Tony who breaks the silence.

"Michelle, as in your twin?" I nod as he whistles. "How did her scent get on something with Daisy's and Jackson's? Did she ever meet Daisy?" he asks. Carl and Richard look at me for answers. Marcus gets up and starts pacing. He's been struggling with this since I told him separately after Mum. I hadn't even let Jon or Daisy come with me, I knew he would struggle with the news, and I was right.

"No, Daisy never met Michelle. Jackson made her wear Michelle's clothes as they had her scent. He thought it would encourage a mating bond to form," I explain, trying not to look at Marcus or Jon.

"But how did he get Michelle's clothes? Why would that form a mating bond?" Tony asks, making me realise how little he knows.

"Because Jackson killed Michelle when she rejected him as her mate. He then stripped her and left her in nothing but her underwear before disappearing." I hear Marcus growl from the patio door. The sound of the doors opening fills the room, quickly followed by the unmissable sound of fabric shredding. When I turn around, Marcus has gone, and all that's left are his ruined clothes.

"I take it Marcus was close to Michelle?" Tony asks; Carl looks from the pile of shredded clothes to Tony and nods as he answers for me.

"He loved her more than any wolf could love someone who wasn't their mate. If any couple had the strength to ignore their fated mates, it was them. What they had was ..."

"Something stronger." Jon finishes. I nod because he's right; I'll never understand how they weren't fated mates. The bond they had together was something else entirely. It even beat mine and Daisy's, and ours is truly unique.

"All of this doesn't explain why he tried to kill Daisy, though. Why not leave her alone if he wasn't going to get her? Why make a pack full of enemies by killing a single wolf?" Richard asks from where he is sitting next to Carl. I turn the box around on the table and open it. What I find inside makes me relax for the briefest moments until I realise what it truly means.

"He wasn't trying to kill Daisy," I whisper, looking into the tub.

"What?" a few different people ask at the same time. I pick up the contents of the box and look at it.

"Daisy got this out of the car; I always keep them in there as I get one out for breakfast during my first class every day. Kellan knows that." I answer as I feel one side of my mouth lift in a half smile.

"So, you're saying that wasn't intended for Daisy?" Stuart asks. I shake my head.

"No, it was intended for me."

)D●((

Ten minutes later, I'm in the woods outside our home, listening out for my pack brother. It doesn't take me long to find him, as I knew he would stay close in case anything happened; no matter how much he wanted to disappear, he would never leave his post.

I find Marcus lying on the forest floor, still as his wolf. I place a pile of my clothes next to him and step back. He looks from them to me and is back in human form instantly.

"Thanks." He mutters as he picks up the clothes and starts pulling them on.

"Want to talk about it?" I ask as I lean against a tree. Marcus shakes his head whilst avoiding eye contact.

"What's the point? It doesn't change anything," Marcus

replies, with no feeling or emotion in his voice.

"Tell me what's on your mind," I push. Marcus turns to look at me with his what was once bright brown eyes, but they lost their spark four years ago when he lost the love of his life.

"She was meant to be mine, not his. Mine!" He yells, "I should have been her mate, not some sadist psychopath with an authority complex. He'd have never loved her. I LOVED HER! NO. I STILL LOVE HER!" All I can do is watch as my oldest friend punches a tree, the crack of the bark and his knuckles can be heard from all directions. "FUCK!" He roars as he drops to the ground of the tree, not holding his hand but his head. I walk over to him and lower myself to sit next to Marcus; our backs are leaning against the tree he's just punched. I reach into my pocket and pull out a hip flask. I unscrew the top and take a sip before offering it to my pack brother.

Marcus takes it from me and has a drink. I lean my head back against the tree and sigh.

"Every day for the last four years, I've wished that you were her mate. You'd have protected her with your life. You'd have carried on making her as happy as you did, and she wouldn't be dead. He wouldn't have killed her as she wouldn't have mattered to him." Marcus takes another sip from the flask and hands it back to me. I take a sip and close my eyes as the liquid burns down my throat.

"And now he's trying to kill your mate," Marcus replies next to me. I shake my head as I sigh and take another sip from the hip flask.

"Take, not kill." Marcus turns and looks at me, frowning. "It was one of my cereal bars that were poisoned; Daisy had gotten it from the car before going to Tony's. The poison was meant for me, not her."

"Fuck." Marcus curses next to me. "How do you feel about that?" I look at him and laugh.

"Relieved he's a shit assassin. Devastated and guilty that Daisy was poisoned and nearly killed by something intended for me. Angry that he took our Michelle and turned my mate into a wolf and abused her as he did. Amused that he dared to try and kill me." I take a deep breath and try to calm myself a little.

"I want the prick dead, Marcus. I want my mate to be free of him once and for all. I need to know that he can never get near her again. I want him to suffer for what he did to Michelle and Daisy."

"Then we do it, Mikey. When we find him, we ensure that the council doesn't intervene and try to keep him alive. No matter what, we kill the bastard and make him pay for doing this to the women we love. We ensure he feels the pain he has caused us all. By the time we have finished with him, he will be begging for death." Marcus commands next to me, he holds out his hand, and I grab it. "I swear to you, Mikey, he took your sister from us, but he will not take your mate or you or anyone else. We end him together."

Chapter Twenty-One

Michael

Marcus and I start making our way back to the house when we hear the unmissable sound of raised voices. We look at each other for the briefest second before sprinting back to the house, scared of what's occurred whilst we were gone. We stop when we find Stuart and Will confronting Tony in the back garden.

"You should have fucking told me!" Stuart yells at him. Marcus and I approach them as Carl, Richard, and Jon rush from the house.

"What's going on?" I demand as I approach the three of them. Tony instantly looks away from me. "Tony?" I ask again, a little firmer.

"I messed up yesterday, and it's my fault Daisy was poisoned," Tony mumbles. I look at him, frowning.

"Unless you poisoned the bar yourself, I can't see how it was your fault," I answer. Tony finally looks up at me, and I can see the tears in his eyes. I take a step toward him. "Tony, speak to me," I whisper as I place a hand on his shoulder.

"He's to blame because he saw Kellan and some guy in the car park yesterday and didn't tell anyone!" Stuart shouts behind him. I let go of his shoulder and take a step back.

"What? He better be mistaken, Tony." I warn. Marcus steps up next to me; I can feel the anger radiating from him.

"I didn't think it was actually him! I promise I would have said something if I'd known it was." Tony declares, looking at me with pleading eyes.

"Even if you weren't sure, you should have fucking told Michael or me!" Stuart shouts behind Tony; I hear Will telling Stuart to calm down as he places a hand on Stuart's arm. But Stuart shrugs him off.

"No, I won't calm down. You didn't see her, Will. You weren't there when Daisy and Michael both nearly died. When Daisy *did* die! I was, and it could have been prevented if that dickhead had just told someone what he fucking saw!" Stuart goes to take a step towards Tony, but Marcus and I both step between them and face Stuart; he stops in his tracks and then looks at us, outraged.

"Are you seriously going to defend him? Michael, because of him, your *mate* was nearly gone forever, and you're defending him! Are you insane?" Stuart roars at me.

"Back the fuck down, Stuart." Marcus bellows as he gets in Stuart's face. I don't take my eyes off him as I cross my arms over my puffed-out chest. Stuart looks at me and instantly bows his head in submission. "Have you forgotten who you are speaking to?" Marcus asks as he takes another step towards him.

"No, Marcus," Stuart replies, still looking at the floor, but he looks up and towards me. "Forgive me, Michael, but I stand by what I said. How can you defend him?"

"I don't need to justify myself to you, Stuart. Who I defend and why is not your concern. But I will ask you this. Would Tony purposely cause any harm to come to *my* mate?" Stuart looks at me, shaking his head. "Also, how would Daisy feel if she could see you now, threatening her best friend?" Stuart bows his head again. "Go for a walk and check the grounds. Take the time to cool off." I demand as I point towards the woods. Stuart nods and leaves without even glancing in Tony's direction. I turn and look at Carl and Richard.

"If you guys want to head off, feel free. I'll keep you updated on how Daisy's doing; there's nothing else that can be done for now." I take a deep breath and turn to face Tony.

"Go with them; I'll be in touch when she wakes up or if there are any changes. Check that Beth is okay, as she was upset this morning. As for seeing Kellan, the damage is done but learn from it and tell us from now on what you suspect. Even if it's just a gut feeling, you were fortunate this time; we all were that Daisy was saved. But next time, we might not be so lucky. Think about that. Now go." I turn away, and I hear Tony walk toward the others.

"I'm sorry, Michael, I really am," Tony whispers as he leaves.

"I know," I reply without turning to face him, worried that I'm still on the verge of losing my shit. I hear the garden gate open and close then I finally turn around to see who's left in the garden.

Jon, Will and Marcus are all looking at me. I let out a sigh and run my fingers through my hair.

"Mikey?" My head spins round to the sound of my mum's voice.

"Daisy?" I ask as I quickly stride towards her; she nods as I race past her into the house, taking the stairs at a record speed. I rush into the room and see Edward sitting beside Daisy as he tries to hold her to the bed. She's thrashing around and moaning loudly.

"What's happening?" I demand; Edward looks up at me.

"I think the wolfsbane is causing nightmares. Can you hold her and see if it helps?"

I rush to the other side of the bed and climb on, scooting over until I'm next to Daisy; I pull her into my arms and lie down with her as we do most nights when she has a nightmare. Her head on my chest, one of my arms under her shoulders. She starts to relax as soon as she is against me, and I run my fingers through her hair.

"Shhh, darling, I'm right here. You're safe. I have you, I promise." I whisper into her ear; she relaxes further until she's finally sound asleep again.

"You have to do that often, don't you?" My mum asks as she sits on the edge of the bed next to Daisy and takes her hand. I nod and plant a kiss on my girl's head.

"Too often; she doesn't even wake most of the time. She tries to convince everyone she's over it, but that's far from the truth. She won't admit to others how much she's still hurting from what he put her through." I look at my mum and see her staring down at Daisy with such sadness in her eyes.

"Sometimes, I'm glad he killed Michelle. Not because he took her from us, but because I dread to think what kind of life she'd have had with him if she had accepted him as her mate." Mum whispers. Since finding out who killed my sister, I've thought the same thing.

"Michelle was always going to reject her mate for Marcus, Mum. There's no way she'd have ever walked away from him." Mum looks at me and nods.

"I know; that's why he'll always be my son. They only had a few months until the wedding; they wanted to try for a baby as soon as possible. Marcus has never been the same since he lost her; none of us has." I look from her down at Daisy in my arms and sigh.

"Many things should be different for our family right now, Mum. But they are what they are. I've been wondering what would have happened to Daisy if Michelle hadn't rejected Jackson, she would have never been bitten, and I may have never found her. She said she would have never studied law without experiencing what she did. She hadn't even planned on university before she was taken. She'd have never crossed my path, and I'd have grown old mateless." I run a knuckle over Daisy's cheek as I watch her now sleeping peacefully in my arms.

"You two would have found each other, Daisy was destined to take over from her uncle, and you're destined to be alpha. You'd have met at council meetings eventually. Even without her feeling the mate bond as she does now, she's a wolf. She'd have loved you the moment she laid eyes on you. You can see it in the way she looks at you now. I don't think anything or anyone could have kept you two from finding each other." I look at my mum and smile.

"Thanks, Mama," I whisper as she smiles back at me. She takes my hand and squeezes it.

"Why don't you take advantage of the fact Daisy is settled there in your arms and get some rest yourself. From what I hear, you were up all night watching Tony's, and I know you must be exhausted with everything that's happened since." As if to prove a point, I yawn and then smile.

"I think I might. Can you tell Marcus to take over for a few hours? But let me know if anything important comes to light. The guys can all leave if they want. You can stay here or go home too, Mum. There isn't much more we can do but wait and see how Daisy is when she wakes up." Mum looks at me, frowning.

"As if you think I could go home when one of my children is so ill. I'll be sleeping in the spare room until Daisy has recovered; I need to ensure you eat and rest too." I knew she would insist on staying.

"Thank you, Mama."

"Now go to sleep, and don't worry about anything, Marcus has everything under control, and I'll give Nigel and Mary an update for you." I thank her again as she leans over and plants a kiss on my head and then on Daisy's before leaving the room. I take a deep breath and inhale Daisy's scent. It's still not right, with the added wolfsbane and the medication in her system. But her scent is there, and it still calms me as I close my eyes and drift into an uneasy sleep with my strong, brave mate in my arms.

Chapter Twenty-Two

Daisy

My body's so heavy; why does everything ache? I try to open my eyes, but I can't. I can hear voices around me and remember I'm at Tony's. I woke up with the flu. Did I fall back to sleep?

"How much longer do you think she'll be out for?" Hang on, that's Jon's voice.

"Jonathan, I might be a healer, but I'm not psychic. Daisy will wake up when she's ready." I must have been ill if they called Edward. I try to open my eyes again, but my eyelids are still too heavy.

"I'm thinking of Mikey; he's going out of his mind with worry." Jon moans.

"Mikey's doing better than I thought he would. Now stop; the more you fret, the worse your brother gets." Barbara scolds her son. I feel the mattress move next to me as if someone stands up from it. If Barbara and Jon are here, where is Michael? Suddenly I feel his presence and relax.

"Any change?" I hear him ask; it sounds like he has just walked into the room. Hang on, am I at home? Did Michael bring me back? Of course, he did. He would have never left me there.

"Michael, you were gone less than ten minutes," Edward sighs next to me. I feel the bed move, knowing it's Michael sitting next to me. I can feel him through the bond and smell his scent. He takes my hand and squeezes it.

"I can feel you getting stronger, darling." He whispers in my ear as he kisses me on the temple.

"I'm here," I reply quietly down the bond.

"I can hear her," Michael says as he lets out a sigh of relief; I hear Barbara and Jon exhale too.

"Is she in any pain Michael?" I hear Edward asks.

"My head and throat hurt; my whole body aches too. Why can't I open my eyes?" I moan. Michael relays everything to

Edward.

"I'll give her an injection of pain relief to see if it helps." I hear Edward's reply as I feel a sharp scratch on my arm. "That should help with the pain. She'll be able to open her eyes when her body is ready." Edward adds.

"Take your time, darling. You're safe; that's all that matters." I don't want to take my time, though. I want to open them now, so I keep trying to move various body parts. The first to move is my fingers. I can feel Michael's hand in mine, and it's as if his touch gives me strength. It doesn't take long until I can squeeze his hand back when he squeezes mine.

"Don't rush it, darling. You'll come back to us when you're ready." Michael whispers. But I want to wake up now. I eventually feel my eyelids start to flutter.

"Mikey."

"I know Mama she's fighting; she's being stubborn."

"You're being stubborn." I sigh as Michael chuckles, which makes me happy. I feel my hand being lifted before Michael presses a kiss to its back.

"Edward, if she's fighting to wake up, will it make the recovery process harder on her?" I hear him ask.

"I can't see why it would. I've no idea how that connection of yours works, but if you can hear her and she's fighting to wake up, I can only see that as a positive sign." Edward responds.

"You're just enjoying not having to deal with my cranky ass," I reply, which causes Michael to laugh out loud.

"Darling, I will never moan about your cranky ass again after the last twenty-four hours."

"Twenty-four hours?" I ask, shocked.

"That's how long you've been unconscious for." That's all I need to hear to give me the last push to open my eyes.

As soon as they open, I have to close them again quickly. The room is so bright. I hear Michael asking someone to close the curtains. As soon as I hear the sound of the curtains closing, I try to open my eyes again, slowly this time. I have to blink a few times before things start coming into focus. The first thing I see is Michael's face. He looks like he hasn't slept in days, there's more stubble on his face than usual, and his hair looks like he's been running his fingers through it continuously, as he always does when he's stressed. I reach up and place a hand on his cheek.

"Hey." I croak as Michael leans into my touch. His eyes close as his whole body visibly relaxes.

"Hey." He replies just as quietly as he looks me in the eye. I open my mouth to say more, but I start coughing.

"Sit her up and get her to sip some water." I hear Barbara whisper as she comes into view. I look over at her as the coughing stops and smile. Between Michael and his mum, they manage to help me to sit, propped up by pillows. Michael keeps his arm around my shoulder as Barbara lifts a small glass to my lips. As soon as the water touches my throat, it feels like I'm swallowing barbed wire, which causes me to start choking.

"Slowly, Daisy dear, one tiny sip at a time." I hear Barbara whisper as she tips the glass to my mouth again. I do as I'm told and slowly drink a little water. Michael gently lowers me back onto the pillows and then moves until he sits next to me; he places his arm around me again so I can lean into him and rest against his shoulder.

"How are you feeling?" Edward asks as he starts checking my pulse and listening to my chest.

"Like death." I chuckle; I feel Michael tense next to me and see I've instantly upset everyone.

"What do you remember?" Edward continues; I think for a second.

"I woke up at Tony's with what I thought was a hangover. I tried to eat, but it instantly made me feel worse. I quickly realised it was the flu. I don't remember anything after getting back into bed." I look at my family around me and notice they all look pale, worried and tired.

"I'm sorry if I scared you all," I whisper. Everyone turns to me, frowning.

"Why are you apologising, darling?" Michael asks next to me. I turn my head and look at him.

"Because you all look upset." I sigh. Michael reaches up and cups my face in his hand.

"We're only upset because we very nearly lost you." He says as his thumb runs over my cheek.

"People get flu all the time Mikey," I whisper, rolling my eyes.

"You didn't have the flu; you were poisoned," Michael says softly.

"What?" I ask, confused.

"The cereal bar was injected with wolfsbane; when you ate it, you were poisoned, and we nearly lost you." Michael takes a deep breath and looks back at me. "Your wolf was so busy battling the wolfsbane your body gave up. For a few brief seconds, you stopped breathing. I had to rebuild the bond so my wolf could help yours." I can feel Michael's hold on me tighten, but I pull away from him. I open my mouth to speak, but the words won't come out as my throat contracts and my chest tightens. I can't speak aloud, so I open the bond.

"It wasn't meant for me."

Michael shakes his head to reply, his eyes not leaving mine. My heart starts racing as I stare at him.

"You would have had the full dose before realising something was wrong. You inhale those bars." I point out. Michael nods as my body starts shaking violently; I've never felt anger like this. I can feel my wolf coming to the surface. She wants revenge; Michael seems to pick up on my internal battle to stay in control.

"Mikey, what's happening?" I hear Jon say behind me. Michael takes my hand and places it on his chest so that I can feel his heartbeat.

"Calm down, darling. I'm here, and I'm safe." Michael whispers through the bond. Not once taking his eyes from mine.

"Michael, I need to know what's happening." I hear Edward ask.

"She realised the poison was intended for me," Michael says, still refusing to look anywhere but at me.

"He's dead," I say aloud through gritted teeth, the hatred dominating my voice.

"I'll kill him for hurting you." Michael nods. But I shake my head.

"No. I'll kill him for trying to hurt you," I growl; Michael looks at me, shocked.

"Mikey, what do you expect? She's as protective of you as you are of her." I hear Barbara say next to me.

"We'll discuss this later. You need to rest," Michael says, running his thumb over my cheek before pulling me against him. I sigh as I lean into his chest before sitting back up suddenly.

"Darling, what's the matter?" Michael asks worriedly, I try to move my legs, but they still feel heavy.

"The feeling will come back soon; your body's still waking up," Edward explains as I try and force my legs to move. I manage to shuffle them to the edge of the bed before Michael's in front of me.

"You need to rest." He says as he grabs my shoulders. But I shake my head.

"No, I don't; I need to pee." I moan, wiggling as I feel like my bladder is about to explode. Michael laughs as he scoops me up in his arms.

"Come on then, but then you rest." He chuckles as he carries me into our bathroom.

Chapter Twenty-Three

Michael

It's been a couple of hours since Daisy woke up, and I haven't left her side. I'm still terrified she will react further to the wolfsbane and she will be taken from me again. Edward keeps trying to reassure me that she will make a full recovery as she now has complete control of her body, can drink without choking, and has kept down some toast. It just seems too good to be true after the last twenty-four hours.

I sent everyone a message that Daisy had regained consciousness and asked them to be at ours at midday to discuss our next move. Jackson has upped the game by trying to poison me, which means we also have to.

Whilst Daisy is talking to Nigel and Mary; I hear the front door opening, followed by the sound of everyone entering at once. I get up from the bed where I have been sitting with Daisy and signal for Jon to follow me. I also want to discuss something with Marcus and Jon before the team meeting.

Once downstairs, I get the two of them to follow me into the dining room and close the door behind us.

"What's going on, Mikey?" Jon asks, frowning at me.

"I'm going to try and get Mum to go and stay with Auntie Sherri," I say quietly. I look at the two of them, and they seem to relax a little. "With everything going on and the pricks determined to get to Daisy and now me, I want Mum out of the way and safe. They won't find her there but may find her at home."

"You know she'll fight you over it, don't you?" Jon points out, and I nod.

"I tried to talk her into it when you were down in Cornwall, but she was having none of it," Marcus says from where he is standing. "I think if anyone has a chance of getting her to listen to reason, it's Daisy," he adds. But I shake my head and lean back against the table.

"I'm not adding to her stress levels right now. She's still

recovering. Since finding out that it was me, he wanted dead; Daisy has been unsettled, to say the least." I sigh as I rub the bridge of my nose.

"So, what do you suggest then?" Jon asks next to me. I turn and look at the two of them.

"We corner Mum and try and get her to listen to the three of us together. Hopefully, we can get through to her." The two of them nod in agreement.

"Why is it always you three hiding in a room conspiring against me?" We all turn around and see Mum standing in the now open doorway.

"We're not conspiring." I sigh, rolling my eyes.

"And we're not against you," Marcus adds next to me. Mum crosses her arms over her chest and walks over to Jon.

"And you? Are you conspiring against me?" Jon looks down at Mum and nods.

"I want you safe that's all that matters to me. If you stay here, you aren't. I won't let anything happen to you." Jon says as his eyes soften.

"I'm as safe here as the rest of you, if not safer, as I have that giant lump of a wolf playing guard dog every night." Mum moans, pointing to Marcus. I frown as I turn to him.

"Is that why you're never free at night anymore? I thought you might have met someone." I chuckle. Marcus shrugs, smiling.

"I thought I was being subtle, obviously not."

Mum walks up to him and taps his cheek. "You wouldn't know subtle if it hit you over the head with a shovel."

Jon and I can't help but laugh as Marcus smiles down at Mum.

"You've hidden in the same spot since you were fifteen; the only difference is that you've grown quicker than the bush. I knew you were there then and when you are there now. So no, you're not being subtle." She adds, smiling up at him.

"You mean you left me in the cold and rain all those times and never said a word or let me in?" Marcus exclaims wide-eyed, making Jon and I laugh harder. Mum leans up and cups Marcus's cheek.

"Why do you think you always got the biggest portion of porridge those mornings before school or the first cup of coffee in the morning." She replies, smiling.

"Mama B, you're one of a kind." Marcus chuckles, "but don't think I haven't noticed you've completely changed the subject. You need to go and stay with your sister." Marcus says as he leans down and kisses Mum on the cheek.

"I'm not going, and that's final," Mum says as she crosses her arms over her chest again and walks out of the door, only to freeze when she sees Daisy standing on the bottom stairs.

"Please Mama, for me," Daisy whispers with tears in her eyes. I rush to Daisy's side, reaching her at the same time as Mum, who throws her arms around Daisy and holds her tight.

"Dear Goddess, what are you doing out of bed?" Mum asks her. I place an arm around Daisy's back as Mum steps away, and I feel Daisy lean against me slightly. I turn to pick her up, but she shakes her head before turning back to Mum.

"I heard what you all were saying, and I had to come down to say my piece."

"You can say it sat in bed," I say as I pull her towards me to lift her again, but the look she gives me stops me in my tracks.

"Adams, if you put me back in that bed, it will be you needing bed rest," she warns. I hear Stuart chuckle behind me and see that the others are now standing in the hallway.

"Looks like Daisy's back to her usual self." Carl laughs as he leans against the lounge doorframe.

"Back to making Mikey's life hell," Richard adds, smiling at her as he leans on Carl's shoulder. I look around, and it's hard not to smile when everyone looks relieved and happy to see Daisy up and about again. I know they can't tell that she's leaning on me for support or that her heart rate's still a little faster than usual. I look back at Daisy and feel my eyes roll as I scoop her up in my arms.

"Adams, I swear I will kick your ass if you take me back up those stairs." She protests in my arms; I look at her and smile playfully.

"As much fun as that sounds, I'm not taking you upstairs. I

won't make you get back into bed, but you will get off your feet. Is that understood?" I answer sternly. Daisy looks from me to my mum before placing her arms around my neck.

"Fine, but if I have to stay off my feet, does that mean you're doing all the cooking and cleaning?" she asks me with that mischievous glint in her eye.

"Yes, it does, so no different from any other day." I laugh and quickly curse as she slaps my chest. "Glad to see your strength is coming back, darling." I cough as I put her down on the sofa and rub my chest. I take the blanket my mum passes me and wrap it around her as I talk to her through our bond.

"You're not fooling me. Why did you come downstairs if you still feel so weak?"

"I don't want to be on my own right now, and I want Mama to be safe." I look from Daisy to my Mum.

"I think you need to hear what Daisy has to say," I whisper. Mum sits down next to Daisy and takes her hand.

"I'm not leaving when you are ill," Mum says.

"But it's being around me that puts you in danger. The best thing you could do is get as far away from me as possible," Daisy replies, quickly followed by everyone protesting.

"That's not what you just said to me. This isn't your fault." I protest.

"Isn't it?" Daisy replies, looking at me before looking around the room. "If none of you was associated with me, would you be here right now? Would your life be turned upside down by all this bullshit?" Everyone just stops and looks at Daisy, no one knowing what to say, myself included.

"You're right. None of us would be dealing with this shit if we didn't know you." I spin around and stare at Stuart, who is looking at Daisy. "But that doesn't mean we don't want to be here," he continues. Stuart moves until he stands beside me before crouching to be at eye level with her.

"We all want to be here. Not as Pack Protectors, but as your friends and family." He adds. Stuart looks at Daisy before looking up at me and standing.

"Michael has said we can walk away at any point, and we all vowed to protect you and support you because we love you," Will says as he stands beside Stuart. Daisy looks at them and me as if for confirmation. I nod before squatting in front of her and cupping her hand between mine.

"Darling, Will's right. Everyone is here because they want to be." Daisy looks at me and shakes her head. Before she turns to face everyone, I try to figure out what she's thinking but can't.

"I love you all too. But it doesn't change that Mikey would be dead now if I hadn't taken that bar. It could have been any of you if you had just seen it lying in the car and picked it up." Daisy looks at Mum, and I can see the tears in her eyes. "What if next time it's something that you eat? What if you're poisoned and alone? Edward told me he has no idea how I survived, and I didn't eat the whole bar. I'd never forgive myself if anything happened to you because of me." Daisy turns and looks at everyone. "If anything happened to *any* of you, I'd never live with myself. But you guys are stronger and able to protect yourselves more." Daisy turns to look at our Mum. "You, Mama, are on your own more than any of us. What if something happened and you couldn't get in touch with somebody? We can't lose you." Daisy reaches out a hand and takes Mums.

"Which is why if you don't go to your sisters, then I'm leaving," she states.

"What?!" I gasp as I feel like I've been punched in the stomach.

"You'd leave Mikey?" Mum asks, looking desperately between Daisy and me. Daisy's head drops, and I see her shoulders shake slightly as she tries not to cry. Slowly she nods, and I feel my insides freeze.

"You're not going anywhere. I'll not let you leave, not without me." I say as I place a finger under her chin and force her to lift her head so I can look her in the eye. But when I look into her eyes, it's sheer determination I see.

"I will do whatever it takes to make sure Mama is safe. Jackson has already taken enough from your family. I won't let him take anyone else." Daisy replies as she looks at me.

"But you'll let us lose you? Let *me* lose you?" I demand as

I look into those green eyes. "Say the word if you want to leave, and we're gone. I will take you anywhere you want. But don't leave me again; we promised no more running." I beg. Daisy reaches over and places a hand on my cheek.

"I don't want to leave you, but Jackson will use everyone we love to get us back if we run together. You know he will. But if I go on my own, he'll assume I don't care enough to stay, and he'll leave you all alone. You're all safer without me." She answers.

"And who's going to look after you?" Marcus asks from his seat; I turn and stare at him.

"I will, as she isn't leaving without me!" I state firmly as I stare at Daisy, trying to get my point across.

"I'll be fine," Daisy says, looking at him. There's no conviction in her voice though, and she knows she won't be able to outrun Jackson forever. Not that I'll ever let her leave without me.

"You're not going anywhere. End of conversation!" I snap as I jump to my feet. Daisy instantly recoils from me, and for a second, I can see fear in her eyes, and I hate that I'm the one putting it there.

"Mikey, you need to calm down," Jon says behind me.

"Calm down? I know what she's really thinking; how can I calm down?" I shout as I turn and storm out of the lounge and throw open the cupboard under the stairs. I grab a rucksack hidden at the back and carry it into the lounge, dropping it at Daisy's feet. Daisy looks up at me wide-eyed.

"How?" She whispers as tears roll down her cheeks.

"How do I know about the bag? I found it. Did you know you talk in your sleep?" I snap, pointing at the bag.

"Michael," Carl whispers as he places a hand on my shoulder, which I shrug off.

"Why don't you share your big plan, darling? Why not tell us all how you plan on sneaking off and handing yourself over to Jackson to protect all of us." I snap. Marcus walks up next to me and stares at Daisy, who is still looking at me.

"I won't be to blame for one of you getting hurt or killed." She whispers like that is all she needs to say on the matter.

"How do you plan on surviving Jackson and hiding from us? Because I can promise you we'll never stop looking for you." Marcus says as he crosses his arms over his chest. I stare at Daisy as I answer for her.

"Oh, she has no intention of surviving, Marcus. She plans to kill him or die trying." I snap. Daisy stares at me; she didn't know how much I had worked out.

"Do you know how hard it is knowing that the love of your life, your mate, would rather die than let you protect them?" I shout.

"Wrong." Daisy snaps at me as she pulls the blanket off her.

"Tell me how I'm wrong?" I ask as I point to the bag, still at her feet.

"You're wrong because it's not about not letting you protect me. It's about me protecting all of you!" Daisy screams as she jumps to her feet, "Especially you!" she yells as she pushes me backwards, and I stumble back a step in shock from her outburst.

"You're all still grieving, Michelle. Do you think any of you will cope with losing someone else from your family? Because I know I can't!" She shouts, looking around the room at every one of us.

"We won't survive losing you either!" Stuart yells behind me. Daisy laughs as she turns to him.

"You've known me for less than six months. You have known each other your whole lives. In the grand scale of things, I'm nothing." She yells at him.

"You are my EVERYTHING!" I roar as I step towards her when I suddenly notice she's gone pale, her face soaked in tears, and her body shaking.

What am I doing? I need to get out of here; this isn't good for her after being poisoned. I turn and storm towards the backdoor.

"Where are you going?" Marcus asks.

"I'm going to calm down." I snap as I throw open the door. I stop and turn around to face Jonathan before pointing in Daisy's direction. "Don't let her out of this house." I don't give him time to answer; I shift and run off.

Daisy

I watch as Michael leaves, and my legs go from underneath me. I don't know who grabs and places me back on the sofa. I hug my knees to my chest and cry into them. I can feel Barbara's arm around my shoulder, but I can't bring myself to lean into her.

I had no idea Michael knew so much. It wasn't a plan like he made it out to be. It was more of a backup option.

"Did you think you could hide all that from Mikey? The man knows everything." Jon whispers as he kneels in front of me.

"I just want you all safe." I sob.

"I'll go."

I turn and look at Barbara as she takes my hands. "I will go and stay with Sherri. I'll stay away until this is all over. But don't leave Mikey and the guys. They need you as much as you need them. Mikey won't survive losing you, and you'll not survive leaving him. So I will go." I look at Barbara, and I don't know what to say. Barbara reaches over and hands me a box of tissues. I take one to wipe my nose and face.

"Marcus can take me home to pack, and then I'll leave. You're right. I'm safer there than I am at home." Marcus walks over and places a hand on Barbara's shoulder.

"I'll take you anywhere you need to go if it means you'll be safe, Mama B." Barbara looks up at him and smiles.

"I know you will, Son." She turns back to me and places a hand on my cheek. "But you need to promise to call me every day and keep me posted on everything. I know I won't be away long, as the lads will have this all fixed and sorted as soon as possible." I look at Barbara and nod, the tears flowing down my face in a continuous river.

"I get why you think handing yourself over to Jackson would work. But I promise you it won't. Mikey would never, ever give up looking for you? That male would pull the world apart to find you. You need to realise that everything you feel for Mikey, he feels for you. Stop trying to protect him by doing this independently; it won't end how you think it will." Barbara says as she wipes the tears from my cheek. I look to the backdoor and feel a tug in my chest to follow him.

"Thank you, Mama," I whisper as I stand up and walk toward the door. Jon jumps up with me and grabs my arm to stop me.

"You heard him. You aren't to leave this house." He snaps with a look of determination I rarely see on his face.

"I'm going to him." I point out, but Jon shakes his head.

"You aren't strong enough yet; you need to stay here. He'll be back." But I just look at him before turning away, pulling my arm out of his grip.

"I'm fine," I snap as I walk to the back door and pull off Michael's t-shirt I'm wearing before shifting.

The shift isn't as easy as it has been; it hurts; I haven't felt a shift for a while.

As soon as I land, I rush towards the woods, following the tugging in my chest, knowing it'll lead me to Mikey. Every step hurts, and every bone in my body feels heavier, but I don't care. I need to find him. I need him to know I don't plan on leaving.

I follow the tug until it is almost gone, and I feel he's close.

"Darling?" I hear him before I see him. Michael rushes out of the trees next to me. *"What do you think you're playing at? You aren't strong enough to shift yet,"* Michael curses as I drop to my knees, shifting as I go.

*"*I'm sorry, that whole stupid plan was a last resort. One I made up when in a blind panic one day. I'd have never been able to go through with it because I'd never be able to walk away from you.*"* I sob. Michael shifts and kneels in front of me.

"Did you really think I would let you go?" Michael asks as he takes my face in his hands.

"No, that's why it was a stupid idea," I say through tears.

"Then why make it at all?" Michael asks as he looks into my eyes.

"Because I'm terrified one of you will end up dead because of me, and I don't know what to do! I'm not as strong as you,

Mikey; I can't lose you. I can't sit and watch you recover from being poisoned. It would tear me apart, and I'd die with you." I shout as my emotions erupt, and the fear I've been trying to hide from Michael comes to light.

"Darling, what makes you think I'm any stronger than you? I didn't handle you being ill at all. I went to pieces a few times. I never want to come that close to losing you again." Michael replies as he runs a thumb over my cheek.

"But you *are* stronger than me," I whisper.

"But not when it comes to you!" Michael yells. I feel him sigh as he pulls me onto his lap and holds me tightly against his naked body. I tuck my head under his chin and listen to his racing heart.

"I am trained to deal with anything life throws at me, but it's impossible to train yourself for the love of your life, your mate, to be that close to death. I can't lose you, darling. I can't." Michael sighs as he kisses the top of my head.

"So, what do we do?" I ask as I look up at him.

"I don't know. We need to think this through carefully. I only know that we don't trust anyone outside our family. We find Jackson and Kellan, and we end this." Michael says. If only it were that easy.

"I'm scared, Mikey," I whisper, finally admitting it out loud for the first time.

"I know, darling, so am I. But you have to stop trying to protect the guys and me. We're trained for this. You need to trust us. I can't lose you, baby." Michael says as he pulls away and looks me in the eye.

"I'm not going anywhere," I promise as I lean up and press my lips lightly against his.

"One place you are going is home. Come on." Michael says as he stands up and places me on my feet. I go to stand on my own, but my legs are jelly and can't hold my weight, but Michael grabs me and lowers me carefully. "Are you okay?" He asks, looking down at me; the worry etched on his face.

"You and Jon were right; I shouldn't have shifted," I admit giving Michael a half smile. Michael huffs next to me and, in a flash, stands with me in his arms; I press my face against his chest as he carries me effortlessly towards home.

"I'm sorry," I murmur as my eyelids become too heavy. I feel Michael rub his nose into my hair.

"Sleep, darling. I'll get you home."

Michael

I'm curled up in bed with Daisy fast asleep in my arms. She has hardly woken since I carried her home. Everyone has left except Jon, who I can hear watching TV downstairs. Marcus has taken Mum to Auntie Sherri's; I knew Daisy would get her way with that. I just didn't expect the conversation to take the direction it did.

Daisy moans in my arms, and I tighten my hold on her as I kiss the top of her head. I'm exhausted; I hardly slept last night while waiting for Daisy to regain consciousness. I've found myself jumping at each little sound, worried Jackson or Kellan will make an appearance whilst she's in no fit to fight. Not that I would let her anyway.

I look down at the woman sleeping in my arms and can't help thinking about everything I have done to get to this point. I've worked relentlessly to build my reputation within the shifter community. Every pack and rogue wolf knows me as *The* Protector, the one to be feared, the one who is willing to do *anything* to protect his pack and all who can't defend themselves.

But then this woman entered my life, and I realised I'm no longer *The* Protector; I'm *her* Protector and our children's in the future. It's a role I take great honour in and am willing to give my life to uphold.

But first, I have to be able to protect her without fear of repercussions. The more I've thought about it during the last twenty-four hours, the more I've realised that my role in the university is, in a way, a godsend. I'm able to be close to Daisy when she is there studying. If I were to leave and our relationship exposed, they could stop me from being on campus, leaving Daisy vulnerable. We have no idea how long we will get away with Stuart being on campus before someone realises he isn't a student. When that happens, we'll need to think of something else, which is what I've been doing.

In two weeks, the Supernatural Council will be meeting for their six-monthly conference. I'd planned on sending Marcus in my place as the Alpha's lead security and Will as Marcus's second. But the Alpha feels that this may send the wrong message, and he wants me there, and I think he's right.

I pick up my phone and quickly type out a message.

Michael: I'll be at the council meeting, but I want a chance to speak to the council myself. Can you organise it?

Alpha: I have already put you on the agenda as I knew you would. We will speak tomorrow.

I smile as I put my phone down and rest my head on Daisy's. I should have known the Alpha would foresee me speaking to the council. He is always one step ahead of me.

For the first time in two days, I close my eyes, feeling relaxed enough to risk getting some much-needed rest.

Chapter Twenty-Four

Daisy

I slump onto the bed and cross my arms over my chest so that Michael can see how much of a mood I'm in. He looks at me with a raised eyebrow.

"Darling, don't look like that; you agreed to this the other week." He sighs as he places his overnight bag on the bed.

"That was the other week, but now I have to spend three days and two nights with Stuart," I sulk. "Can't I come with you? I'll hide out in the spa or the gym." I throw in the puppy dog eyes for good measure; for the briefest of seconds, I think I might get my own way, but then Michael shakes his head and looks away, growling in frustration.

"No. Because I'm not only going to talk to the council about us, I'm also there to protect the Alpha. I can't do that properly if I'm worrying about you."

"Jackson wouldn't do anything with that many witnesses." I point out.

"I'm not willing to take that risk. You're better off here away from it all." Michael argues, not looking at me as he packs his bag.

"You mean stuck here as a prisoner. I need a change of scenery, Mikey." I huff as he shoves another top into his bag. I don't know why I'm bothering to argue with him. There's no way he's going to let up on this.

Michael's been a nightmare since I was poisoned. I know he's worried, especially as that cereal bar was meant for him, plus I did kind of die. But other than when I am in class, Michael or a team member is always with me. Michael won't even let it be just me and Tony anymore after Tony didn't report that he thought he had seen Kellan. It's so suffocating at times.

I watch Michael as he puts his toiletry bag into the one on the bed and sighs before looking over at me.

"I know you hate this, but help me out here, okay? I'm struggling with the thought of leaving you for three days when

I still have no idea where the arseholes are and what they're planning next. I'm constantly fighting my wolf, who wants to lock you up and throw away the fucking key until they've been dealt with. It's wearing me out." I can see he's exhausted; the whole team is. They're working around the clock, trying to track Jackson and Kellan down, doing their usual protector duties, and guarding the Alpha whenever he needs it. They have been called out more frequently to rogues being near pack territory. They are all stressed and fed up.

I look up at Michael and hold my arms out for him; he chuckles as he climbs onto the bed so I can curl up against him.

"I wish you didn't have to go," I whisper into his chest as he starts playing with my hair; I feel his lips touch the top of my head as he inhales deeply. "It's not so boring when you're here with me."

"Trust me, baby, it's the last place I want to be right now. I want nothing more than to spend my weekend here with you. But confronting the council myself may be the only way I can get them to relieve me of my duties as a supernatural advocate at the university." Michael places a kiss on the top of my head again before continuing.

"Not only that, but I have to set an example to the team and the council. I have to show I deserve their respect when we take over the pack. Plus, the demons are always looking for an excuse to make out our pack can't be trusted."

"Are there nymphs at these meetings?" I ask; Michael looks at me and nods.

"Do the nymphs and demons ever ... well, you know?" I ask, wiggling my eyebrows at him. Michael bursts out laughing. It's well known that demons and nymphs are sex mad.

"I've never attended one of these meetings where there hasn't been a falling out between them because a nymph has ended up having her heartbroken." I look up at him with a raised eyebrow.

"And how many of them have tried it on with you?" I ask. To my surprise, Michael blushes.

"At least Nigel and Alex will be there this time. Now your uncle is representing the witches and sorcerers. They've agreed to help me state my case."

I sit up and look at Michael.

"Don't change the subject; how many nymphs usually try it on with you?" I ask again. Michael grabs me and rolls me onto my back so he can lean over me. I feel his knee nudging my legs to make room for him, my body disobeys me, and my legs open willingly.

"Does it matter? I never took them up on the offer before, and I certainly won't now I have the most beautiful wolf in the world waiting for me at home." His lips brush against mine as his breath warms my face.

"Cheeseball," I whisper before lifting slightly to press my lips to his harder. Within seconds the kiss deepens, I brush my tongue gently over his lips, and he allows me access greedily. We have just pulled each other's tops off when we hear someone letting themselves into the house.

"I hope you're both decent or upstairs this time," Stuart calls out. I let out a moan as I sink into the pillows. Michael chuckles over me as he lowers his lips to my stomach and continues to kiss it gently.

"Tell him we'll be down in a minute." I hear Michael whisper through the bond. I feel a smirk spread across my face.

"Just helping Mikey pack, go in the dining room and find the Chinese menu. It's in the take-out drawer." I call.

"Alright, but hurry up. I'm starving." Stuart calls back.

"So am I?" Michael whispers as he pushes my skirt over my thighs, his lips moving further down my stomach. Suddenly Michael lifts his head and frowns at me. "That menu is in the car."

I wink at him, "I know. I reckon I brought us at least ten minutes."

"I better make them count then," Michael replies with a devious grin before lowering his head between my legs and moves my thong to the side. My eyes roll to the back of my head as Michael's lips land exactly where I want them. I have to bite my bottom lip to stop myself from moaning out loud.

"You always taste so perfect," Michael whispers as he licks and sucks my core. It doesn't take long before I'm shaking as I

get closer to losing all control. I don't want to come in Michael's mouth. I need him in me now.

"Stop." As always, Michael does instantly. He looks up at me, worried for a second.

"I need you in me now," I demand as I sit up, so he has no choice but to move. I grab hold of his trousers and undo the zip, freeing him. Michael grabs hold of my legs and drags me to the edge of the bed so my legs hang off.

"Get on to your hands and knees." I quickly do as I'm told as Michael pulls down his trousers, freeing himself further. I feel Michael slide my skirt over my hips and rip off my thong before slinging it across the room. He takes my ass cheeks in his hands as he kneads the soft flesh.

"You always look perfect in this position." He growls through the bond as he positions himself at my entrance, waiting for permission.

"Please," I beg; Michael doesn't need telling twice as he rams into me, filling and stretching me. I have to bite my lip hard to stop myself from moaning loud enough for Stuart to hear.

"Oh, baby, you feel so tight and perfect this way; you know I won't be able to last long," Michael growls.

"I'm so close, Mikey, please." Michael starts moving, and it's not long before we find the perfect pace; working together, we quickly head towards orgasm.

"Fuck, baby, I can't last," Michael gasps. Knowing how close Michael is pushes me over the edge as we climax together, and we both collapse onto the bed shaking and panting.

"As much as I love it when we go at it for hours, sometimes these quickies are by far the sexiest moments with you," Michael whispers as he pulls me into his arms and kisses me deeply. I can still taste myself on his lips, sending a shiver of pleasure through me. I kiss him back before pulling away slightly to look at him.

"I had to ensure you were satisfied before sending you away to be surrounded by sexy nymphs." I run a hand over his chest before continuing. "This is all mine; no one else can touch it." Michael takes my hand and places it over his heart.

"Darling, this is yours and yours alone. No one will ever be able to steal me away from you. With or without seductive powers."

I lean over and place a kiss on his lips. "Good answer, Cheese ball," I mumble before extracting myself from Michael's arms and heading for the en-suite. "I'm going to clean up; you need to finish packing." I turn my back on Michael but squeal as he rushes to me and lifts me into his arms before carrying me into the bathroom.

"I have a better idea, but you won't be getting very clean." He whispers in my hair as he kicks the door closed behind us.

Chapter Twenty-Five

Michael

"Sorry, Stu, I got side-tracked," I call as I walk down the stairs twenty minutes later. I'm met with silence, I stick my head into the dining room, where I expect to find Stuart, but it's empty.

"Stu, where are you?" I call, but still nothing. I enter the lounge and find him sitting with his back to me, lying with his legs up on the sofa, drawing in one of his sketchbooks.

"You ignoring me now?" I ask as I walk up behind the chair he is sitting in; as I lean over his shoulder to see what he's drawing, Stuart jumps up from his seat.

"Where the fuck did you come from?" He curses loudly. I frown until I see the earbuds in his ears. He seems to remember, quickly removing them and muttering an apology.

"I hope you don't plan on wearing them all weekend?" Stuart looks down at the buds in his hand and chuckles as he shakes his head.

"Jon warned me about you two and how it's better to have something else to listen to if you're both upstairs." I can't help laughing as I walk away and sit on the sofa opposite the one he's back sitting on.

"Yeah, Daisy can get pretty loud." I chuckle; Stuart raises an eyebrow at me.

"It's not Daisy that everyone hears, boss." I stare at him, open-mouthed. I'm about to protest when I hear Daisy laughing hysterically from the landing.

"Told you, you were louder than me," she calls as she walks down the stairs.

"Well, as long as Daisy isn't complaining, I don't give a shit," I laugh as Daisy waltzes in and jumps onto my lap. Daisy wraps her arms around my neck and kisses me quickly as I pull her against me.

"Handsome, the sound of you enjoying what we do is the biggest turn-on ever; let's face it, neither of us has ever been

left disappointed." Daisy's hand rubs along my chest and up my neck as she runs her fingers through the hair at the back of my head.

"Be careful, darling; I will take you back upstairs." I squeeze her hips and push mine up slightly so she can feel how aroused I am.

"Oh, for fuck's sake, you two are doing that weird mind chat thing again, aren't you? Stop it; it's freaky, especially when you're talking dirty to each other." Stuart moans. I look over at him and give him my best alpha look; he instantly sinks back into his chair submissively. Daisy laughs and moves to get up, but I hold her in place.

"I want a coffee." She protests but stops as she feels how hard I am underneath her. Daisy instantly starts to smirk and wiggle on my lap. Knowing full well what she's doing. I growl in her ear as I lift her with me as I stand. Moving her so she can wrap her legs around me, hiding where my trousers have become uncomfortably tight from my rock-hard cock.

"Put your headphones back in, Stuart," I growl as I carry Daisy and head back to the stairs.

"You're too much." Daisy giggles as she tightens her legs around me. Just as I'm about to answer, the front door opens.

"Oh, for fuck sake, put her down, Adams." We both turn to the sound of our alpha's voice. I instantly go to put Daisy back on the floor so we can bow, but Desmond puts his hand out to stop us.

"It's bad enough I can smell your arousal; I don't need to see it too." He groans before smirking. I can't stop the laugh that bursts from my lips. Daisy, on the other hand, hides into my shoulder with embarrassment.

"Oh goddess, kill me now." She whispers as I walk into the kitchen and put her on the breakfast bar before kissing her on the cheek.

"I was going to ask for a coffee, but if you've had sex on that, I don't want anything that has touched it." Desmond laughs as he follows us in; I turn to the Alpha, grinning.

"If you don't want to touch any surface we've had sex on, I suggest moving away from that doorframe." I point out.

"For the love of the goddess." He exclaims, pulling himself away from the door frame and heading towards the lounge where I can hear Marcus talking to Stuart.

"I'd avoid the sofas and floors, too," I call after him.

"Michael!" Daisy exclaims as the three guys all groan out loud.

"I don't remember him being like this with Carly." I hear the Alpha sigh from the lounge.

"That's because he wasn't," Marcus laughs. "Plus, she was a controlling bitch. Daisy brings out the fun side of him and the horny side too." I laugh as I look at Daisy and kiss her gently.

"He's not wrong," I whisper in her ear before I nibble on her lobe as she pushes me away, smiling.

"I'm going to go over a few things with them; I don't suppose you'd mind making coffees for everyone, would you?" Daisy smiles at me as she nods. "Thank you, darling." I kiss her gently one last time before grabbing her hips and helping her down from the bar.

I head back to the lounge, where Marcus and the Alpha are sitting on one sofa, Stuart on the other, his sketchbook now discarded on the floor next to him. I walk over to the fireplace and take my regular spot, leaning against it.

I stand here as it gives me a view of all the seats to make it easier to address everyone. I can also see the entrance hall, kitchen, and patio doors, so I can get to Daisy quickly if there are any issues. When did protecting my mate in our own home become such a priority? This should be the one place she's the safest, but at the moment, nowhere is safe. I hate it.

"You ready to go, or do you still need to pack?" Marcus asks from his seat. I look over at him and nod.

"I'm packed, but I don't think it's possible to be ready with everything going on," I admit. I see the Alpha look at me with an understanding nod. With the Luna being so close to giving birth, I know this meeting is the last place he wants to be.

"You're doing the right thing in coming, I know how hard this is, but with everyone knowing the situation here, you have to show how strong and dedicated you are to your role and your mate. I'm sure that asking them to replace you at the university in person will help, as well as wanting confirmation you can terminate Jackson." I nod as it's the same thing I had told Daisy.

There are times like this when I seriously consider walking away from it. The position of leader of the protectors, the reputation I have built as a protector and a professor. Those roles are constantly in the way of me being able to look after and protect my mate. But they are also helping me get any extra help I need to keep an eye out for Jackson and Kellan. It's a catch-twenty-two situation, and there is no easy escape.

"I know" I sigh. I turn to Stuart, "you know what you need to do here?" Stuart looks at me and nods.

"Babysit the little lady whilst the big bad wolf plays with the nymphs and demons," Daisy answers as she carries a tray of mugs into the lounge.

"You told her about the nymphs that climbed into your bed?" Marcus asks from his spot; I spin around and stare at him wide-eyed. Fuck.

"What?" Daisy shouts as she stares at me. I'm suddenly happy there is a coffee table between the two of us; she has that look.

"I'd take that as a strong no Marc." Desmond answers as he leans back in his seat, smirking.

"Nymphs?" She asks, emphasising the S. "As in more than one?" She demands as she puts the tray down on the coffee table and stands at her full height with her hands on her hips. "In your bed? I thought you said you never slept with any of them?" Daisy asks, frowning at me.

"I never!" I protest as I look at Marcus, who's snickering like a child, "Thank you, prick." I hiss before turning back to Daisy, who's still waiting for an answer. I rub my face with my hand before offering one.

"Nothing happened. I woke up one night to find two nymphs trying to crawl into bed with me; I quickly made it clear I wasn't interested, and that was the end of it." I look her straight in the eye. "Nothing happened, I swear," I add firmly.

"So how did they get into your room?" she asks; I let out a deep sigh closing my eyes.

"I had heard a disturbance in the corridor beforehand; when I had gone to investigate, I found nothing; Marcus had heard it too and popped in for a moment as we waited to see if we heard it again. When he left, I forgot to check the door as I was tired and, to be honest, drunk. I should point out that I have double-checked every time since," I declare. Marcus and Desmond are both laughing from their seats; I quickly flip them off, making them laugh louder. Daisy turns and stares at them; they abruptly stop as they look up at her.

"You're going to be one scary alpha, lady," Desmond exclaims. Daisy keeps looking at him before she addresses them both.

"You two were the ones that made sure they got in, weren't you?"

I turn and stare at the guys in disbelief as they both share a look and burst out laughing, even harder than before.

"What the fuck, guys?" I demand as they both laugh uncontrollably, leaning against one another.

"How come it took her two minutes to work out what's taken you two years," Marcus cries hysterically.

"You're both arseholes," I exclaim, not knowing how to react. As if I never realised it myself.

"That's exactly what I meant by Daisy having the brains and you having the muscles." Desmond laughs. I look over at Stuart, who's laughing so hard he can hardly breathe; even Daisy is smirking at me, trying not to laugh.

"Mikey, you were so wound up we figured getting laid might help you out." Marcus laughs.

"Help me out? What the fuck?" I yell over their laughter.

"Hey, I wanted to send in a demon, but Marc promised it was the ladies you were interested in." My alpha declares as all hell breaks loose. All four of them burst out laughing at my expense. I don't have the words to deal with this shit. As if they were so convinced I needed to get laid, they helped two nymphs sneak into my room, also that they even considered I would prefer a demon.

"You're all fuckers," I exclaim as I walk over to the coffee table and grab my favourite mug while they continue laughing at my expense. I casually drink my coffee whilst watching Daisy.

I wish I could say I am pissed off with them all, but it's made Daisy laugh louder and harder than she has in a while; I can't find it in me. If me nearly getting jumped on by two nymphs is what it takes to make her laugh like that and forget everything that's going on, then so be it.

Daisy picks up her mug and walks over to me as I hold out an arm so she can lean into my side whilst drinking her coffee.

"If you turned them down whilst single, I guess I have nothing to worry about." She says, winking whilst sipping her coffee.

"You weren't worried, were you? That man worships the ground you walk on; there will never be a threat of him cheating." Marcus says from his seat as he retrieves his cup of coffee and passes Desmond his.

"I know he wouldn't; it's the nymphs I was worried about. But if he could chuck them out when he was single, I know he'll be able to do it now he's taken." Daisy replies, smiling up at me.

"Oh, he didn't throw them out," Marcus says. I watch as Daisy's smile slowly disappears from her face.

"What did you do?" She asks carefully. I take a sip of my coffee and shrug casually, smiling.

"They seemed to be enjoying each other's company, and it seemed rude to interrupt, so I left them to it and slept on the couch in Marcus's room." Everyone burst out laughing again, me included, as I lean in and kiss her.

)) ● ((

Twenty minutes later, Desmond, Marcus and I are preparing to leave. I've said I'll drive, and we'll take my car. Desmond and Marcus are talking to Daisy as I turn to Stuart.

"You know what to do if anything happens; get the call out and protect her, no matter what." He nods.

"I promise everything will be fine; you know I'd never let any harm come to that woman." I nod as I believe him.

"Thanks, Stu. Jon will be back by tomorrow afternoon.

Remember, no matter what Daisy says, she's not to go out anywhere without you. She hates this and will fight you whenever she can. She doesn't open the door; she doesn't go to Tony's or the bar, nothing without you." I remind him.

"Sure thing, Boss. Don't worry; everything will be fine." He reassures me.

"It better be because I'll kill you if anything happens to her," I warn.

"I'm well aware. Nothing will happen, I promise." I shake Stuart's hand before heading over to Daisy, who is now watching the others leave as they head towards the car; Marcus already has my keys in his hand. I wrap an arm around Daisy's waist and pull her towards me so that I can kiss her.

"Do as you're told, *please*; whilst I'm away, follow the rules and keep yourself safe." I can see she's desperately trying not to roll her eyes at me.

"I promise, but only as it's you. I'll keep myself safe if you promise to do the same thing." Daisy replies, winking as she places a hand on my chest. I lean in and kiss her again.

"I always do now that I have you," I reply quietly as I look deep into her bright green eyes.

"Cheese ball." She whispers, grinning. I lean in and chuckle.

"But whose cheese ball am I?"

"All mine." She replies, smiling. I kiss her one last time before picking up my bag and turning towards the door. "Give my love to my uncle and Alex for me." She calls after me. I don't turn until I'm in the car and putting my bag in the trunk.

"Of course, I will. I'm looking forward to having a few beers with them whilst you're not there; apparently, they have loads of stories to tell me." I wink at her as she steps out of the front door. Stuart quickly grabs her around the waist to stop her. She keeps trying to leave as he pulls her back, causing everyone in the car to laugh loudly.

"Don't believe a word they say, Adams. I'm a freaking saint." She calls out; I laugh as I climb into the driving seat.

"Baby, I have lived with you for three months, and the only time you have ever been saint-like is when you are after something or have done something. Now, be good." I call as I close the door. I open up the bond as I look at her, smiling.

"*I love you, darling. Keep safe.*"

"*I love you too, handsome; come back to me.*"

"*Nothing could ever keep me away,*" I whisper as I pull off the driveway and head off to Birmingham, leaving my whole world behind me and praying no harm will come to her whilst I'm away.

Chapter Twenty-Six

Michael

"We're here, darling; just heading to the restaurant now for some food. Everything okay there?"

"Yeah, all fine; Stuart's driving me mad and can't pick a film to watch, so I'm upstairs studying whilst he decides." Daisy sighs down the line. She sounds so fed up and bored I can't ignore the pang of guilt in my gut. She's twenty-three years old. She should be enjoying herself, not stuck in on a Friday night with another wolf. At least when I'm home, I can distract her in other ways, and the weekend flies by in a haze of lovemaking and general messing around. When it's just the two of us, there are never enough hours in the day. But when we're apart, time seems to go a little slower.

"I'm sorry, darling; I promise to make it up to you when I get home." I sigh.

"Oh really, and how do you plan to do that?" Daisy teases as a smile spreads across my face.

"How would you like me to make it up to you?" I tease back.

"I can think of a few ways, Adams; want me to list them now or send you a mental image?"

"I swear to the Goddess, if you list them out loud, I'll puke." Marcus moans next to me as he heads towards the table I point out, where Alex and Nigel are already sitting.

"Marcus, stop listening!" Daisy gasps down the line. I chuckle as Marcus rolls his eyes at me.

"Wolf hearing Dais, when will you learn we hear everything!" He points out.

"Oh, Gods." She curses; I can't help laughing as I picture her throwing her hands over her face in embarrassment.

I approach the table and shake Alex and Nigel's hands quick in greeting.

"Well, that's put a damper on my mood; I think I'll leave you to it now; I'm far from horny." Daisy sighs.

"Daisy Angela, I hope I heard that wrong!" Nigel exclaims. I hear Daisy gasp.

"You never told me my uncle was there! Adams, I'm going to kill you!" She yells as the line goes dead; I glance at the now blank screen, chuckling.

"Well, that's one way to get her off the phone." I laugh as I take a seat between Alex and Desmond. I quickly make the introductions before pulling the drinks menu towards me.

"I hope that Goddaughter of mine is behaving herself," Alex says, grinning; Marcus bursts out laughing.

"Behaving isn't in that woman's vocabulary! She's driving us all around the bend. How haven't you killed her yet?" He asks Nigel.

"Oh, I've considered it a few times." Nigel groans as he takes a sip of his pint. "I swear she gets worse the older she gets." He adds, shaking his head.

"At least you never have to deal with her and Clare at the same time! There's no end to their stupidity and the drama it causes." Alex says, looking at his friend with raised eyebrows.

"Why do you think we always insisted that Daisy came to you and not the other way around. There was no coincidence that *all* sleepovers happened at your place." Nigel replies before turning to me, "never allow Clare to stay with you unless her parents are there too. I hope you have a good decorator and carpenter in your pack if you do. You will need them." Nigel says with arched brows.

"Are they that bad together?" Marcus asks as he pours himself a glass of water.

"Worse." Alex and Nigel say together. I laugh as I sit back in my chair.

"Yeah, I heard about when Clare put the gagging curse on Daisy." Alex turns and looks at me with an angry expression.

"Don't go there, Adams. I nearly killed her that day. They were only sixteen, and Clare was already bringing boys home with her." Alex shakes his head whilst Nigel chuckles next to him.

"Yeah, that was one thing we never had to deal with when it came to Daisy. She wasn't interested in sleeping with anyone."

"And now she's at it continuously." I hear Desmond sigh. Nigel, Alex and I all choke on our drinks whilst Marcus roars laughing, slapping the Alpha on the back.

"WOW!" We call together as Desmond looks up from his phone at me innocently.

"Oh, I'm sorry. Did I forget to mention this is Daisy's uncle and godfather?" I ask sarcastically, holding my hand towards Nigel and Alex whilst looking at my alpha with raised eyebrows. Desmond just looks at me with a wicked grin on his face. Knowing what he's just done, he isn't going to drop it, either.

"Well, you have no problem discussing your very active sex life in front of us. We've all heard you …."

"Enough, I've heard enough!" Nigel declares, holding his hand up as I punch Desmond on the arm.

"You can't hit me. I'm your Alpha!" Desmond laughs, wide-eyed as he rubs his now bruised arm.

"You're being a bigger dick than an Alpha, so yes, I can," I reply through gritted teeth.

"I think that's my cue to go and get a round of drinks. What's everyone having? Except you, Adams, you're buying your own." Alex says as he flips me off. Marcus roars, laughing from his seat.

"Now I know where Daisy gets her manners from."

I nod my head towards Alex whilst looking at Marcus.

"I've been told he's to blame for every aspect of that woman that keeps me on my toes. Whenever she insults me or refers to me as Adams, I hear this guy."

"I taught her to fight too, so be warned, she isn't as weak as she makes out," Alex says proudly.

"That she isn't, I held the pads for her once, and I swear my arms ached for a week," Marcus replies.

"A new protector in the making?" Desmond asks, looking at my second, who nods.

"Possibly," Marcus replies, smiling.

"Nope, not happening," I declare as I stand up.

"Oh come on, Mikey, you know she'd be good." Marcus

starts.

"She's better staying in uni and finishing her studies. She's not becoming one of us. End of conversation." I reply sharply.

"For once, I agree with him," Alex says, pointing in my direction.

"I'll give you a hand at the bar. Desmond's paying anyway; it's a business expense, so we get the best stuff." I say to Alex as we both grin at each other.

"Not after last year, Michael. We have a limit this time." Desmond calls as we start walking away from the table.

"Yeah, a limit of how much of your bullshit we can put up with before we lock you in your room," I reply as I flip him off before turning my back to him and heading to the bar.

"Bastard." I hear my alpha mutter under his breath as I chuckle to myself.

"I thought you all had to show your alpha the utmost respect at all times?" Alex laughs next to me. I look at him and nod.

"We do, but you get away with a little more than most when you've spent as much time together as Desmond, and I have. It also helps that Des doesn't rule with an iron fist." I look around, spot the Dark Sun Pack at the back of the restaurant, and nod in their direction to Alex.

"Can you tell which one at that table is the Alpha?" Alex glances over and nods.

"The guy who has a whole side to himself. Red top and black hair." I nod in confirmation.

"See how his guards are keeping their heads down and not eating? That's because the Alpha demands *complete* respect and to be treated like a medieval king. No one is to look at him unless spoken to. The guards will have their meal in their rooms when he's asleep. He has the second biggest pack in the UK, thirty-four members, and rules with an iron fist." I look over at our table, where Desmond, Marcus, and Nigel are laughing and joking. The atmosphere is the complete opposite.

"Desmond believes that if he treats us with the respect we deserve, we'll be loyal to him and his pack. Yes, we all bow to him and most only address him as alpha. But we also know that if we have any personal or pack-related issues, his door is always open, day or night, no matter who you are or what your rank is. But everyone also knows what will happen if they disrespect him. A pissed-off Desmond is not something you wish to see. That's when my role comes into play, I've had to dish out punishments whilst he stands behind me." I admit.

"And what will you be like when you're alpha?" Alex asks as he leans on the bar. I look at him and shrug.

"I want to believe I'll be respected like Desmond. I don't plan on ruling with an iron fist like some. But things will be different when Desmond steps down. We haven't discussed it much, but Daisy and I could rule together with us both having the alpha gene, or either could take control and the other stands to the side." I explain.

"What does Daisy want to do? She hasn't mentioned much to us on the matter. Only when explaining your unique bond." Alex says. The bartender comes over, interrupting, and I order a bottle of bourbon, five glasses and a bucket of ice. This gets a raised eyebrow from Alex, but I just wink before carrying on the conversation.

"Daisy wants to be my luna; she says she isn't interested in being recognised as an Alpha. But I think she'd make the best Alpha, a fair one. In times like this, I think she could strive and make such a difference with the meetings. We all joke about her way with words and how she's the least patient woman we've ever met. But when we're deep in discussion in class or even just the two of us at home, she shows such passion for rightful justice and her intelligence and maturity shine through. I think it'll be a waste for her not to lead either beside me or instead of me." I admit.

"You would step down and let her lead on her own?" Alex asks, surprised.

"Of course, I would. I've thought about it a lot. I'd happily be her beta and let her grow into the leader I know she could be. But I also know I can't force her to take that role. She has to decide it herself." I take the bottle and ice bucket, giving the waiter the Alpha's room number as Alex grabs the empty glasses.

"You really do love her, don't you?" Alex says next to me. I turn and look at him.

"Was that ever in doubt? Because if I ever gave you a reason to question that my love for Daisy is genuine, then .." I start, but Alex puts his hands up.

"No, not at all. I think we, as in Sara, Clare, and I, worried it was all due to the mate bond, that without that, you wouldn't have even fallen for each other." I watch as he shakes his head. "That's come out wrong; I just mean that it was so fast, and we don't know what it's like for wolves with their mate bond," Alex explains as I relax.

"I get that. But even with the mate bond, there must be some attraction. We don't fall for someone purely because of the bond. It just makes it more intense. I may have known Daisy was my mate the second I saw her, but it took me getting to know her to realise how much I love her. It didn't take long granted. But it wasn't instant love at first sight; it was deeper. It's Daisy I fell in love with, not the bond. I really would give everything up for her. I've offered to many times. I've told her I'd move with her if she wants to concentrate on her witch side and move to be with the coven when Jackson is no longer a threat. What she wants and needs is the most important thing to me. Not any of this alpha crap, not the pack or the team. She is, and after everything she's been through, I want to be there when she grows into the incredible woman I know she is, and I love watching as her confidence grows and the leader side of her comes to the surface." I say, meaning every word.

"Thank you."

I look at Alex, smiling softly at me as he pushes himself away from the bar.

"What for?" I ask, confused.

"For encouraging Daisy to be who she wants to be and not just getting her to follow whatever plan you had set out for yourself. I guess, in a way, I thought maybe the Alpha gene and the bond could be used as a way of controlling her. Not that I think you would be abusive with it, not like that prick Jackson. But now I get it. I get that her happiness is as important to you as your own."

We start walking back to the others as we carry the drinks. We are just reaching the table as I answer Alex.

"It's not that her happiness is *as* important. Her happiness *is* my happiness. I could never be happy if Daisy were miserable. Like now, for example. As much as I'm enjoying your company and know we'll all have a laugh and a few drinks tonight. Inside I'm feeling guilty as fuck."

"Why?" Nigel asks as I take my seat.

"Because my twenty-three-year-old mate is stuck at home studying on a Friday night because she can't be out with her friends like she should be at her age. She should be taking full advantage of me being away and out drinking and dancing. Most of her friends have stopped messaging her to see if she will go out. Even Beth has become distant because Daisy can't tell her what's really going on. Daisy only has the team and Tony now."

"That's not your fault, though; that's all on Jackson," Desmond says as I pour his drink and hand it to him.

"I know that, but it doesn't mean I don't feel guilty. Why should I be enjoying myself when she's stuck inside?"

"Because you deserve it, you work bloody hard, Mikey," Marcus says from across the table; I look at him with a raised eyebrow.

"So does Daisy. She's never missed a deadline with uni. Her work's always in early. She studies harder than any other student I've ever met, and every shit thing that gets thrown at her for the past three years, she takes in her stride. She's dealt with every blow I have. We find out that Jackson has always known where she was; she was the one whose life he violated, not mine. Kellan tried to poison me, but it was Daisy who nearly died, not me. Daisy can't go anywhere without one of us being with her, I'm free to go where I want when I want. She doesn't even run anymore. She used to run for miles every day.

"The bottom line is whenever someone says to me, 'you're handling this all so well.' They forget that Daisy is the one who is handling it better." I turn and look at Marcus.

"When we went to tell Mum about who killed Michelle, Jon and I froze, but Daisy looked her in the eye and told her. I thought for a moment Mum was going to take her anger out on Daisy; I tried to get between them, but Daisy stepped around me and stood in front of Mum as if to say, 'you can't hit him, so hit me instead', like she felt she was to blame for what that prick did to Michelle before he had even taken Daisy and turned her. She carries more guilt over that than you'd believe, even though Jackson would have never turned her if Michelle had accepted him as her mate.

"Which is why I'm taking my girl anywhere she wants to go when we finally get rid of Jackson for good. I'll be leaving you in charge for a month, Marcus, and we will travel, and I'll spoil her as, for the first time in three years, she won't be looking over her shoulder, and she'll be free to enjoy herself. No threat, no worrying about who sees us. It will just be her and me. I have no idea where we'll go, but I know we'll not have our phones with us, and we will do whatever she wants as she deserves it and so much more."

I look at the guys around the table and see that they all get it, as they've all seen what Daisy has been through. I turn and look at her family, and even though I always felt accepted by them, at this moment, I know they are finally seeing how much I genuinely love her.

"I think that sounds like the perfect plan, Son," Nigel says as he holds his glass up towards me before taking a sip. Alex nods in agreement and lifts his own. I hold my glass up towards them before taking a sip of my drink.

"I'll drink to that," Desmond says next to me before reaching over and pulling a menu towards himself. "Now, can we please order some food, as all this seriousness makes me bloody hungry?" I turn to my alpha and laugh.

"When aren't you hungry?" I ask.

"When I'm eating, now shut up and take down my order. It's going to be a big one if we're going to be here drinking for a while." Desmond states grinning.

"Oh, I have a feeling we are going to be here a long while." Marcus laughs next to him as he picks up his own menu.

"You think you can keep up with us?" I ask Nigel and Alex, smirking. Alex looks at Nigel, who rolls his eyes at him.

"You ready to show these pups how it's done?" Nigel asks him with a devious grin on his face. Alex just grins back at him before answering.

"Let the fun commence."

Chapter Twenty-Seven

Michael

The meeting only started an hour ago, and I'm already bored. I lean against the wall in my usual spot, where I have sight of both the Alpha and the exit; Marcus is on the opposite side of the room and has his eyes on the Alpha and the entrance.

In the centre of the room is a large conference table; on it are two representatives from each of the main supernatural species of the council. These include wolves, vampires, witches and sorcerers, demons, nymphs, and necromancers.

"Are these meetings always this dull?" I turn to the sound of Alex's voice next to me and smile.

"They can go one of two ways. One, they remain dull, and all will be wrapped up by tonight so we can go home early."

"Or?" Alex asks; I grin at him showing all my teeth.

"Or two, all hell breaks loose, and we get to play," I whisper. Alex looks at me, grinning.

"As fun as that sounds, the first option would be preferred today." Alex sighs, looking around, "how many of these have you been to?" Alex asks, leaning against the wall next to me

"Six as my predecessors second, and six as a leader. This is Marcus's fourth. As my previous second moved away two years ago." I look over at Marcus, who looks more bored than me.

"Couldn't he hack working under you?" Alex chuckles next to me.

"*She* could handle anything I threw at her and more. Natalie left for personal reasons. She moved away from the whole pack and is greatly missed." I reply, smiling fondly.

"You were close?" Alex asks. I can't miss the suspicion in his voice.

"Not like that. She was one of my sister's best friends. She spent as much time at our house as Will, Marcus, and our luna Jayne as we all grew up." I reply as I turn to face Alex, who nods before looking back at the large round table in the centre of the room where all the leaders are sitting.

"So if Daisy becomes alpha, will you be on guard duty or sit beside her?" Alex asks next to me. I look at him with an arched brow.

"Do you think I would trust anyone else to guard her? You know she'll start some kind of argument." I watch as Alex cringes.

"You sure you don't want to ensure that it's you sitting at the table and not her?"

I look at him and grin. "But where would the fun be in that? She'll be far more entertaining than this lot." Alex chuckles and nods.

"That girl has never taken being told 'no' lightly; I'll never know how you keep her in line with all of this. I once told her she couldn't have a new Barbie, and I swear the whole town knew about it." I laugh and quickly turn it into a coughing fit as everyone turns to look at me.

"She's making my life hell, that's for sure. You should've seen the sulk over this weekend when I said Stuart would be staying with her and watching her every move. I'm half expecting her to sneak out at some point." I sigh as I run my fingers through my hair.

"Wouldn't surprise me; she never was good at being grounded. She made poor Mary and Nigel's lives hell every time." Alex looks over at Nigel, who looks like he is on the verge of falling asleep and laughs. "And there's my cue to go and wake the lazy bastard up. He's useless when he's hungover."

"That's what happens when you try and stay up drinking with the wolves. You two have much to learn." I reply, smirking.

"You're an arsehole, Adams," Alex says through gritted teeth as he walks away. I turn to him and wink.

"Yet you approved of your goddaughter being mated to me." He flips me the bird and walks over to Nigel. I watch as he leans over and whispers something in his ear; Nigel subtly glances my way and scratches the side of his face with two fingers in my direction. I can't stop grinning as I turn back to find my alpha, grinning at me with a raised eyebrow. I casually shrug and go back to watching professionally.

)) ● ((

Three hours into the meeting, and I'm glancing at my watch, waiting for a lunch break. It's nearly one in the afternoon, and nothing interesting has happened or been discussed. Desmond's planning on approaching the topic of my post at the university this afternoon, as well as asking for permission for us to terminate Jackson. We get away with rogues as we only kill them if there is no other option. But to hunt for one, we need the council's approval.

"What's the chance of these arseholes letting us grab some food soon?" I turn to see Marcus now standing next to me. I shrug and look around.

"Who knows, but I'm starving. Anything going on over there?" I ask. Marcus shakes his head.

"Just the usual mumblings about everyone being bored and hungry or wondering like me if it's lunchtime yet." Marcus sighs, rolling his eyes. "Is it me, or is that prick Prince Draven looking at you more smugly than usual?" He adds, looking at the main table.

"You noticed too?" I ask, looking over at the Demon Prince, with his black spiked hair and smug face.

"Couldn't miss it."

"Hopefully, he will give me a reason to break that pretty little face again," I reply, grinning at Marcus, who chuckles next to me.

I notice movement on the other side of the room and mutter a curse.

"Somethings up, the demon guards are now stationed at both doors." Marcus looks between the two and curses before heading back to his spot in case of trouble. As soon as he's back in his place, I give him a nod and start walking over to the Alpha. He must sense me coming as he looks up at me and then at Marcus, who is obviously on high alert.

"Michael?" Desmond whispers as I get to him; I lean down and whisper into his ear.

"Two demons, one at each door. I'm going to stay close just in case." Desmond nods once, not once taking his eyes off the vampire currently discussing the database they have in place for recognising new vamps and who has changed them.

I stand up and step behind the Alpha as the vampire finishes the discussion. Desmond looks at me and nods before addressing the room.

"I don't know about anyone else, but I'm starving. Shall we break for lunch and restart in two hours?" there's a chorus of "yes" as people start to stand.

"One second, please, Alpha Desmond; I'd like to address something before we all disperse." I see Prince Draven standing, leaning against the table. Desmond sits forward a little in his chair and smiles at the demon.

"Surely there's nothing of great importance that you will delay people from eating any longer. Could it not wait until after lunch?" Desmond asks. Draven looks at the Alpha and grins.

"You would try and put off this discussion, as it involves your pack and the leader of your protectors who happens to be standing behind you now." I glare at the Prince, who grins at me. "Not forgetting, of course, his rather beautiful mate. How is the lovely Daisy, Michael?" My arms are crossed over my chest, so he can't see how my hands are curled into fists.

"You would be wise to leave individual members of my pack out of this Prince," Desmond warns as he stands and leans against the table; I can feel his alpha magic radiating from him. I glance up and see Marcus has moved closer to the table, as has Alex; Nigel's face is bright red as he struggles to contain his temper. I've been warned that his temper can get the better of him as he is very protective of his niece, especially after everything she has been through.

"Even when those individuals are the topic I would like to discuss? Now, how about we all sit back down, and I can discuss the matter at hand? We can all disperse for lunch once I have concluded." He looks around the room, grinning at everyone; his eyes fall on me last. I hear people mumbling in agreement as they take their seats, but my eyes don't leave the Prince's.

The Prince is the first to break eye contact as he looks around and smiles once everyone is back in their seat; this time, the guards are all a little closer to their leaders; you can't miss the feeling of magic building in the air as everyone waits for trouble.

My alpha is the one to break the silence as he sits straight in his chair and leans his folded hands on the table.

"It seems you have your wish, Prince; the floor is yours. Now, pray tell what is so important we should all starve." I can hear the slightest change in the Alpha's voice, and I know he is pissed off. He'll come across as his usual calm and collected self to anyone else. I watch the Prince's smile as he takes his seat, leaning back in it casually.

"It's come to my attention that the Blood Moon Pack wishes to discuss the termination of another alpha. An alpha all wolf packs are refusing to acknowledge. This pack has brought several grievances to my attention, and I wish to address you all on their behalf and ensure their safety." Draven announces, not taking his red eyes off me.

"And which pack would this be?" The necromancer across the table from us asks.

"The Luna Dais Pack, of course." A knot forms in my stomach so tight that I wonder how I'm not throwing up. I knew he'd discuss Jackson the second he mentioned Daisy, but to hear the pack's name, her name, it's taking every ounce of self-control not to rip Draven's fucking head from his shoulders. He's trying to provoke me, and it's working.

"I'm sorry, I've heard of no pack under that name. You'll have to enlighten us on where they are based and who their alpha is." Desmond replies calmly. I risk a glance at Marcus, standing nearer to Alex and Nigel. Alex's hand is on Nigel's shoulder to help keep him under control. Draven is still grinning at me, daring me to react.

"It's a fairly new pack; their alpha Jackson has had to keep things quiet as it seems his luna has been taken and is now residing in your pack. Jackson fears that any attempt to reclaim her will result in his death at the hands of your lead protector,

Michael Adams." Draven answers, grinning like the idiot he is.

"A wolf is within its rights to defend its bonded mate by any means necessary; this is a law followed for thousands of years. As I know you're well aware." Desmond answers. "The wolf you are referring to as alpha has not to be recognised by the wolf council as they have not followed the correct procedures to form a pack. This "alpha" is currently wanted for a string of offences, including killing Michelle Adams on her pack territory and the number one rule of our kind that is punishable by death. We do not change humans without their consent." Desmond states firmly. The Alpha of the Dark Sun Pack nods next to him in agreement.

"Ah yes, he said you would try to use that old rule. Is there proof that Daisy Andrews did not consent?" Draven asks, smirking.

"Are you calling my niece a liar!" Nigel roars, jumping to his feet. Both Alex and he stand shoulder to shoulder now, and both are on the verge of losing control. I nod to Marcus, and he is by their side instantly in case of trouble. I need them to stay calm. Draven smiles as he turns to face the sorcerers.

"How silly of me; I forgot about the family connection. How are Mary and Sara, gentlemen?" the Prince looks up at Alex, "and your lovely daughter Clare." Fuck this.

"You leave them and their families out of this, Prince," I demand as I step forward. I stand to my full height, pull my shoulders back, and hold my head high as I address the Prince. At six foot eight, I tower over his six foot two, and he knows it.

"If you want to know anything about my mate or where she stands regarding this new pack, you address me, and I will answer for her. If you want further confirmation, I'll organise a phone call to be made between the two of you. But I will not allow you to disrespect her, her family or our pack. If you want to know what the so-called Alpha did to my mate, you need to only ask the other leaders in this room, as I'm aware they've all seen the reports and the evidence that proves, without a shadow of a doubt, that Daisy Andrews was turned into a wolf without consent and has been fearing for her life as well as her families ever since." I lean on the table and look at the Prince as I allow the anger to radiate off me and allow others to feel the effects of the Alpha gene as I issue a final warning.

"I would think carefully about whom you pledge your alliance to, as I can promise you, you won't want to be on the losing side when justice is paid for what that prick did to Daisy and my sister."

"Are you threatening me, pup?" The Prince growls, leaning on the table, his face red with anger. His eyes are glowing brightly.

"If he isn't, then I am." Nigel answers as he crosses his arms over his chest, "If you so much as question my niece's accounts of what that fucking arsehole did to her, you will feel the wrath of the whole magical community." Next to Nigel and Alex, I see the other representatives stand and their guards flag them, facing the Prince and willing to fight for their sister.

"As well as ours," Desmond adds as he stands, the Alpha of the Dark Sun pack next to him and his guards. Suddenly the whole room faces the demon Prince, who looks less sure of himself.

"If you feel so strongly about one individual, then who am I to question your loyalty." He turns to me and grins, and I know he has more up his sleeve.

"I hope Daisy is worth the drama Michael. But I wonder, who's watching the lovely lady in question if you are here?" My insides freeze, and I shrug, hiding my fear.

"Daisy doesn't need protecting; she's perfectly capable of defending herself. She was trained by the most powerful coven in the UK and my team. She's a force to be reckoned with, and I feel sorry for anyone who pisses her off." I look over at her uncle and godfather and nod, smiling; they smile back. As I turn my attention to the demon Prince, I stand tall again.

"Is there anything else regarding Jackson? If there is, I strongly suggest waiting until my alpha's appointed time slot later today, where as you know, we have planned to discuss and provide evidence of his law-breaking. Until then, can we all finally go and get something to eat?" I ask. The Prince looks around, realises he's outnumbered, and wisely decides to drop it.

"I think I could do with a bite." He replies as he turns and sulks out of the room.

Chapter Twenty-Eight

Michael

I turn on the spot, storm away from the table, and into the shadows as I open up the bond.

"Baby, are you okay? Where are you?" I call frantically as every possible scenario rushes through my mind.

"Mikey? I'm at home. What's the matter?" My whole body relaxes as I hear her voice.

"Tell Stuart code red. I want you to ensure all the doors and windows are locked, and neither of you answers the door to anyone." I command.

"Mikey? What's happened?" I can hear the panic in her voice, and by the gods, I hate it.

"I'll phone you as soon as I can, I promise. As long as you are both locked in, you're safe. Give me ten minutes." I add quickly.

"Okay, Mikey," I hear her whisper back before I cut off the connection.

I see Alex, Marcus, Nigel and Desmond all talking together. I head straight over to them, all turning to face me as I approach.

"She's fine; they're at the house; Stuart knows to be on alert. I promised I'd call her in ten minutes so let's make this quick." They all nod as we head off to Nigel's suite, as it's the closest.

"I've sent a message to Jon and Will; they're both en route to the house. Carl's also on standby." Marcus explains as he walks the other side of the Alpha. As soon as we get inside Nigel's suite, Alex starts pacing.

"What the hell was that all about?" Alex asks, his phone in hand as he messages Sara.

"He wanted to push my buttons," I say as I look out the window for any sign of danger.

"But why?" Marcus asks. I turn to face him.

"Because then he would be able to prove that we're

keeping Daisy away from Jackson; he wanted to make out I'm controlling and preventing my mate from being where she wants to be. Plus, he's still sulking over me, breaking his jaw a few years back," Marcus curses as Nigel laughs.

"Just shows he's never met our Daisy," Alex says from the table as he sits down.

"I can't shake the feeling there's more to this, though; why did his guys move to the doors? I watched them the whole time, and it was like they were waiting to block everyone in." Marcus mentions as he checks his phone.

"Who knows? I think he likes to feel superior." Desmond says from his seat. I nod in agreement as I feel the connection open on Daisy's side.

"Your ten minutes is up Adams, spill." I can hear the irritation in her voice and can't help but chuckle.

"Sorry, guys, I need to make a phone call before she loses her shit and gives me a headache. I'll go check out our rooms for anything dodgy." I turn and point at Desmond before continuing. "Stay here, and don't leave until I get back." I turn to Marcus, who signals that he won't leave the Alpha's side.

"And there was me thinking you were the boss," Alex says as he hands the Alpha a beer from the fridge.

"Oh no, when Michael's in "The Protector" mode, I do as I'm told because I don't fancy fighting him. He'll win." Nigel and Alex both laugh and look at him.

"And you want to leave the pack to him and Daisy?" Nigel asks. Desmond looks at me, and I can't miss the pride in his eyes for a moment.

"After his performance today and seeing how Daisy handles all of this, I think they'll be just fine."

"Thank you, Des," I whisper,

"ADAMS. Call me now before I come there and find you myself." Daisy snaps as her voice fill my head,

"Two minutes!" I snap back before turning to her uncle.

"Do you know how lucky you are not to have her in your head shouting at you constantly?! You sure you won't take her back?" Nigel holds his hands up.

"No returns or refunds. She's your problem now." I look at

Alex pleading with him. He shakes his head, smirking.

"What he said, you had your chance to run."

"Pricks, the pair of ya." I turn and walk out of the room. As I pull my phone out of my pocket, it starts ringing, and Daisy's name appears on the screen.

"Yes, Darling, I was just calling you." I sigh as I answer.

"What took you so long? Are you all okay?" Daisy demands, but I can hear the panic in her voice.

"We are fine, I was trying to get your uncle to take you back, but he refused." The line fills with the sound of her cursing at me, and I can't help but laugh. I'm still chuckling at her when I get into my room and see an envelope has been slid under the door. I open it carefully and pull out the contents. My insides freeze.

"Darling, as much as I love you calling me every name under the sun, kindly pass the phone to Stuart. Now." I hear Daisy calling Stuart before passing the phone to him.

"Hey, what's happening?" Stuart asks.

"How about you start by telling me why the fuck you were asleep on the sofa last night whilst Daisy was reading in the goddamn garden!" I roar down the phone as I look down at the photos which were in the envelope.

"What?! Michael, she never went outside last night! I'd have known." I can hear the shock in Stuart's voice.

"Then why the fuck have I been sent two photographs, one of her lying on the blanket in the garden reading and another of you sleeping surrounded by beer bottles. I swear I'll kill you when I get back there, Stuart."

I hear Stuart protesting that Daisy never went outside when the phone gets snatched from his hand.

"Don't shout at Stuart; I jumped out the back bedroom window," Daisy admits.

"You did what?!" Stuart and I shout simultaneously.

"I felt trapped; I haven't been on my own for so long. It's why I've been so cranky. So I waited for Stuart to fall asleep and jumped out the window, making sure I put a silencing spell on the lounge so he wouldn't hear me. I used to do it when I was grounded as a kid." I start pacing around the room, not trusting myself to speak.

How the fuck could she be so stupid? I joked about her sneaking out to Alex, but that was all it was, a joke.

"Mikey, say something," Daisy whispers down the line. I can hear her voice breaking.

"I've got to go. Stay in the fucking house, Daisy." I growl through gritted teeth as I hang up, not giving her a chance to speak. I gather the photos and storm out of my room. I quickly check the Alpha's room and Marcus's before returning to the others.

I walk into the room, letting the door slam behind me as I close it.

"Just in time, lunch arrived," Alex calls as he looks up; Nigel looks at me too, and they both freeze.

"What did she do?" Alex asks, letting out a deep breath.

"Want to know how she snuck out when grounded? She'd climb out her bedroom window and use a silencing spell on any rooms which would hear her." Nigel looks at me, shocked.

"She hasn't?" He asks, but I can tell he knows the answer; he doesn't want to admit his niece would be that stupid.

"Oh, she fucking did, just in time for someone to snap some pictures and send them to me." I throw the photos down on the table for the others to see. Marcus picks up one of Stuart and growls.

"I'm going to fucking kill him."

"Get in line. He knows he's in the shit; I just went berserk at the kid; he had no idea. Apparently, Daisy made sure he was asleep before she did it."

"I take it back. I'm going to kill her," Marcus replies, throwing the picture back onto the table.

"Not if I get there first," Alex growls as he storms out of the room. Before I can say anything, I hear him in the bathroom. "Daisy Angela Andrews, what the fuck did you think you were playing at, you stupid girl?" I go to walk in after him, but Nigel grabs my arm, shaking his head.

"If anyone can get through to her, it's him. Trust me," Nigel says, nodding towards the closed door as Alex's voice fills the room again.

"I don't give a shit that you thought you were safe; you obviously weren't. Michael's here arguing with demon fucking princes on your behalf; the whole fucking council is standing up to the demons for you, and what are you doing? Sneaking out of fucking windows like a child because you want some space. You will have no space at all if you carry on, as I'll be shipping you off to the Irish coven and getting them to lock you in the old basement cells you would hide in as a child."

"That would work." I hear Nigel chuckle from his seat.

"Well, if you won't go, then maybe cut your mate some slack and do as you are told. Because now he has to deal with a whole new threat, and the fact that someone was obviously outside your house and knows he's not there and can't come home ... I know he can't come home because he has a demon prince trying to make it seem like he's holding you against your will and stopping you from being with Jackson and his pack. He has to stay here and show that he won't back down to threats against the two of you. What do you think that's doing to the poor guy?"

"Shit, I never even got to tell her about all that," I mumble as I rub my face.

"Yes, like I said, he's dealing with a lot of shit you don't even know about, and it's all for you. What are you doing to repay him, being a child and adding to the stress. Do as you are told, stay in the goddamn house, or I *will* be coming to get you and will deal with you myself, is that understood?" Before we hear any more, the bathroom door opens and Alex storms out; he looks ready to murder somebody.

"She knows now." He says as he walks over to the table and starts rubbing at his beard.

"Do you take requests? Because I have a wayward eighteen-year-old who needs telling," Desmond says from his spot on the sofa. "I'm willing to pay big for him to receive some of that." Alex looks at Desmond and shakes his head.

"If he drives you as mad as Daisy and Clare drive me, I'll do it for free." Alex looks at me, "She is sorry; she was crying when she answered. I think this has given her a bit of a scare." I slump down next to Desmond and put my head in my hands.

"I know it sounds like I'm a bastard, but I'm glad. She seems to forget she nearly died two weeks ago, but hopefully, this will make her realise that the threat to her is still real. That I'm not being paranoid," I sigh.

"Has she made contact since I got off the phone with her?" he asks; I know he means through our bond; I shake my head.

"It's probably a good thing. I'm too furious to risk speaking to her right now," I admit.

"What do you want to do? Do you want to head back?" Desmond asks next to me; I look at him and shake my head again.

"Alex was right, someone here is communicating with Jackson, and it's not like we have to guess who. So if I leave, they'll make it seem like the confrontation spooked me before, and I've gone running off with my tail between my legs. I have no choice but to stay." Even though it's the last thing I want to do.

"You're making the right decision Michael, even if it doesn't feel like it," Nigel says.

"I feel like I'm failing here, I should be able to ensure that she's safe in our own home, but instead, I may have no choice but to move her as she isn't safe. People keep finding her, and I don't understand how."

"You're far from failing, Michael; you're constantly being handed a new challenge and rising to them all. There's no way you could've foreseen this." Alex says from his seat; I look up at him with a raised eyebrow.

"I should have foreseen Daisy doing something stupid and putting herself in danger." Alex and Marcus chuckle from where they're sitting.

"So, are you going to confront anyone about the pictures?" Desmond asks; I turn and face him; I can see a sparkle in his eyes, and I know he's thinking the same as me. I look back and grin at him.

"I think it's time to remind the Prince what happens when you piss me off."

Chapter Twenty-Nine

Michael

I'm standing outside the conference room, where everyone else has taken their seats inside. Marcus has called Daisy and Stuart to tell them the plan and to play along. He's going to text when things start. I made him make the call as I was still too furious to speak to either of them.

"Alpha Desmond, I notice you are down a guard. Is there a problem?" Prince Draven asks smugly. I hear the Alpha chuckle.

"No, nothing that isn't being handled. I'm sure you'll hear all about it when Michael gets here." That's my cue.

I walk up to the conference room doors and push both open, so they slam into the walls on either side with a bang. I storm into the room and stand next to my alpha, pulling the photos out of my pocket before throwing them onto the table for all to see.

"Who would like to explain how pictures of my mate relaxing in our garden have found their way into my hotel room?!" I growl. I look around the room and see the only people reacting in any other way but shocked are the demons.

"Michael, what are these?" The necromancer elder asks as she lifts one. I stand tall and fold my arms across my chest.

"That picture in your hand is my mate, relaxing in our garden last night reading. As you can see from the other one, one of our friends staying with her for company was sleeping in the lounge."

"Friend or keeper?" The Demon Prince asks; I look at him and frown.

"If he's a keeper, he's a piss poor excuse for one. Stuart may be on my team, but like the rest, he's also a good friend to Daisy and me. He's there to keep her company."

"Did any harm come to your mate? How is she after this invasion of her privacy?" The vamp next to me asks. I look at her and see that she's genuinely concerned.

"She's unharmed but livid; this is our home and the place she should be the safest. Instead, someone's trying to scare her." I look down at my phone as it starts ringing; I look up at the room, "It appears Daisy would like a word." I say before putting her on loudspeaker.

"Have you calmed down yet, darling?"

"What do you bloody think! I've been out in the garden and found the trail of the individual who took the photos; we're following it now, Will and Jon have joined Stuart and me. Stuart reckons it's a demon, is the Demon Prince there?" Daisy asks, the anger evident in her voice.

"He sure is, and you're on speakerphone," I answer, smirking at Prince Draven, who's looking a little less cocky.

"Oh, good. Tell me, *Prince,* what is the penalty for trespassing onto another species' territory and violating their privacy?" Daisy demands.

"They're to be dealt with by whatever means the individual they wronged feels is necessary," Draven answers sounding less sure of himself and looking pale.

"And if that individual is in a particularly bad mood and decided the only acceptable punishment would be death, you would be powerless to stop them, right?" she asks.

"Yes." The Demon Prince replies through gritted teeth.

"Okay then, I'll see what mood I'm in when I find them. Right now, their death will be the only solution." Daisy replies coldly.

"NO!" My head shoots up, and I look to the corner where the sound came from—a demon steps out of the shadows and heads towards the table.

"What was that?" Daisy asks; I don't take my eyes off the demon as I answer.

"It seems one of the prince's guards does not agree with your choice of punishment, darling," I reply.

"Oh, really and why not?" Daisy asks.

"Because he's my brother and was only following orders." The demon declares.

"Whose orders?" Daisy demands. I can hear her voice changing as her alpha gene kicks in.

"Prince Draven's. He ordered my brother to take photographs of the house and yourself this weekend."

"Why?" Daisy and I ask at the same time.

"Because the Demon Prince is in debt to Alpha Jackson. The prince has been helping him track you; they planned to kidnap you this weekend." I feel a growl escape my chest as I turn and glare at the Demon Prince, who's shaking as he stares back at me. I watch as he pulls a piece of paper towards him and writes on it. Whilst they are distracted, I see Desmond typing on his phone under the table; I know he is messaging Daisy instructions.

"As you are not here, darling, would you like me to handle this?" I ask with my jaw clenched. I can feel everyone looking between the prince and me. I risk glancing at Nigel, who has Alex and Marcus standing on either side of him again. All three look murderous as they stare at the demon. The Prince holds out a piece of paper and beckons Marcus over to him. Marcus looks at me, and I nod. Marcus walks to the prince.

"Yes, please," Daisy's voice falters for a second as she takes in the confession. She quickly remembers she is on the line. "I won't kill the guard's brother right now, message him and tell him I'd like to talk. No harm will come to him if he comes to me and behaves appropriately." Daisy continues on the phone, unaware of what's happening in the room. I watch as Marcus is asked to give the note to me. I hold out my hand as he approaches and hands me the note. I open it cautiously.

I will tell you everything, but you don't want the team member with Daisy to hear it.

I hand the note to the Alpha, who frowns and nods.

"He will be there; he isn't far away." The demon agrees, pulling out his phone.

"I'll leave you to deal with things on that end then, darling. Please remember to play nice with our guests." I add, looking down at the phone. My heart is racing; I need to end this call and find out what the prince won't discuss in earshot of Stuart.

"You're no fun, handsome. I'll speak to you later." With

that, the line goes dead. I look up at the prince.

"Want to explain what this is about?" I ask, holding up the note.

"There are things you need to know about your team members that may change your mind about who you leave your mate with," Draven replies. I hear Marcus whispering to the Alpha, who hands him the note.

"Is Daisy still in danger of being kidnapped?" I ask, trying to work out a plan in case she is.

"No. Not now." Draven answers.

"Why should we believe you?" Alex asks as he steps forward; Draven turns and faces him.

"Because there's no way his brother could do it now. I'll call him myself and tell him to abort the mission." Draven replies.

"Tell him to avoid telling anyone at the house the information you are so eager to tell me," I add; Draven looks at me and nods.

"That would be wise." He replies as I look around the table.

"Would anyone mind if I questioned the Demon Prince Draven and his guards to find out exactly what's going on and how they've been giving Jackson information on my pack and its members?" Desmond says next to me as he stands up and leans on the table.

"I would like to know the answers to these questions as well, as they concern my niece, who is still a coven member," Nigel says from his seat.

"I think we should all be aware of what he's been up to as who knows who else he has been selling secrets to." The vamp next to me adds. The sounds of people agreeing around us fill the room. Desmond holds his hand up, and everyone falls silent. He sits back in his chair and looks at the prince before speaking again.

"Very well then, Prince Draven; I believe you wanted the chance to speak before; I think you should start now as we are all desperate to hear what you have to say, before Michael breaks your jaw for a second time."

Chapter Thirty

Jon

I enter the bedroom and find Daisy sitting on their bed; her knees tucked up to her chest and her chin resting on them. I sit on the edge of the bed, where we stay silent for a while, neither of us knowing what to say.

"You did well; you showed no fear and demanded respect. The demon near enough shit himself in fear." I look at my baby sister as she shows no sign of hearing me.

"I fucked up, Jonny." She whispers, still not looking at me.

"Yes, you did," I reply honestly.

"He won't talk to me. He hasn't messaged or called. Mikey's never given me the silent treatment before. He's so angry with me," Daisy says, her voice breaking as she tries to stop the tears from falling.

"Well, it was going to happen eventually; let's face it, you love to push his buttons." Daisy looks up at me as a single tear rolls down her cheek.

"I didn't think." She whispers; I tilt my head to the side as I look at her.

"That's the problem, Daisy; you never do, whereas Mikey can't help but overthink. It's embedded in him to think and assess all dangers. I know you think he's just being overprotective, and it's a wolf thing, but that male can spot a threat a mile away. If he says there's a risk of danger, you listen to him because he'll be right."

"How do I make this right, Jonny?" Daisy asks as she puts her forehead on her knees.

"You grovel, make him see how sorry you are, and you do as you're told. I'm warning you; it's going to be tough. As you said, you fucked up and destroyed his trust in you." I point out.

"He called me Daisy." She whispers as she keeps her head down.

I look at her frowning. "Well, it's your name." But Daisy shakes her head at me before putting it back on her knees.

"Mikey *never* calls me Daisy unless in class. It's always

darling or baby, never Daisy." She says as her voice breaks.

"Ahh, I see. It just shows how much you need to grovel then, doesn't it?" I move so I'm sitting on the bed with my back against the headboard; I put an arm around her and pull her to me, so I'm holding her as she cries into my chest.

"Why are you being so nice? Stuart and Will are furious with me. Marcus is going to make my life hell when he gets back." Daisy sobs as she uses the sleeve of her top to wipe her face.

"Stuart has every right to be furious. You've put him in an impossible situation. Marcus and Mikey are going to kill him." I point out, which makes Daisy cry harder.

"But it wasn't his fault." She gasps.

"Yes, it was. You shouldn't have been able to get outside, let alone stay out. He was also drinking on the job. He should have picked up on the demons watching the place. He didn't because he allowed himself to get distracted." I run a hand over her head and let that sink in before continuing.

"I know you don't like it, but believe it or not, we're all working our asses off trying to keep you safe. We're still keeping tabs on activity in Exeter; Mikey's calling in every favour to keep your family and you safe. We're exhausted, Daisy, none of us are doing anything but working and running around trying to protect you, and last night you threw all our hard work in our faces. It hurt." I admit as she continues to cry.

"I'm sorry, Jonny." She sobs into my chest. I kiss her on top of her head and sigh.

"I know you are; we all do. It's just going to take some time for everyone to calm down. Especially Mikey, who's hurt the most." She nods into my chest, and I hold her as we continue to talk until she falls asleep, emotionally exhausted.

Not long after, I hear Michael's car pull up outside. Daisy is still in my arms, so I gently lay her down and quickly leave the room, hoping not to wake her. As I close the bedroom door, I meet with Marcus.

"I take it she's asleep?" He asks. I nod and point towards my room. I close the door and find him sitting with his head in his hands.

"Was it that bad?" I ask. He nods without looking up. "How's Mikey?"

Marcus looks up at me, and I can see how exhausted he is.

"Furious. Not just at Daisy but at the whole situation. Jackson has had the Demon Prince doing all kinds for him and knows more than we thought he did. The whole thing's a mess, and the fact that Daisy pulled that trick last night was just the icing on the cake. I had to drive us home. He crashed out in the back seat most of the way."

"Fuck. Where is he now?" I ask, hoping for a few moments alone with my brother to check on him.

"In the dining room, waiting for Stuart to return from his rounds."

"I'm going to speak to him quickly before he does," I say as I turn towards the door.

"Okay, I'll speak to Daisy as she'll be awake in a minute anyway; Michael will struggle to hold back when he gets his hands on Stuart." I nod as I know what Michael is like when one of his team fucks up, I've been on the receiving end of my fair share of bollockings. Michael may be a strict leader, but he's also fair and will never pull the leader card unless it's deserved. I stop at my door and turn to face Marcus.

"Don't go too hard on her; she knows she fucked up and is punishing herself." He nods as I leave the room and head downstairs.

I find Michael in the dining room, looking out of the patio doors and into the woods behind their garden.

"Is she okay?" He asks without turning around.

"Not really, but she knows she only has herself to blame," I reply as I lean against the door frame with my arms crossed. "How are you doing?" I ask, watching as Michael takes a sip from a glass, and then I notice the bottle of bourbon on the table.

"I honestly don't know. I don't know who I'm angrier with right now; Jackson, Kellan, Draven, Stuart, Daisy or myself." My brother sighs.

"Mikey, you can't do any more than you are already

doing." He spins around and looks at me, his eyes black, where his wolf's so close to the surface.

"So, everyone keeps telling me Jonny, yet they keep finding ways to get near her. The kicker is that she's putting herself in their fucking path. It was so close last night, Jonny." His voice gets louder as his emotions come to the front. "Every time I relax just a little thinking she's safe, I get proven wrong, and they get closer to her. I can't even keep her safe in our own home. This was the last place, Jonny, the last place they hadn't found her, and now they fucking have." He slams the glass down on the table before leaning over it, his whole posture screaming defeat.

"Maybe Alex didn't have the worse idea of sending her to Ireland. At least Jackson wouldn't expect that, and she'd be safe." He sighs.

"I'm not going to Ireland." I turn to find Daisy standing in the doorway behind me, pulling her cardigan around herself as if cold. Michael doesn't look up at her, and I can see its effect on her. "You can't make me go," Daisy adds in a whisper.

"You will if it is the safest option," Michael says in a slightly calmer voice but remains looking at the table.

"You said you would never force me to do anything I didn't want to," Daisy argues, looking at Michael.

"And look where that has fucking got us, Daisy!" He bellows as he stands tall; Daisy jumps at the change of tone. "I can't do any more to protect you; I can't physically do anything else to ensure you're safe. What more can I fucking do?!"

"I fucked up; I know that." Daisy whispers, and a laugh bursts from Michael's lips.

"Fucked up is an understatement; there's no words for how badly you fucked up, and the kicker is you don't realise how close you were to being taken. How close I was to losing you!" I watch Michael's posture change again as he leans back over the table and looks down.

"Daisy, I love you more than you could ever know, but right now, I need you to go upstairs and give me space. I've had a fuck full this weekend, and I'm not up for arguing with you. Especially as I have to rethink the whole team's assignments, deal with Stuart and the information the demon gave me, and try to keep you from doing anything else that might put you in further danger."

I squeeze Daisy's hand; she looks up at me as I nod, signalling for her to do as he asks. I can see the pain and defeat in her eyes; I know she'll be going straight upstairs to cry.

"I'm sorry, Mikey." She whispers before heading up the stairs at speed.

"Fuck." Michael curses as he stands tall and stares at the now empty doorway. I can see he wants to run after her. It's written all over his face. When Marcus walks into the room, he spots it too.

"Go sort this out with her; I'll deal with Stuart; you're not in the right mind to discipline him and deal with everything else." As if on cue, Stuart walks through the front door with Will. Michael sees them and straightens up.

"No, we will do it together." He instantly goes into leader mode; Stuart pales as he sees Michael and Marcus standing in the dining room.

"Stuart, sit down." Marcus barks as he points to a chair at the far end of the table as he stands next to Michael. I turn to leave, but Marcus stops me.

"Jon, Will, we need you to hear this too as it will save us repeating ourselves," Michael says as he crosses his arms over his chest. I nod and lean against the door frame again as Will stands beside me.

"Michael, Marcus, I know you're pissed off with me; you have every right to be; I fucked up." Stuart starts; Michael shakes his head and looks at the ceiling.

"If one more person tells me that they 'fucked up' this weekend, I'll lose my shit completely." Michael looks down as he moves back to leaning on the table, looking across at Stuart, who's trying very hard not to show his fear, but it's there in his steel blue eyes.

"Stuart, you're lucky I'm not kicking you off the team; you fucked up that badly." I can see the verbal blow hit Stuart as Michael intended.

"Not only were you drinking on the job, but you also didn't

even notice that the house was being watched all weekend. The demon arrived two hours after we left and was camped out until I contacted Daisy and told you to be alert. You noticed nothing, and why? Because you were too busy enjoying time with my mate and playing house whilst I wasn't here." Both Will and I turn to Stuart at the same time and frown. As I turn back to face my brother, I see the hatred in his eyes. I can't remember the last time my brother looked like that at another individual.

"I ... I don't know." Stuart stammers.

"You don't know what I mean? Stuart, I've always known about your feelings for Daisy, and I don't mean as a friend." Michael states; I hear Will curse next to me as I stare at my brother, shocked, as he continues.

"I've never called you out on them as I also hoped you would never act on them. But this weekend, you let those feelings get in the way of you doing your job; you put Daisy in danger. That's neither professional nor appropriate." Michael looks over at Marcus and signals for him to take over. Michael's temper is starting to get the better of him.

"We found out a lot this weekend. Jackson has a few more people working for him than we could have ever anticipated. His pack has grown and now has about twenty members; he's had people watching us who have been careful to do so when we are most vulnerable. When we're at home or in our day jobs when we aren't looking out for trouble." Marcus looks at Stuart, "he's singled you out as our weakest link because apparently, Daisy can get around you the easiest. Jackson knows that you're the most likely to do whatever she says because of how you feel about her." Fuck, how did I miss that? I never picked up on any of this, even with all the time I've spent with Stuart and Daisy, either together or apart.

"Shit." Stuart curses as Michael turns and glares at him. "Michael, I'll be honest; yes, I developed feelings for Daisy. But I've never, ever, acted on them. I would never act on them as I have far too much respect for you." Stuart declares, looking straight at Michael. The guy has balls; I'll give him that.

"The issue remains that these feelings make you a risk to

the team and, most importantly, to Daisy," Michael replies.

"Please don't kick me out of the team because of this; reassign me, take me off guarding duty; I'll train harder than I already am; I'll do anything, but please don't kick me out," Stuart begs.

"I'm not kicking you out, Stuart. If you had been in front of me when I first received the pictures, you would have been out of the team instantly; as soon as they told us they knew about your crush on Daisy, you were nearly in a body bag. It's one thing for me to know but a complete other for others to realise. But you'll be taken off guarding duty and have to prove to me that you deserve your spot on the team, and you'll need to work your fucking arse off to regain my trust. Because right now, the only thing going for you is I know you're an asset to this team when you put your mind to it." Michael walks past me and moves to lean over Stuart, one hand on the back of his chair and one on the table. Stuart instantly leans away from him.

"But take this as your last warning; you will be gone if you ever mess up again." I watch as Michael's face changes and realise that all professionalism has gone, and so does Marcus as I notice him take a step forward and uncross his arms, ready in case he has to intervene.

"This part is personal." Stuart leans back further as Michael gets right in his face. "You ever put Daisy in danger again because she has fluttered her eyelashes at you, and I will make you wish you had never been born. You even think about acting on your feelings, and I will kill you. I don't care if Daisy hates me for it. Do you have any idea how humiliating it was to hear how strangers knew that my pack brother, a guy I trust with mine and my mates life daily, is so obsessed with my mate that she can wrap him around her little finger and if she says jump, you ask how high? How those sketchbooks you carry around are filled with pictures of Daisy or things you know she will like so that she smiles at you. I had to stand there and pretend I didn't care when I was fucking fuming. I have never been so close to losing my composure as I was at that moment. You were lucky I had a three-hour car ride to get to you because Marcus would be burying your cold dead body right now if you had been to hand." Michael stays there and stares at Stuart before moving away from him and moving back to where Marcus is standing.

"For the next month, you don't come within sight of this house. You're off guarding duty, and you'll be given new assignments. There will be no contact with Daisy or Michael; you will contact me directly daily. *If* an emergency concerns Michael and Daisy directly, you can contact Michael or the house, but not Daisy." Marcus explains to Stuart as Michael returns to looking out of the patio window towards the woods.

"Be warned, Stuart, you're lucky Michael has been so lenient as I wanted to kick your sorry ass off the team, but he refused; why is beyond me. Personally, you don't deserve your spot or to even be allowed within ten miles of Daisy; if it were my mate, you would be dead." Marcus warns. I do not doubt that threat as I remember how protective of Michelle Marcus could be.

"This is why they referred to me as the calm one," Michael says from his spot. Marcus shrugs, but I can see a slight smirk on his face. Marcus looks at Stuart before continuing.

"Go home and wait for my call in the morning. I'll move a few things around and give you your new assignments. You're off duty until nine a.m." Stuart nods and stands from his seat. I watch him take a deep breath before speaking.

"Can I say something to you, Michael, before I leave?" Michael takes a deep breath and turns to face Stuart before nodding.

"I know it was wrong to develop feelings for Daisy; I tried to pretend they weren't there. That they didn't exist, I honestly never considered acting on them. I have far too much love and respect for you. Not just because you're my leader, but also my friend and brother, I'm sorry I let you down, but no harm would have come to Daisy on my watch; I would fight until my last breath to protect her." Michael stares at him for a moment before charging forward, his eyes ablaze; luckily, Marcus puts an arm out to stop him as he holds Michael in place.

"No harm would have come to her? They nearly took her!

I nearly lost her! They were seconds away from grabbing her, and you would have been none the fucking wiser! Five seconds Stuart. That was how close it was!" Michael roars as he tries to get past Marcus, but I step up to help hold him back, knowing that he'll kill Stuart if he gets to him.

"Get out, Stuart, before I punch you for him." Will snaps behind me. Stuart walks out of the room, picks his bag up from the hallway and leaves.

"Fucking prick!" Michael shouts as he turns away from us all.

The four of us stand there in silence for a moment as Michael attempts to calm down, and the rest of us try to process what just happened.

"Well, I wasn't expecting that." Will sighs from his spot by the door. Michael shakes his head where he's standing; he puts a hand on Marcus's shoulder and squeezes.

"You can take over a bit; I need a break." Michael picks up the bottle and now empty glass and walks out of the room. Marcus glances at me and nods for me to follow him. I pat Will on the back as I leave; I find Michael in the lounge and sit on the opposite sofa.

"You going to talk to Daisy?" I ask as he pours himself a drink. He nods slowly before holding up the glass.

"Dutch courage." He says before knocking it back and pouring another one. I chuckle and sit back in my seat.

"How was she with the demon?" he asks as he sips his drink. I can't help but smile.

"She was amazing; you'd have been proud. She never once let him see she was scared or worried; she was pure alpha. Even I was scared by how calm and collected she was. The demon didn't mention any of that Stuart stuff, though." Michael shook his head.

"His brother told him not to. Not with Stuart and Daisy both being here." Michael explains. I nod as it makes sense.

"How do you feel about it all? Got to say I never noticed." I admit. Michael sits back and runs his fingers through his hair.

"I've known since Daisy ran off to Cornwall. But like I said to him, I hoped he wouldn't act on it, so I tried not to let it bother me. I even used it, thinking it'd make him a better guard as he would never let anything happen to her; I guess I was wrong." He takes a sip of his drink and looks at me. "It was humiliating hearing the demons say that they knew all about his crush and that Stuart was the weaker link because of it."

"Do you think Daisy knows?" I ask; Michael shrugs.

"I like to think not as otherwise; she's played him; I'm not alright with that." Michael downs the rest of his drink and lets out a deep sigh.

"I can't put this off anymore. I need to talk to her."

"Go easy on her, Mikey. She knows how much she's fucked up and has been delicate since Alex called her." I look up at the ceiling to where their room is; I know Daisy will be even more upset than she was if she heard everything that just occurred in the dining room.

"He let her have it, that's for sure; It wasn't pretty," Michael says as he stands up and heads towards the stairs. He stops at the bottom and looks up anxiously.

"Just have it out and make up; you know this isn't worth losing each other over," I say, hoping to reassure him. Michael looks over at me and nods before heading up out of sight.

Chapter Thirty-One

Michael

My heart stops as I walk into the bedroom to find it empty. I open my mouth to yell to Marcus that she's gone when I hear the sound of water coming from our bathroom. I let out a sigh of relief as I walk up to the door, take a deep breath and knock.

"Who is it?" Daisy asks quietly.

"It's me," I reply. I hear her say it's open, and I let myself in. I look over to the large bath and find Daisy sitting in the middle of the tub with her knees pulled up to her chest as she leans her chin on them.

"Hey." She whispers as she looks at me, and my heart breaks. Her eyes are swollen, bright red and bloodshot from crying. She's been chewing on her lip to the point it's bled. She looks so lost. I walk over to the bathtub and sit on the edge.

"Hey, what you doing in here?" I ask gently. As cross as I am with her, Jon's right; she's learnt a harsh lesson today and had an even bigger scare.

"I ran the bath as I didn't want to hear you shouting at Stuart. It seemed a waste not to use it." I run my fingers through the water and realise it is only lukewarm.

"Did you hear anything that was said?" I ask as I shake the water from my fingers.

"Only when the shouting started." She whispers as she bows her head and looks at the water. I run my fingers through my hair and let out a deep sigh.

"Stuart won't be around for a while, and he isn't to contact either of us," I explain as I watch her eyes fill with tears.

"Did you kick him off the team because of me?" Daisy asks. I open my mouth to tell her no, but decide honesty would be best here.

"Stuart hasn't been kicked off the team, not yet anyway. But some factors prevent him from doing his job properly, especially when protecting you. His feelings for you being the biggest issue." Daisy looks at me and frowns.

"Feelings?" It seems I was right, and Daisy's had no idea about Stuart's feelings either.

"Stuart has strong romantic feelings for you and has for a long time. Because of this, he's been distracted from time to time when he's meant to be looking out for danger." I rub the bridge of my nose before continuing.

"The Demon Prince told me a lot today, including how the demons have been watching us all for a long time; they've even sat near Stuart at the university, and he hasn't noticed or questioned them. They singled him out as the weakest link, and they've been waiting for the two of you to be alone so they could kidnap you for Jackson. They thought it would be easier this weekend when they realised Marcus and Jon, and I were all elsewhere." I look at Daisy and wipe away a tear from her cheek as my chest tightens as I think about how close they came to taking her last night.

"The only reason I didn't lose you this weekend was that the guy couldn't get hold of the prince to get confirmation; they were to grab you. The prince was busy fucking a nymph and didn't answer the call. The guy got the go-ahead as you closed the bedroom window after climbing in. If it had been seconds earlier, you would have been taken. When Draven realised they'd missed the opportunity, he used the pictures to taunt me as we have an unpleasant history." I tuck a stray section of hair behind Daisy's ear and wipe the fresh tears from her face.

"I was so angry when I heard that the demons and Jackson knew about Stuart's feelings for you and that they made you an easy target when in his care." I stand up from the bathtub and walk over to the sink. I lean against it to try and calm down. I'm still fighting my wolf, who wants to go after Stuart and rip him apart for being in love with our mate.

"Today, when you admitted to purposely climbing out that window and blocking any sounds from inside the house, I was fucking furious." I look at Daisy, who has turned around and is looking back at me. "Why did you do it? Why not explain to us how you were feeling? I knew you felt trapped and suffocated; I even said how guilty I felt about it last night. We could have come up with something so you could at least be in the garden like last night, but you would have been safe." I turn and look at Daisy, who's still crying quietly to herself.

"I know things have been intense since you were poisoned, but we nearly lost you. *I* nearly lost you!" I walk over and kneel by the bathtub; I reach out my hand and cup her cheek as I lean forward and press my forehead to hers; I close my eyes and try to relax, but I can't.

"I'm hanging on by a thread here, baby; I feel like every time I've made you safe, something else happens, and they find a new way to get to you, and I don't see it coming. I even joked to Alex this morning about expecting you to sneak out, but I never thought you actually would; not once did it seriously cross my mind you'd do that to the guys and me. After everything we've been doing to keep you safe. You just threw it all in our faces." I exclaim.

"I know, and I'm so sorry, Mikey. I'd had a few drinks and felt so trapped; Stuart was asleep, so I decided to see if I could do it. I never dreamt there would be anyone out there. I'll never be so reckless again, I swear." Daisy gasps as she bursts into tears, and my heart can't take it anymore. I grab her around the back and under the knees before I lift her out of the bath and hold her on my lap, against my chest, as tightly as possible as her heart breaks. I reach over to the stool and grab her towel to wrap around her before picking us both off the floor and carrying her into the bedroom.

I place Daisy on the bed and climb beside her to hold her against me, to remind myself that once again, even though I was close to losing her, I didn't, and she is still here, even if it was just sheer dumb luck that kept her safe. After today, Prince Draven will think twice about to whom he pledges his alliance. At least for a couple of months anyway, as his jaw mends again.

I know Daisy's sorry and didn't think, and I can see how scared she is now after hearing how close she had been to being retaken. But it still hurts that she failed to follow simple instructions for one night; maybe I'm not used to being ignored after the guys always follow my orders without hesitation.

"There wasn't anything going on between Stuart and me.

You know that, right?" Daisy's voice pulls me out of my thoughts. I look down at her, frowning.

"It never even crossed my mind that there was; why would you say that?" I ask.

"Because I was worried you'd think there was. I've never treated him any differently than I do the others. I have no idea why or when he started getting feelings for me, but they weren't reciprocated." She says, looking up at me. I reach down, cup Daisy's face again, and make sure she looks into my eyes before answering.

"I've known for a long time that Stuart has feelings for you, and not for one second did I *ever* think you returned them; if I had, I'd have killed him." Daisy slaps my chest, finally showing me a small smile. I laugh before pulling her tighter into my side and kissing the top of her head.

"Seriously though, I'd have said something, and I certainly wouldn't have left you two alone for a moment, let alone all weekend. So please don't doubt my trust in you regarding that."

"But you don't trust me with other stuff anymore," Daisy whispers into my chest; I sigh, fighting the urge to lie.

"Not to keep yourself safe, no. We need to discuss where we go from here." Daisy sits up suddenly and looks at me, the tears still in her eyes.

"You're not leaving me, are you?" I bolt upright and grab her, pulling her back into my arms and holding her tight.

"Gods, no! I don't mean that; I will never mean that. I've told you; that you're stuck with me until my last breath. I don't care how angry you make me; you will never make me mad enough to leave you. Ever." I promise her.

"Then what do you mean?"

"As much as I hate to admit it. Stuart was the ideal guard, he fits in at the uni with him only being twenty-five, and he had more time on his hands due to being unemployed. It will take a lot of juggling to keep someone with you. I know you'll argue and fight me on it, but we have no choice with what we now know. It's not safe to leave you on your own." I lie back on the bed and pull Daisy down with me so that she's back, leaning against my side; I start running my hand over her head trying to soothe her. We lie in silence for a few minutes, trying to compose ourselves and come to terms with everything that has happened.

"What have the others said about the whole Stuart thing?" Daisy asks after a while.

"Not much; Marcus had guessed and thinks I should kill him; Jon and Will had no idea and were both shocked; Stuart tried to hide it from everyone." I look over at the door as someone knocks. I quickly glance down and check Daisy is covered before calling for them to enter. Marcus sticks his head around the door.

"You both doing okay in here?" He asks as he enters the room; I look down at Daisy in my arms and nod.

"We will be," I reply before looking up. "What's up?" Marcus looks at me and nods towards the door.

"Carl's on his way so that we can sort out the schedules and assignments; we could do with you being downstairs for it. I tried to put him off to give you guys some more time, but he's short of time himself as they have the bar, and it's Saturday." I shake my head.

"No, it's fine; give me five minutes, and I'll be down." Marcus nods and leaves the room; I kiss Daisy quickly and climb off the bed. As much as I want to stay there and hold her, I still have responsibilities to the team to sort this mess out. I also need to get out of these wet clothes after picking Daisy up from the bath. I glance at the bedside clock and see it is nearly seven pm.

"Have you eaten?" I ask her as I change out of my jeans and into some dry sweatpants. I look over as she shakes her head. "Want me to bring you up something?" I offer; Daisy sits up, holding the towel over her chest as she chews her bottom lip.

"Would it be okay if I come down? I feel like I should since this whole mess is my fault." I walk over to the bed and sit down by her side. Daisy looks up at me, and I gently press my thumb against her bottom lip and pull it from her teeth before leaning over and softly pressing my lips to hers.

"First stop chewing your lip; it's been bleeding. Second, if you are up for coming down, please do, but know that we'll be discussing everything that has happened with Stuart, and I don't know how much you want to know about what the demons had planned." She looks up and makes eye contact.

"I want to know everything the demons told you." I lean over and kiss her gently again.

"Then get dressed, darling, as you're not sitting down there in just a towel."

Chapter Thirty-Two

Stuart

What the fuck was I thinking?! Why did I think I could hide my feelings for my best friend's mate? I should have been honest from the beginning and told Michael everything, but now I've lost both Michael and Daisy's trust and friendship. Worst of all, I've lost Daisy.

She'll be mortified when she finds out how I feel about her. She's going to think I'm a fucking idiot. Which I am.

I throw my bag onto the floor and drop down onto the sofa. My phone rings in my pocket, and I pull it out, scared to see who it is.

"If you are phoning to take the piss fuck off." I snap as I answer.

"Why would I take the piss? I'm phoning to see if you're okay?" I hear Jon sigh.

"I'm far from okay, Jon."

"How bad is it?" He asks as I lean back into the chair with the phone to my ear.

"Couldn't get any worse," I admit.

"You love her?"

"Yeah." I sigh.

"Fuck Stu."

"Yep," I answer abruptly cause what else is there to say?

"I get it, Stu; she's beautiful, funny and amazing, but she's Mikey's mate; she is everything to him. They're so in love; it's not like there was ever any chance for the two of you." He might as well stick a knife in my heart.

"You think I don't know how fucked up this is? I have to watch the two of them together every single day. I watch her face light up by the sheer mention of him; it kills me. But I can't explain it, Jon. I'm drawn to her. I have been since the moment I met her. If I hadn't known she was Michael's mate, I would have thought she was mine. The things I feel for her are so intense. It's going to be hell trying to stay away." I can hear Jon sighing down the phone.

"You have to, Stu. You have to do as Mikey has asked. I'd be honest if you were in love with my mate, I'd have kicked your arse. Mikey needs time to calm down," Jon says softly.

"I don't know how he didn't. When he said he knew, I thought I was done for." I reply, shaking my head.

"Yeah, well, Mikey's calmer than most of us. But as you saw, he's struggling with this. You'll have your work cut out for you, that's for sure. You must prove to him that you're trustworthy enough to be around Daisy."

"How is Daisy?" I ask.

"Should you be asking?" Jon replies, I know he's right.

"I can't not," I admit because I need to know that she's alright and how she's reacted to everything.

"She's not good. Mikey tore her a new one when he first saw her before you returned. They're talking now, though. I don't know how she'll react when she hears about your feelings for her. Do you think she knows?" Jon asks as I pull my hair from the top knot; it's been in all day.

"No, she's never treated me any differently from you guys anyway," I reply.

"She never led you on to get her way?" Jon asks carefully.

"Gods, no, Jon! Her whole world revolves around Michael. He's everything to her." I sigh as I run my fingers through my hair. "I would have never acted on my feelings, Jon."

"I know." I can hear voices in the background. "Look, I need to go; Marcus has called a meeting. I'll call later. Want me to pop round?" Jon offers; I think about it for a moment before answering.

"I want to be on my own tonight, Jon. I need to sort my head out."

"Alright, dude, but if you need a chat, message me. Everything will work out, I'm sure of it." Jon says in the hope of reassuring me.

"I wish I had your confidence," I sigh as I hang up.

At the moment, it's hard to be positive. All I can see is how much of a messed-up situation this is. I screwed up big time, and I know it will take a long time for my friends to see anything but that.

I honestly don't know how this is going to work out. It will be so hard staying away from Daisy. We text continuously usually, but now my phone lies silent on the coffee table. I pick up my bag and head into the bedroom to unpack. I'm hoping to crash for a bit and pretend I haven't destroyed two of the best friendships I've ever had for a few hours.

Chapter Thirty-Three

Michael

I down the rest of my drink and sit back in my office chair. It's eleven at night, and everyone has gone home. Jon's in his room, and Daisy had fallen asleep shortly after the others left and is now in our bed. I'd curled up with her for half an hour, but my mind was working overtime, so I came in here to do some marking. Not that I'm getting much done.

Since speaking to Daisy about what she did, I've calmed down a lot. I knew she felt trapped, yet I didn't realise how much. The biggest issue for me to deal with now, other than the information the demons gave me, is Stuart.

It makes my blood boil every time I think about how obsessed over Daisy he has become. Even I had no idea it had become this much of a problem. I thought maybe I was paranoid, but I guess I was right to be.

There have been times I've wanted to call him out on it, like when Daisy was poisoned; it was almost as if he wanted me to leave him looking after her. Or the time she healed me at Mums, and he had the nerve to tell me off for allowing her to do it. There have been little comments here and there that have left me feeling unsettled. The only consolation was having complete trust in him not to act on his feelings. Mainly because he knew I wouldn't hold back if he did. I also trust Daisy completely, as I know she would never cheat on me; that was never a worry.

Daisy's close to all the guys and says they're like brothers to her, which I guess they are. Marcus the protective big brother, Jonathan the joker, and Will, the one you know always has your back. But for her, Stuart is the one she turns to when she needs someone to talk to and if she needs a little advice. When she was angry and wouldn't speak to me, Stuart talked her around, and I know he made her realise how much I love her. Daisy will miss him, but she agrees that giving us all space is for the best as she doesn't want to lead him on. I hope we can all move past this one day, as I know their friendship means a lot to her, and he has been a good friend to me too.

I place my glass on the desk and refill it from the decanter. I have drunk more tonight than I have in a while when at home. Jon's keeping an ear out for trouble so I can attempt to relax as much as possible; I'm not entirely sure I can, though. I lift my glass to sip my drink when my phone vibrates across the desk. I pick it up and see a text.

Alex: Hey, I wanted to check in and see how you're doing. Give me a shout if you need anything. You dealt with a lot today, and I could tell it was taking its toll.

Michael: Alright. It's been a shit one, that's for sure. Everyone only went home a couple of hours ago. Let me know when you're next free for a chat. Been thinking through a few things they told us and have a few magical questions. Thanks for checking in; I appreciate it.

I place the phone on the desk, and it instantly vibrates. I pick it up and answer, chuckling.

"I didn't mean you had to call right away."

"I know, but I can't sleep anyway, so I'm sitting in the study having a drink. How you doing?" Alex asks. I sip my drink and lean back into the chair, groaning.

"Been better, to be truthful. It was tough keeping my cool when I returned and dealt with Stuart," I admit. I hear Alex hiss down the line.

"I bet. Is he still breathing?" he chuckles.

"Just about. He's lucky I had three hours to calm down and get my head around it all, and that Marcus and Jon were able to hold me back. Everyone here was shocked, Daisy included. He's been told not to contact Daisy or me until further notice. Marcus is going to be the go-between for a while."

"Sounds like it's for the best, though, especially after everything they said today," Alex replies. He had been furious when he heard how close they had been to taking Daisy. I had to hold him back from hitting Draven himself at one point.

Daisy may not be Nigel or Alex's daughter, but they have both stepped up and taken her father's place since he was killed. There is no mistaking the lengths they will go through to protect her.

"Yeah, I think so. Daisy's going to miss him as they are close. But she's said she doesn't want to lead him on any further, so she understands," I add with a sigh as I take another sip of my drink.

"And how is my adventurous goddaughter? Grovelling, I hope."

"She's broken, Alex. Apparently, she was amazing when questioning the demon when he arrived. Jon and Will said it was like she had turned all her emotions off; it proves what I was saying last night about her being an amazing alpha. But as soon as he left, she went to our room and didn't leave until I returned. From how she looked when I saw her, she'd cried the whole time." I quickly take another sip of my drink as I look towards our room, where Daisy is hopefully sleeping peacefully.

"She needs to realise how badly she fucked up, Michael," Alex says down the phone; I know he is right.

"Oh, she knows. She hates herself for what she did. I was so angry when I first saw her I shouted at her to stay out of my way. But we've talked, and she's promised never to be so reckless again. She's had a fright which made her see I'm not just being overprotective."

"Well, hopefully, she's learnt her lesson. Anyway, what did you want to ask me about?" Alex asks.

"Is it possible for somebody to cast a spell over a distance?" I hear Alex thinking about it as I wait patiently for an answer.

"I guess with the right tools, then yes. Why? What are you thinking?"

"Somehow, Kellan and Jackson always seem to know where Daisy is. The demons said the sorcerer with Jackson has been helping them to hide, but they had no idea who it was. They must be doing it from a distance if they are not around to perform the spells. I don't believe it's Kellan, as I'm sure Daisy would have known if he was a sorcerer." I explain.

"It would make sense. I wonder if they are somehow blocking Daisy's magic as well? Nigel said it felt like someone else was involved, but with everything that happened down in Cornwall, he didn't have time to investigate it." I hear Alex moving about and wait. "Did you say you're both off from classes for the next week?" He asks.

"Yeah, the students all have a few weeks off to study, so I'm working from home most of the time." I answer.

"I could do with visiting Daisy and seeing if I can pick up on something Nigel missed. I could also look around and see if I can find a talisman or something that might explain how someone is projecting their magic around there."

"That'd be great. When are you thinking?" I ask as I pull my diary towards me to double-check we're both free.

"Day after tomorrow? I'll bring Clare and Sara up with me. I know they want to see Daisy, and it might be a good distraction for her." Alex replies as I check my diary.

"We're both completely free this week, so that's perfect. I appreciate it, thanks. We only have one room here, but I know the pack houses are all empty, so I'll ask Desmond to lend us one of those for you to sleep in. It's fully kitted out and saves paying for a hotel." I say as I quickly jot down a note on my writing pad to message Des in the morning.

"Yeah, he said last night we could use one if we come up. I'll message him tomorrow when I know the timings and so on," Alex replies.

"Thanks Alex, will speak to you then. Oh, and let's keep it from Daisy. It'll be a nice surprise for her." I say, smiling for the first time since I received the photos.

"Does she deserve nice surprises?" Alex jokes.

"She may be a pain in my ass, but she still deserves something good to happen," I chuckle back.

"Fair enough." Alex laughs. "Take care of yourself, Michael, and get some sleep."

"You too, Alex. And thanks for calling," I say quickly before hanging up.

Knowing he's coming to see what's going on with the magic around here has put my mind at ease. I feel like I could sleep for the first time since getting home.

I shut down the computer and switch off the lights before stretching and heading back into the bedroom. Daisy's still curled up and asleep in bed; she doesn't look like she's moved. I slip out of my clothes and slide onto the bed next to her. Daisy instantly turns to face me and places her hand on my chest as she lifts her head and rests it on my shoulder, giving me a chance to slide my arm underneath her. I pull her closer to me to kiss her head and smell her sweet floral scent.

"Where did you go?" she whispers. I look down at her and smile. I can never sneak out of bed without her knowing.

"I couldn't sleep, but I'm tired now," I whisper into her hair.

"I love you, Mikey." She sighs as she falls back to sleep in my arms.

"I love you too, darling," I reply as I close my eyes and let the sound of her breathing lull me to sleep.

Chapter Thirty-Four

Daisy

"Mikey, a car's pulled up outside," I call down the stairs from the office, where I've been studying all morning.

"Can you get it, darling? It's for you anyway." He calls from somewhere downstairs. I frown to myself as I stand up and walk down the stairs. The car doesn't sound like any of the guys, and Michael hasn't let me answer the door in weeks. Somebody knocks as I reach the door, and I falter for a second before opening it. I've been so nervous and anxious after everything that happened this weekend with the demons.

"It's about time. I'm busting for a pee!" My best friend and coven sister Clare yells as she barges past me into the hallway.

"What the hell are you doing here?" I scream as I grab her and pull her into a hug laughing.

"Your Dom told dad you're being a brat, and we have to come and sort your ass out," Clare calls, laughing as she rushes into the downstairs toilet; I point out to her.

"For the last time, Michael is not my Dom," I call back as I roll my eyes.

"And I never called Daisy a brat," Michael adds as he walks into the hallway, laughing. "But if you want to play that way, I'm more than willing to." He smirks as he slaps my ass, making me squeal.

"Adams, I advise you to stop right there. That's my goddaughter you're talking to." Alex calls as he walks into the house with Sara behind him. I rush to my godmother and throw my arms around her neck as she hugs me tightly. Michael laughs as he shakes Alex's hand before kissing Sara on the cheek.

"Did you find us alright?" Michael asks as he closes the front door; I don't miss him quickly, looking around outside, checking for threats.

"We sure did. Michael, this is a beautiful house." Sara says as she looks around. Michael places an arm around my shoulder and pulls me to him as he looks down, smiling.

"Thank you, we think so," Michael replies. I look around and frown at my extended family.

"Is no one going to answer my question? What are you all doing here?" Alex smiles at me as he answers.

"Michael thinks something magical is happening around here, which is why the demons and others can locate you so easily, but we can't," he explains.

"We also think that something is going on with your magic, so Alex suggested coming up to look into that as well," Michael explains next to me. I look up at him frowning.

"We know it's the shifter gene, right?" I ask. But Michael shakes his head.

"I think it's more than that," Alex chimes in as I turn to look at him.

"Why don't we move this into here, and I'll explain over coffee," Michael says as he shows the others into the lounge. Before I can enter, he pulls me to one side.

"Are you mad at me?" He whispers.

"Why would I be mad?" I ask, frowning.

"I wanted to surprise you, but maybe I should've pre-warned you they were coming," Michael replies nervously. I lift onto my tip toes and kiss him gently.

"You worry too much. Now let's get the coffees sorted so you can fill me in on what you think is going on." I reply as I grab his hand and pull him into the kitchen.

Once we are all sat down, Michael starts to explain.

"Darling, you once told me that you couldn't use your magic when Jackson kidnapped you because he was blocking it."

"Yes, with an anklet," I reply; I turn and look at Alex.

"I remember that. It extended so that when you shifted, it didn't break." Alex says. I nod in agreement.

"Alex, you were the one who worked out how to take it off," Sarah adds. I watch as Alex nods.

"Is there any chance something else could be working as a barrier? Or even as a signal?" Michael asks. As we all look at him, my stomach tightens with worry.

"What do you mean by 'a signal'?" I ask quietly. Michael reaches over and takes my hand off my lap.

"No matter where you are, they always seem to find you. Like when we were down in Cornwall or at the gym. I can't help wondering if there's some kind of beacon or signal they're following." Michael explains, looking from me to Alex, who is nodding at him.

"Couldn't they just be using a tracking spell?" Clare asks, but Alex shakes his head at her.

"No, Daisy can't be tracked like that. Nigel and I have tried many times." Alex answers his daughter before turning to look at me.

"I'm thinking that if they can track you, there may be a way that they can use your magic, too," Michael adds as he holds my hand tightly; as I realise I am tapping my fingers against my thumb like I do when I am anxious.

I look at Alex, "What do you think?" I ask him.

"It's certainly possible. I'll look into it. I could also see if we can work out if something is blocking your magic. You wouldn't let us before, and we never pushed you to do it."

"But now I'm stronger and more cooperative?" I offer with a smile.

"While I wouldn't go as far to say cooperative," Alex replies, smirking, I grab a cushion and throw it at him. He stops it with his magic and sends it flying at Michael too quickly for him to block, so it hits him in the face.

"Hey!" Michael protests as he moves the cushion back beside me. "What was that for?" he asks, laughing.

"For even considering introducing my innocent goddaughter to the dominatrix world," Alex replies. Michael bursts out laughing as I grab the pillow and hide behind it.

"I love the fact that you think she's innocent." Michael laughs as Clare chuckles from her seat.

"What? I am." I protest, turning to Michael, who looks at me with one arched brow.

"Baby, the only innocent thing about you is your name," Michael replies.

"Well, whose fault is that? I was a sweet innocent girl until you corrupted me." I smirk at him. I can see the heat and desire in Michael's eyes.

"Adams, I will warn you to consider how you respond in front of me." We both look at Alex, who's gone into dad mode. Sara's bright red, and Clare's smirking, trying desperately not to laugh aloud.

"Fair enough." Michael chuckles before looking at me with that lopsided grin I love.

"We will finish this later," Michael says down the bond. I look at him, grinning, before responding.

"Yes, we will. In the woods against a tree."

"See? Point proven," Michael replies, smirking. He plants a kiss on my forehead before returning his attention to Alex.

"Anyway. What do you need to do to help tap into Daisy's magic?"

)) ● ((

Half an hour later, Alex and Sara are setting up everything they need in the garden. I'm anxious, so I start folding some washing in the bedroom whilst Clare sits on the chair by the window.

"So, how's it been playing the little housewife?"

"In what universe am I a little housewife? I'm in uni, and Michael does just as much around the house as I do." I point out, frowning at Clare.

"Okay, so what's it like living with a man?" she asks.

"It's the best," I reply, unable to stop myself from grinning.

"And the sex?" Clare asks, wiggling her eyebrows at me.

"Out of this freaking world," I reply, as my grin spreads further.

"God, I need a man." Clare moans, leaning back into the chair, "I've not had any action for months."

"What happened to Lawrence?" I ask, surprised. Clare and Lawrence had been dating for two years; I was sure they'd be together forever.

"He wanted the whole this is it for me no one else ever crap. Who wants that at twenty-three?" Clare declares, scrunching up her face in disgust.

"Hey! I have that at twenty-three, and I couldn't be happier," I point out. Clare looks at me and rolls her eyes.

"That's different, though. You're a wolf now; you mate for life."

"I would be with Mikey, even without the bond," I answer honestly.

"Really? You never wonder what it'd have been like if you were single?" Clare asks, surprised.

"Hell no! I love what Mikey and I have. Although the stress of hiding our relationship wouldn't be missed," I add, shaking my head.

"And the stalkers," Clare adds as I roll my eyes.

"Yeah, they can fuck off, but I'd never be without Mikey. He completes me." I reply, smiling to myself.

"When did you get so cheesy?" Clare moans at me, grinning.

"She learnt from the best," Michael says as he walks into the room. He pulls me into his arms and plants a kiss on my lips.

"Why are you doing the washing? I said I would." He pulls the trousers out of my hands and places them on the bed.

"Because it needs doing. Why are you still here anyway? I thought you were going to meet with Marcus?" I ask as I pick the trousers back up and put them onto the hanger in my hand.

"We're meeting here instead," Michael replies casually as he hangs up a shirt.

"In other words, Stuart was meant to be on guard duty, and now he can't be, so you have to meet here," I add for him. Michael looks at me and shrugs.

"Something along those lines."

"Who's Stuart?" Clare asks, causing Michael and me to turn and look at her.

"Just a team member, he usually watches Daisy, but he's busy at the moment," Michael says as he looks at me quickly. I give him a sad one-sided smile before nodding at Clare.

"Oh wait, isn't he the one who's in love with you, Daisy?" Clare asks. Michael turns from her.

"Yes," Michael growls. I place a hand on his chest before

looking at Clare.

"Leave it, Clare," I warn gently.

"Sorry, but you have to admit it's funny." Clare chuckles as she pulls out her phone.

"It's not," I answer as I turn my back on her and Michael and return to putting the clothes away.

"Are you okay?" I hear Michael asks; I nod, not trusting myself to answer. I feel Michael's arms wrap around me from behind. *"I know you're not, and I get it, darling. You and Stuart are close."* I lean back into him as his arms tighten around my waist.

"I feel terrible. I must have led him on somehow. I didn't mean to," I sigh.

"You didn't, darling. Jon has spoken to him about it all. Stuart said he knew you would never even look at him that way as you love me as much as you do." Michael leans his head to the side and kisses my cheek.

"I hope we can get past all this without it damaging any of our friendships. You and he have been friends longer than him and me." Michael plants a kiss on my cheek again and pulls away from me. I turn in his arms and wrap my arms around his neck.

"You always put others before yourself, don't you?" Michael says as he looks at me softly.

"You do too. It's one of the reasons I love you so much," I reply, smiling.

"Uh, guys, are you doing that weird telepathy thing? Because it's bizarre to see in real life." Clare asks from where she is sitting; I turn and smile at her.

"Yeah, sorry, we sometimes forget," I answer, leaning into Michael.

"Must be a weird thing to get used to."

"I don't know," I reply, smiling at Michael as I step out of his arms. "It can be fun as well as convenient." I send a quick image of myself in nothing but the red bra and thong set I'm wearing. Michael growls as his eyes darken with desire before launching himself at me, tackling me to the bed and causing me to squeal, laughing.

"Convenient for whom?" He growls as he kisses me on the lips before climbing off me.

"I don't even want to know what you just said to him, but I bet it was hot." Clare laughs as she stands up and walks out of the room. "I'll leave you to it, but we'll be ready to start in five minutes, so you don't have much time unless Michael is a two-minute wonder." She calls as she leaves smiling, closing the door behind her. I burst out laughing; Michael looks between us, shocked. He lifts an arm and points to the bedroom door.

"Tell her I'm not a two-minute wonder; tell her right now!" He demands dramatically, which makes me laugh harder. "Darling, tell her right now!" he shouts over my laughter; we hear Clare laughing as she walks down the stairs.

"Thou doth protest too much, Adams," Alex calls up the stairs, which causes me and Clare to lose it completely. Michael grabs my hand and pulls me to my feet.

"Your goddaughter has never had any complaints." He calls out; I hear Alex choking on something and hide my face in Michael's chest as he roars laughing.

"You're going to hell, Adams." Alex calls up the stairs, "and sooner than you expected." He adds as I hear him wandering away from the bottom of the stairs.

"You love winding him up, don't you?" I laugh as I step back from Michael, who shrugs at me, grinning.

"He makes it easy." Michael leans over and kisses me gently on the lips. "Come on, let's get you downstairs and find out what is going on with your magic," Michael whispers as he pulls away from me and takes my hand. I take a deep breath and let him guide me out of the door and downstairs before heading into the garden where Alex and Sara are waiting.

Michael

"What do you think they're doing out there?" Marcus asks as he sits across the table from me, both of us looking out of the patio doors and into the garden from the dining room.

Daisy sits with her legs crossed in the middle of the garden;

her hands pressed into the grass around her. Clare and Sara sat on either side of her facing inward as Alex faces her. Around them are several different burning herbs, candles, crystals, and incense. Alex has been whispering various incantations for the last hour.

"The amount of magic in that garden is unlike anything I've ever experienced before," I admit as Marcus moans in agreement.

"You can feel it deep in your bones. Every hair on my body is standing on end," Marcus replies. I turned to face him, nodding.

"Alex must be one hell of a powerful sorcerer," Marcus adds as he sips his coffee. His words hit home hard.

"Daisy should be even more powerful than him," I sigh. Marcus looks at me wide-eyed as I nod for confirmation.

"Daisy was already the most powerful witch in their coven before she was turned, and she hadn't even fully come into her powers," I add.

"But now she can hardly use them," Marcus sighs. I sigh too, unable to take my eyes off her. "No wonder she resented her wolf as much as she did initially; Jackson really did take everything from her," Marcus adds.

"They believed she would have been the strongest witch in the UK. She was destined to lead the magical council," I explain.

"Do you think that's why he chose her? Why he's so determined to get her back?" Marcus asks.

"If Jackson can unlock her true potential and unlimited powers, he'll have the most powerful luna known to our kind," I answer as Marcus whistles beside me. I take my eyes off my mate and look at him. He is watching her as closely as I have been.

"If Daisy's powers can be unleashed, she'll still be able to return to the coven to lead, won't she? Will you follow her?" Marcus asks, looking at me.

"Daisy doesn't want to lead the coven in Exeter. She doesn't want to leave here. She won't take me away from the pack and you guys."

Marcus looks at me and smirks playfully. "She says it's for you, but she'll miss us the most."

"You would miss her just as much, don't kid yourself." I chuckle. Marcus laughs as he looks out at Daisy; I can't miss the smile he gets when he looks at her. It's a smile I've noticed a few times recently. Daisy is slowly bringing back the Marcus we haven't seen since Michelle was killed.

"Yeah, I've grown quite attached to the little witch." I hear him admit. I laugh and turn to reply when I see Marcus's face drop.

"Mikey, look." He whispers. I turned back to the garden and see a light glowing around Daisy. Alex, Sara, and Clare shield their faces as the wind picks up around them. It's like they're sitting around a tornado, and Daisy's in its eye. We rush for the door. Suddenly Daisy lets out an ear-piercing scream. I throw the doors open and get hit by the force of the wind.

"Alex!" I yell. He's now on his feet, trying to reach Daisy. Clare and Sara have moved away; Marcus and I grab them and rush them to safety before returning to the garden.

"What's happening?" I shout.

"We need to wake her up now!" Alex yells over the noise from the wind. I try to get near Daisy, but a wall of wind surrounds her, and I can't penetrate it.

"Wake up!" I shout as I try and push against it.

"The bond Michael!" Alex shouts behind me. "Try and wake her through the bond!" I reach through it and find it's blasted wide open I can hear her calling out on the other end.

"You have to wake up!" I cry out to her.

"I can't stop it", Daisy yells back.

"Yes, you can. You need to stop and wake up!" I can feel how scared she is. I haven't felt her like this since she was poisoned.

"I can't control it, Mikey; it's too strong."

"Then shift!" I shout before I even realise I'm thinking it. Of course, it makes sense. *"Your wolf will make you stronger! Shift, now!"* I watch, terrified, as Daisy falls forward and shifts into her wolf; my wolf instantly connects with hers. The wind disappears as soon as they connect, and she collapses to the

side. I throw myself beside her and run my fingers through the fur on her head as she whines slightly and leans her head against my leg.

Alex drops beside me and reaches for her. My wolf races to the front as I grab him by the t-shirt collar and pin him to the ground, growling.

"Don't fucking touch her!"

Alex stares at me wide-eyed, holding his hands up in defence.

"What the fuck did you do?" I shout through gritted teeth, trying desperately to stop my wolf from taking complete control in the fear he will kill Alex.

"Somebody has control of Daisy's magic. Just as we regained control, they did that to kick us out." Alex explains calmly. I searched his eyes but can only find fear and sadness. I let go of him and turn back to Daisy, as my wolf stays close to the front, ready to defend her whilst she is weakened.

She's almost asleep, still in her wolf form. I pressed my forehead to hers and inhale her scent.

"Darling, I know you're tired. But you need to shift back. You can rest all you want then." I whispered into her ear. I can tell she's too tired as she whines but doesn't shift or wake up enough to respond properly.

"She's reached full magical exhaustion. We need to give her some energy to help her heal." Sara whispers beside me as she places a hand on my shoulder. My body's still stiff, and my wolf is on full alert.

"Michael, if we don't give her some energy, she'll suffer," Sara adds. I don't look at her as I nod in agreement, too scared to take my eyes off Daisy for fear of something else happening to her.

From the corner of my eye, I see Sara kneel next to me and place a hand on Daisy's chest. She closes her eyes, and I feel the magic building within her. As Sara exhales slowly, a light travels from her chest down her arms and into Daisy. After a few seconds, I watch, amazed, as Daisy shifts slowly back into human form. Clare is beside Daisy instantly and places a blanket over her now-naked body. I place an arm around Sara as she sighs and loses her balance.

"Thank you. Are you okay?" I whisper. Sara looks at me and smiles.

"I will be," she replies as she leans into me slightly.

"I've got her; you take Daisy," Alex says to me as he helps his wife up onto her feet. I lean over and pull Daisy into my arms before standing and carrying her into the house. Marcus is holding the back door open for us.

"Get them anything they need," I say to him, not trusting myself to say more as I pass everyone and head toward the stairs.

Chapter Thirty-Five

Daisy

"Daisy. Daisy, wake up now!" I open my eyes and look around me. I'm lying in an empty space. I sit up and see Kellan.

"What the fuck? Where am I?" I ask, panicking as I jump to my feet.

"Hi, nice to see you too," Kellan replies sarcastically, rolling his eyes. He looks different than when I last saw him. He looks tired and like he has lost weight. His usual short brown hair is hanging limply around his ears.

"Where the hell am I?" I ask again, firmer this time as I storm towards him.

"Don't panic. You're still at Michael's. You're asleep; I had to talk to you." Kellan says as he holds his hands out.

"You're invading my dreams? How?" I demand.

"Look, we don't have much time. You need to listen to me now," Kellan replies, pushing himself straighter as if he'd been leaning against an invisible wall.

"I don't need to listen to anything you have to say! Get out of my head now!" I shout as I stamp my foot.

"Stop being a drama queen and listen. I'm trying to help you!" Kellan sighs.

"Help me?" I laugh sarcastically.

"Yes. What the hell do you think I've been doing?" Kellan yells, throwing his hands up in the air. "Look, stop trying to tap into your magic. It's being dampened for a reason. It's to keep you safe; trust me. As soon as I can, I'm coming to get you. You have to trust me and run with me. Leave everything and everyone."

I stare at Kellan, gobsmacked that after everything, he thinks I will just do as he says. "I'm not going anywhere with you."

"You have to; no one else can keep you as safe as I can," Kellan says as he steps forward.

"Michael can protect me." I point out.

"Adams can't do shit against Jackson! He can't protect you, not like I can," Kellan replies as he takes another step.

"I'm not going anywhere with you, Kellan. Not now, not ever!" I shout, standing my ground.

"If you love Michael and your family and friends, you'll come with me when it's time. It's the only way to save them all." Kellan replies softly.

"Go to hell, Kellan." I hiss back at him, and Kellan's face breaks into a grin.

"Princess, thanks to Jackson, I've been there every day." Kellan stops just in front of me. "Be ready, princess. I'm coming for you soon." He whispers as he kisses my head.

I push him away as I feel two hands grab my shoulder, pinning me to the wall. I fight back, screaming.

"Get off me. Don't touch me!"

"It's me, darling; wake up." I throw my eyes open and look up at Michael leaning over me, pinning me down. As soon as his grip loosens, I throw myself into his arms, wrapping mine around his neck and burying my face into his shoulder as I inhale his scent to calm my racing heart.

"Shh, darling, you're okay. I've got you," Michael whispers as I feel his hand running over my head. I hear the bedroom door open and smell Alex's scent, but I don't turn to face him; I need Michael and his woody pine scent to help me calm down. Michael keeps holding me and reassuring me whilst I breathe into his shoulder.

Slowly Michael pulls away from me as my breathing settles. I realise I'm on our bed in one of Michael's t-shirts.

"Are you okay?" Michael asked quietly as he runs a thumb over my cheek. I slowly nod my head.

"What were you dreaming about that scared you so much?" Michael asks. I open my mouth to tell him, but I freeze.

"I don't remember," I admit, confused. I look to the side and try to recall. "It was important. I hated it and was angry." I look back at Michael. "Why don't I remember?"

"Because it was just a dream, darling. You've been through a lot, and your mind needs to recover as much as your body." Michael whispers into my hair as he plants a kiss on my forehead.

"Daisy, you need to rest longer. Your magic must be at an all-time low." I turned to Alex's voice, frowning.

"I feel fine. My magic is at its normal level," I reply. Alex walks up to me, looking confused.

"That's not possible. Only fifteen minutes ago, you were completely drained. Sara only gave you enough energy to shift back. It should be a full day of rest for your levels to recharge." I can see him assessing me, looking for signs of magical exhaustion.

"How's your head feeling?" Michael asks. I can see the confusion and concern on his face too.

"Honestly, I feel fine," I promise. I turn and look at Alex.

"What happened? Did you say I shifted?" Alex nods. He looks at Michael, who is still watching me closely.

"Michael told you to shift as you lost control. You were in danger of hurting yourself," Alex whispers.

"So, I have been losing control of my magic? That's why I've been feeling so drained at times?" I ask. Alex shakes his head.

"No, it's not that simple." I watch as he takes a deep breath as if composing himself. Alex looks nervously at Michael again.

"No." Michael growls as Alex takes another step towards me but stops in his tracks.

"Michael, I know you're upset, but..." Alex starts but stops as Michael's head snaps up as he glares at my godfather.

"Upset? You almost killed her! I'm not upset, Alex. I'm fucking murderous. I told you, you don't come near her until I say so!" Michael snaps through gritted teeth.

"Mikey, calm down. Alex would never hurt me intentionally. Whatever happened was not his fault." I whisper as I reach for Michael. His eyes are black; and I can feel the power flowing from him as his wolf comes to the surface, trying to push the shift. Michael's jaw is so tight I'm surprised he hasn't cracked a few of his teeth. I turn to Alex and give him a reassuring smile.

"Can you give us a little time, please? We will be

downstairs in a bit." Alex looks at me and nods slowly. He turns around and walks to the bedroom door. He stops but doesn't turn as he closes it.

"I'm sorry I couldn't prevent that, Michael. I love her as if she was my own child." He sighs as the door closes.

As the door clicks closed, it's like something snaps in Michael. He jumps to his feet with absolute murder on his face. The growl that escapes his chest is terrifying. At that moment, I see why every rogue is terrified of Michael Adams, *The* Protector. I jumped to my feet and stand before him with a hand on his chest.

"Mikey, stop," I whisper calmly down the bond.

"How fucking dare he!" Michael bellows. "How can he say he loves you when he nearly killed you!" Michael roars as he tries to take a step towards the door. But I stand my ground, knowing he will never forcibly remove me.

"Mikey, look at me. I'm here, and I'm fine; I'm completely unharmed." I whisper. Michael looks at me, and I see his pain as clear as day in his eyes.

"But once again, you nearly weren't! Once again, I nearly lost you!" I witness the moment everything becomes too much for my strong, unbeatable mate, and he crumbles to the floor, his head in his hands as a roar escapes his lips like none I've heard before. I feel his heartbreak through the bond as mine follows suit. I drop to my knees and throw myself on him, holding him tightly as he crumbles.

All those months of him being my rock, holding me together, running his team, worrying about Jackson and Kellan and what they're planning next all come crashing down on him in one fail swoop.

I wrap my arms around him as he buries his face into my neck; I can feel his shoulders shaking as he cries into mine, holding me tightly against him.

"I nearly lost you again. I can't lose you. I can't," he sobs. I want to tell him that I'm not going anywhere and that I'm safe. But I can't because Jackson has repeatedly proven how determined he is, how hard he's willing to fight to get me back, that he's not giving up.

"Mikey, look at me," I whisper as I pull away from him slightly. I place my hands on his face and look into his tear-soaked eyes. My big macho man looks like a lost child, and I hate it. I hate what all this is doing to him, to us.

"I wish I could promise you that everything will be fine. I wish I could take away all your pain. I would do anything for none of this to be happening to us. But I can't. But I can tell you that every time something has happened to me, every time I've been hurt or scared, you have saved me. Your love and strength have made me fight to come back to you and be strong." I lean over and place a kiss on his cheek. Tasting the salt of his tears on my lips.

"No matter what happens, I will always fight to return to you. I'll never give up on us or our future. Because no matter how bad things are at the moment, no matter how bleak they seem, I can see the most amazing future with you by my side," I whisper.

Michael tries to look away from me, but I move so that I can look back into his eyes.

"Handsome," Michael's face softens as our eyes meet, and I give him a soft smile. "Do you know what I see in our future?" I ask; Michael shakes his head.

"I see us being able to walk around together, no hiding, no sneaking. Just a couple out and about in love." I reached down and take his hand in mine, entwining our fingers. "I see nights out with friends and family with lots of laughter and love." Michael looks up at me, and I see a glimpse of a smile on his face.

"I see you in a long white dress as you walk down an aisle looking like a queen," Michael whispers. I lean over and kiss him.

"What else?" I ask, smiling; Michael places his hand on my stomach.

"Kids. I want to see a baby growing in here, our baby," he whispers.

"Will you still love me when I'm big and fat with a belly that takes up most of the bed?" I ask, unable to stop the giant smile that spreads across my face as Michaels lights up.

"I will love you even more then, than I do now," he replies. Michael's face drops slightly as he places a hand on my cheek before resting his forehead against mine.

"But we need to survive this to get to that, and sometimes I feel like the odds are against us, darling. It's like the gods are showing us all the ways we could be happy just to take it away." I can feel his anger building again.

"Or they are showing us that we can defeat anything thrown at us, together. Together we are unbeatable," I whisper.

"Do you believe that?" Michael asks as I lean away from him, smiling.

"Michael Adams, I believe you and I could take on the world and win. Because we are our strongest together." I declare, looking deep into his now bright blue eyes. His wolf is finally calm enough to retreat back.

"I wish I had your confidence, darling," Michael whispers as he pulls me into his lap and tucks me under his chin.

"Then it's a good job I have enough confidence for the both of us," I whisper.

"What would I do without you?" Michael sighs as he tightens his hold on me. I turn my head to look at him.

"You probably wouldn't be losing so much hair, old man," I reply, grinning, before squealing as Michael starts tickling me.

"Who you calling old man?" he laughs as I squirm out of his reach.

"Hey, you will always be older than me!" I laugh as I watch Michael relax. I crawl back to him and plant a kiss on his lips.

"You go mad when I hide my feelings from you. Don't do the same to me. We are in this together; talk to me," I whisper. Michael plants a kiss on my head and sighs.

"Okay, darling."

"Thank you. Now, do you think you can be around Alex without killing him? Because he does love me. He would never intentionally put me in harm's way," I point out.

"I guess I took more out on him than he deserved." Michael sighs. "I just didn't cope well with you being hurt, again," he admits, holding me tightly against his chest.

"Neither did he," I point out.

"I'll apologise, darling," Michael whispers into my hair.

"Thank you, handsome. You ready to go find out what's going on with me?" I ask cautiously.

"Can I just hold you for a little while? I just want five minutes when it's just me and you and none of this shit."

"That sounds perfect," I reply, smiling as I lean into Michael's chest and allow myself to breathe.

Chapter Thirty-Six

Michael

"Somebody else is controlling my magic?" Daisy asks.

We're all sitting in the lounge. Alex, Sara and Clare are on one sofa, Marcus, Daisy and I on the other.

"That's right; it's almost like they are syphoning it from you to use themselves. Which must be taking some serious magic in itself to do," Alex explains.

"Could you do it?" Marcus asks next to Daisy. Alex shakes his head.

"No, I'm not that powerful. I can do it if touching the person, but I couldn't without that physical contact." I look to my right at Daisy and see her deep in thought.

"What are you thinking?" I asked quietly. I place a hand on her lower back, and she leans into me.

"If they can control my magic, could they control me?" she asks quietly as I run a hand up and down her back, hoping to reassure her. The contact also eases my own anxiety. I hear Alex take a deep breath as he shares a look with his wife, who shrugs at him.

"I honestly don't know. They could find a way to wield your magic through you, maybe. But I don't think they could take control of your mind or body," Alex replies.

"What about entering my dreams?" Daisy asks. I wrap my arm around her waist and pull her tighter against me as I feel her concern through the bond.

"Darling?" I look down so I can see her better. She looks up at me.

"I think it's Kellan," she whispers.

"Why do you think that?" Sara asks, frowning.

"I think I remember that dream from earlier. It was Kellan; he told me to stop trying to tap into my magic. That it was for the best, it was weakened. He said..." Daisy looks away from me mid-sentence and shakes her head.

"What did he say?" I ask, but Daisy doesn't look at me or

answer. I place a finger under her chin and apply pressure until she gives in and looks at me. "What did we agree upstairs. No hiding anything, we promised," I remind her. I watch as Daisy nods slowly.

"He said he was coming for me and would protect me in a way you couldn't." I quickly take a deep breath in an attempt to calm myself. I inhale her scent as I mentally count to ten. I can feel everyone watching me as they wait for me to explode again. When I open my eyes, the first thing I see are Daisy's bright green ones looking back at me. I put all my focus into them as they calm my wolf and me.

"He will not get near you. He'll have to kill me first," I promise her. Daisy smiles and leans her head against my chest as I pull her against me.

"I know; I'm not worried," she whispers as she places a hand over my heart.

"How the hell do you two keep doing this?" Clare yells as she jumps from her seat. I look up as Daisy lifts her head to look at her best friend.

"Because we have to; what other option do we have?" Daisy sighs.

"If you have any suggestions, please share them, as we are running out of ideas on how to end this," I ask, watching Clare, who is clearly on edge herself.

"Can't you turn up there and kill the bastard? You guys are meant to be good at this shit." Clare curses dramatically, throwing her hands up in the air.

"Trust me; if we knew where he was, we would have done that by now. But the prick is always one step ahead of us. The Exeter packs are trying to locate his den, but they're having no luck." Marcus explains from the other side of Daisy. Clare turns to face her dad.

"Can't we do a locator spell or something?"

"We don't have anything of his to use. When we tried on something from Kellan's, nothing worked," Alex sighs.

"What about those clothes he made Daisy wear?" I feel Daisy and Marcus both tense as I do. Daisy reaches over and takes Marcus's hand offering him the same support she needs.

He looks down at her hand before interlocking their fingers as they share their pain.

"We burnt them. They were a reminder none of us needed," Marcus answers quietly. I watch as his eyes flick to the picture of Michelle on the fireplace.

"But why? You could have used them!" Clare demands, obviously frustrated.

"Clare, those clothes were a constant reminder for everyone of what he took four years ago. None of us needed that," Daisy answers. I can see Clare is about to argue when Sara reaches up and takes her daughter's hand.

"Enough. I completely understand why they did, and I'm glad those clothes are no longer in existence," Sara says to her daughter softly.

"So, what now?" Clare asks, the defeat evident in her voice as she sits next to her mum.

"For now, we all call it a night. I don't know about anyone else, but I'm exhausted, and there's nothing else we can do at this hour," Alex says, stretching as he stands from his spot.

"I'll go get the last of our bits into the car," Sara says as she stands. She looks down at her daughter, "you can help me." Clare rolls her eyes as she stands back up.

"But some of its heavy," she moans.

"Good job I'm here then," Marcus says, smiling as he too, stands, letting go of Daisy's hand. The three of them leave, giving Daisy, Alex, and I a chance to speak. I quickly look up at Alex and feel Daisy move away from me slightly so I can stand up.

"Alex, before you go, I want to apologise for my outburst earlier. I think you can gather I'm stressed, but that's still no excuse for questioning your love for Daisy, and I'm sorry for implying that you didn't have her best interest at heart or that you would purposely harm her."

"Thank you, Michael, but you didn't need to apologise. I'll never know how it's taken you this long to snap. You've shown such unbelievable strength and self-control through all of this," Alex says as he looks at Daisy, who is now standing next to me. "You both have," he adds, smiling at her softly.

"One of us always seems to have the other's back," I reply as I put an arm around her shoulders and look down at her, smiling.

"That's the way it should be. How you are with each other is why Nigel and I have been so relaxed about your relationship and how fast it's moved. I don't think I'd be so calm if it were Clare. She needs a lot more looking after than you, Daisy," Alex laughs.

"I don't know; she's stressed me out a fair bit this last week," I laugh as Daisy backhands my chest. I look at her with a raised eyebrow. "Do I need to remind you about the back window?" Daisy looks up at me sheepishly.

"No, handsome."

"I thought not," I smile at her, my heart full of love for this remarkable woman.

"Dad! Mum wants to go; she's tired," we hear Clare call from outside.

"Clare! Your father is talking. I said I could wait!" Sara calls to her daughter.

"I can't. I'm knackered," Clare calls back to her mum.

"I think that's my cue to leave," Alex laughs. Daisy walks straight into his arms; Alex holds his goddaughter tightly.

"I don't know what I'd have done if Michael hadn't gotten through to you earlier," Alex admits as he holds Daisy close.

"Luckily, we don't need to find out," I say as Daisy steps away from Alex, and I shake his hand before putting an arm back around Daisy's shoulders as she places one of hers around my back. We follow Alex to the front door, where Marcus is already waiting.

"Mind if I shoot? I'm beat after today. Jon will be home soon," he asks. I nod in return.

"Yeah, I've seen enough of your face for one day," I laugh as Marcus flips me off.

"Breakfast here first thing," Daisy calls to her family.

"Sounds good to us," Alex shouts back.

"Yes, you too, Marcus. I know you can't say no to a free cooked breakfast," Daisy laughs; Marcus leans in and kisses her cheek, smiling.

"This is why I'm glad you keep surviving shit," he winks at her before jogging to his car. "Lock up and get some sleep, the pair of you," Marcus calls as he drives off, followed by Alex and his tribe as they head to the pack house.

"Sleep sounds like a good idea. I'm beat." I groan as I close the door. I turn to find Daisy looking at me with a devious grin. "What you got in mind, baby?" I ask as I take a step towards her, grinning. Daisy looks at me, smirking.

"Well, we have the house to ourselves for a while. No one's here to hear us for a change," she points out. Without taking my eyes off her, I pull my phone out of my pocket and make a quick call.

"Hey, Jonny, stay out another hour at least," I hang up before I hear his reply and smirk at Daisy. "You have an hour. We can do a lot in that time." I take another step towards her. Daisy's face lights up as she answers.

"There are thirty lots of two minutes in an hour." I freeze as I remember her and Clare teasing me earlier.

"Oh, baby, I'm going to show you how many times I can make you scream in that time," I growl as I spring towards her. Daisy rushes up the stairs squealing with laughter, as I chase her into our room.

Chapter Thirty-Seven

Stuart

These have possibly been the most challenging four days of my life. Even with Jon coming around daily to check in on me, I've never felt so lonely or distant from everyone. The only other person who contacts me is Marcus, and when he does, it is to bark orders at me. Will hasn't made contact, and obviously, neither have Daisy or Michael. I miss everyone, and as much as I know I shouldn't, I miss Daisy most of all.

How did things become such a mess? Why can't I see what the relationship Daisy and I have is: a very close friendship. She is my best friend, and I miss speaking to her and hanging out with her. I know even without the romantic feelings I have for her, she will always be my closest friend, as I can talk to her about things I can't tell the others.

As much as the guys don't treat me any differently than each other, I still sometimes feel like the odd one out as they all grew up together, in the same year at school and have been friends since birth.

I didn't grow up with that connection to them. My older brother Owen did, and it's because of him I'm on the team. I replaced him when he left to be with his mate Todd in Manchester. Even though I've known the guys my whole life, I was always the outsider, even if they didn't mean to treat me that way.

But since Daisy came along, I have felt more like I belong, and I have had someone to talk to when the guys start reminiscing. It's been easier to be part of the team. But now that's gone, and I've never felt less a member than I do now.

Jon called a while ago, and I could hear everyone in the background laughing and joking. Daisy's godparents are visiting with their daughter, and Daisy's cooking everyone breakfast. It's hard knowing they are all there and I'm not. They're my family, and I've not spent this much time away from them since joining the team three years ago.

I'm currently on the way to a pack house where the Alpha wants me to redecorate one of the rooms and build a new chest of drawers. He removed the other ones yesterday before Daisy's family arrived after realising they were severely damaged.

I'm glad for the distraction and something to do with my hands for a change. I haven't been able to draw since the weekend. The only thing I seem to want to draw is Daisy or things that remind me of her. So I've stopped altogether. I've also burnt most of my sketchbooks. Michael was right; they were all for Daisy in some form. It seemed disrespectful to them both to keep them, as well as a reminder of the time Daisy and I have spent together.

My heart has felt heavy since I walked out of their house on Saturday. Everything is trying to pull me back there, to Daisy. I hate that I feel this way; it hurts so much and disrespects Michael. I always knew it would end in heartache but knowing that she's in danger and I'm not there to help protect her makes it worse. I want my family back, and I'll do all I can to succeed.

I pull up outside the pack house and climb out of the car. The Alpha had called Daisy's godfather and checked that they'd finished with the property and that it was okay for me to go in there. The Alpha has said any of Daisy's family and coven can use the premises whenever they visit, whilst Jon's staying at the house for extra protection. I know this will make Daisy happy as she misses her family a lot. Her godparents and coven sister visiting will cheer her up and give her the distraction she needs.

I walk into the house and instantly know somebody has been cleaning. Cleaning products cancel out nearly all other smells for wolves. Especially me, as my sense of smell is stronger than most. I quickly rush around the small lounge and conjoined kitchen and open the windows and back doors to try and get some of the smell out. If I'm going to be here for a while, I need to eliminate the smell of bleach. I walk out of the house to get my tool kit whilst the house airs.

Opening up the boot, I see one of Daisy's hoodies that she

left the other week. I keep meaning to give it to Jon so he can return it to her, but part of me doesn't want to let it go. I sigh as I try and ignore it and the ache in my heart as I pull out what I need.

Walking back into the house, I feel sick with how much I miss Daisy. Why is this so hard? My heart is broken, and I feel heavy with grief. I walk to the back room where the Alpha has asked me to decorate. I place my hand on the door and sigh, my shoulders heavy as I head to complete the mundane task he has given me to keep me busy.

I open the door and stop in my tracks. The second the scent in the room hits me, my whole-body freezes; everything I've been worrying about, every concern I've had about never getting over Daisy, evaporates as I zone in on what's in that room.

That scent, why is it so familiar? It's like I have smelt it every day of my life and never noticed until now. It's the perfect mixture of citrus, coconut, and magic. Everything I thought I had lost is in that scent. I'm in a daze as I walk into the bedroom and towards the perfectly made bed. I pick up the pillow and bring it up to my nose before inhaling deeply. My back straightens, and my heart races as my wolf jumps to attention.

"Mine."

Chapter Thirty-Eight

Daisy

It's been such a great morning. Since ten, the house has been filled with the sounds of laughter. Word had gotten around about the breakfast, so Jon and Will joined us. Thank the goddess we have a massive dinner table because having eight mouths to feed, five of which are hungry wolves, requires a lot of food. I have no idea how Mama does this by herself, as I'd have never managed it without Sara and Michael's help.

As we sit around laughing and joking, I can't help but miss the people who should be here but aren't. Stuart and Mama are both missing leaving a big hole in our wolf family. It's been weeks since I persuaded Mama to go and stay with her sister, and by the goddess, we're missing her. Everything seems a little duller without her around. I know Michael's struggling with her absence, even though we speak to her at least once daily.

"Hey Jonny, have you been to see Mum this week?" Michael asks across the table. Jon looks up at him and nods.

"Yeah, last weekend. She's asked me to take her some bits next time I go; any chance you could go and see her and take her what she needs?" Jon asks as he leans back in his chair with a mug of coffee.

"Of course, he can. He'll go in the next couple of days," I pipe up, knowing Jon's trying to get Michael to go so Mama can see that her son's okay for herself.

"You know I can't. I can't risk taking you there and won't leave you here," Michael states, frowning at me. But I know he wants to go and see his mum.

"Why don't you go and see the Silver Moon Pack instead of me? I'll stay with Daisy, and you can pop in and see Mama B on the way back." Marcus suggests as he looks at Michael, who looks up at him and shakes his head.

"I'm not risking being away for any length of time," Michael says, although I can see him considering it.

"Mikey, everything will be fine. Will's going to be here, as you were going to pop into work anyway, and I will be close by. I'll ask Carl to pop over to check the perimeter every couple of hours," Marcus says as he pours himself another coffee. I can see Michael pushing food around on his plate and know he's again conflicted between doing what he wants to do and protecting me. I reach over and take his hand that's resting on the table.

"Mama would love to see you, and I know you want to see her. Will and I will be fine here. Alex has put extra wards around the house, so no one will be able to get to me here now. Take advantage and go see your mum. Even if only for an hour," I whisper; Michael looks at me and smiles slightly.

"If I keep fighting it, will you give up nagging?" I smile at him and shake my head playfully.

"Nope."

"If I were you, Michael, I'd go just for the peace from her." Alex laughs from across the table.

"Hey! How many times? I'm a freaking saint!" I protest; Alex looks at me with arched eyebrows.

"Oh, you are, unless you're tired, hungry, hormonal, sulking, bored or grounded. Did I miss anything, Michael?"

"Only hungover or under pressure with uni work. Other than those, I think you got them all." Michael replies, smirking from his seat. I can hear the others laughing around me as I turn to face my mate.

"Well then, if I'm that bad, there's no reason you wouldn't want to take a break from me and go to see Mama is there? I'm sure your Auntie Sherri would put you up for a couple of nights so you can have a real break from my moods." I stand up from my chair to clear the plates, but I feel a pair of arms go around my waist and pull me to the side, so I'm forced to sit across Michael's knees. I look up at him and see a huge grin on his face.

"You know I can't be away from you. A few hours is my limit, baby." He looks down at me, giving me that half-raised smile that makes my core tighten.

"Only because you can't trust her to behave." Marcus

laughs from across the table. I try to jump off Michael's lap as he laughs at his pack brother, but he tightens his hold on me.

"Also, because I can't stand to be so far away from that fine ass, I got to fuck repeatedly last night," Michael whispers through our bond. I feel my cheeks heating as I recall the amazing sex last night. We sure made the most of having the house to ourselves. I don't even know when Jon came home, and I know he would have heard a fair bit of it.

"Play your cards right, and you can have a replay later," I reply, winking at him.

"Guys, you're doing it again." I turn to see Clare rolling her eyes at me.

"What?" I ask as Michael lets me sit up a bit but won't let me off his lap. His arm protectively around my waist.

"Doing that telepathy thing. It's so weird." Clare groans from her seat.

"They do it all the time. But trust me, it's a lot worse if they discuss what they are thinking, out loud. I should know. I heard it once." Will shudders dramatically next to Clare, who turns and smiles at him.

"Have you noticed how those two have been flirting with each other all morning?" Michael asks. I turn and look at him, smiling. When I look back at Clare, she's deep in conversation with Will, who has an arm over the back of her chair.

"Down, Papa," Michael whispers. I look up and see Alex frowning at Will and Clare. He looks back at Michael and flips him off.

"Fuck off, Adams." He mutters back before shaking his head. Michael laughs and shrugs.

"I could, but then you'd have to take this one back," Michael replies, kissing my cheek.

"Nigel and I have already told you no returns or refunds." Alex chuckles; I roll my eyes at the pair of them and look over at Jon.

"Jonny help me out here, will you?" I stop when I see him frowning at his phone and completely ignoring me. I watch as he types out something, then seems to watch for a reply. His phone vibrates quickly. He reads something and jumps to his feet.

"Will, cover my shift here; some thing's come up," Jon says as he looks from Will to me. "Thanks for breakfast; I'll be back as soon as I deal with this," he adds before walking out and up the stairs to his room. Michael taps my leg for me to move off his lap so he can go and check on his brother, but I shake my head.

"Let me," I whisper as I stand up. Michael takes my hand to stop me.

"If it's Stuart, you can't get involved," Michael whispers. I nod and place a hand on his cheek.

"I know, but I can't ignore it either. He's still my friend." Michael pulls my hand from his cheek and plants a kiss on my palm.

"I know that, baby. But we have to give him space." I nod and kiss Michael on the lips gently.

"I just need to know he's okay," I whisper as I turn and walk past everyone.

As soon as I'm out of the room, I rush up the stairs to Jon's. I knock on the door.

"Come in, Daisy," Jon calls. I walk in and see Jon doing up his boots.

"What's going on? Is it Stuart?" I ask; Jon looks at me softly. I know he understands why I need to know, but he won't want to go against Michael and Marcus. "It's okay. Mikey knows I'm checking on him," Jon nods and sighs before pulling on his other boot.

"I don't know; he just asked me to meet him straight away, and it's important," Jon replies.

"Do you think he's in some sort of trouble?" I ask whilst rubbing my hands together. Jon stands up and walks over to me. He takes my hands in his and smiles.

"Stuart is a big boy, and even with all of this going on, he'd contact Marcus or Mikey if there was any real danger. I'm sure he needs a hand with whatever the Alpha has him doing. He'd hate to think you're worried about him," Jon says softly.

"I know; I just miss him. He's one of my best friends Jon," I admit.

"He misses you too, but don't worry, okay. Everything will work out; I'm sure of it," Jon says as he kisses me on the top of the head and starts playfully pushing me out of the door.

"Now go and enjoy the rest of your morning with your crazy tribe before they head back and see if you can get Mikey to go and visit Mum. She misses you both so much."

"I'm working on it." I laugh as we get to the bottom of the stairs. I turn to tell him to give Stuart my love but have to stop myself. Jon looks at me knowingly.

"He knows, hun," He whispers as he plants a kiss on my cheek and smiles at me before standing up. I notice Jon smile at someone behind me before walking out of the front door.

"Everything alright, Dais?" I turn to see Clare standing behind me. I quickly force a smile onto my face and nod.

"Yep," I reply, as my voice breaks. Clare is beside me in an instant and pulls me into a hug.

"Want to talk about it? Girl to girl?" She whispers as she looks at me, smiling.

"You have no idea how much I miss having female company." I chuckle as I try and hide my tears.

"Then come upstairs and tell me all about it," Clare says before leaning forward and whispering in my ear. "Then you can tell me all about Will, as he's a hottie!" I can't help but laugh, as I knew she would like him.

"Go and talk to Clare; you're right. You need more females around you." I hear Michael whisper through the bond.

"I'll talk to her if you promise to go and see the other pack instead of Marcus, so you can visit Mama."

"You aren't going to stop until I agree, are you?" Michael sighs.

"Nope," I answer firmly.

"Fine, I'll go. But you and Will won't be going anywhere all day. You have to stay here." Michael demands, and I know he means it.

"We will do as we are told. Now shut up unless you want to listen to me talking to Clare?" I respond as I head upstairs with Clare.

"No, thank you. Don't rush. We are all fine here."

"You are the best," I answer, meaning every word.
"Only because you make me so," Michael replies sweetly. He is such a cheese ball.

Chapter Thirty-Nine

Michael

"I can't believe I'm going to say this, but can you drive us back, Jonny? I'm knackered," I sigh as I walk into Auntie Sherri's lounge.

"Why do you always have to comment on my driving?" Jon asks.

"Because you have crashed more cars than anyone I know." I point out as I sit on the sofa next to him.

"Have not!" Jon snaps as he punches my arm.

"Have to!" I reply as I punch him back.

"Not!"

"Pack it in now, boys, before I bang your heads together!" Auntie Sherri snaps before turning to our Mum. "Barbara, do they always argue like this?"

"If they do, it's a wonder you don't escape to here more often."

I look at Jon and frown, "we don't argue."

Jon looks at me, smirking, "not as much as Will and Stuart anyway."

I roll my eyes and shake my head, "no one argues as much as Will and Stuart."

"How is Stuart, Mikey? I haven't heard from him in nearly a week," Mum asks from her spot.

"You'll have to ask Jon. Stuart is keeping away from me for his own good." I answer through gritted teeth as Mum looks with a raised eyebrow.

"Do I even want to ask what he did?" she asks.

"Stuart's in love with Daisy." Jon chuckles next to me. I turn around and punch his arm again, which makes him laugh harder. Mum stares at me, shocked.

"Is he serious?" she asks, sure it's a joke.

"Unfortunately, yes," I answer. Mum looks at my auntie, who's trying not to laugh.

"Is he still breathing?" Auntie Sherri asks. I pinch my lips together as I nod.

"Yes, but he isn't to make contact with either of us for a bit, to give me time to calm down; Marcus is the one giving him orders for now," I reply, leaning back into the sofa.

"That can't be fun for Marcus," Mum sighs.

"Marcus doesn't seem to mind. It's not his mate Stuart's in love with," Jon replies, winking at my auntie Sherri, who laughs again.

"Jonathan, stop winding Mikey up. You wouldn't be so calm if it were your mate." Auntie Sherri points out.

"If it were my mate, he'd be six feet under. It's because Mikey's so calm that I'm winding him up." Jon laughs, then jumps away from me as I swing for him again.

"How is Daisy handling it all? She and Stuart are close." Mum inquires whilst shaking her head at Jon.

"She misses him but doesn't want to lead him on, so she agreed he needs to keep a distance from us for his wellbeing." I sigh, knowing that Daisy does miss him. More than she is willing to admit to me.

"Doesn't mean it's easy for her though, or him," Mum points out.

"I don't care if it's not easy for him. He shouldn't have let his feelings for her influence how he acted when he was supposed to protect her. He fucked up, and she could have been hurt or worse due to it." I add quickly before filling Mum in on what happened with the demons and how close they were to taking Daisy.

"I get why you are annoyed, Mikey, but it doesn't change the fact that Stuart may be struggling right now as well as Daisy." I should have known she'd be the logical one out of us. I also know Mum's right.

"Talking of Stuart, he's not messaged since this morning. Which isn't like him." Jon says as he pulls out his phone.

"I haven't heard from the others either." I pick up my phone from the table in front of us. I look at my messages and realise Will has missed his last check-in. I point it out to Jon, who frowns at me. I haven't heard from Daisy for a couple of hours either.

"Will never misses a check-in," Jon points out. I nod in agreement. I quickly type a message to him, my heart racing.

Michael: Hey, Will. Is everything okay? It's gone three, and not heard from you.

I see straight away the message has been sent but not delivered. I turn my phone around and show Jon. He curses and shows me his; the message he has sent Stuart hasn't delivered either. We both quickly try to call them but to no avail. I try Marcus to be sure, and I can't reach him either.

"Mum, something's wrong. We need to get back," I say as I jump my feet. Jon stands next to me.

"Try Daisy," he says, tapping his head. I quickly tried to open our link but hit a wall.

"Shit, I can't." I grab the car keys and rush to the car. I hear Mum shouting to call her later, so she knows everything's okay.

"I thought I was driving," Jon calls as he jogs after me.

"Not at the speeds I'll be hitting," I call back as I climb into the driver's seat. I pull away from the curb before Jon has even closed his door.

"Why can't we get through to them?" I ask in a panic. Fuck. I knew I shouldn't have left today.

"I don't know. Hopefully, it's just that the signal is down. It happens occasionally," Jon replies.

"That wouldn't block me from being able to contact Daisy, though. Would it?" I point out. Jon looks at me and shakes his head. The worry is evident on his face.

"Shit," I curse aloud.

"That has to be magical, Mikey." I nod in agreement.

"Kellan?" I ask; Jon shrugs. "What if they're draining Daisy again to do this?" I panic.

"Alex gave her those charged crystals. They should stop her from becoming completely drained again." Jon points out in an attempt to reassure me.

Alex and Sarah had spent the other morning charging a

bunch of crystals so that if Daisy felt drained again or needed to use her magic, she could use the charge from them. There's a box full in the house, and I hope it will be enough if she's being drained.

"We still don't know what Kellan is; we also don't know where he is or if he is still working with Jackson," Jon says.

"We shouldn't have come today; I should have stuck with my gut instinct," I curse.

"Neither of us expected anything like this," Jon points out. I turn onto the back road that will take us up the mountain before taking us home. It's a longer route, but others hardly use it, so I can hit my car's top speeds and get home quicker.

"Put your seatbelt on, Jonny. I'm putting my foot down," I tell him; Jon rolls his eyes but does as he's told. As soon as I hear it click, I put my foot to the floor, and my car smoothly jumps from sixty to ninety and then to a hundred.

Usually, I grin like a child when I get to drive like this, but I'm too anxious to enjoy it.

"Mikey, there's still no change; where's your phone?" I reach into my pocket and pull it out. As I hold it out to Jon, I see the studs on the road, but I'm going too fast to miss them.

"Shit Jon!" I shout as I feel the tyres burst. The car shakes, and the wheel turns suddenly as I feel myself losing control of the vehicle; the car swerves to the other side of the road and heads straight for the mountain cliff edge.

Chapter Forty

Daisy

Something's wrong. Will's been on edge for the last couple of hours and won't tell me what's happening. He won't sit still and constantly gets up and looks out the windows. I'm about to call him out on it when I hear a car pull up outside; I recognise it immediately.

"Why is Stuart here?" I ask.

"I'm going to find out. Wait in here." Will demands as he walks out of the room, closing the door behind him. As I hear the front door open, Marcus's car also pulls up. Now I know something's wrong.

I leave the lounge and stop in the hallway.

"What are you doing here?" Will's voice rings out.

"I couldn't get hold of anyone. The protocol is to come here. I'll leave if everything is fine," Stuart replies quietly.

"No, you won't. Something is going on, so guard out here, check the perimeter and shout if anything happens," Marcus barks at him.

"Yes, Marcus," Stuart replies; I can hear the sadness in his voice.

"When was the last time any of you heard from them?" Marcus asks.

"Over two hours ago. Mikey contacted Daisy to say they were heading to their Auntie Sherri's and would shout when they left. I tried to message him and you an update an hour ago, and none of my messages are being delivered," Will explains. I feel my heart racing, and I open the bond to check on Mikey. But as soon as I try to communicate with him, I realise I can't. Something is blocking me.

Panic takes hold, and I rush for the door and throw it open.

"Why can't I contact Mikey?!" I shout as I throw open the door. The three of them are standing on the doorstep, and they all turn to look at me. Stuart quickly steps out of view as Marcus grabs my arm and drags me into the house and Will slams the door shut behind him.

"What have you been told about going outside?" Marcus snaps as I pull my arm from his grasp.

"What's going on?" I demand, not giving a shit about anything other than I can't get ahold of Michael.

I'm about to demand answers when I feel my stomach and chest tighten so much that it causes me to catch my breath; I clasp at my chest and double over with the pain. Marcus and Will are by my side in an instant.

"Daisy, what's happening?" Marcus demands in my ear, and the pain intensifies as a scream escapes my lips. I feel pressure on my chest like something heavy is being pushed against it.

"Fuck." I hear Marcus and Will curse together as someone lifts me into their arms.

"My chest." I gasp as they place me on the sofa. Stuart rushes through the door.

"What's happening?" he asks.

"We don't know; call Edward," Marcus shouts as he helps me out of my hoodie.

"I can't. I'll have to go and get him," Stuart points out.

"Fuck," Will curses again. "Fine, go and bring him back here." I watch Marcus nod to Stuart, who rushes out the door.

"He was just looking for a way to get away from me," I try to joke, but my chest hurts too much to laugh.

"Daisy, what kind of pain is it? Have you felt it before?" Will asks. I go to shake my head but stop myself.

"Yes, it's similar to when I ran off to Cornwall, but worse." Marcus and Will both look at each other.

"You don't think he's hurt, do you?" Will asks Marcus.

"What? Why would he be hurt?" I demand. I can see Marcus looking at Will, signalling with his eyes for him to shut up.

"I'm sure he's fine; as long as you can feel the bond, we know he's alright," Marcus answers, looking at me. I nod, telling myself he's right, but I know he's lying and trying to protect me.

The pain remains the same for around ten minutes when

slowly it starts to ease; by the time Stuart returns with Edward, it's a dull ache in my chest. Edward still examines me and tries to give me something for the pain, but I refuse to take it. I don't want anything else blocking the bond with Michael.

I stand up from the couch and move back over to the window; it's two and a half hours until Michael said he would be home; I'm hoping he will be early as I need to know he is okay.

"Everything will be fine, Dais; you know he's going to walk through that door and be surprised you were so worried," Marcus says as he walks up to me. I nod, not trusting myself to speak. I wrap my arms around myself as a cold wave washes through me. I feel every part of my body tense and go on high alert. I search for the threat, but I don't see anything. Stuart's back outside, and Will and Edward are just talking through what to do if I feel the pain again. I look at Marcus, and he knows something's wrong.

"What is it?" he asks. The panic in his voice makes the others stop and look at us.

"Something's wrong with our mate, I don't like this," my wolf chimes in.

"Mikey's hurt or in danger; I can feel it," I say as I rush to the other side of the room and pick up my phone. There's still no signal.

"Try the bond again," Marcus says as he stands beside me. I try and concentrate on it, but the barrier is still there. I try and try to break through it, but I can't. I look up at Marcus and shake my head.

"Why can't I contact him, Marcus? Why do I feel so much dread and fear? Mikey doesn't fear anything," I reply.

"Except losing you," my wolf answers. But he isn't losing me; I'm losing him! My head whips up, and I look Marcus in the eye. He can see the realisation on my face as clearly as I can see it on his.

"He's in real trouble, Marcus; he needs help; the bond feels weaker somehow," I tell him, feeling it in every fibre of my body; Michael is injured and in a bad way.

"Fuck," Marcus curses as he runs his fingers through his

hair and looks around, lost and confused. He looks at me, and I can see he doesn't know what to do.

"I don't know which way they would have gone; I don't know if they have even left Sherri's. How the fuck am I meant to find them when we have no way of communicating with them?" Marcus yells, looking as lost as I feel.

"Don't you have trackers on the cars?" Edward asks; Marcus turns and looks at him.

"Of course we do, but they aren't working; nothing technical is working. It's like we're all in some anti-tech bubble or something," he snaps.

"Then we take a car each, and we all drive a different route!" I yell at him as I march out of the lounge towards the bowl I keep my keys in. I throw the door open, and someone grabs me, blocking my path. I scream as I look up to find Stuart looking down at me.

"You're not leaving this house," he declares. I push him away and snarl at him.

"Mikey is out there hurt; Jonny must be too. Are you going to tell me I can't go to find them, because I'd like to see you stop me?" I growl. Stuart looks at me, and his eyes fill with sorrow for the briefest moment. He looks down at the floor, and I think he's backed down. I go to walk out of the door when I feel arms around me again, and I'm hoisted up off the floor.

"Put me down Stuart! Now!" I scream as I lash out at him; he throws me over his shoulder and carries me upstairs. I try to fight him, but he's stronger than me.

"What the fuck are you doing?!" Will and I shout at the same time. Stuart walks me to the spare room and throws me on the bed; as I jump up and rush towards him, he steps out of the room and closes the door behind him. I hear the lock turn on the handle.

"Stuart, open this door right now!" I scream as I pound on it.

"I'm sorry, Daisy, but I let Michael down once before, and I won't make the same mistake again; you need to calm down and realise that the only thing Michael will want is to know you're safe," Stuart replies calmly through the door.

"What you going to do, Stuart? Lock the door and keep me in here forever? I don't think so. I've got past you before, and I will get past you again!" I yell as I turn and head straight to the window but as soon as I try to open it, I realise that it's locked somehow. I scream in frustration.

"Alex sealed it magically when he came so that you couldn't climb out of it again," I hear Marcus murmur through the door. I storm up to the door and bang my fist against it.

"Open this fucking door now; I can't leave him out there. I can't leave him on his own!"

"He's not alone; he's with Jon; they are amazing fighters and are prepared for any situation; he'll be fine." But as Marcus says it, the pain in my chest increases again, and the tightening in my gut, I lean against the door.

"He's not fine." I gasp as the pain intensifies and the tears I've held back escape. "He's not fine Marcus. I can feel all of it, he's hurt, and he's scared." I sob as I slide down the door.

"The only reason Mikey would be scared is for you, Daisy. Scared something was happening to you." I scream in frustration and bring my knees up to my chest, which hurts so much. "I know it's hard, but you have to stay here, and out of danger; you have to do it for Mikey," Marcus whispers through the door. From the sound of his voice, he's sitting behind the door at the same level as me.

"Aren't you scared for your brothers?" I ask; I hear Marcus take a deep breath.

"Of course, I am Dais, but I promised Mikey I would protect you no matter what; you're my family as much as he is. Jon is watching him, and I'm watching you. I must put my fear for my brothers to one side and concentrate on you." I lean into my knees and cry uncontrollably. The pain in my chest doesn't worsen. But the fear and panic I'm feeling doesn't subside either. Luckily the bond isn't becoming any weaker; Michael isn't getting worse, whatever has happened. That's got to be a good sign, right?

Chapter Forty-One

Daisy

I sit on the floor until the tears subside. The pain remains, but the feeling of dread has at least weakened. I haven't asked to be let out of the room; I know there's no point; they don't trust me to stay inside. Gods, I don't think I trust myself right now. I can only think about Michael and Jon and worry about how hurt they are, because I know now that Michael's hurt. There's no denying it.

I hear the guys whispering outside the door as they take turns keeping watch and ensuring I don't do anything stupid. At one point, I wander to the window and look out to find Stuart standing in the garden, not taking his eyes off the window. He looks up and offers me an apologetic smile; I know it's for more than just locking me in the room. I try to offer a small one back but fail. Instead, I head over to the bed, where Mama sleeps when she stays with us. I curl up on the covers, and rest my head on the pillows, not knowing what else to do.

Will is currently outside the room, guarding the door. I know this will kill him, not knowing what is going on with his pack brothers. I want to tell him they'll be okay and that they'll be back with us soon, but I'm not convinced either of us would genuinely believe it right now. I close my eyes and try to calm my racing heart. Michael's taught me ways to ease my anxiety, so I try some of those techniques.

I have been at it for about fifteen minutes when I hear footsteps on the stairs; Will shushes whoever it is.

"I think she's sleeping," he whispers; I consider correcting him but decide against it when I hear Marcus's voice.

"It's gone five; they should have been back by now."

"I know," Will sighs, "what do we do?"

"I'm going to send Stuart to the Alpha's and give him an update; I'll ask him to get Carl and Richard from The Crow. We need to start considering a search party," Marcus whispers. The sound of someone sitting down fills the silence.

"I tried shifting, but I couldn't hear anyone, not a single person from the pack. Whatever magic has been cast, it's fucking strong," he adds. I reach down and pull my crystal out of my pocket. I know it's drained of magic. Kellan must be blocking my magic again. Thank goddess, Alex charged these crystals to keep me going. I need another and soon.

"This could all be part of some huge trap; I don't like the idea of us being separated, not when that's what they could be waiting for," Marcus says; I can hear the tension in his voice. He's not in control of this situation, which has thrown him out of his comfort zone.

I slowly turn on the bed to lie on my back, staring at the ceiling. I try to think about what I know about Jackson and what he could be aiming to achieve by separating us all. Of course, the obvious is grabbing me and killing as many of the guys as possible.

"Marcus?" I say quietly, knowing he will hear me just fine.

"You okay, Dais?" he asks softly.

"Go and find them. Please. I know something's wrong. I'll stay in this room, I swear." I feel my voice break as I pull my knees up to my chest and lie on my side again. "Just help them, please," I beg as the tears start again. I hear the door unlock, and Marcus's scent fills the room. I don't look up at him. I continue to cry, curled up in the foetal position.

He sits on the bed and places a hand on my head.

"What can you feel?" he asks; I open my eyes and look up at him through the tears.

"It feels like my chest is being pulled open." I feel him run his hand over my head.

"We will find him, Daisy, I promise." A wolf's howl fills the air as I open my mouth to reply.

"That's Jonny," Will calls from the door as he pushes himself away from the frame and rushes out of view.

"Stay here. It could be a trap," Marcus shouts at me as he jumps off the bed and rushes to the door, I try and get there before he can close it, but he's too quick. I bang on the door as I hear him locking it.

"Marcus, open this door now. Let me out." I scream, but I

know it's falling on deaf ears. I can hear a commotion downstairs, and I stop shouting, hoping to hear what is happening.

"Get him in now," Marcus yells.

"What's happened to him?" Will asks.

"Has he run all the way here?" Stuart adds.

"Jonny, can you shift? Where's Michael?" Marcus asks; my heart stops. Why is Jon here but not Michael? I can hear a wolf crying. It doesn't sound natural for him to be crying out; Jon never moans; he must be in a bad way.

"Jonny shift back; I can't communicate with you if you don't shift," Marcus demands. But all that follows is the sound of Jon's wolf crying out.

"Shift; you may be able to hear him," my wolf points out. But Marcus said he couldn't hear other wolves when he shifted.

"Are you a witch or not?! Shift and cast a spell; see if you can hear Jon." I quickly strip out of my yoga pants and vest top and shift whilst chanting a communication spell. Almost instantly, I can hear him.

"Jon, what's happened?" I demand.

"Daisy, where are you? Are you safe?" Jon asks, panicking. His voice cracks as he moans in pain.

"They've locked me in the spare room. They won't let me out." I hear him chuckle but then hiss in pain again.

"You been causing shit again?"

"Fuck off; I'm an angel. What's happened? Where's Mikey?" I demand, again.

"They knew we were away from here. We were ambushed on the way home. We fought them off, but Mikey was injured. He forced me to run home to get help," Jon explains. *"I'd promised to protect you over him."* I can hear the pain in his voice from having to leave his brother injured and vulnerable.

"Can't you shift back and tell them where he is?" I ask in a panic.

"Too tired. You'll have to tell them for me," he sighs, the tiredness evident in his voice.

"Tell me, Jon, so that I can get him help."

Less than two minutes later, I shift back and start banging on the door whilst pulling my clothes back on.

"I know where Mikey is! Open the door! Marcus, Will, Stuart. Open this fucking door now!" I yell until someone rush's up the stairs.

"I know where he is! You need to get to him now; he is hurt and alone!" I growl as I pound on the door again.

"How do you know where he is?" I hear Marcus ask.

"Jon told me. I found a way to communicate with him. Open up, Marcus."

"You can't rush off after him, Daisy. You need to stay here," he tries to tell me calmly.

"I know! I need to look after Jonny. Mikey needs you now!" I hear more footsteps rushing up the stairs.

"Jon says they were ambushed on the mountain road about an hour from here. They fought some rogues, and Mikey is injured. You need to go now!" I yell.

"I'm going, Daisy, I promise; why didn't Jon drive him back?" Marcus asks.

"The cars totalled, it's..." a sob forms in my throat; I quickly swallow it down, fighting to stay in control. "It's fallen off a cliff or something; Mikey and Jonny were in it." There is silence on the landing as what I'm saying sinks in.

"Is Mikey...?" Marcus can't seem to get the rest of the sentence out.

"He's alive. I can feel him. But you have to go now!" I hear the lock click on the door; I step back as it opens; Marcus is standing in the doorway.

"I'm going, don't do anything stupid." I rush forward and throw my arms around his neck.

"Bring him home. Please," I beg as he holds me tightly.

"I promise." He whispers into my ear. Marcus loosens his hold on me and kisses the top of my head. "I'm taking Stuart; Will is staying with you. I'll try and get word to Edward to come back."

"Go, now!" I shout and start pushing him towards the stairs. We all rush down; Will rushes into the hallway.

"Carl and Richard's place is on the way; go in there and get them to notify Edward before coming here. Daisy and I will see to Jon until they arrive." Marcus nods before he and Stuart rushes out the door. I turn to Will to say something, but Jon's whining from the lounge has me rushing to be by his side.

As soon as I see Jon, my heart skips a beat; he's lying on his side, panting. I can't see his right-hand side, but his left is a mess. Even in his thick caramel fur, I can see blood, leaves and twigs stuck to him. I drop to my knees next to him and run a hand over his head. I press mine to his gently before whispering in his ear.

"I'm no healer, but I can help. Trust me?" Jon lifts his head slightly and licks my face. I can't help but laugh as I wipe off the drool his tongue has left. "I'll take that as a yes." I turn and find Will, pale and sick with worry.

"Will, there's a large first aid box in the main bathroom under the sink. Grab it as well as a bowl of water from the kettle. Make sure to refill it and re-boil it. I have a feeling we are going to need quite a bit." I stare as Will stands there looking at his pack brother as if he has gone into shock.

"Will, now!" I snap. Will looks down at me and shakes his head a little to bring himself around. "I need you to stay with it, Will, I'm terrified too, but they need us to stay calm and focused. Can you do that?" I command. Will nods slowly and takes a deep breath.

"I'm here; sorry, I'm going." He turns around, and I hear him rushing up the stairs to the bathroom. I turn back to Jon and lean my head against his again.

"If I give you some energy, will you be able to shift?" I ask; he huffs and shakes his head. "It won't drain me. I have the crystals from Alex." I can see him thinking about it, then slowly nodding like he isn't happy with the decision.

Gently, I place a hand on Jon's chest and close my eyes. I concentrate on my breathing and keeping calm. Carefully I reach within myself and feel the energy slowly forming in me as if it was a ball of light, starting off the size of a tiny seed and gradually growing. Once I have gathered over half of my energy, I slowly start feeding it from myself through my hand, resting on Jon and into him. The process takes a while but slowly, I feel his heart rate slow down to normal and his breathing as he heals a little. By the time Will returns, Jon is lying on the floor in his human form. He looks up at me, and I can see the worry in his eyes.

"Are you okay?" he asks; I nod and sit back on my heels.

"I'm fine. Tell Will, what you told me." I whisper as I pull myself onto my feet and try to hide that the room is spinning. I wait until I know Will and Jon are deep in conversation before heading to the dining room, where there are a few more charged crystals. I sit at the table, pulling a crystal over before cupping it in my hands and allowing the energy to fill me.

"You overdid it, didn't you?" I hear Will whisper behind me. I turn to him and smile weakly.

"Something has been draining my magic all afternoon. I hadn't realised how much until I was healing Jon." I touch the necklace that Michael had given me as a mating gift. Alex had charged it to ensure I always had something to hand if I needed any energy. It's empty, as are the two crystals I had in my pocket. I place them on the table, pushing them to one side with the crystal I've just emptied.

"Is it that bad?" Will asks; I force a smile.

"I'll be fine; concentrate on Jon. I'll be back in a minute." I hear Will sigh as he moves from the door. "Will?" I whisper as I turn to look at him. Will stops and faces me. "Don't tell him I'm being drained. He may need me to do more for him, and he won't let me if he thinks I'm in danger."

"And are you?" Will asks. I shrug whilst I think of the best way to answer.

"I'll stop if I think I am, I promise." I can see Will wants to argue, but he doesn't have a choice. He needs to allow me to continue doing as I am, especially as we're isolated and have no idea when help will reach us.

I watch Will walk from the dining room and back into the lounge. I hear him telling Jon I'm just upset about Mikey, and I'll be back in a minute. I rest my head on the table and try my hardest to calm my racing heart.

"They'll find him; they will bring him home," my wolf whispers. I feel a tear roll down my face as I try the bond again

to see if I can reach him.

"I love you, Mikey. Please come home."

)) ● ((

What feels like hours later, I hear Marcus's car pull onto the driveway and rush for the door. Will is ahead of me and forces me to wait inside until he knows it's safe. In minutes Marcus and Stuart stumble through the door carrying Michael between them. For a moment, I freeze when I see my unconscious mate, black and blue, covered in mud and dried blood. I snap out of it and switch into calm and collected mode; the freak-out can come later once I know he's safe.

"What's wrong with him?" I ask as I try to see where he's injured. "Get him upstairs and onto the bed; Jon's in his room," I say as I use a spell to help lift Michael before the guys drop him.

"Pack it in. You're going to drain yourself." Marcus growls when he realises what I'm doing.

"Just get him upstairs quickly." I snap back.

"Don't think I won't tell Mikey when he wakes up," Marcus warns as he glares at me; I glare right back.

"Tell him what? That I helped you get him up the stairs before you dropped him? Get a fucking grip Marcus and get him on the bed." I snarl, shaking my head.

"Stop arguing the pair of you, or I will kick you both out," Edward snaps. I turn to him and glare. I would like to see him try and keep me away right now. I turn back to Michael and brush his hair off his face as I take his hand.

"Mikey, can you wake up, handsome? We need to know where you are injured. Please, Mikey." I try to communicate with him through the bond, but I can't hear him even though the way is no longer blocked.

"It's okay, Daisy. I can see what the problem is. Can you grab another bowl and some more towels? We need to clean him up so I can assess everything," Edward says next to me as he places a hand on my shoulder.

"Would be easier if you'd let me heal him," I murmur from our en-suite; Jon has ordered that I can't do any more healing, thanks to Will admitting I was being drained. I hear Edward groan. "Michael, when you wake up, remind me to give you a medal for putting up with her. She's a much better patient than a helper."

"Oh please, old man, you would have never gotten Jon up those stairs without me earlier." I point out as I walk back into the bedroom with the bits Edward had requested. "Plus, you said yourself, I'm great in a crisis. Now sort Mikey out, so I know he's okay." I add a bit of pleading in the last few words as Edward starts working on Michael.

)) ● ((

"Daisy, you need to sleep; it's gone one in the morning. You look exhausted." I hear Marcus sigh from the doorway. I don't look up from my spot on the side of the bed next to Michael's sleeping form.

"I'll sleep when I know Mikey's okay," I whisper as I run my hand over his head for the millionth time.

"Edward said he won't wake until the morning, not with the drugs he's given him. Get some sleep, please." I can hear the frustration in Marcus's voice.

"I'll curl up next to him once I have rechecked on Jonny," I whisper as I climb to my feet, trying desperately to hide that my legs are feeling like jelly.

"You better as you look ill." Marcus sighs as I walk past him and onto the landing. "You've drained all the crystals, haven't you?" He demands, grabbing my arm as I sway on the spot.

"It wasn't just me," I confess. He pulls me into a hug, and I lean against him more than I usually would.

"Check on Jonny quickly, then go to bed. Mikey will kick your ass and then mine if you are still struggling when he wakes up," Marcus whispers as he puts an arm around my waist and leads me into the room where Jon is resting.

Chapter Forty-Two

Kellan

"What the fuck was that?!" Jackson roars as he punches me in the jaw sending me flying. My head bounces off the wall beside me so hard I see stars. I slump to the floor and hide behind my hands, cowering from him.

"The wards around her were too strong! I couldn't keep the blocking spell up and teleport through them all. It would take at least a few hours to break down all those wards, or I need to have more energy than I did today!" I yell, not daring to look at my brother.

"What's the point in keeping you around when your powers are so weak?" Jackson yells.

"They aren't weak, just stretched, you know that. You have me placing the invisibility cloak around this huge premises, the tracking spell on Daisy, and that huge signal blocking spell on the whole pack territory; it was too much, Jackson; I couldn't take down the wards as well. They've been advanced since the demons failed attempt to take her," I answer back, risking a look at my brother. I see the boot flying toward me and attempt to block it, but it still makes contact with my ribs, which crack under the pressure of his foot.

"You are fucking useless, you piece of shit. Give me one good reason why I shouldn't kill you now," Jackson growls.

"Because you need me, you know you do. There's no way you can get her away from them all without me," I point out as I gasp in pain.

"It seems I can't get her even if I have you." He roars as he kicks me again.

"Kicking the shit out of me isn't going to help! You're making me weaker!" I yell back as I heal my ribs before they damage my lung.

"Shut up. Stop whining. I'm trying to come up with a new plan. Again." Jackson curses as he paces around my room.

I watch and think of all the ways I could kill him. It would be so easy, he'd never expect it, but then I'd have to get away from here before his 'pack' realised what I'd done because they're loyal to him. Why I don't know; over half of them are stronger than him.

"I have an idea," I whisper. Jackson huffs and carries on pacing. "No, I do, and I think you'll like it," I add. Jackson doesn't stop, but he signals for me to continue with his hand. I take a deep breath and start talking.

Ten minutes later, I'm alone in my room. Jackson agreed that my suggestion was for the best and left me to heal myself and rest whilst he gets everything ready. Gods, my whole body hurts. Even with the added magic I syphon from Daisy, it's hard to keep up with all Jackson has me doing for him. My magic was close to being drained today. I don't know how Daisy kept going. Every time I'd feel her magic becoming dangerously low, it seemed to refill again. She must have some magical source in her house. I'm guessing the person who tried to tap into her magic has left her ways to recharge.

It's for the best, as recharging her after I drain her is exhausting, especially over this kind of distance. But there's no way I'd allow her to suffer, especially when it's my fault.

The worst was when Jackson got me to assassinate the men that Adams and his team had captured. I had no idea Daisy was already suffering from exhaustion until it was too late. I almost killed her. I recharged her as quickly as possible, but luckily, she had already started the process.

I need to get her away from all of this; we need to escape and get far enough away that I can allow her to have her magic back or at least enough to protect herself. She's much more powerful than she knows, but she'll be an easy target for Jackson with that amount of power, which is why I've been using it for so long. Daisy's safety has always been my priority and always will be. The sooner I can get her away from all these wolves, the sooner she can have the life she deserves with people who love her, for her.

Chapter Forty-Three

Daisy

I wake up to the feeling of someone running their hand over my head. I moan slightly as I open my eyes and am met with the bright blue eyes of Michael.

"Hey darling," He whispers as a smile spreads across his face.

"Hey handsome, how are you feeling? Do you need anything?" I ask as I sit up; Michael grabs my hand and pulls me back towards him.

"Only you. Come back here for two minutes," he says softly. I smile as I lie back down on my side, keeping a little distance between us. Michael frowns at me. "Uhh, what are you doing over there, baby? Come here?" he says playfully. I slowly shake my head, smiling.

"You broke your left arm in two places yesterday. I'm not risking knocking it." Michael looks at me and rolls his eyes. "You can look at me like that all you want Adams, but you were in a mess when the guys finally got you home last night. I'm not risking hurting you." I reach over and cup his cheek in my hand.

"I was so scared; I was sure they wouldn't find you. That something had happened after Jon had left you." I close my eyes before continuing. "I felt it all." I hear Michael gasp as he grabs my hand.

"Oh, baby, please tell me you didn't." I open my eyes and see my pain reflected in his own. I look down as I nod.

"We think I felt the initial crash and when you were attacked. I could feel how scared you were and that you were in pain. I hated not being there. I fought against the guys to get to you, but they wouldn't let me. Stuart locked me in the back bedroom." I look back up at him.

"You were so scared, and there was nothing I could do to help you. What happened that made you so terrified?" I ask.

"I couldn't get to you, darling. I didn't know if you were

safe or not. Every possible outcome was running through my mind. Had they broken down the wards? Had they gotten to you and taken you whilst I was away? Were the guys hurt? I had no idea what was happening here, and it terrified me. I wasn't scared for me, darling; I was terrified for you."

"That's what we kept telling her, but it took her a while to listen." We both turn to see Marcus standing in the doorway. He walks in and sits on the bed beside me, looking over at his brother. "How you feeling?" he asks. Michael smiles at him playfully.

"Like I could still kick your arse."

Marcus looks up at the ceiling and sighs. "Dude, I'd let you so that I knew you were alright. You had us fucking worried there for a while."

"Think we were all worried for a moment. What the hell was happening here? Why couldn't we contact any of you?" Michael asks as he pulls himself up into a seated position. Hissing and groaning as he holds his ribs, which were broken when he was brought home last night. I'm beside him, trying to help, but he manages independently.

"We don't know what happened exactly, but all forms of communication were blocked in a ten-mile radius. We couldn't use phones; we couldn't communicate when we shifted, and Daisy couldn't even reach out to you. There was some powerful magic being used." Marcus explains as Michael looks at him, shocked, and then turns to me.

"Was your magic being used?" he asks; I nod slowly.

"Every one of my crystals has been drained, and my necklace and rings," I explain as Michael places an arm around my shoulders and pulls me to him. I try to keep from leaning into him, but he looks at me with that raised eyebrow.

"I swear to the goddess Andrews, if you fight me one more time, I'll lose my shit. I need you to keep me calm right now." I sigh dramatically and lean against him as gently as possible; I feel Michael bury his nose into my hair as he does whenever he needs to relax.

"How quickly did it drain your crystals?" he asks.

"It took nearly all day," I reply.

"Wouldn't have drained them all if she hadn't insisted on healing, you and Jon with Edward," Marcus adds. I look at him, frowning.

"Snitch," I mutter as I feel Michael's chest vibrate with a low growl.

"I told you never to heal me again."

"What was I meant to do leave you to die? You both had internal injuries that were slowing down your healing," I point out.

"We're wolves. We'd have healed ourselves." Michael snaps, which earns him a look from me.

"In over a week! Edward couldn't speed up your healing himself, and I figured if you came to find out you had to stay in bed for a week, you'd throw a hissy fit and do more damage. Tell me I'm wrong!" I snap as I glare at Michael. Michael stares at me but doesn't say a thing; his jaw clenched tight and his breathing heavy. I smirk at him and shrug whilst sitting back next to him.

"That's what I thought." I look over at Marcus, who's desperately trying not to laugh at his friend.

"How is Jonny?" Michael asks.

"He's good, still resting in his room. He's been up and about, though. No permanent damage. Again, Daisy's magic helped with that." Marcus says, winking at me.

"Not helping the situation," Michael growls. Causing Marcus to roll his eyes.

"Okay, put it this way, if we'd left you to heal in your own time and was attacked, how well do you think that would have gone down? We need you two up and fighting fit. Alex will be here tomorrow to recharge all of Daisy's crystals and completely heal the two of you," Marcus answers. I turn and look at Michael.

"There was no other option. I didn't risk healing either of you completely, as I don't know when my magic will be used again."

"Is everything back to normal now?" Michael asks. Both Marcus and I nod. "That's one thing, at least." He replies he closes his eyes, and falls quickly back to sleep.

Chapter Forty-Four

Michael

I stretch out on the bed and listen to the sound of the shower coming from our bathroom. Knowing Daisy is in there naked and wet from the water is enough to make me forget about my injuries and want to join her. Just as I start to move from where I'm lying, I hear a knock at the door. I consider ignoring it for a moment, but I know I have no choice when the person knocks again.

"Come in." I groan. I watch the door open as my brother sticks his head in, with his eyes tightly closed.

"You both decent?"

I roll my eyes. "Would I have said come in if we weren't?!" I watch Jon chuckle before looking around the room.

"Where's Daisy?" he asks.

"In the shower. What's up?"

Jon walks into the room and stands by the bed as I stand up and stretch again. Feeling all the aches and pains in my back, arms and legs from yesterday's misadventures. I still have a lot of healing to do.

"Stuart's downstairs and wants to speak to you alone before he goes." I look at him with arched brows, but he holds up his hands, signalling for me to wait. "You need to hear what he has to say. He doesn't want to speak to you in front of the others; trust me; it's for the best. Hear him out."

"Jonny, I get why he was here, but what I said still stands. He needs to give us both space. He needs to give *me* space as I'm still pissed with him."

"He knows that, but trust me on this one, please. It will help if you hear him out. It'll take two minutes; then he'll leave and stay away as long as you want. But *please* hear him out first." I look at my brother. It's not like him to get involved in team dramas, and if he's so desperate for me to hear what Stuart has to say, I will.

"Tell him to meet me in the garden in two minutes." I sigh.

"Thank you, Mikey," Jon says before leaving the room. As he leaves, Daisy walks out of the en-suite with a towel wrapped around her whilst drying her long hair with another.

"What was that all about?" she asks as she nods towards the door.

"Stu wants to talk to me about something. You stay up here, and I'll see what it is. Don't come down until I say, please," I whisper as I walk toward her.

"Mikey, this is ridiculous; Stuart had to come here yesterday. Don't give him shit for that."

"I'm not going to. He did the right thing. But everything still stands. I can't just forget that he's in love with you, darling. I'm sorry." I walk over to her and place my finger under her chin, lifting slightly, so she tilts her head and looks into my eyes.

"Call me what you want, but you are mine, and I can't stand the thought of him being near you and fantasising about what you look like naked or what it would be like to make love to you. I'm a patient wolf, baby, but I don't like the idea of another male wanting what's mine." I lean down and kiss her passionately, wrapping my arm around her waist and tugging her so she's pressed tightly against me. I hear her heart begin to race as I pull away from her, grinning.

"I like being the only one who gets to do that," I whisper, smirking as she tries to steady her racing heart.

"You are." She whispers back, smiling.

"Good," I reply before pressing my lips to hers lightly. "Now get dressed, and I'll be back as soon as I find out what Stu wants to talk to me about."

"Okay, handsome," she whispers as she lifts onto her tiptoes and kisses me quickly before walking towards the chest of drawers. I slap her ass as she passes me, making her squeal laughing.

I'm still chuckling as I walk out of the bedroom to find Marcus standing on the landing, waiting for me.

"You really okay speaking to him?" he asks.

"It's fine. I want to thank him anyway. He was the one to stop Daisy from escaping and coming to find me yesterday," I explain. Marcus nods, and I know he understands.

"Okay. I'll go and speak to Daisy and make sure neither of us is earwigging then." He chuckles.

"Knock before you enter; she's getting dressed," I reply as I head towards the stairs.

"And you're the only one who gets to see that," Marcus chuckles, rolling his eyes.

"Hell yeah, I am," I call back, laughing as I walk down the stairs and head to the garden.

As I get to the patio doors, I see Jon and Stuart whispering outside; Stuart's back is turned to me. I take a deep breath and remind myself I can't beat the shit out of him before stepping out into the garden.

"Mikey's here now; just be honest with him," Jon whispers as I approach.

"Be honest about what?" I ask. Stuart turns around to face me; he keeps his head bowed and looks at the floor. "What's so important that you need to speak to me now whilst I'm still healing," I ask, not attempting to keep the frustration out of my voice. Stuart looks up at me, and I see how nervous he is. It instantly gets my back up. If he starts admitting how much he misses Daisy right now, I will likely lose control.

"I need to speak to you about this mess with me and my feelings for Daisy," Stuart blurts out. I feel my jaw clench as I cross my arms over my chest to stop myself from punching him.

"I told you, I don't want to talk about this. I get why you came yesterday, and I thank you for doing as you were told and staying out of the way of Daisy. Also, for keeping her from coming after me. But your orders still stand, and if you think, I'll let you near Daisy whilst you're in love with her..."

"I'm not in love with her anymore." Stuart declares, interrupting me. I stop and frown at him.

"What?"

"I said I'm not in love with her anymore. All my feelings like that for her no longer exist," Stuart blurts out.

"So in six months, you couldn't get over your feelings for her, but a little over a week was fine. Is that what you are telling me?" I ask carefully.

"Well, no, obviously it's more complicated than that," Stuart says, flustered.

"Want to know what I think? I think you figured that I'd believe you and let you start hanging out around here again, and all would be forgotten so you can go back to fantasising about my mate." I growl, taking a step forward.

"I found my mate." Stuart almost yells as he holds his hands up.

I stop and stare at him. "What?"

"I found her, my mate," Stuart says again.

"Who?"

"It's complicated. So, I don't want to say." I watch as Stuart goes back to looking at the floor.

"Stuart, I don't believe you. I'm sorry, but you must tell me if you have," I answer honestly.

"It's Clare," he replies quietly.

"Clare, who?" I ask, frowning.

"Daisy's coven sister, Clare. I smelt her scent at the pack house when the Alpha sent me to change the chest of drawers there, and I just knew." I watch as Stuart turns away, places his hands on his head, and starts pacing.

"I didn't want to say anything as she's messaging Will, and she's planning on coming to see Daisy tomorrow as an excuse to see him as well. I don't know if she will feel the bond because she isn't a wolf. I don't know what to do." Stuart turns and faces me; I'm lost for words. I stand and stare at him.

"The one person I wanted to contact when I realised was you, as you've been here, you know what this feels like. When you met Daisy, you couldn't tell her how you felt as you didn't know if she felt it or understood what the bond was, plus she was your student. But I couldn't contact you as you told me to keep my distance, so I did, and I messaged Jon."

I turn and look at Jon, watching his friend fall apart.

"That's why you ran off from breakfast the other day?" I ask; Jon looks at me and nods.

"Michael, when I smelt her scent, it was like a release button was pushed. All those feelings I had for Daisy just disappeared, and all I could think was I needed to find the person to whom this scent belonged. But then I realised who it was, and I planned to wait until she next came up here. But this morning, I heard Will on the phone with her, and I realised they're kind of dating, and once again, I have feelings for one of my best friend's partners."

"Okay, Stu, calm down," I say as I step towards him with my hands up. All the anger I feel towards him evaporates as I see how cut up he is about everything.

"What if she doesn't feel it, and my one mate doesn't want to be with me?" Stuart asks desperately.

"We don't know what she'll feel yet. Just breathe and take a seat. We will work this out." I say as I point towards the table and chairs. Stuart nods as he pulls out a seat and sits down.

"I'm sorry, Mikey, I really am." He whispers, looking at me.

"I know. This may even explain why you had such strong feelings towards Daisy. She's linked to Clare magically through a sisterhood spell they did when they were kids; maybe that link is what intensified your feelings for her."

"Do you think?" Stuart asks hopefully.

"I do. Have you spoken to Will?" Stuart shakes his head and looks up at me.

"Will won't speak to me unless to give me an order. He hasn't since the whole thing last weekend." I nod as I know Will has struggled with the fact that Stuart never confided in him about his feelings for Daisy. He thought they were closer than that.

"I'm sure if you spoke to him and explained about Clare, he'd step aside and let you see if she does return your feelings," I say, placing a hand on his shoulder.

"I always thought this was meant to be easy, you met your mate, and you lived happily ever after." Stuart sighs as Jon and I both burst out laughing.

"Yeah, didn't we all." I laugh. I look at Stuart, and I don't want to punch him for the first time in just over a week. I feel sorry for him as I remember the first few months of seeing Daisy every day and being unable to hold her or tell her how I felt, watching everything she did from the side-lines. Fuck, it hurt and was so hard. Knowing that my pack brother is going through that now makes everything else seem mute.

"Thank you for listening to me, Mikey. And thank you for not punching me when I'm sure you wanted to," Stuart says, looking at me sheepishly.

"Oh, I wanted to kill you, Stuart; now I'm sure you can understand why," I answer as Stuart nods.

"I guess I do. What should I do?"

"For now, I think you need to go home and rest. Will has already gone, and Marcus is staying here for a few days as we have no idea what yesterday was about. Jackson and Kellan may still attempt to grab Daisy, so Marcus is here to help."

I turn and look at Stuart. "We'll all meet back here for lunch in a couple of days. You can speak to Will and take things from there. For now, I won't say anything to Marcus or Daisy but keep the no texting going with Daisy. I'm not as angry anymore, but I need a little more time before you two go back to being as you were," I explain.

"I get that. Thanks, Michael." Stuart says as he climbs to his feet. "I'm going to shoot off as I'm knackered. Let me know if you need anything." I nod and hold out my hand; Stuart looks down at it before shaking it.

"Thanks, I'll let you know. Take care, Stuart. Daisy's missed you, and I know she'll be so happy for you if this works out."

Jon says he'll walk Stuart to the car and be back in a minute. I watch them walk out of the garden gate and head back inside. Why can't these things ever be easy? I'd never give up what I have with Daisy in a million years, but I do wish life was more straightforward for us, for her. I want to enjoy every second with her without worrying about what's coming around the corner this time to ruin our fun. I take a deep breath and head back into the house. I hope we can have one day where we get to relax and heal after yesterday, as I'm exhausted physically and mentally.

Chapter Forty-Five

Michael

"Any idea what this is about, Marcus?" I watch as he steps away from his car, and we both head towards the Alpha's front door together.

"Not a clue, but he sounded pissed off on the phone." As soon as we get to the front door, it opens, the Alpha's son Joshua stands back to let us in.

"Alright, guys, dad said to go straight to his office. He's on the phone."

"Cheers, Josh. Any idea what's going on?" Marcus asks, but Josh just shrugs his shoulders.

"Your guess is as good as mine. All I'm saying is good luck; he's been yelling for the last half an hour," Josh replies before walking out of sight.

"Here goes nothing," Marcus mutters as he opens Desmond's office door, and we see just how angry our usually calm alpha is.

"You've got a lot on your plate? Fuck that! You're a pack of fifteen wolves! I've got forty-three wolves, a pregnant wife who's due any day, and a pack member whose life is in danger due to your negligence, and I'm still able to pick up on the unwanted attention a rogue is causing in your area. You better have some answers by the time I fucking get there!" The Alpha slams the phone down on the table.

"Shit!" He curses as he leans against his desk breathing heavily. I can see his body shaking as his wolf threatens to take control.

"That didn't sound good. The Exeter pack, I assume?" Marcus states. The Alpha nods his head and signals for us to sit down. From what I know about the Exeter pack, their alpha is completely incompetent. I can gather my alpha will be heading over there, which means he will need us to go with him. But I don't know if I can leave, not with things as they are with Daisy and what we can only assume is the most recent attempt to abduct her.

When Alex arrived yesterday, he confirmed someone had tried to tamper with his wards, but luckily, there seemed to be too many for them to remove altogether. It's hard to believe that some invisible magic was all that stood between Daisy and Jackson and did a better job at protecting her than the physical strength the guys and I rely on.

"How's Daisy, Michael?" Desmond asks.

"Scared. After the crash the other day, she is jumpier than before. She's been struggling to sleep and eat." I watch as Desmond sits down and leans back into his chair.

"I'm going to be frank with you both. There's a chance we've found Jackson's den, but his numbers may have doubled in the last three weeks. We need everyone." I watch as the Alpha sits back up and places his folded hands on the desk, signalling he means business.

"There's been ongoing reports of guys disappearing in and around Exeter. They disappear for a week and then return, acting differently. They then leave their family and friends, telling them not to follow them and that they won't be back." Desmond explains while not taking his eyes off me; I can feel Marcus watching me as well, both waiting for me to explode as the red mist descends through me.

I feel my anger surge as I jump to my feet, my chair toppling behind me; Marcus jumps to his feet to restrain me if he needs to, but I hold my hand out, signalling I'm still in control, for now at least. I start pacing, unable to stay still. My wolf's on edge, ready to take over.

"How many?" I ask as I pace the room, trying my hardest to stay in control and think logically.

"Nine that we know of," the Alpha replies. "The demons had said he already had about fifteen."

"Shit." I hear Marcus curse from his seat.

"Mikey, we have to consider the possibility that there are more." Desmond sighs. I spin around and face my alpha, my blood boiling.

"You think I don't know that, Des? Do you think I'm not fully aware that the bastard who killed my sister, tortured, raped and turned my mate would be turning these guys to outnumber us and take her? What am I meant to do? What if this is some trap to distract us and take Daisy? Am I meant to leave her unprotected here and hope for the best? Our team is good, but it isn't enough to take on that many rogues alone." I turn to start pacing again, but Marcus steps in my way, placing a hand on my shoulder to stop me.

"We aren't on our own with this, Mikey. The Silver Sun pack has offered full assistance, as well as Daisy's coven and the Exeter packs. Call in all the favours you're owed. You've always helped those who need it. Now it's their turn to help you. Accept it," Marcus says calmly as he squeezes my shoulder.

"I'm scared, Marcus. I'm scared of letting her down again and what could happen whilst we are away," I admit.

"That's only natural, Michael. But if we end this now, Daisy will be safe, and you can start living the life you both want. Alex is here to help protect her; let him," Desmond points out. I nod, knowing he's right, but I can't fight the feeling that something will go wrong. I don't like any of this, and neither does my wolf.

))●((

An hour later, I'm heading home to prepare. I've contacted Nigel and given him an update; he's promised the coven is on standby should we need them. I've also called Alex and asked him to come to the Alpha's in two hours for a briefing.

I pull up in Jonny's car outside the house, and instantly Daisy's standing at the door.

"What have I told you about opening the door?" I call as I quickly search for any threat.

"I saw the car," she replies as I approach the door.

"That's not the point, darling, and you know it." I walk through the door and see Jonny standing directly behind her.

"I tried to tell her, but she didn't listen." I pull Daisy into my arms and inhale her scent to calm my racing heart.

"What's happening?" Daisy asks as she wraps her arms around my waist; I know she's picking up on how stressed I am.

"I'll explain everything now," I answer as we walk into the lounge, where I find Will sitting on the sofa.

"What are you doing here?" I ask. He points to the pile of books on the floor.

"I picked up some new books from the library for Daisy."

"Well, good job, as it saves me a phone call," I reply as I sit down on the other sofa. Daisy goes to sit next to me, but I pull her onto my lap; I need to hold her. She seems to realise and doesn't refuse.

"Mikey, you're scaring me. What's happening?" she asks again, looking at me.

"The Exeter pack thinks they've found Jackson's den. It also seems he's been turning guys to increase his pack numbers," I explain, looking at the three of them.

"Shit." Jon curses next to Will as Daisy gasps leaning into my chest.

"How do you know?" Will asks. I quickly update them on the strange behaviour of the guys in and around Exeter. All remaining silent until I have finished. Everyone sits and absorbs the information for a moment afterwards. All knowing what this will mean but not wanting to be the one to say it. Will is the one to break the silence.

"What's the plan?" Will asks as he looks at me.

"We're all heading to Exeter in three hours," I answer.

"Are we going to be enough?" Jon asks. I look at him shaking my head.

"No. Which is why I've called in extra reinforcements. Carl is coming, as are members of other packs. They're meeting us on the way," I explain.

"No," Daisy says from in my arms; I look at her and can see the fear in her eyes.

"I don't have a choice," I say softly as I run my hand down her cheek.

"Yes, you do. Get another pack to deal with them; get them to send their team. It's a trap. I know it is; you can't go." I can hear her heart rate rising, and the tears in her eyes as her breathing quickens.

"She has a point, Mikey. It sounds like a trap," Jon says.

Daisy jumps out of my arms and onto her feet, pointing at my brother.

"See! You can't go. I won't let you."

"Darling, I have to go. Our team is the best. The Silver Sun pack is coming too. It will be okay."

"You are not going. He will kill you!" Daisy screams. I jump up and grab her as a full panic attack hits. Her legs go from underneath her as she crumbles to the floor. I scoop her up into my arms and carry her to the back door. Jon's there in an instant, opening it for me. This isn't the first time he has seen how bad she can get in recent weeks. I look at him and Will and nod, signalling for them to prepare. They know the drill by now; I don't need to tell them what to do. Jon mutters he will go and get Stuart before I walk away from them.

I walk into the garden with Daisy, still hyperventilating and crying in my arms. I sit down on the grass, still wet from the morning dew, and place her between my legs holding her close to me but allowing her room to move. Her back pressed firmly to my front.

"Tell me five things you can smell," I whisper. I feel her shaking in my arms, gasping for breath.

"Mikey." She sobs as she tries to turn in my arms, but I hold her in place even as it rips my heart into pieces.

"Five things, darling," I repeat a little firmer.

"Grass." She says as she gasps for air.

As encouragement, I run a hand over her head and kiss her tear-soaked cheeks.

"Roses."

I tuck a stray section of hair behind her ear and kiss her temple.

"Dew," her breathing is still ragged but easing a little, her body shaking with every gasp for air.

"Two more, darling." I coach softly as I run my hand over her head.

"Pine trees."

I kiss her cheek again.

"You." She whispers. I take her hand and place it on the wet grass. She is still sobbing uncontrollably, the panic still overpowering her.

"Five things you can feel now, baby," I whisper.

"Grass, dew." She lifts her hand and picks up a daisy as her hysterics subside, but tears stream down her face as her heart continues to race.

"Three more, baby. Come on." I kiss her cheek as I wipe the salty water away.

"Petals, leaves." I see her looking around for something else. I take her hand and place it on the one thing I know will calm her quicker than anything.

"Your heart," she whispers, her bottom lip quivers as I hold her hand against my chest

"It's yours, darling. It's always been yours." I whisper as I look into her green eyes.

"I can't let you get hurt because of me." She sobs. I pull her into my arms as she cries into my chest. I feel her reposition herself so that she can hear my heart.

"Count them, baby," I whisper. Daisy sits in my arms, counting each heartbeat through the bond. I hold her, running my hand up and down her back, soothing her as she pulls herself out of the panic attack.

Slowly her voice becomes quieter in my head as her body relaxes.

"*I love you*," I whisper through the bond.

"*I love you too*." She whispers back as we sit silently for a few minutes, trying to calm our aching hearts.

"I understand why you have to go. It doesn't mean I have to like it," Daisy whispers in my arms. I tighten them around her and kiss the top of her head.

"I don't like it either, darling. The last thing I want to do is leave you right now. But this is personal. I hate him for what he did to my sister and you. He has to be stopped. Plus, I want you free of him forever."

"I know." I feel Daisy move and watch as she twists in my arms to face me. She kneels up and places a hand against my cheek. She looks at me with such seriousness my breath catches in my throat.

"Promise me you will come back. If it means letting

someone else kill him, you let them. Please, I need you, Mikey. I need you to come back to me in one piece." I place a hand over hers.

"I promise. Nothing or no one will stop me from returning to you." I wrap my arms around her as I gently kiss her soft lips. What was only meant to be a simple kiss quickly develops into a full deep passionate one. I don't have to think as I pick her up in my arms, and she wraps her legs around my waist as I carry her into the house. Kicking the door closed behind me, I lock it and double-check it, the whole time not allowing her lips to leave mine.

Daisy moves in my arms, and I reluctantly lower her to the ground, breaking the kiss. She steps back and looks around.

"They've left to prepare," I explain. Daisy walks up to me without saying a word and takes the bottom of my T-shirt. Slowly she pulls it off and discards it onto the floor as she looks at my now naked torso. Daisy lifts her hand and presses it against my heart; she starts to run her fingertips over my body, her eyes following them as if storing each centimetre to memory. She takes another step forward, and I feel myself inhale deeply as her lips brush against my chest.

"Baby," I murmur. But she places a finger against my lips.

"No talking, handsome," she replies, looking deep into my eyes. I can see the pain and longing in them. I pull her into my arms and lift her again to carry her around the lounge, past the sofa, and onto the soft rug in front of the fire.

Slowly I lower us down before stripping her of her clothes. As I look down at her completely bare in front of me, and I realise why she needed to look deeply at me. Because as I look at her, I take in every inch of her body, her smooth sun-kissed skin, the colour her nipples go when she's aroused, and every scar on her perfect abdomen left by the bastard Jackson. I take it all in like it's the last time I'll see her. I feel Daisy undoing my jeans and let her help me to remove them. As I lower myself back to her, I let my fingers run over her sex and feel how wet she is already.

"Eager as always, baby," I whisper, smiling softly at her. I can see the longing in her eyes as I move down her body, kissing my way down her stomach across her hips.

"Mikey." She gasps as she tries to pull me back up towards her, but I look up at her as my lips brush against her, tickling her clit with my breath.

"Please, darling, let me taste you." I watch as she nods, and my tongue skims over her swollen clit. Instantly, Daisy relaxes underneath me as she moans. I devour her, licking her, sucking her just the way she likes it. I insert one finger into her, curling it just right, that has her screaming my name. I quickly insert a second to help push her over the edge. I love the taste of her cum on my tongue. I love to lick her clean as she squirms underneath me. But today, it's not enough; I need to be in her. I move up her body and position myself so the tip of my rock-hard cock is at her entrance. As always, I look to Daisy for permission.

"Please, Mikey, I need you." That's all I need as I painfully slowly slide into her. Even after months of making love to her almost daily, I'll never get used to the feeling of her tightness around me.

"Fuck, baby." I groan as she moans my name; her eyes roll to the back of her head.

I start moving in and out of her wanting to take it slow, wanting to savour every inch of her, but it's soon apparent that it's the complete opposite of what we need. I grab Daisy's hands and pin them above her head as she wraps her legs around my waist; together, we move in perfect sync.

Here I can forget everything, as nothing else matters but her and me, here in this moment. The closeness I feel to Daisy as we make love is like nothing I have ever felt before. We really do become one when we are here, like this, lost in each other's touch and love.

I release her hands as she pulls against my hold, and she grabs my back. Her nails digging into my skin, pushing me close to the edge. I can feel her tightening around me as she gets closer to her own climax.

"Come with me, baby. Please." I beg through our bond.

I instantly feel her contract around me, and my name spills from her lips. Her orgasm is my undoing as I instantly follow suit. I pour everything into her as her tightening milk every last drop from me. I roll to the side and pull her into my arms as I bury my face into her neck.

Both of us slick with sweat, and breathless, I hold her close, unable to let her go. Daisy wraps her arms around my chest, pulling me to her.

"Please come home." I hear her whisper as she breathes deeply. The smell of saltwater fills my nose as she starts to cry silently in my arms. I hold her as tightly as possible as I whisper my reply.

"Nothing can keep me from you, baby, nothing."

Chapter Forty-Six

Michael

I'm standing in the Alpha's office with Daisy in my arms, and I don't know if I'll ever be ready to let her go. I know I promised to come back, but there's a real possibility that I won't. Looking around the room, I take in the scene in front of me. My whole team is here, plus the Alpha and his beta Alaric. Alex, Clare and Sara are also here whilst we put our final plans together.

I spot Stuart standing to one side, talking to Jon; I lean down and kiss Daisy on the top of her head.

"I need to speak to Stu, darling. I'll be right back," I whisper as I kiss her gently on the lips before walking away.

"Jon, can you give us a minute, please?" Jon looks at me and nods. I see him wink at Stuart before heading off to stand by Daisy. I've already discussed this with Stuart and told him he isn't coming with us.

"I know you probably think me telling you to stay here is a sign I don't trust you out on the field or that it's a form of punishment. But in fact, it's the complete opposite." Stuart looks up at me, frowning. "I'm leaving you in charge of the most important thing to me. You don't have the experience in large pack fights. But you are outstanding in one-to-one, and I need to know that whoever's watching Daisy can defend her physically in case the wards fail." I explain, desperately trying to ignore the constant feeling in my gut that this is a mistake.

"I would die before I let anyone harm my pack sister and best friend," Stuart says as he looks at me.

"And that's why I need you here because I believe you; you've learnt from your mistakes," I reply.

"It's probably for the best I stay anyway. I'm not sure I could concentrate without knowing what was happening here." I watch as he glances at Clare standing in the corner with her parents. I catch her looking in our direction and quickly looking away again. I can't help wondering if she does, in fact, feel something.

"Have you spoken to anyone about it yet?" I ask; Stuart shakes his head slowly as he glances at Will. "Make sure you do, don't wait as Daisy and I did; life's too short." I squeeze his shoulder gently, "but Stuart, remember to protect them both. I know it'll be hard but remember, I'd do it for you."

"I know you would," Stuart says whilst forcing a smile. "I won't let you down, Michael."

"I know you won't."

I'm about to say more when a loud knocking comes from the front door. We all turn to the sound; Stuart instantly leaves my side and grabs Daisy positioning her behind him. The Alpha steps in front of everyone, Marcus and me joining him. As we approach the door, it swings open with a bang. I'm blinded as the sun pours through the gap for a second.

"I told you they'd started the party without us!" There in front of me is a beautiful blonde woman, six foot four, with pure badass vibes pouring from her, her hands resting on her curvy hips. She screams danger in her tight black jeans, thick black boots, and a t-shirt under a black leather jacket.

"Michael Graham Adams, as if you thought you could leave us out of the fun!" she calls as she walks up to me.

"Natalie? What the fuck are you doing here?" I step forward and pull my old second into a tight hug. I look behind her and see Carl, Richard, and two other ex-teammates. Owen, Stuart's brother, and Luca, my predecessor.

"Carl called. He said it was an all-hands-on-deck job. Did you really not call us yourself? Remind me to kick your ass when all this is done." Owen curses as he pulls me into a one-armed hug. Natalie's face is lit up behind him. I watch her smile fade as she bows to the Alpha who has walked up behind us, as all the newcomers follow suit.

"You came back to help?" the Alpha asks, smiling.

"This is still our pack is it not, Alpha?" Natalie answers with a grin.

"This will always be your home." Desmond steps forward to hug Natalie. As they step back, I see Natalie's face and posture change.

"Jonathan."

I turn to see my brother standing behind us.

"Natalie. It's good to see you." He answers quietly.

She nods before turning back to me.

"Is it true this guy threatening your mate is the same one who killed my best friend?" Natalie asks. I nod, not trusting myself to speak. I watch Natalie take a deep breath to let it sink in and calm herself before looking at me again with a smile. "So where is this amazing mate I've heard so much about?" I turn and nod to Stuart, who lets go of Daisy's arm as he stares at his older brother before heading towards him and pulling him into a hug. Daisy walks up to me and stands by my side, smiling.

"Natalie, this is my mate, Daisy." I watch as Daisy smiles at Natalie whilst leaning into me.

"So you're the one who threw Mikey into the wall in the gym. Girl, you need to train me!" Daisy demands, smiling; Natalie bursts out laughing.

"From what I hear, you can handle yourself just fine when it comes to this lot," Natalie replies, nodding to my team behind me.

"I try my best, but I could be better after some training from you." Daisy shrugs.

"No!" Will and Jon are protesting behind us, which makes me smile as I imagine the havoc Natalie and Daisy could cause together.

"We'll discuss a plan over some wine when all this is over." Natalie winks at Daisy before turning to me, "right, where do you want us? We're at your disposal."

)D●((

Half an hour later, everyone has their assignments. A plan's in place; all three newcomers and Carl will come with the team and me. Richard has gone with the Luna and Joshua, as well as Sara, as she is the coven midwife. Desmond is worried that the stress will bring on labour and wants her to have extra protection. The beta will stay at the Alpha's house to ensure everything's running smoothly. Most importantly, Daisy will be escorted home by Alex and Stuart; with the wards holding up the other day, we decided it was the safest place for her. Clare will also be joining them in the hope of keeping Daisy distracted and from worrying about us. Tony's unfortunately away at his uncle's and won't be at ours until later tonight. At least, if we aren't back, he can help keep Daisy calm.

It's time for us to leave. I see everybody saying goodbye to their partners and family, and I can feel the anxiety in the air. Everybody's worried that somebody won't come home. I see Jon holding Daisy with Will and Marcus to their side. Daisy lets go of Jon and hugs each of the other two.

"Watch each other's backs. You hear me; make sure you all stay safe." She whispers, looking at each of them.

"We promise," they all reply; Marcus leans over and kisses Daisy's forehead.

"You know what to do? You know how to stay safe if you need to?" she nods at him. "Do whatever you need to do; fight or run." He kisses her again and then looks up at me. I nod to them all as they leave my mate and me.

I feel the Alpha beside me as I pull Daisy into my arms; I hold her tightly, pressing my nose into her hair and inhaling her scent. I slowly release my hold of her and move so my forehead rests against hers.

"You listen to me, Daisy Andrews; if anything happens to me, I want you to run." Daisy steps away from me, and I can see the fear and pain in her eyes as I try to push back my own.

"What?"

"You heard me. You run. And you keep running. You take your coven and Stuart, and you hide. Forget the pack, forget uni, run, and keep yourself safe." I watch as Daisy straightens up and turns to Desmond.

"Who leads this pack if anything happens to you?" She asks as my chest tightens. I can hear everyone around us going quiet.

"Michael would. He's the next alpha," Desmond answers.

"And if anything happened to Michael?" I hear her ask.

"Technically, you are the next person with the alpha gene. But you haven't been sworn in; no one would think any less of you if you didn't accept the role. Michael's right. If you feel you need to run, you run." I watch as Daisy's back straightens further. There's the faintest hint of magic in the air.

"Are you saying I'm not fit to lead?" she asks him. I watch a grin creeping onto Desmond's face, and my stomach plummets.

"The complete opposite," he replies.

"Then, if neither of you returns, I will lead this pack. I will not run or hide; I will lead." I grab hold of her shoulders as my hands start to shake; I quickly swallow the bile that fills my throat.

"No, darling, you run." But my strong-headed mate turns to me and smiles.

"Would you run?" My stomach clenches.

"It's not the same," I reply, shaking my head.

"Isn't it?" Daisy asks with arched brows.

"No, I've been training since I was sixteen for the role of alpha. You've had none, plus Jackson will come for you." I watch as she looks at Desmond, who nods once at her. As if it's all the reassurance she needs, she stands to her full height, her head held high, her shoulders back, and the room fills with magic.

"This is my pack, my family, and if I'm next to lead, then goddess be damned, I'll lead, and I will ensure the safety of every wolf in my family. If Jackson manages to hurt a single one of you, the Gods help him when he faces me," she declares. Desmond places his hand on his heart and one on Daisy's cheek.

"I have never been prouder to call somebody my pack daughter," Desmond declares. Daisy smiles at him as she steps back, and her voice raises a little more to address the whole room filled with many of our loved ones who are here, ready to defend my mate and our pack.

"This whole conversation will be mute anyway as you are all coming home." She looks around the room, and I watch as every single wolf stands taller and nods to Daisy.

"Yes, ma'am." Her eyes settle on me, and I step forward again, resting my forehead against hers.

"Remember your promise," she whispers with her eyes closed. I close mine as I breathe in her scent one last time and pull her into my arms.

"I will come home to you," I whisper in return. Daisy lifts her head slightly and brushes her lips against mine gently.

"You better. Because I will track you down and drag your ass back even if I have to kick down the pearly gates or the gates of hell to do it, is that understood, Adams?" I smile proudly at her.

"Yes, ma'am."

"I love you," Daisy whispers as she pulls me against her again.

"I love you more," I reply, holding her tightly. I place a kiss on her head and step out of her arms. "I promise," I mouth once more before turning and walking away. Every step killing me; every step away from her feels like a mile. But I know everything I'm doing right now is to protect her, to give us the life we so desperately dream of.

"Fallout," I call as everybody heads out of the building with me. I can't bring myself to look back at Daisy because I know I'll crumble if I see a single tear fall from her eyes. I have to do this and be the leader and mate she deserves; her protector.

I feel somebody nudge me with their shoulder.

"Get it out of your system Nat." I sigh.

"What? All I was going to say is I like her." I look at Natalie and can't help smiling,

"Everybody does," I reply.

"Well, when this is over, I'm going to make that girl my new best friend, and I'm going to corrupt her." Natalie declares proudly. I laugh as I push her away from me and towards a car.

"If we all make it through this, I look forward to watching you try." I wink; Natalie laughs at me as she jumps to the car next to Jon's, which I'm driving and pulls Will out of the driving seat, pointing to me.

"You go with him. I'm driving this one, asshole." Will looks put out until he sees Jon sitting in the passenger seat of his car. Natalie blows Will a kiss as she pulls out of the parking space. Carl, Owen and Luca are all in the car with her.

"But that's my car!" Will protests. I look at him and laugh, nodding towards the back seat.

"Come on, let's go and get this over and done with."

Will jumps into the back of the car as I pull away from Daisy and towards one of the biggest fights of my life.

Chapter Forty-Seven

Michael

We're minutes from taking the den, and my heart is pounding. But not in the way I thought it would be.

"Michael, everybody's in place. Nat's reporting no signs of life at the back. Will says the same at the left entrance," Marcus whispers down the earpiece. I look up at the front entrance and see two guys outside it. Neither pays any attention to what's going on around them.

"Two guys at the front. They have no idea we're here or what they're doing," I reply before looking to Jon, who is crouched down beside me.

"What are you thinking, Mikey?" Jon whispers. I shake my head and look up at the building again. For something so big with so many scents surrounding it, it's too quiet.

"I don't like this, Marcus. Something doesn't feel right," I say quietly, and not for the first time.

"It's too quiet," I hear Natalie whisper through the earpiece.

"Agreed. If I didn't know better, I'd say this building's empty," Marcus adds. I hear Jon curse next to me. I look around again and realise I need to get closer and see inside.

"Will? How accessible is the basement?" I ask.

"No padlock or keyhole visible. It's old, and hinges are rusted, so it could be accessed even if locked on the inside," he whispers.

"But it may be noisy," Natalie points out. "There's a window here I could easily fit through," she adds. I can hear the longing for action in her voice.

"How much training have you been doing?" I ask; I can feel the tension radiating from Jon but ignore it.

"Please, I could still kick your ass, Adams," Natalie replies. I can hear the challenge in her voice.

"Okay, go. I want radio silence from everyone but Natalie. Nat, you know what to do," I order.

"On it, boss." I hear her pulling off her leather jacket; she must hand it to someone as I hear her threatening them. "Anything happens to that jacket; it won't just be rogues dying here today. Good boy."

"Natalie, focus. Get in, look around, get out. No heroics." Jon snaps next to me. I turn and stare at him with a raised eyebrow.

"Who died and made you my keeper, arsewipe?" Natalie growls as I hear Will and Marcus chuckle.

"Do your thing, Natalie, and be careful." I snap before adding quickly, "complete radio silence from now. Natalie, you go silent for longer than three minutes, and I'm sending Jon in."

"Fuck, boss. I used to like you. I'm going in." I take a deep breath and pray to the goddess to look after her.

For a few moments, I hear Natalie moving and cursing quietly as she slides through the window. Suddenly there's a loud thud, and Natalie curses through gritted teeth.

"Nat?" I whisper.

"I'm fine; got to lay off the wine, though. My hips are bigger than they used to be." I roll my eyes, shaking my head. I glance at Jon, who looks as stressed as me.

"All quiet down here, heading to the hallway," Natalie whispers. The only sound I can hear is the occasional creak of floorboards or rustle of her jeans. It's still far too quiet.

"Found a door. Going to look inside as there's a peephole." There's silence for a moment before I hear Natalie curse again.

"Nat? Are you okay?" I ask.

"I am, but this prick won't be when I get hold of him. I found a holding cell; I'm guessing it's for Daisy," Nat replies; I hear Jon growl next to me.

"Don't tell me yet, Nat," I reply. I know if I hear what's in there, I won't be able to keep control of my wolf, who's already begging to rush the building and find Jackson.

"I'm going up a level. But I have a feeling that I'm not going to find anything. It's far too quiet, Mikey," Natalie whispers. Radio silence commences for a while. Other than the occasional creaking of a door being open, there's no other sound. I'm about to tell Natalie to call it quits when I hear Jon curse.

"What the fuck?"

I turned to look in the direction he's staring and see Natalie skip out of the front door between the two guys.

"Hey guys, where's the party at?" she smiles. Both guys look at Natalie in shock before she punches one, turns on the other, and kicks him to the floor.

"Natalie. I'm sure we're taught not to kill the informants." Marcus curses as he jogs up next to her.

"The building's empty. No sign of life other than these arseholes." Natalie calls out for all of us to hear.

"We've been set up." Jon curses next to me.

"Get them in the van and get back to ours now!" I bark as I turn my back to everyone and rush to the car. Opening the link to Daisy as I run.

"Baby? It was a diversion. They're coming for you!" I shout down the link.

Her voice makes me stop in my tracks; as she answers calmly.

"I know, handsome."

Daisy

I look around me, and my insides freeze. Clare is in Jackson's arms as he holds her at knifepoint in my front garden; Kellan stands next to him. Stuart's on the ground to my left, bleeding and with more broken bones than I wish to count after being attacked again and again by Kellan's magic. The only thing that stopped him was when they got hold of Clare.

"Get your fucking hands off, my MATE." Stuart roars. Alex, who has had his magic drained to the point of exhaustion, stares at him dumbfounded from the floor. I look between Stuart and Clare, and my heart breaks for my mate. As if he knows, I feel the bond opening.

"Baby? It was a diversion. They're coming for you!" I can hear the panic in Michael's voice, and tears fill my eyes as I look

at the scene in front of me.

"Stop! Everyone stop!" I scream. Everyone turns and looks at me.

"I know, handsome," I reply calmly.

"What? Run, run now!" Michael demands.

"It's too late. I'm sorry."

"What? What do you mean? Run!"

"I can't. They're here and have Clare."

"Let her go, and I'll go with you," I call out, looking at Jackson, I can hear Stuart and Alex shouting behind me, but I use what little power I have left to freeze them in place.

"Don't you fucking dare, Daisy!" Alex screams behind me, but when I look at him, I can see a dad about to lose his only child; a goddaughter is better than a blood one.

"Darling, don't," Michael begs through the bond. I can hear the desperation in his voice.

"I'm sorry, Mikey. I love you so much; remember that," I whisper, hoping he can't hear the pain in my heart.

"I will find you!" I can hear and feel his pain as he roars, but I shut the bond down completely; he doesn't need to feel the fear that courses through me.

I walk up to Jackson and stand before him as he looks triumphant.

"Let Clare go unharmed, and I'll come with you; I won't fight." I can feel the tension pouring from Kellan, but I daren't look at him. I look at the knife in Jackson's hand and watch it move slightly from Clare's side.

"You have made the right choice," he says, grinning. He pushes Clare away from him as he grabs me instead. He holds the knife to my throat; I watch as Stuart rushes to Clare's side and pulls her behind him, protecting his mate.

"You won't get far with her. You're a dead man walking," Stuart snarls. Jackson laughs as Alex reaches his daughter and holds her as she cries into his shoulder whilst holding on to Stuart's shirt. Keeping hold of him to make sure he doesn't leave her.

I look at the few members of my family and whisper, "I love you." All three look heartbroken as they look back at me.

Stuart somehow manages to take a step forward, but Kellan blasts him with another spell, and Stuart crumbles to his knees, his broken leg finally giving out on him.

"If you want to take me, just go," I shout, knowing Stuart will keep fighting until they kill him. I won't let him die for me.

I feel Jackson's hand slide over my stomach as he holds me close to him. His touch makes my skin crawl. I may be leaving willingly with him, but he will *never* touch me again, and I swear that to every god and goddess of this world.

"Take it, and then we leave." I hear Jackson say. I frown, wondering what he means, until I feel another hand grab the necklace around my neck, the one Michael gave me as a mating gift. They pull it, and I watch it fall to the ground as the world turns black, and my stomach drops as my family disappears.

Chapter Forty-Eight

Clare

Dad and I help Stuart lie on the spare room bed; he's covered in cuts and bruises. I quickly assess his injuries and realise one side of his body has taken a beating. His left arm and leg seem broken, plus a few ribs. My heart aches from seeing him in so much pain.

"Are you sure you aren't hurt?" Stuart asks as he looks up at me; I nod before answering.

"I'm fine, physically at least," I answer as I try to pull up some power to help heal him, but I'm running on empty. I turn to my Dad, who's standing by the door in shock.

"Dad, can you help him at all? I'm drained," I whisper; my Dad looks from me to Stuart before shaking his head.

"No. I'm drained too, sorry."

"It's fine; I heal quickly. I need to call Edward to get him to help me speed things up," Stuart says, wincing in pain as he pulls his phone out of his pocket. I go to help him, but he looks at my Dad and then at me and shakes his head.

"Clare, let's leave Stuart to make this call, and we'll check in with your mum and others," my Dad says as he walks to the door.

"I'm staying with Stuart," I reply as I turn my back to Dad.

"No, go with your Dad. I'm fine," Stuart says, smiling, which causes his split lip to reopen.

"I'll be back in a minute," I say as I walk out of the room and close the door.

"What's your problem?" I snap as I storm past him and into Michael's office. Dad stands on the landing looking at me; I beckon him with my hand, rolling my eyes. As soon as he's in the room, I close the door.

"So?" I ask.

"My problem is I've just watched my goddaughter being taken from me by a fucking wolf; I'm not about to lose you too." He snaps. "You are too young to be 'mated' to that boy;

you don't even know him."

"And you do? What's the difference between Daisy finding her mate and me finding mine?" I ask, raising my eyebrows for emphasis.

"I have no say in Daisy's life; I do yours. You're not being mated to a guy who was in love with Daisy a week ago." I stand in front of my Dad and stare at him.

"You've lost a goddaughter, and I've lost my oldest friend, who's like a sister to me. I'm not interested in completing the bond or whatever they do; there are more important things on my mind, like finding Daisy and bringing her home in one piece before he breaks her again. But I know that's not going to happen in the space of a day, Dad, and right now, I need someone, and I feel deep in my heart that Stuart is the one who can help me handle all of this." I look at my Dad as the tears spill from my eyes and the adrenaline wears off.

"I can't lose her, Dad; I can't lose my best friend again. And as much as you and Mum will try to be there to help me through this, I know Nigel and Mary will need you more. So please don't give me a hard time if I turn to Stuart for support or try to support him, as it feels like the most natural thing to do." I watch Dad's face soften before he pulls me into his arms. As soon as I lean into him, I feel the floodgates open, and I start crying; my Dad's arms tighten around me.

"I'm sorry I couldn't stop all of this. I let you both down, sweetheart." My Dad whispers into my hair; I shake my head and pull away.

"No, you didn't; we had no idea what we were up against. I didn't even know what he did was possible." I whisper as I wipe my face trying to brush away the tears. My Dad reaches out and wipes my cheek.

"Me neither. I've never felt so weak." My Dad sighs. My Dad is among the most powerful sorcerers; he has never known life without magic. To find himself powerless like that would have been hard for him.

"I promise I will stop giving you a hard time about all this mate business, but please take your time with it all. I don't want you jumping in because you need the distraction or getting caught up in it because it worked out so well for Dais..." I feel my Dad's arms tighten around me again as he struggles to hold it together.

"She will be okay, Dad. She's much stronger this time," I whisper; I don't know who I'm trying to convince more, him or me.

"Gods, I hope so, sweetheart, I really do." He sighs. "Take it slow with Stuart, okay. Like really slow."

"I'm not an idiot," I sigh. My Dad laughs and kisses the top of my head.

"I know, just hard-headed like your mother." He lets out a deep sigh and pulls out his phone. "Talking of which, I need to call her. She's going to be devastated."

"Want me to call Mum? So you can call Nigel and Mary," I offer, but Dad shakes his head.

"No, I'll do both; you go back and check on *your mate*." As I slap his chest, he rolls his eyes and gives me a small smile.

"You will always be my number one guy," I whisper, smiling, through the silent tears still flowing.

"Oh, I know I will be; that position isn't up for grabs." My Dad pulls me in for one last hug. "Go check on Stuart, and I'll get these calls done. I'll try and get some order to things downstairs before Michael gets back. This is going to kill the poor guy," he says as he rubs the back of his neck.

"We will get her back, Dad. I know we will. The wolves will find her quicker than we could." I can't imagine how Daisy would cope if she were there for five months like last time.

"Michael won't stop until he does. I know that much," he whispers as he walks past me and out the door.

I watch as my Dad walks down the stairs, looking for some privacy to make these calls. I don't envy him as I don't even want to think about how everyone will take the news.

I walk back to the room where we placed Stuart, take a deep breath, and wipe my face before returning. I don't know why I bothered because Stuart looks at me as soon as I open the door, and I know he's aware I've been crying.

"What's happened? Are you okay?" he asks; I shake my head and walk over to the bed. Stuart tries to sit up, but I quickly grab his good shoulder to stop him.

"Please don't hurt yourself further. Did you call the healer?" I ask as I kneel on the floor by the head of the bed to be at head level with him. Stuart nods.

"Yeah, he's on his way. I've told him to keep everything quiet until your family has been told." I close my eyes and lean my head against the mattress. I feel Stuart move, and his hand touches my head. "I called Marcus too. Daisy had contacted Michael before being taken, so they already knew. They are on their way back," Stuart says as I feel his thumb running over my head.

"How's Michael doing?" I ask. From the look on Stuart's face, I can guess the answer.

"Not good. I could hear him in the background. This is killing him." Stuart answers as he holds back his tears.

"Dad is calling Mum now and then will call Nigel and Mary."

"I'm sorry I didn't stop him from taking her," Stuart whispers. I lift my head and look at him.

"It's not your fault. Everything happened so quickly. Dad and I aren't used to being without our powers," I admit. Stuart takes my hand in his.

"Why didn't you run when I told you to? Why did you follow me out? You could have been killed. I was trying to give you time to escape," Stuart says as he holds my hand.

"Because all I could think was I have only just found you; I can't lose you now," I admit. Stuart reaches up with his good hand and cups my cheek.

"Really?"

I nod before looking into his hazel eyes.

"I don't usually care what happens to people outside my family and coven. But as soon as I laid eyes on you, I knew you were what was missing in my life. The thought of never seeing where this could go scared me more than what was happening."

"You may not think like that later on when you hear a few things about me," Stuart sighs as he lowers his hand and closes his eyes.

"That you are in love with my best friend?" I ask, terrified of what he will say, wondering if it's possible to have your heart broken before knowing someone.

"I'm not in love with Daisy; I thought I was, but ... it's hard to explain."

"Try."

"Ever since I met Daisy, I have felt like I was linked to her somehow like she was meant to be in my life. I even wondered if she had met me first, would I have been her mate. But then I smelt your scent in the bedroom at the pack house, and all those thoughts and feelings disappeared as quickly as they had formed. Michael thinks my feelings for Daisy were due to her connection to you. That I was feeling our bond through her," Stuart explains.

"And you don't feel anything for her now?" I ask carefully.

"I do love her, but not romantically. I love her the same way Jon, Will and Marcus do; as a sister, she's my best friend, and that hasn't changed; but do I love her the way I feel I could love you if we got to know each other? No, not at all," Stuart whispers. I feel the tears roll down my cheek, and Stuart reaches up towards me, but I quickly wipe them away.

"I don't know what to do here; I don't know if you want me to comfort you or leave you alone. I wish we could have met under different circumstances, and none of this was happening." Stuart sighs as he places his head back on the pillows and looks up at the ceiling.

"I do too, but I could do with a friend I can lean on right now," I admit. Stuart turns and looks at me and offers me a sad smile.

"I can be that if you will let me."

I nod and place my head back on the mattress as Stuart runs his hand over my head again.

"I can't lose her, Stuart."

"I know, neither can I."

Chapter Forty-Nine

Daisy

The next thing I know, I'm standing in a large, grassed area surrounded by trees, with a manor-type house directly in front of us. I lean over and empty my stomach contents onto the grass. Fuck, the human body is not made to travel like that. I feel someone's hand on my back and instantly move away.

"Don't fucking touch me." I hiss as I throw up again.

"Dais, it will pass in a minute, I promise," Kellan says softly next to me; I spin around and push him away as hard as I can.

"Don't speak to me, don't touch me, or even better, just fuck off, Kellan!" I growl as Jackson chuckles from behind me. I spin around and punch him, hitting him straight in the eye. The bastard flies backwards, landing on his ass.

"You fucking bitch!" Jackson roars as he jumps up, holding his face. I look at him smugly as I place my hands on my hips. "You will pay for that!" he warns.

"I'd like to see you try, arsehole." I laugh as Jackson comes charging towards me, and I ball my hands into fists whilst planting my feet in a better stance, ready to defend myself, but Kellan jumps between us and stops Jackson before he can get to me.

"Kellan, take her to the cell. I'll deal with the bitch later." Jackson smirks at me. "I'm sure you remember how well I can deal with you," he adds as those grey eyes brighten.

"You will never touch me again. Never!" I laugh as I feel Kellan grab my arm, and we appear in a white room. I look around and curse.

There's a single bed, a sink and a toilet. That's it.

"What, no sheets? Worried I'll hang myself?" I sigh as I walk away from Kellan and sit on the stained mattress; luckily, it doesn't seem to smell too bad.

"Are you trying to get yourself fucking killed?" Kellan roars at me. I stare at him with arched brows.

"What's the alternative? Stay here and be forced into

being a birthing mule for his pups and live under his thumb for the rest of my life? Fuck that shit! It ain't happening." I answer as I lean back against the wall and fold my arms over my chest.

"No, it isn't, because you won't be here long." Kellan hisses through gritted teeth before looking around to check we're alone.

"Why, where am I going?" I ask as I frown at him.

"Keep your voice down. There are guards outside this room!" Kellan curses through his teeth as he points to the door. "I'm not letting him hurt you again. Why do you think I've been working with him? So, we can get out as soon as possible."

"I'm not going anywhere with you unless you take me back to Michael." I hiss back, leaning forward a little.

"You aren't safe with him! What you had with him was fun, but it ends now. You need to forget him." Kellan sighs as he crosses his arms over his chest. The move makes me think of Michael, which causes my heart to hurt more.

"I'll never forget him; he's my mate, and he *will* find me," I answer firmly.

"Not without that necklace; he won't," Kellan says as he walks over to the wall opposite mine and leans back against it.

"What's that got to do with anything?" I ask, confused.

"If you don't know, then it doesn't matter now. Michael won't find you here. Jackson has so many wards around this place that nothing will get through. His own wolves can't communicate with each other when in wolf form. Face it, Princess, you're on your own now, and I'm your only ally." Kellan stands, placing a foot against the wall behind him, I consider getting up and beating the shit out of the prick, but he's not worth the energy.

"I guess I'm on my own then, as I sure as hell don't want a snake like you trying to help me," I snarl. Kellan pushes himself away from the wall and takes a few steps towards me as I sit back, trying to look as relaxed and carefree as possible.

"Well, if you decide you want my help after all, just whisper my name, and I'll come to you. Otherwise, good luck as I know what he has planned for you and trust me, you'll need more than that smart mouth and a good right hook to get you through it." He vanishes into thin air again before I can jump from the bed to hit the smug bastard. Fuck.

I look around and feel the panic building inside me.

"Marcus has trained us for this. Think. What did he tell you to do if you were taken?" my wolf says, trying to calm me down. I close my eyes and lean back into the wall, working through the mental list Marcus drilled into me.

1. ***Breathe and remain calm.*** I keep my eyes closed and take a few deep breaths, attempting to push the building anxiety down.

2. ***Any doors and windows? What can you see out of them? Can you get through them safely?*** I look around and see one door. I get up from the bed and walk over to it. I place my hand against it and feel the cold touch of the metal. There's no windows, but there is a small hatch at the bottom of the door. I'm guessing that's where the food will be posted through. It's certainly too small for me to climb through, and Kellan said there were guards outside.

3. ***Any cameras? Any way of watching you?*** I look to the ceiling and find two cameras watching me. I instinctively stick up two fingers whilst grinning. I can hear Marcus chuckling in my head.

4. ***Anything you can use as a weapon?*** I look around again. The only thing I can see is the bed and mattress. The toilet doesn't even have a lid on it. Great. I walk over to the bed and lift the mattress. The bed has metal slats, but they would see me breaking one off. Looking at the camera, I wouldn't be surprised if it had night vision. Fantastic.

5. ***Do what you can to stay safe. Shift if you need to.*** I don't plan on shifting yet; I will if I have to. I've been practising, so I can do it instantly and on-demand. The only issue I have is the lack of clothing. If I shred my clothes, it leaves me more vulnerable. Fuck my life.

I sit on the bed and push myself back against the wall. I consider contacting Michael, but what can I tell him? I have no idea where I am as I wasn't outside long enough to pick out any landmarks or road signs. Until I know where I am, I need to keep the bond shut tight. Michael has spent months protecting me; now it's my turn to protect him.

I look up at the camera and swallow deeply. I refuse to cry and let him see that he's winning because he won't. Not this time. I know Michael will find me, and when he does, he will end Jackson, and we will finally be free. I have to hope that Jackson doesn't kill me first, as I have no plans to do as I'm told or being well-behaved. He wanted a luna, but he got a bitch who will fight him every second of every day.

Chapter Fifty

Jon

"Mikey! Stop him!" I yell as Michael barrels out of the car and rushes for the house. Marcus, Will and the Alpha all dive to stop him but fail to reach him in time.

Michael has lost control; his whole body is bulked up as his wolf has taken over his human form. His mate is missing and in harm's way, fuck everything else; nothing else matters. I'm a few steps behind him as he barges through the front door, almost taking it off its hinges.

"STUART!" Mikey roars; I swear the whole house shakes. Clare and Alex are there at the bottom of the stairs. "Where the fuck is he?!" Mikey roars.

"Michael, you need to calm down." Alex starts, and I cringe, knowing it is the wrong thing to say.

"CALM DOWN?! HE HAS HER!" Michael bellows in a way I have never heard from him before.

"I know. I was here. There was nothing more Stuart could have done." Alex says, taking a step towards Michael with his hand held out in front of him defensively. "He shattered one side of his body whilst trying to protect her," Alex adds.

"He still let him take her!" Michael yells as he tries to storm past Alex but freezes. I can see his eyes moving. "Fucking release me now, Rogers! Or I swear to the gods I will make you regret this."

"It's not Dad, it's me." I see Clare standing behind her dad, her hand held out in front of her.

"Release me, Clare," Michael growls through gritted teeth.

"No, he's hurt enough. This isn't going to get Daisy back, and you won't feel better for beating the shit out of your pack brother. Calm the fuck down, Adams." Clare replies, and it was like Daisy's there for a split second, only she speaks to Michael like that. Michael looks at Clare; her face is pale, and her eyes are bloodshot and swollen. She hasn't just cried; she has broken her heart. I see the realisation in Michael's eyes as he looks at the woman Daisy refers to as her sister.

"Let him go, Clare."

We all look to the stairs where Stuart is walking down them with the aid of the healer Edward. His left arm is in a sling, and he has a brace on his left leg. His face is covered in bruises; you can see the beating he took.

"No, he will kill you," Clare argues.

"It's what I deserve. I failed him," Stuart says, looking at Michael.

"Too right, you deserve it. You fucked up again. Because of you, our sister is back in his hands." Will yells at Stuart.

"You think I don't know that? You weren't here, Will! You didn't see how it unfolded!" Stuart yells back. Will takes a step forward, but Marcus grabs his shoulder. Alex steps beside Stuart.

"I didn't need to be here to know your mind was probably preoccupied whilst Daisy handed herself over!" Will shouts, straining against Marcus's grip.

"Of course it was! Because all we could see was that prick holding my mate at knifepoint!" Stuart roars back. The silence that fills the room is intense. Fuck.

"What?" Will says, stunned as he frowns at Stuart and tries to work out what he's said. Stuart looks down at the floor and then back at Will, staring at Clare as she stands beside Stuart, looking guiltily at Will.

"Clare, is your mate?" Marcus asks, still holding Will back. Stuart looks at him and nods before he faces Will, his face softening.

"I didn't want you to find out like this." Stuart rubs his face with his right hand. "This isn't what matters now. What matters is finding Daisy and getting her back," Stuart adds as he looks at Michael, still frozen to the spot.

"Michael, I tried to protect her; I was willing to die to stop her from being taken, but everything happened so quickly, and Kellan had powers none of us expected," Stuart explains quietly.

"Tell me what happened?" Michael says, sounding surprisingly calm; he looks at Clare. "I won't hurt him, I promise." Clare looks from Michael to Stuart, who nods. I watch as Clare lowers her hand, and Michael falls forward as if he had been leaning against an invisible wall, only just managing to catch himself before falling completely. Everyone holds their breath and watches for a moment as Michael stares at Stuart, all waiting to see if he'll attack, but he doesn't.

Michael's hands are still fisted at his side, and I know there's a real chance he could still flip. Michael nods once at Stuart, who takes a deep breath before recounting what happened.

"We were all in the lounge when it started. Daisy knew Jackson was close without even seeing him; he caused an explosion which shattered the front lounge window. Alex told me all the wards had been destroyed, so I said for him to get Daisy and Clare out. I headed out the front to keep Jackson distracted whilst they escaped. I didn't care if he killed me or not; I just wanted them to be safe. But things went downhill from there."

"It was my fault," Clare says as she steps next to Stuart. "I couldn't face Stuart going out there alone; I panicked and ran after him. I should have known Daisy and my dad would follow." Clare says as tears roll down her face. Stuart reaches out and places a hand on the bottom of her back for comfort.

"So the four of you were outside against how many?" Marcus asks. It's Alex who answers.

"It was only Jackson and Kellan. But Kellan is a powerful magic wielder. In seconds he syphoned all our powers, I managed to wield a little to protect the girls for a minute or two, but that's it. He knew what he was doing. I've never seen or felt anything like the power he used to throw Stuart around like a rag doll. Stuart kept getting up and advancing, but Kellan didn't even break a sweat; he threw power ball after power ball at Stu, sending him flying each time whilst syphoning our magic from us."

"I saw my dad drop and panicked; I left Stuart and ran over to him; that's when Kellan grabbed me. One second I was running to my dad. The next, I was in Jackson's arms on the other side of the garden," Clare explains.

"How?" Marcus asks, frowning.

"It was as if he teleported. One second he was on the other side of the fence, the next, Clare was in his arms, and he pushed her to Jackson. It took less than a second," Stuart explains.

"That must be how he can get into locked buildings," Marcus says quietly to no one in particular.

"Everything stopped when we realised he had a knife to Clare's side. He said he would take her; as an alternative to Daisy. He knew grabbing Clare would make Daisy stop fighting him. Daisy handed herself over to protect Clare. We tried to stop her, but she wouldn't listen. She somehow used her power to freeze us all in place; we attempted to get her to see sense but failed. The second Jackson had hold of Daisy; he had a knife to her throat; I couldn't risk fighting him; he was crazy enough to kill her and grab Clare again. There was no way to beat him, not without one or both girls dying," Alex says quietly, looking at the floor, his shoulders hunched in defeat.

I look at Michael, who's trying to take it all in. He looks up at Alex, "she'd never have let you lose your daughter. Or let Clare go through what she did."

"But I lost her," Alex whispers as a single tear rolls down his cheek.

"At least we're one step ahead of him this time," Michael sighs. Alex takes a deep breath and looks Michael in the eye.

"We're not."

"What?" Michael asks, frowning at Alex.

"He knew somehow; he knew what we'd done." I look at him, confused. I glance at Michael and see he knows exactly what Alex is talking about. He starts shaking his head; the look of pain and disbelief is heart-breaking to witness.

"No. Please don't tell me he knew about *that*." Michael begs as Alex nods and pulls something out of his pocket; I watch as he holds up his fist with Daisy's necklace hanging from it. Michael's pain rips through the whole house as he falls to his knees, his head in his hands.

"How?!" he howls as Alex shakes his head.

"I don't know; I have told no one what we did. Not even

Nigel."

"What's going on?" I ask as I look between them, everyone around me looking just as confused.

"Michael asked me to place a tracking spell on Daisy's necklace before giving it to her. One that was so strong that no matter how many wards were around her, we would still be able to track the necklace; it would work as a beacon," Alex explains.

"If only you two knew about it, how did he know to leave it?" Will asks, speaking for the first time.

"I don't know. As I said, I told no one, and there was no way he could have seen me do it. It was down in Cornwall when Michael and I first met." Alex sighs.

"I told Daisy I had gone to train the pack there, but before I did, I met up with Alex, and we worked out a plan for if she was ever taken; I gave him the necklace, and he placed the spell on it," Michael whispers from his spot.

"That's why you went for that early morning walk that day?" Clare asks her dad, who nods.

"We decided that the fewer people who knew, the better," Alex explains as he looks at his daughter. "We had discussed it at the BBQ the night before."

"But we didn't know Jackson was a threat back then." Will points out; Michael shakes his head.

"No, but I had a gut feeling he was out there somewhere. Why go through all the trouble of turning and abusing her and then just letting her go? It didn't make sense, so I wanted a backup plan," Michael answers.

"That's why you didn't tell me," Marcus says. Michael nods his head.

"Alex knew that if anything happened to me, he was to tell you or Jon what we'd done. Daisy was never to know." Michael holds out his hand, and Alex places the necklace into it. Michael looks at the pendant and exhales. "There's no way of tracking or knowing where he has taken her." The defeat and exhaustion are evident in his voice.

"What about the place in Exeter? Did you find anything or anyone there?" Stuart asks. We all shake our heads.

"There were two guys; we've left Natalie to try and get some info out of them and search the place for anything that might say where they've relocated to. But so far, nothing." Marcus sighs. I look over at Michael, who is trying to rise to his feet, I rush to his side and to help him, but he pushes me away.

"I need a minute. Just leave me." He whispers as he walks toward the stairs. Stuart steps out of his way, but Michael looks at him and grasps his shoulder. "I don't blame you, not really. I should have never left you on your own."

"I'm sorry, Michael," Stuart whispers; Michael looks from Stuart to the stairs and lets go before heading up.

"Me too." He sighs as he walks out of view.

Chapter Fifty-One

Michael

I walk into our room and close the door behind me. My back slides down it as my heart pounds in my chest. I can't breathe, and when I do, all I can smell is Daisy. Her scent's everywhere. I can't catch my breath as my throat contracts, and the tears I've somehow been holding in escape.

He has her, and I have no way of finding her. What the fuck am I meant to do now?

I look over at the bed, where I made love to her only this morning; I can still smell the mixture of our scents and arousals in the air. There had been no sign that we would be apart by the end of the day, that I would be here without her. Everything changed when the Alpha called. But even after that meeting and coming home to prepare, I believed that if either of us were missing tonight, it would be me. That it would be me badly injured or dead. I never dreamt Daisy would be the one missing from our home.

I rest my head on my bent knees and feel my body shake as I break down. I open the link as I have so many times since she told me she loved me. But as before, it's blocked off from her. There's no Daisy at the other end, only silence.

"They call you The Protector, yet you couldn't even protect your own mate." My wolf howls in my head.

I know.

"Do you, though? Do you realise what this means? He has her, and we have no way of finding her!"

I know.

"Is that all you've got to say on the matter? That you know?"

What more is there to say? I know what he is probably doing ... I can't finish the sentence, the thought of him touching her, hurting her, abusing her, and worse is too much. I grab a bin and throw up.

I can't take it; I can't let him do all that to her again. There must be a way of finding her, of working out where he's taken her and what I can do to get her back. I promised her she would be safe, and I've failed her time and time again. But this time, it's worse. This time he's won, and he's taken her from me.

"We have lost her before, and we managed to get her back," my wolf points out. I shake my head as I move the bin away from me. That was different; we had some idea where she would have gone. This time we have nothing. There's no way of finding her.

"Of course, there is. There's always a way. The guy's an idiot. He must have left something in the den. There's no way he managed to get everything out of it." I won't know more until Natalie and the guys I left with her get here with anything they find. I take a deep breath and regret it as Daisy's scent fills my senses again.

Fuck, I have no idea what to do. I told myself I was prepared for this. I had a plan; I knew how to find her if she was taken. I hold her necklace in front of me and run my finger over the pendent. The two wolves, one for her and one for me. How did he know? How did he know to leave it? Daisy hadn't even picked up on the magic stored within it.

I take a deep breath through my mouth before pulling myself up onto my feet. I walk into our bathroom and splash cold water onto my face. As much as I feel like I'm about to fall apart, I can't, not now. I need to keep it together, find my mate, save her, and bring her home.

As I walk down the stairs, a few minutes later, everyone comes into the entrance hall to meet me. I look around at my alpha, team, Alex and Clare, until I spot Marcus; I immediately go into protector mode as it's the only way I know how to handle this.

"I want EVERYONE here in the next hour. All who are available to fight are to be on standby. The dining room becomes HQ and tell Natalie and Owen to grab everything and get it here. I want any piece of paper they find gone over with a fine-tooth comb. The bastard is not clever enough to have completely hidden his tracks. There has to be a paper trail somewhere." I turn to Alex.

"Have you made the call to Nigel and Mary?" I ask as he nods.

"I had to; they are on their way." I take a deep breath and nod once. I'm not looking forward to facing them. But at least I can prove I won't stop until I find her.

"Tell them to come straight here." I turn to Desmond, standing beside Alex, my team behind him. "How many pack houses are available?" I ask.

"All four, they are at your disposal," he answers. I tell Alex to take the one he had before and that Nigel and Mary will have another. That leaves two for anyone who doesn't live close by and wants to help, like Natalie and Owen.

I look at Stuart and Will, standing behind Desmond in the doorway to the lounge.

"If you two need to have it out, do it outside. I want you both on full alert and focused on finding Daisy and not squabbling over Clare. You have ten minutes. Beat the shit out of each other for all I care but then move on." Stuart turns to Will, who nods towards the back door. He starts to follow him, but Clare grabs his good arm. Stuart looks at her and smiles softly.

"It's fine. I promise." He whispers as he leans in and kisses her on the cheek before following Will; I turn to Alex.

"If you need to join in the beating, then go now. I don't want any distractions." Alex looks at me, shaking his head.

"Me and the wolf have made a deal; we will deal with it after this is over."

"Dad, please don't start. You promised," Clare sighs behind her father.

"I'm not, for now," Alex replies to his daughter. I look at Alex and almost smile.

"What did you say about being glad Clare wasn't in a serious relationship?" I tease.

"Adams, sometimes you are a real fucking arse," he replies as his jaw clenches. I place a hand on his shoulder and give it a reassuring squeeze.

"Welcome to the family, Papa Bear." Alex walks away, cursing all wolves under his breath; I know if Daisy were here, she would be smiling and teasing him too, if not worse.

"I never understood when Daisy said how intense the bond is." I turn to find Clare standing next to me, looking out into the garden where Will and Stuart are having a rather intense discussion. She looks up at me, her eyes filled with tears. "I get it now. I knew the moment I saw him that he was special to me." Clare looks back outside. "Did you know about us?"

"Yes," I reply, watching Will and Stuart.

"Did Daisy?" Clare asks; I shake my head.

"No, only Stuart, Jon and me. No one else," I answer, looking down at her.

"She knows now. Stuart screamed for Jackson to let go of his mate. That's when I finally understood why I felt this way about him. It made sense. He should have told me," Clare sighs.

"We weren't sure if you would feel it with you not being a wolf. That's why Stuart never told you, you seemed happy with Will, and Stuart didn't want to ruin that for you if you didn't feel what he did," I answer honestly.

"That wasn't his decision to make; I had a right to know." She snaps before turning to face me, her face softening. "I'm sorry, Michael, your whole world has been turned upside down, and I'm here bitching. It wasn't where I planned on this conversation going." She sighs as she reaches out and places a hand on my arm. "How are you doing?" She asks, softly.

"I'm falling apart, Clare; I need to keep busy until I can work out how the fuck to get her back. I refuse to think about anything but bringing her home." I take Clare's hand and squeeze it, "when I bring her home, she'll want to know everything about you and Stuart, you know that, right? As well as giving you both hell." Clare looks up at me and smiles.

"I know. I also know you'll find her, Michael. You'll find her quicker than we could anyway." I squeeze her hand as I pull her into my arms.

"I hope so, Clare. I really do," I whisper into her hair as I plant a kiss on the top of her head.

Chapter Fifty-Two

Daisy

The light shines brightly above me, luckily not enough to get into my eyes and block my target. Sweat drips down my neck and back as I hit the pad repeatedly.

"What are the points to aim for?" Marcus snaps.

"Chin." Punch. "Nose." Punch. "Stomach." Punch. "Balls." Knee. The pad moves with each point.

"Good. Again."

We go over it five more times until Marcus stops me.

"Punch and dodge; go until I tell you to stop." He barks as he holds the pads up; I punch when they are stationary and dodge when he tries to hit me.

"What do you do if you're taken?" Marcus barks.

"The five rules," I declare as I dodge a punch.

"Which are?"

"Breathe and stay calm."

Punch.

"Viewpoints and exit."

Punch.

"Cameras or spy holes."

Dodge.

"Possible weapons."

Dodge.

"Stay safe."

Punch.

"Good. What do you do if you can't escape?" Marcus asks.

"Never give up, fight. Don't show I'm weak." Punch. Punch. Dodge.

"Are you weak?"

"No." I gasp, out of breath, as I barely dodge the pad as it flies towards me.

"Are you weak?!" Marcus demands louder.

"NO!" I roar as I kick the pad with the ball of my foot, sending Marcus flying backwards. I look amazed at him lying flat on his back on the ground. He looks around, shocked and then bursts out laughing. I smile as I hold out my hand and help him up to his feet.

"No, you are not." He laughs as he dusts himself off. I lean over with my hands on my legs and try to catch my breath. I'm done in; we've been at it for hours. I check my watch and realise the time.

"We better get back and shower before Mikey gets home and wonders why we both smell so bad." I stand up and start stretching my arms whilst rolling my neck. I look up at Marcus and notice a smile on his face. "What?" I ask worriedly. Marcus isn't a big smiler; I always feel uneasy when he smiles at me.

"Nothing, just thinking how far you've come."

"Think I will survive if he takes me?" I ask quietly.

"He won't take you," Marcus replies with certainty.

"But if he does?" I ask again, knowing realistically there's a chance. Marcus looks at me before pulling me into his arms and holding me tight, throwing me off guard by the sudden display of affection. It takes me a second before I relax and hug him back.

"If he does, then I think you will be just fine."

)) ● ((

The lights in my cell come on, suddenly blinding me. I shield my eyes with my hand; as I look at the door and see the prick coming in. I have no idea what time it is or how long I've been here, but I must have fallen asleep at some point.

I look up at him and burst out laughing.

"How's the eye, arsewipe?" I tease as it's swollen shut; by swollen, I mean it is massive. Marcus would be proud. Jackson dives for me, but I jump off the bed and move to the middle of the room. *"Don't let yourself get backed against a wall."* One of the many things Marcus drilled into me over the last two months during our secret training sessions. Jackson turns around and snarls at me.

"What's the matter? Not up for a fight?" I know I'm tormenting him, and I don't give a shit.

"You know I will get my way in the end, sweetheart. Don't

pretend you haven't missed me." Jackson smirks as he moves off the bed and stands in front of me.

"Oh, I've missed you like a hole in the head!" I taunt. Jackson tries to grab me again, and I easily dodge out of his way.

"You want to play Daisy? Let's play." He tries to grab me repeatedly, and I jump out of his reach each time. The problem is I'll be backed against a wall in a minute if I can't get around him. I assess and realise I need to move to the left; he can't see out of that eye. As Jackson jumps for me again, I manage to get around him, but I trip and land on the floor.

"Fuck!" I curse as I fall. I'm almost back up again, but Jackson quickly grabs my leg and pulls me back down. He's on me in a flash. Double fuck. I swing my fist and connect with his jaw.

"Stop fucking fighting, you little bitch." He snarls at me as he tries to grab my hands.

"Fucking make me, prick," I growl as he gets hold of my wrists. He smiles as he pins them above my head, but he doesn't realise I'm letting him. If he would move a little ...

"Ahhh, my nose!" Ha! I headbutt the bastard. It hurts like a bitch, but the bastard lifts off enough to give me the opening I need. I bring my knees to my chest and kick them out with all my strength, sending him flying across the room. I jump to my feet and get into a defensive pose.

"You bitch, you broke my nose." Jackson curses as blood streams down his face.

"That's not all I'll break if you try and come near me again," I warn him.

"I thought you'd prefer it without the chains; I guess I was wrong. Enjoy being able to move whilst you can, because you will be chained to the bed when I return, and you'll have no way of fighting me." Jackson growls as he holds his bleeding nose. I can't help myself; I burst out laughing, causing Jackson to look at me, confused.

"You are so pathetic. You call yourself an alpha? You can't even attack little old me without having your ass handed to you, does chaining me up give you a fighting chance?" I mock.

"Oh, I won't need the chains for long. Once you realise that Adams is never coming to save you or even cares, you'll give up fighting me and realise I'm your best option." I walk up to him until I'm an arm's length away, looking into those dark grey eyes that have haunted my nightmares for three years, and realise I am no longer afraid.

"I will never stop fighting you, and I will never give up on Michael, as I know he will never give up on me. So, you can tell your lies, as you might fool all the idiots out there, but I know the truth. I know that you are a pathetic little male who hides behind his wolf, which is just as weak. You will never be an alpha worth following."

"I AM YOUR ALPHA! You will show me the respect I am due!" Jackson roars.

"You are not *my* alpha! My alpha is Desmond Gibbs, who is a million times the male you claim to be. I will NEVER abandon my pack, and they will never abandon me," I reply, grinning at him.

"They have abandoned you; they aren't even looking for you. I am your alpha now, and you will bow to me." Jackson roars. I stand tall as I step closer to the male I once feared.

"I am the mate of Michael Adams, a member of the Blood Moon Pack, and I bow to no one but MY alpha!" I reply, feeling my pride in every single word. Jackson stares at me speechless; he'd expected me to be scared and weak again, but I'm not; I am no longer that terrified nineteen-year-old who took the beatings and didn't fight back. I take a step closer and am amazed when Jackson takes one back.

"I'm no longer weak, and you will never touch me again," I growl, allowing my wolf to come to the front, so my eyes darken. "Now get out. I'm bored of you." I cross my arms over my chest and stare at him. Letting my wolf remain upfront.

"This is not over," Jackson warns as he backs up to the door. "I will be back, and you will regret disrespecting me."

I shrug and take a step towards him.

"We will see who regrets what," I reply calmly as I smirk at him wickedly. Jackson bangs on the door, which opens from the outside.

"See you soon, sweetheart; enjoy your freedom whilst you can," He adds as he walks out of the door. I stand and wave whilst smiling.

"See you soon then. It's been a blast," I throw in for good measure.

As soon as the door's closed and I hear the locking mechanism click, I walk over to the sink and run the tap. I know when I stand here that the camera only sees my back. I close my eyes and breathe. *"Inhale slowly, 1 2 3 4 5. Exhale 1 2 3 4 5. Again, repeat until you feel calm."* I follow the memory of Michael's voice as he talks me through a panic attack. My heart is aching to be in his arms, smell his scent, and feel his breath on my head as he holds me.

"Remember, you are braver than you believe and stronger than you seem," Marcus whispered to me one day after training. I can't help but laugh.

"Are you, of all people, quoting Winnie – The – Pooh at me?"

Marcus frowns at me, "no, I just made it up." I shake my head and smile at the big lump of a man in front of me.

"Unless you are a fat yellow bear in a red top, which is too small to go over his belly, I beg to differ."

I smile at the memory and know I may have won this battle with Jackson, but I need to keep my wits about me for the next.

Chapter Fifty-Three

Michael

"Mikey, you need to try and get some rest. It's been nearly twenty-four hours." I turn to see Marcus standing at the patio doors. I've been sitting outside in the garden for the last hour. Needing a break from the house and Daisy's scent that's embedded into every fibre.

"You've been up as long as me." I sigh as I go back to looking out into the woods. Everyone's gone to bed. Alex has taken Clare back to the pack house to be with Sara. Mary and Nigel arrived an hour after we returned and went with them. Natalie and Stuart are working through some paperwork she found in the den. They've both had a few hours of sleep. Jon's asleep on his bed, Mum in the spare room and Will on the sofa. The only ones unable to sleep seems to be Marcus and me.

"I'll sleep if you do," Marcus answers next to me. I don't bother to reply as I know he has as much chance as me. I hear Marcus pulling up a chair and sitting down, but I don't turn to face him.

"Daisy wouldn't want you running yourself to the ground, Mikey. She'd expect you to look after yourself to a point." Marcus sighs.

"I know." That seems to have become my response to everything. If only I knew something important, like where she is.

"Then please, for her; if not, the rest of us, get some rest."

"I can't, Marc; I've tried. But every time I close my eyes, I see what he's doing to her. I can hear her begging me to find her, and I can't. I can't save her from his touch, his abuse." I look at my oldest friend as the tears roll down my face. "I never trained her like I promised to. I kept finding excuses because I didn't want to accept she needed to learn to defend herself. If I accepted that, it meant I was failing her, that there was a chance he would get her. But now he has, and she can't protect herself because of me." My throat and chest tighten as I admit the guilt that has been riding me since Daisy was taken.

"Mikey, Daisy can defend herself. She's prepared for this." Marcus says next to me quietly. I roll my eyes and look away, shaking my head.

"She likes to think she is, but she isn't. You don't have to lie to me."

"I'm not lying, not about this. Because..." I hear Marcus take a deep breath and turn to face him, frowning. "Because I trained her myself." I stare at him for a moment, shocked.

"What?"

"Daisy knew why you were reluctant to train her, and she understood, but she wanted to be prepared. So she asked me to meet with her here twice a week when you were at work. She trained her fucking ass off for two months, Mikey, she has a plan, and I have no doubt he'll be in for the shock of his life when she attacks."

A laugh burst from my lips. "I said she looked more toned, and she said it was all the sex." I turn and look at Marcus, "you really trained her?" He smiles softly and nods.

"She knows ways to escape and how to defend herself. She pushed herself to the point she was sick a few times," he explains.

"Do you think she has a chance of defeating him?" I ask hopefully. I watch as Marcus looks at the floor, smirking before looking back up at me with what can only be described as pride in his eyes.

"She knocked me on my ass."

"Fuck off!" I exclaim loudly. Marcus chuckles and nods. Only I've ever knocked Marcus off his feet; no other team member has managed it, no matter how hard they've tried. It's become a friendly challenge within the team.

"Yep, knocked me right off my feet, my ass hurt for days, my pride even longer." Marcus reaches over and places a hand on my shoulder. "That mate of yours is something else, and I know she'll be giving him fucking hell wherever he has her. If not with that smart mouth of hers, then with those fists."

"Thank you, Marcus. Thank you for stepping up where I didn't." I say, genuinely grateful for my friend.

"You gave her everything she needed, Mikey. Don't ever doubt that. You two have dealt with more shit than anyone I have ever known. But know that Daisy's well prepared for this, and she will defend herself until her last breath, and we'll find her long before it comes to that. I promise." I look at Marcus and sigh.

"Any ideas on how we're meant to find her yet? Because he could be holding her anywhere in the UK, fuck he could have left the country, and we'd be none the wiser."

"I know he won't take her out of the country. Daisy would make too much of a fuss, and they would get caught," Marcus points out. I know he's right; Daisy would not go quietly.

"But if he can get Kellan to teleport?" The thought has been playing on my mind.

"I don't think he can teleport; I think it's more of a time or speed spell. Alex has been looking into it; he'll know more by the morning. But we're both sure you must keep within a certain distance of your starting point. Mikey, please stop and try to rest." I look back at the house and know Daisy would want me to rest. I need to be strong for her and keep going because I'm never giving up on her; I will keep looking for the rest of my life. But I'm useless if I don't rest.

"Her scent is everywhere in there. I can't move without smelling it." I whisper. I turn to Marcus, who nods.

"When Michelle was killed, I couldn't go into our room for weeks. All I could smell was her, and fuck, it hurt. But I was also scared that her scent would fade if I kept going in there, and I'd never smell her sweet cinnamon and nutmeg scent again." Marcus looks at me and smiles.

"That's when I started sleeping more regularly in your garden in my wolf form. I slept there when we were younger to be closer to Michelle until we were eighteen and got our own place. When she died, I told myself I was doing it to keep an eye on Mama B and you guys. That you needed me there. But in truth, *I* needed to be there. I needed to be where Michelle had been, but her scent wasn't overpowering; it was enough to take away some of the pain." Marcus looks at me and nods towards the woods.

"Shift and go to sleep in there. Your wolf will know you need to rest and take over your senses. You're no good to any of us, especially Daisy, if you're not firing on all cylinders." I look at my watch and see it's five AM. I glance from my pack brother to the woods and know he's right. I can't think straight or help find Daisy if I'm dead on my feet.

"The alternative is me getting Alex to knock you out with a sleeping spell or Edward giving you a draft. Either way, I will make sure you sleep soon. How you fall asleep is down to you," Marcus warns.

I take a deep breath and sigh as I stand up.

"Alright, I'll try it your way. I've told everyone to be back here at nine. If I'm not back by eight-thirty, find me. I want time to shower before I face them all," I say as I face my second.

"Mikey, sleep; and worry about everything else afterwards. There are a few of us still working through all the paperwork. If anything comes up, I'll come and get you myself." Marcus states to reassure me.

"Try and sleep as well, Marcus; as I said, you've been up as long as me. If I'm not functioning properly, I need to know you are." Marcus stands up and nods.

"I'll sleep in your study for a bit. Now go and get yourself some rest. We'll all still be here when you get back." I nod before walking into the woods as I address my wolf.

Alright, I'm leaving you in charge now. Do you think you can help us get some rest?

"Yes, you know I can." He sighs; My wolf is struggling as much as I am without its connection to his mate. I strip down and place my clothes in the tree before shifting.

I run a little from the house until I find a spot to curl up. I cautiously sniff the air and instantly find Daisy's scent. But it's mixed with all of ours and the natural woodland smells. It still hurts as I can smell her every time I breathe, but it's not as overpowering as it is in the house.

I curl up on the ground, and the image of Daisy instantly fills my mind, but this time she's smiling at me the way she was the other morning after we made love and had breakfast together. It's a happy smile as if my wolf is showing me what I need to see and remember. I slowly fall asleep, her beautiful eyes being the last thing I see.

Chapter Fifty-Four

Michael

Marcus, Natalie, Stuart, and I are all sitting around my dining room table, going through the hundreds of pieces of paper Natalie grabbed from Jackson's former den when I hear the front door bang open.

"Michael!" I jump up to the sound of Alex's voice.

"In here," I shout as I watch him, Nigel and Clare rush into the room.

"Where's Stuart?" Alex demands as soon as he sees me.

"I'm here," Stuart says from beside me; Alex takes a step towards him; I instantly stand between them and hold my hand out.

"Step down; I'm not dealing with *that* yet," Alex declares, rolling his eyes. I step out of the way and observe as Alex stops in front of Stuart, who is now on his feet.

"When Kellan grabbed Clare, what did you notice?" he asks. Stuart looks at him, frowning.

"Nothing, it was so quick. One second, I was grabbing for her. The next, she was on the other side of the garden."

"Did you and your wolf senses pick up on any scent, light, or shimmer? Anything that was out of the ordinary?" Alex asks. I watch as Stuart replays the scene in his head. Suddenly his head shoots up as his eyes widen.

"Yes, the smell of flowers stood out from those around us. There was also a shimmer around Clare as she disappeared." Stuart looks over at Clare as he continues. "As my fingers reached what would have been her cardigan, there was a strange tingle up my arm, almost like pins and needles but without that fuzzy feeling you get." Alex looks at him and surprises me by placing a hand on Stuart's shoulder before facing me.

"Kellan did teleport; it wasn't a type of speed spell," Alex declares.

"How's that even possible?" Marcus asks from behind us.

"There's only one type of magic that can do it, fae magic." Alex sighs.

"The fae don't exist; they're just fairy tales," Natalie says slowly. Alex turns to look at her and shrugs.

"You could say the same about shifters, sorcerers and witches. The fae are as real as us, demons, necromancers, and all supernatural races; they just stay in their realm. I can't remember the last time a fae was seen in ours," Alex explains.

"Then how is there one here now?" Stuart asks, voicing the question on all our lips.

"Because somehow, he came through from his realm. If Kellan is fae, he could be hundreds of years old, and we'd never know the difference. They age slowly; he could be over five hundred years of age and look about twenty-five in our eyes," Nigel adds.

"Would the fact that he's fae explain the lack of scent and how he can control Daisy's magic even when he is not close?" I ask. Alex turns to me and nods.

"I was too scared at the time, so I don't remember much. But I thought Stuart's wolf might have picked up on something," Clare says as she steps next to her dad.

"He must be blocking his scent magically, but it would also take an incredible about of magical energy to teleport as he did. When he teleported to get to Clare, Stuart could pick up on his scent." Alex says as he quickly glances at his daughter as if to check she is, in fact, still next to him.

"He could not keep it masked and teleport," Marcus says from beside me. Alex nods again.

I turn and look at Stuart, "Do you think you'd recognise the scent again if you smelt it?" Stuart looks at me and nods, his eyes widening.

"I've smelt it before in Mama B's garden; I'm sure of it."

"Go pick out the scent and bring whatever is back here so we can all smell it. There might be a time he messes up again and can't mask it. We all need to know it." Stuart nods and grabs his keys from the table in front of him.

"There are herbs in the garden, right?" Clare asks next to me. I turn and nod.

"Mum's in the lounge. Tell her what you need, and she'll let you know what she has. She's been adding to them with Daisy's help." Clare turns, but Alex grabs her arm. I feel Stuart tense beside me, but I throw him a warning look, and he instantly relaxes.

"What are you thinking?" Alex asks her.

"We need more herbs and mixtures; we don't have anything. If I can at least make up some healing lotions and some teas for magic exhaustion, I can help the healer if we need to." Alex looks at her for a moment and nods. Clare rushes off into the lounge as Alex turns to Stuart.

"If any harm comes to that girl, wolf, you will see why I'm one of the most powerful sorcerers around," he warns.

"Stuart will never let any harm come to Clare, and you know it," Nigel sighs from behind Alex.

"I swear she will always be safe with me." Stuart declares, looking straight at Alex. Alex nods once and moves out of his way. Stuart glances at me quickly before rushing off to get Clare.

"You need to get your head about their bond Alex, as fighting it will do none of you any favours," Nigel says as he places a hand on his friend's shoulder. Alex huffs and steps out of the room. Nigel watches his friend disappear before looking back at me. "He'll come around; Clare's always been his little girl, and the thought of her growing up has been a tough battle for him. He wasn't overly pleased with you to start with, but after he heard how well you looked after Daisy that day, he agreed to play nice." I look away and try to blink back the tears as I remember the last time I had to search for Daisy and how I had found her crying in her uncle's arms in her room down in Cornwall. I thought it was hard to find her, and I managed it; I just have to hope someone helps me this time.

Nigel steps up to me and holds out a small bottle. "This is from Mary; it's to help you get some rest as she knows you won't have been able to." I shake my head and point towards the table covered in paper.

"I don't have time. I need to go through all of this and see if we can find something to lead us to her. I won't give up." I point out.

"We know you won't, but how much of that is going in, Michael? You're exhausted; you can't seriously expect us to believe you're capable of thinking properly?" Nigel says as he tips his head to one side, just like Daisy does when she's calling me out on my bullshit. It makes my heart ache for her even more.

"I'm fine, Nigel. I got some sleep early hours of this morning." I say as I hope he won't see through my white lie.

"How much?" he asks.

"Enough," I answer, still refusing to look at him.

"He got three at the most. No more," Marcus says from the other side of the table. I turn and frown at him, but he shrugs as I hear Nigel sigh.

"It's not enough. As much as I hate to say it, the chances of anything happening in the next four hours are minimal. Please, Michael, you have to sleep. If you don't and Daisy finds out we did nothing to help you, she will make our life hell for years. So do this old man a solid and have a sleep. The draft will only last five hours, but it will be like sleeping for ten." Nigel says, holding the bottle out in his hand again.

"And the dreams?" I whisper as I avoid eye contact.

"It will be dreamless; Mary made sure of it. We both had to take some ourselves last night," Nigel says. I take the bottle and look down at it in my hand, knowing I should do as he requests. But I'm terrified to sleep and miss something important.

"If anything comes to light, we'll be able to wake you; it's just to put you into a dreamless sleep. It will help, I promise." Nigel says softly, obviously understanding my apprehension.

"Okay, I'll take it." I turn to Marcus, leaning on the back of Natalie's chair, looking over a pile of papers.

"Can you two take over for a bit?" I ask, even though I know I don't need to.

"I'll happily take over," Nat says, grinning before pointing her thumb at Marcus. "Been a while since I got to give this one orders."

"Umm, I think you'll find I'm his second now, which means

I'll be giving the orders." Marcus points out as he looks at her.

"You're only his second because I left. I was second first." Natalie responds, looking up at Marcus, frowning.

Marcus stands tall, crossing his arms over his chest. "This is true, fine. You can be in charge." I can't miss the mischievous grin on his face.

"Yes!" Nat cheers quietly as she fist pumps the air.

"That means you have to deal with the reason you left. And by reason, I mean wolf," Marcus adds. I watch Natalie's face drop as she curses under her breath.

"Fine, you can be in charge. Arsehole." She growls under her breath and looks up at me before adding. "Go to sleep Mikey; you look like shit."

"Thanks, Nat, a pleasure as always." I sigh as I roll my eyes and look at Nigel, who has a smile for the first time since he got here yesterday.

"I can see you have your hands full with these two." He chuckles; I look at him and can't stop the slight smile on my face as I look back to my previous and current second.

"They're good at their jobs; it's the only reason I keep them around." I look down at the bottle in my hand and gently close my fist around it.

"If you learn anything," I whisper, not addressing anyone in particular.

"We will wake you, I swear," Marcus says from his spot next to Natalie. I nod and walk up to our bedroom. I take a deep breath before entering.

Inside I slowly look around. The bed's still made. The bin I threw up in yesterday has long gone after Jon threw it out for me. I see Daisy's favourite hoodie thrown over the end of the bed from where she decided it was too warm to wear it. Is she cold now? Is he giving her clean clothes? I pick up the hoodie and place it on the chair. I lie on the bed and open our bond; again, I hit that barrier Daisy has put up.

"I'm being forced to sleep, but I miss you and won't stop until I bring you home. I love you, darling." I open the bottle and drink the contents. It's a sweet draft, not like the one Edward makes. This one has a subtle taste of honey and

chamomile. I will have to remember to ask Mary to make me some more, to have ready for Daisy when she returns.

I lie back before turning to face her side of the bed. On her bedside cabinet is a photo of the two of us, taken when I went down to Cornwall just before we were mated. I found her then, and I can find her now. I look at her smiling face as I drift off into a dreamless sleep.

Chapter Fifty-Five

Stuart

I'm wandering around the garden, trying to separate the smells, to pick out the one closest to Kellan's scent, but it's not working; my senses are so overwhelmed, everything is jumbled up.

"For fuck's sake," I growl as I look at the flower bed.

"What's wrong?" Clare asks behind me. I turn to her and see the bundles of herbs she already has in her hands.

"I can't separate the scents enough to find the one I'm looking for," I explain. Clare looks around, nodding.

"There's a lot of different flowers and herbs in here; it must be overpowering." She agrees. Suddenly her blue eyes light up as she smiles at me. It's the same look Daisy gets when she has an idea, and I can't miss the prang of sorrow that hits my heart at the thought of my missing best friend.

Clare carefully places the bundle of herbs on the ground and walks up to me.

"Close your eyes," she whispers. I frown down at her wearily. "Don't you trust me?" she asks, grinning.

"You grew up with Daisy as an influence. Do you blame me for being cautious?" I reply, smirking. Clare bursts out laughing, shaking her head.

"Fair enough, I'll give you that one. I promise I won't do anything bad."

I smile down at her before closing my eyes. I feel Clare take my hands and lead me away from the flower bed.

"Where are we going?" I ask as I start to open my eyes.

"Keep them closed, or I will blindfold you," she exclaims.

"Kinky," I reply, wiggling my eyebrows whilst keeping my eyes closed.

"Behave," Clare giggles as we come to a stop. "How overwhelming are the scents now?" she asks softly.

"They aren't too bad," I reply. Clare turns us around, and I feel something touch the back of my knees.

"Sit down and keep them closed," she whispers. I do as I'm told, wondering what she's planning. "Wait here. No peeking," she whispers as I feel her hands slide out of mine. I hear her walking away from me, followed by the sound of leaves and bushes being touched and moved. Using my advanced wolf hearing, I listen carefully and wait for the sound of her soft footsteps on the grass to get louder as she comes back to me.

"I'm going to hold out a few different plants, and I want you to see if you can pick out the scent you're looking for," Clare explains as she stops in front of me.

"Okay," I reply.

I hear Clare moving around again before a scent fills my nose.

"Roses," I answer quickly. "That's not it," I add.

"I didn't even get it by your nose. Your sense of smell must be amazing." Clare chuckles as I hear her move again.

"I have the best nose in the team," I say with a shrug.

"That must be why you picked up on Kellan's scent when Dad and I didn't," Clare say quietly as another scent overwhelms my senses.

"Rosemary and thyme. Not the scent."

It goes on like this for a few more minutes until I hear Clare sigh.

"If you take a deep breath, does *anything* stand out?"

"All the scents I've named already, plus you," I answer as I smile; I feel Clare place her hands on my knees and lean on them slightly. I lift my hands and place them where I guess her hips will be, judging by the feel of her legs against mine.

"And what do I smell like?" she whispers seductively, her breath tickling over my ear. I keep my eyes closed as I turn my head and feel my nose run along her shoulder and up her neck.

"Coconut, citrus and magic," I whisper as I rub my nose along her skin and inhale her mesmerising scent. I hear her gasp, and blood rushes to my head and cock. Her scent is intoxicating, but as I rub my nose against her neck and feel my lips brush her soft skin, I notice her scent changes slightly, and I smile.

"Do you like that, baby?" I whisper as I tighten my hold on

her hips and let my lips brush her neck again, causing her to inhale sharply.

"Maybe," Clare whispers back as I run my hands down her hips and move them around the back of her thighs before tugging her onto my lap. I instantly feel the heat from her sex which confirms my suspicions.

"I think it's more than a maybe." I tease as I let my lips brush her silky soft skin again. I feel Clare shift on my lap and rub against me in the right place.

"I don't think I'm the only one," she whispers into my ear as she takes the ear lobe between her teeth. I can't stop the groan that escapes my lips, causing her to giggle. Suddenly she jumps off my lap, and I open my eyes and search for her. She's standing in front of me, grinning. She looks radiant in the sun as it shines behind her. Her honey-coloured hair glows as it falls over her shoulders in waves.

"You are the most beautiful woman I have ever seen," I whisper before I can stop myself. Clare blushes and then looks me in the eye.

"You should see me naked." She winks before spinning around and walking quickly into the trees at the side of the garden. I jump to my feet and rush after her as the sound of her giggling fills the air. As soon as she is in reach, I grab her around the waist and spin her around, pressing her body against mine. Clare screams, laughing as she places her hands on my chest and looks up at me with the biggest smile on her face.

"Stuart?" she whispers as I stare into her deep blue eyes.

"Yes, baby girl?" I whisper, unable to tear my eyes from her beautiful face.

"Kiss me," she whispers. I don't need telling twice. I lean forward and press my lips to hers. Instantly she threads her fingers into the hair at the top of my neck and deepens the kiss. Fuck I could get lost in this remarkable woman; I've never felt so much from one kiss; every fibre of my body comes alive from the touch of her lips and the way her tongue sweeps across mine; it's just perfect. I reluctantly pull away from her and smile.

"If I don't stop kissing you now, I'm not sure I'll ever be able to." I sigh as Clare chuckles and leans her head against my shoulder. The top of her head rests perfectly in line with my lips. I turn my head slightly and kiss her forehead.

"We should be getting back anyway," she replies softly. I put my forefinger under her chin and lift her head so she looks at me as I step back a little.

"I won't push you into anything, I know at the moment you need a friend, and I am more than happy to be that for you. But once Daisy returns home, I want to try being more," I admit honestly as I look down at her. Clare looks back at me and smiles.

"You're already more," she whispers before pressing her lips to mine again. I slide my hand to the back of her head and tighten my other arm around her. I feel the breeze shift around us and inhale the sweet scent ... I pull away from Clare quickly and sniff the air.

"What's the matter?" Clare asks as I take her hand and pull her against my back protectively as I turn us around. Keeping her hidden and safe behind me as I sniff the air again and look in the direction from which the scent is coming. I take a few steps forward, the scent getting stronger with each one until it comes into view.

"That's it. That's part of the scent!"

)) ● ((

I help Clare out of the car before taking her hand and leading her into the house.

"Michael?" I call as soon as I enter; Marcus quickly comes out of the dining room with a finger on his mouth.

"He's finally asleep." He whispers, waving us into the dining room; we quickly follow him.

Around the table, I notice Natalie, Alex, Nigel, and my brother Owen.

"What are you doing here?" I ask him, frowning.

"Marcus called me in to go through all this paperwork. Where the hell have you been hiding?" Owen asks before looking down at my hand, which still holds Clare's. He looks back at me, frowning. "Who's your girlfriend?"

"That's his mate, Clare." Marcus corrects him as he looks over, smirking, knowing full well he's winding up Alex and teasing me.

"Congrats, little bro," Owen grins at me before turning to Clare. "Welcome to the family." He says with a smile.

"They aren't mated yet." Alex pipes in with a look my way.

"Pack it in, Dad." Clare sighs as she takes hold of my arm; I tighten my hold on her hand before turning to Marcus.

"I found a part of Kellan's scent, but something is missing, which I can't quite work out. Now and again, it smells closer to it, but I can't work out how." I explain as I hold out a cutting of the plant.

"Something's better than nothing," Marcus says as he looks at it. "That's not from Mama B's garden," he points out; I shake my head.

"No. It's from in the woods next to it," Clare answers.

"What were you doing in the woods?" Alex asks, glaring at me. I glare right back, refusing to be intimidated by him.

"Dad, we were looking for the scent; enough," Clare warns as she stares at him. He moves his eyes to look at her before huffing and returning to the papers in front of him.

"What's going on in here?" Will asks as he walks into the room, holding a plate of cut up fruits. I grab some from his plate. "Dude, first my girl, now my breakfast? Stop stealing my stuff." Will protests smirking, as Marcus and Natalie both stifle a laugh. I sniff the fruit in my hand before pulling Clare closer to me and sniffing her neck.

"What the hell do you think you are doing?" Alex growls as he jumps to his feet.

"That's why I said it smelt the closest to his scent in the car. It was mixed with the citrus from yours," I explain, looking at Clare before turning to Marcus. "Kellan's scent is a mixture of these two things."

Chapter Fifty-Six

Daisy

I want to go home. I want to get out of this hell hole, find Michael, return to our little house, and never leave again. I'm taking back every strop, moan and tantrum I had about having to stay there whilst hiding from Jackson. After this, I swear I am never leaving Michael's side again. I'm going to climb on his back like a baby monkey and never ever let him go. Adventurous Daisy, who climbs out of bedroom windows, is long gone. This home bird is never leaving her nest again!

I promised Marcus I wouldn't be weak if taken, but it's getting harder and harder the longer I'm away from Michael. My wolf is pining for him constantly. I need him to know I'm okay, that Jackson hasn't been able to hurt me, not yet, anyway. But the thought of hearing his voice through the bond and not knowing when I can be back in his arms will be harder than not hearing him at all.

I'm currently curled up on the bed. The air conditioning has been turned up, and it's freezing. I know Jackson's doing it on purpose to try and weaken me, but it's not going to happen. I'm not backing down.

Luckily, I'm still not chained to the wall or bed. Jackson and two goons did come in and try, but I was prepared, and I had shifted, knowing that the second I shifted back, the chains would be loose, and I'd be able to get out of them.

Jackson had been livid when he realised I could shift on-demand now and had cursed me something ugly that day. But I was too busy laughing at his eye, which he still couldn't open properly. Plus, his nose is wonky after I broke it. I thought his little buddy Kellan would have healed it for him because he has some serious magic skills. I haven't seen or heard from Kellan since he dropped me off in this cell. Not that I want to see the prick. I'll know I've hit an all-time low if I start wishing for him to visit.

I have no idea how long I've been here as there are no

windows or any way for natural light to come in. It could be the middle of the night, for all I know. I could have been here twenty-four hours; I could have been here one hundred. Why did I stop wearing a wristwatch? Note to self, buy one as soon as I get out of here and never take it off. Not that I ever plan on being abducted again.

I'm so concerned for Michael as I know he'll be going out of his mind with worry. For the millionth time I consider opening the bond, but saving him from my internal feelings and panic is all I can do to help him. I hope Marcus has told him I am more prepared than he's aware.

I know I should have told him about Marcus training me, but I didn't want him to think he had failed me, because he hasn't. I understand why he was reluctant to do it himself. I did this for my benefit; I had to prepare myself to ensure I could survive long enough for Michael to find me because I know he will. I hope he isn't too mad at us for hiding it from him.

Suddenly, the cell door opens, and Kellan waltzes in, followed closely by Jackson.

"Oh, look, it's Beavis and Butthead, or is it Dumb and Dumber? I can't decide." I sigh as I sit on the edge of the bed.

"Just shut up for once in your life." Jackson groans at me. I laugh, holding my hands up.

"Sorry, someone obviously got out of bed on the wrong side this morning. Is your eye still bothering you? Or maybe your nose?" Jackson flies towards me, but Kellan stops him before he reaches the bed.

"Pack it in; there's no point beating the shit out of her; you're just letting her win that way," Kellan points out. As he turns Jackson away from me, he quickly glares over his shoulder, trying to tell me to behave, but I wink and smile in return.

"Get the hell off me," Jackson growls as he shrugs Kellan off. "I'm not here to antagonise her; I'm here to talk to her about something."

"Then why insist that I'm here?" Kellan asks, frowning. Before I even see it coming, Kellan teleports me from my bed to the other side of the room. He presses me to his back as he stands between Jackson and me.

"Fucking stop doing that," I growl as I nearly lose the little food I've eaten since I got here.

"What the fuck are you up to?" Kellan growls. I try to move away from him, but he holds me tight. I know I could fight him, but I can't be bothered.

"I should be asking you the same thing, Kellan. Did you think you were going to get away with it?" Jackson growls.

"Get away with what? I've done everything you ask of me." I feel his hold tighten on me and realise I may be in trouble here, as I can tell Kellan is worried about something.

"Oh, I know you have, but I also know that now we have Daisy, you're trying to work out a way to run with her. How stupid do you think I am?" Jackson growls.

"Very," I mutter under my breath; I swear I hear Kellan chuckle under his before he answers him.

"How am I meant to run with her when I can't teleport out of this fucking building after you put the rest of the wards up. I can only teleport around the room I'm in."

"Why do you think I have done that, you idiot. Seriously, Kellan, you may have built up the muscle mass in the last few years, but your brain cells are dying quicker than a fish out of water." Jackson snaps.

"Would someone like to explain to me what the fuck is going on?" I ask, rolling my eyes.

"Shut up, Daisy." Kellan and Jackson both snap together. I almost laugh to myself.

"Well, if I'm not allowed to participate in the conversation, can you kindly take it out of my cell. Some of us have a headache," I moan. Kellan turns around and frowns at me.

"Why have you got a headache?" He asks, looking concerned. I roll my eyes at him.

"Oh, I don't know, maybe because two idiots are arguing in my cell like a couple of spoilt brats." I sigh. Kellan looks at my face and curses before spinning back around to Jackson.

"What the fuck are you doing?" Kellan shouts at him. I look at Jackson, who's grinning,

"What I should have done as soon as we got her here."

I open my mouth to comment when I feel the room spin; I grab hold of Kellan, expecting to find he's teleported us, but instead, he looks down at me, his brown eyes wide with surprise.

"What the fuck?" I mutter as I feel my legs go from underneath me; Kellan grabs me and holds me against him.

"Jackson, you've had your fun. Now pack it in. Leave her alone. She's about to pass out." I hear Kellan shout.

"That's the point; you aren't the only one with powers." I try to look at Jackson. What the fuck? Does he have magic? I can hear the two of them arguing before everything goes black; as much as I try to fight it, I can't stop myself from drifting into a heavy sleep.

Kellan

"Fuck." I curse, catching Daisy as she passes out. "What the fuck are you playing at Jackson?" I turn and face my brother with Daisy in my arms; I quickly carry her to the bed. I hate that this leaves her vulnerable, but I know there's no way of safely getting her out of here. I can feel Jackson causing her to slip into a coma-like sleep.

"What's your big plan here? Why am I still alive if you're convinced I'm here to take her? Why not just kill me?" I demand as I turn back to face my brother, keeping myself between Daisy and him.

"Our darling mother made me take a blood oath that you would never die by my hand. If I just let you go, I know you'll run to that dickhead Adams and tell him where we are. So I have come up with my plan to keep you in line. Which in turn will get Daisy to do as she's told." My brother explains as he grins at me with that evil look in his eyes.

"Fuck you, Jackson. What you mean is you can't do jack shit without me. You need me to keep the wards around this place and keep Daisy from kicking your ass again," I reply, shaking my head.

"Why do you think I said I'm not going to kill you. As much as I hate to admit it, your magic is stronger than mine. It always has been. I need you to keep the wards up and active so that bastard Adams and his band of merry wolves can't find her."

"And if I refuse?" I ask.

"Every time you refuse, I will harm Daisy, whether I break a finger or cut something off. Yes, she'll survive, but how much disfiguration will she endure before breaking completely?" Jackson lets out a whistle as the door bursts open. Three of his goons come in and form a barrier between him and me. My back is against the bed, protecting the still unconscious Daisy. I want to teleport, but I know he'll hurt her if I do.

"Grab him," Jackson growls; the three guys step forward, and I swing my fist towards the one closest to me and catch him in the jaw. But I'm outnumbered as two of them advance toward me; the third is heading for Daisy.

"Don't fucking touch her!" I growl as I turn towards him.

The other two grab me as my back is turned to them, and I feel a foot connect with the back of my knees, forcing my legs from underneath me. Two of Jackson's men hold me down by the arms as soon as I'm on my knees, ensuring I can't move. I notice a knife in the third guy's hand, which he hands to my brother, who smiles wickedly at me.

"Don't hurt her, you arsehole; she's unconscious, for fuck sake," I yell at him as I try to fight off the guys holding me, but every time I move, it feels like my arms are going to be ripped from their sockets.

"I know; it's the only way I was going to be able to do this. I need you both together for the next bit, and she hates being near you almost as much as I do. And if she were awake, she would fight, and I would kill the little bitch," Jackson explains, grinning at me.

Jackson cuts my hand, reaches over, and cuts Daisy's, who moans but remains unconscious. The guys drag me to the bed and force my bleeding hand into hers. Jackson starts chanting a spell in old fae, which I don't recognise at first. But slowly, the words start to make sense as my insides turn to ice as I realise what he's doing.

"Fuck, no, not that. What the hell are you doing?!" I yell as I try and fight against the guys holding me. But they tighten their hold, mine and Daisy's hands together as I feel our blood mixing, the connection between us becoming stronger. I fight and shout, but it's no good; the spell is too far along. If I end it now, I put Daisy at risk. I stop fighting and accept the inevitable.

Eventually, my brother stops chanting, and his men let me fall to the floor. I instantly look up at Daisy and then at Jackson.

"What the fuck did you do?" I gasp, praying I'm mistaken.

"You know full well what I did." He replies with a casual shrug of his shoulders. Shit.

"But why? What the hell do you achieve from *that.*" I ask as I look down at my cut hand.

"With her linked to you, I have a way of controlling you both because..." Jackson turns and punches me in the face. Daisy screams and clenches her face as if she had been the one punched. "Your pain is her pain, and her pain is yours. What's done to one is done to the other," Jackson explains smugly.

"What the fuck was that for?" I turn and see Daisy lying on the bed, holding her face. I slump further to the floor, unable to look at her.

"He linked us, which means if one of us is hurt or killed, the other is too," I whisper as I look up at her and see her trying to process it.

"You sick son of a bitch!" Daisy yells at him as she jumps up, but one of Jackson's guys pushes her back down. "Why have you linked me to him? Why him!" she demands, pointing to me.

"This way, he won't try to escape and get word to your lover boy. Because if Adams sees him, he won't be able to control his temper and will beat him within an inch of his life or even kill him. What will happen to you, Daisy, if Kellan is killed?" Jackson asks.

"You sick fuck!" she hisses as she throws herself at him again.

The next few seconds happen in slow motion as I watch on in amazement. One of Jackson's guys tries to stop her, but this time she's ready for him, and she punches him in the stomach before kicking him between the legs; as he doubles over, she grabs his head and brings it down hard onto her advancing knee, I swear I hear his skull crack with the impact. Daisy throws him to one side and charges towards Jackson again. The two other guys that had hold of me grab her but she sidekicks one in the stomach, and the other gets a broken nose for his trouble. I feel every kick and punch, and I know how much power she puts into each. I have no idea where she has got this strength from, as I know he hasn't been feeding her.

Daisy grabs Jackson with a look of murder on her face. "Undo it, now!" she snarls in his face. Jackson smiles at her, but I can see the fear in his eyes; she just took out three men and hasn't even broken a sweat.

"No can do, darling."

"Don't call me, darling!" Daisy hisses as she brings her head back and head-butts Jackson, breaking his nose further. I can't help but smile as I watch her take on my brother.

Daisy's so much stronger than she was the last time he took her, physically and mentally. Jackson shouts, and more of his pack rush into the room, surrounding the two of them. But she doesn't let him go.

"I will call you whatever I want as you are mine. I own you now. If I want to stop you, all I have to do is hurt Kellan there." Jackson gloats as he points to me. Daisy's anger surges, and she knocks him to the ground. I can't stop the laugh that bursts from my lips as she pins him. His men all advance to pull her from him, but she's fighting to keep hold of Jackson, who's trying to hide how scared he is. But I can see it, and I know some of his men will as well.

I've been so caught up in watching Daisy that I haven't noticed one of the guys she had taken out before, getting up and making their way to me. It's not until I feel the knife's sharp edge against my shoulder as he slices into the flesh I realise he's there. Daisy screams and falls to the side as blood gushes from her new wound. Jackson laughs at her as she turns and looks at me, holding her arm, seeing that my arm is bleeding too.

"That's one way to get you to stop." Jackson laughs. He nods towards two of his guys, who grab Daisy by the arms and pull her, so she's kneeling in front of Jackson. Even though she's injured, she is still trying to fight them. I also know if she wanted to, she could break free.

"You will pay for this, you bastard. When Michael gets his hands on you, he'll make you pay for every mark you leave on my body, no matter how small. That's if I don't kill you first!" She growls.

"When are you going to get it into your thick head?" Jackson snarls as he leans over Daisy. "Your precious Michael will never find you; there's no way he can save you now. So you might as well accept that you *will* be the Luna of this pack. You *will* use your magic when I tell you to, and you will help me overthrow the magical council and all that stands in my way." I watch as Daisy stares at him for a moment before she bursts out laughing.

"You have no idea, do you?!" She laughs, and I panic, hoping she doesn't tell him I have use of her magic. Jackson looks at her frowning.

"My magic has been weak since I escaped you last time. I'm barely a level one. Just casting a simple healing spell drains my magic to full exhaustion. Do you really think I can help you overthrow the council? I can't even throw a fucking pancake with my powers. All your plans are fucking useless."

Daisy looks over at me and shakes her head laughing as she gets up and shrugs off the men still holding her. "I'm not going to touch him, you idiots; he's not worth my energy." Daisy snaps before they step back from her, there's something in her tone I haven't noticed before, but suddenly a lot of things make sense. Fuck, she's an alpha and a fucking strong one too. How did I miss that? Does Jackson realise? Does he know she is stronger than him?

"As for Michael giving up on me, he never will. He will have the whole supernatural council working with him to find me. There's nowhere you can hide." Daisy turns and sits on the bed as she looks around.

"You can all get out now. I'm bored of you all." She looks at Jackson and smiles. "What time is it? Too late for coffee or too early for gin? If any is going, I could do with a drink of both." I can't help laughing as Jackson growls at her, as she smiles at him smugly. He turns to face me before pointing in my direction.

"Get him in his room and lock it. I will deal with them both later." I continue laughing as the guys drag me to my feet and push me from the room. I glance over my shoulder and see Daisy giving us a little wave as we go.

I might not like Michael Adams, but I can't deny he has helped Daisy become a hell of a fighter and how she's dealing with Jackson has him written all over it; she's acting just as arrogant as him. If it isn't that he has taught her to be stronger, it's that he makes her simply by being her mate.

I can see she is never going to give up on him, and from what I've seen over the last few months, he isn't going to give up on her, either. Maybe it's time to admit defeat and accept that Michael Adams isn't as wrong for her as I initially thought.

I'm pushed through the door into my room as Jackson smiles at me from the doorway, his face again covered in blood and his nose looking even more swollen than before, after Daisy headbutted him for the second time.

"If I were you, I wouldn't think about running and getting help because if you go anywhere near the Blood Moon pack, you'll be killed on sight, and if they don't kill you, they will beat you. If bruises start to appear on her body, I will move her to another location," Jackson says with a grin.

"This is a big risk, Jackson. What if they kill me when they find you?" I ask.

"I have a plan. If anything should happen to you, I will go for my second option: Daisy's little coven sister. She'd be the perfect consolation prize." Jackson laughs as he closes the door. I hear the key turn and know I'll be left here for a while. Jackson's favourite punishment is to leave me for twenty-four hours without food and drink.

I walk to my window and look out. I'm on the third floor of the manor house, too far to jump and thanks to the wards, I can't teleport out of here. I look over at the tree and the large branch that is within reach of my window. If I can climb onto that, I can make my way to the trunk, and I should be far enough away to teleport.

I open my window and climb onto the ledge. I quickly check no one's watching and jump to the branch. I only just manage to catch it before I fall to the ground. I tighten my grip and take a deep breath before pulling myself up, praying it doesn't snap.

As soon as I'm safely sitting on the branch, I make my way over to the trunk. I can feel myself walking through the wards I have around the building. Luckily, it will only be me who feels them as I put them up; Jackson can only control the ones inside the building.

I look around and decide to test my theory; I teleport to the next tree. I look back at my bedroom and realise I've left the window open. Shit. I try to use my magic to close it, but I'm on the wrong side of the wards. Fuck. I'll have to do all this a damn sight quicker than I planned because as soon as someone sees that window open, they will check on me and find my room empty. I close my eyes and picture my next stop.

I open them outside of the blood moon pack territory. Even I know it's not safe for me here. I have to plan this next move carefully. I close my eyes and teleport to the roof of the building I need. I listen carefully with my advanced fae hearing and can hear the voice of the wolf I need inside. From what Daisy says of him, he is the only one who won't let his feelings overpower his ability to act rationally. I close my eyes take a deep breath to steady my nerves, and teleport into the office below.

"What the fuck?!"

I open my eyes and see two men standing at a desk; the bigger of the men, with his broad as fuck shoulders and olive skin, pushes the other, older guy behind him. I look up at the dark brown eyes as I gasp for breath; teleporting has taken it out of me. Marcus steps away from the Alpha as he advances towards me, snarling. I quickly throw up my hands.

"Don't hit me; it will hurt Daisy, and she needs you now!"

Chapter Fifty-Seven

Michael

It's been five days since Daisy was taken. Five days, fourteen hours, and seventeen minutes since I last heard her voice.

"I'm sorry, Mikey. I love you so much; remember that." I hear it constantly on repeat, like a stuck record. How could I ever forget how much she loves me? I just hope and pray that she knows how much I love her too.

The longer she is missing, the more I'm struggling to stay in control, to the point a few hours ago, Marcus declared enough. They've moved the whole operation out of the house, and Desmond has ordered me to step down. He's promised I'll get an update every couple of hours, and if anything comes up, they will call me in. But I'm now stuck at home with Mum and a 'babysitter', as Daisy kept calling them.

Jon has just left to interrogate the rogues we found at the den again, and Will's downstairs, giving me space. I'm sitting in my office, ignoring Marcus's order to do nothing and trying desperately to find somewhere big enough for Jackson to move his pack. Nothing indicates he has taken them abroad, which is a relief.

We've found evidence from the paperwork taken from the den that Jackson's looked at premises in Cornwall, Scotland, London, South Wales, Manchester, and Nottingham. He's purposely left that trail so our team would be as stretched as possible as we check them out. It shows how little he knows of our pack as we haven't had to check any of these premises ourselves. The closer packs have checked each one and recorded and documented what they found, which is absolutely nothing. Each one is a dead end. We can't seem to catch a break and are no closer to finding her than we were five days ago.

So now I'm looking for what's been available around those properties, anything in a twenty-mile radius that may house around twenty wolves. I know he may have more, and there's no way for us to have the exact number of his pack. We also have no idea what Kellan has in place to stop us from getting to Daisy. That kid is powerful as hell; how none of us picked up on it before is beyond me.

Alex and Nigel have discussed the fae with the Magical Elders to see what they can find out. They've learned that teleporting is a scarce gift, even for the fae. But it can be traced back to one bloodline in particular. The Mournmoon bloodline.

This particular fae family has many known historical warriors and leaders within it. The history of this noble bloodline alone could fill a library. They're renowned and believed to hold the highest position within the fae courts. However, we have no idea how Kellan was born into the family as none of them has been rumoured to have travelled to the human realm in nearly five hundred years.

Tony and I have sat down while reviewing textbook after textbook from various contacts, and we can't find any mention of a child born in this realm. Tony said he asked Kellan once about his family, and he just said, "They aren't around much," and that was the end of it. Tony never pushed in case his own parentage came up.

Demons, when born, are handed over or taken by their fathers to be brought up, as they are always male. Once a child comes of age, at eighteen, the father lets them live their own life and will offer to help cover their expenses until they can stand on their own. Tony has no idea who his real father is, as his "uncle" brought him up.

I look at my screen and realise I can no longer see the display; my eyes are too tired. I've hardly slept since I took that sleeping draft four days ago and have refused any others. I stand up and stretch before heading downstairs to make a fresh coffee.

I walk into the kitchen to find Mum stirring a large pot on the oven. She's been keeping everyone supplied with food since day one. I know it's her way of keeping busy, as she is struggling as much as the rest of us with Daisy being gone. Looking at her now, I can tell she's been crying. She might have wiped away the tears quickly when she heard me on the stairs, but her eyes are red and swollen. Her hair, which usually hangs in its thick tidy bob, looks ruffled as if she has run her fingers through it just as much as I have my own. It's a trait I picked up from watching her over the last twenty-eight years.

As I walk past her to the coffee machine, I plant a kiss on her cheek and squeeze her shoulders.

"What do you need, Mikey?" she asks, her voice croaking to the point she has to clear her throat.

"Just a coffee Mum, I'll get it," I reply, needing to keep busy. I look over my shoulder and hear Will in the lounge; he's been pacing since he arrived, not knowing what to do with himself. We are all struggling without Daisy; we cannot relax enough to sleep. We all need her home.

"Want a coffee, Will?" I call. He appears at the kitchen door.

"Please. Make it two sugars instead of one." I nod as I get two mugs off the draining board; I've purposely avoided going in the cupboard, as seeing Daisy's mug sets me off every time. Has she had a coffee since she was taken? Is he at least giving her food and drink? Or is he starving her?

"Mikey?"

I snap out of my thoughts and look at my mum, watching me with that concerned look on her face.

"I'm fine, Mama," I whisper in response.

"You don't have to lie to us, Mikey," Will says from his spot on the other side of the breakfast bar. I open my mouth to tell him I know, when I hear two vans stopping outside the house and the sound of people running up the path; I'm just getting past Mum when the front door flies open.

"Mikey!" Marcus shouts as he and the Alpha rush into the entrance hall. Will and I stop in the doorway at the sight of them, both in their mission gear.

"What's happened?" we ask together.

"We know where she is!" Desmond declares. I freeze. It's the last thing I thought I would do when I finally heard those five words, but I'm terrified I'm dreaming. Marcus steps up to me and places a reassuring hand on my shoulder.

"We found her, Mikey; we're going to get her and bring her home. Get your shit. We move out in five minutes when everyone gets here." I drop the mug in my hand as I spin around and race up the stairs, not caring when I hear it smash as it hits the floor.

In less than three minutes, I'm rushing down the stairs in my black cargo trousers and black t-shirt we wear on missions, with my boots in hand as Marcus and Will, now in his gear, are talking in the hallway. Stuart and Alex rush through the front door. Marcus turns and looks at them both.

"Are they safe?" Marcus asks.

"Yes, they're in the warehouse with enough wards to kill anyone who tries to tamper with them," Alex answers.

"What's going on? Who's in danger?" I ask as I drop down on the bottom step to tie my boot laces.

"Clare," Stuart growls. Alex places a hand on his shoulder as if to calm him.

"What?" I ask, jumping to my feet; Marcus turns and faces me, nodding.

"Looks like Daisy is doing exactly what she planned to do and is making Jackson's life hell; the problem is he's making alternative plans," Marcus explains.

"How do you know all this, and how do you know where she is?" I ask as I walk up to my second.

"I'll explain in the van, we don't have much time, and it's a four-hour drive." I go to rush out of the door but feel a hand on my arm stopping me. I turn to find Mum looking up at me with tears in her tired eyes.

"Be careful; make sure you all come home and that you kill the son of a bitch," she demands. I lean over and kiss her on the cheek.

"I promise Mama, can you get everything ready for when we bring her home?" Mum smiles at me, nodding. I storm out of the house and see three vans and three cars outside; I start heading to the van in the front when Marcus grabs my arm.

"You're in the second one."

"Why?" I ask, frowning.

"Just trust me, Mikey," Marcus states; I look at my second

and nod as I make my way to the next van. I'm surprised when Marcus and the Alpha follow me. Will heads to the front van, where I see Owen behind the wheel; Alex joins Will as Stuart jumps behind the wheel of our van.

These are our mission vans. They're adapted in the back with benches and two holding cells. As I climb into the back of the van, I hear Marcus calling for Owen to drive around and get behind us.

As soon as Marcus and I are sitting in the back, the Alpha next to Stuart in the front, I hear Marcus giving him the go-ahead to start driving. As soon as we pull away from the house, I turn to him.

"Right enough, I want to know what you know and how you know it now," I demand. Marcus and Desmond share a look as Desmond nods.

Marcus takes a deep breath and looks at me.

"Kellan told us."

"WHAT?!" I roar as I go to jump to my feet; Marcus pulls me back down before I hit my head on the van's roof. "How the fuck did you find him?"

"We didn't; he found us. He teleported into the Alpha's office about an hour ago, begging us to save her."

"And where the fuck is he now? How do you know he isn't running off to tell Jackson we're on our way, and this is some big trap to lure us away from them?" I demand, as there's no way I will ever believe a word that comes out of that arseholes mouth again.

"Because he's in the other van, guarded by Jon, Natalie, and Will. Plus, Alex has put a spell on the van to stop him from teleporting."

"Stop this van right now, Stuart," I demand as I go to stand up again.

"Stuart, keep driving." The Alpha commands as he looks from Stuart to me, "Michael, if you don't calm down, I will have Marcus put you in that cell."

"Calm down? Are you fucking kidding me right now?"

"Adams, I mean it, calm the fuck down; that's an order!" Desmond snaps at me using his Alpha tone, making me sit instantly, bowing my head in submission. "Thank you." He sighs as he turns to Marcus, who's watching me.

"As I was saying, Kellan teleported into the office and begged us to save Daisy. She's been making Jackson's life hell, and he's quickly concluding that he may need to up his game or find an alternative. He has singled out Clare as a possibility."

"Daisy would never allow that," I say through gritted teeth as my body freezes out of fear for my mate.

"We all know that, so Kellan wants us to kill Jackson before he breaks Daisy down."

"How can we trust him after everything he's done?" I ask. I see the Alpha and Marcus share another look before Marcus continues.

"We believe him as it seems Jackson has magically linked Daisy and Kellan to each other."

"What do you mean?" I ask cautiously.

"I mean whatever harm is done to one is done to the other. If I let you punch Kellan, you'd be hurting Daisy, which is why I have kept you both apart," Marcus explains.

I wait for the punch line, but from the look of Marcus and Desmond, there is none.

"You're serious, aren't you?" I ask carefully; Marcus nods and places a hand on my shoulder.

"I am; Alex has checked it out and confirmed it. He is in the other van trying to find out what he needs to undo the spell."

"Fuck." I growl as I lean forward and place my head in my hands. This is too much to take in in one go. "I want to speak to him." I sigh as I lift my head and look at Marcus.

"What do you plan on saying to him?" Desmond asks; I look up at him and take a deep breath.

"I want to know why and what his overall plan is here," I admit. Marcus looks at Desmond, who nods and hands over a tablet. I watch as he opens an app and Jon's face comes onto the screen.

"Everything okay in there?" Marcus asks.

"Yeah, how you doing, Mikey?" Jon answers as Marcus hands the screen over to me, and I look at my brother.

"I honestly don't know, Jonny. Can you put Kellan on?" I

ask; Jon looks to the side before moving the screen so I can see Kellan sitting on the cell floor. He looks at the screen and gives me a sheepish wave, his hands tied together with a cable tie.

"Alright, Michael."

"Kellan," I growl as I feel my temper rise.

"Long time no see," Kellan answers.

"Cut the pleasantries. Why Kellan? Why did you turn her over to him?" I look at him and see a broken kid for the first time.

"It all went wrong; I was meant to get away with her." He looks up at me, and I see his eyes change. "If you had walked away and left her alone, none of this would have happened. She was safe with me. She has always been safer with me. She was mine to protect."

"She was never yours, Kellan," I growl at him.

"Yes, she was. Who do you think nursed her through her transition after he bit her? Who helped her after her first full moon? Who cleaned her up when he beat her until she was unconscious? It was me, always me. I was the reason she escaped. I unlocked the door that night, "Kellan declares.

"If that's true, why doesn't she remember any of it?" I ask, knowing Daisy would have told me if she knew.

"Because I made her forget me," Kellan answers. I don't know if that would even be possible.

"Who is Jackson to you?" I ask, trying my hardest to stay calm. Losing it with Kellan now would be the same as losing it with Daisy.

"I told Marcus all of this." Kellan sighs, rolling his eyes.

"And now you're telling me," I growl as my patience is thinning.

"He's my brother."

I look at him, amazed. "Your brother? But you're not a wolf. So he was bitten?" I ask.

"Obviously, dumbass." Kellan sighs, making my temper rise further.

"Kellan, I might not be able to punch you without hurting my Daisy but don't think I will take being spoken to like shit. The second your life's not linked to hers, I'll have free reign to kill you. The less you piss me off, the better." I warn as I look at him, and he keeps his mouth shut.

"Where has he taken her?"

"South Wales. I thought it would throw you off if he went somewhere different," Kellan answers.

"It worked. Why can no one track her magically, but Jackson always seemed able to find her?" I ask.

"It's me who can track her, using her mother's ring. It also works as a blocker from anyone else. I did it so Jackson would never find her," Kellan says.

"So you haven't been working for Jackson?" I ask. Kellan shakes his head.

"Working for that arsehole? Hell no. I've been as much his prisoner as Daisy. When I tried to scare her away from you in March, I did it thinking she would run back to Cornwall. I never thought she would go back to Exeter.

"I placed the spell on her mother's ring when he first took her three years ago because it hasn't left her hand since she was sixteen. So I would always know where she was. It linked me to her magic and allowed me to use it when needed. To keep her safe." Kellan explains.

"Can you communicate with her? You did it before through a dream," I ask, sitting back, amazed with how wrong we've had things. Kellan shakes his head.

"It's too dangerous. He'll move her if he realises I can contact her or I'm gone. He'll block me, and we lose her, possibly for good." I start breathing heavily, my anger getting the better of me. What I would give to punch something right now.

"Who linked you?" I'm trying to get as much information from him as possible as I need answers.

"Jackson."

"Why? Surely, he knew we would kill you if we found you," I ask, frowning.

"He did it to ensure I didn't come to you myself. Plus, he'll know you have me if bruises appear on her. He will move her," Kellan states.

"It's a hell of a risk coming to us; we could have just killed you on sight." I point out. Kellan shrugs.

"It was a risk I was willing to take. Things have gotten out of hand, and Daisy needs more help than just mine. Plus, Jackson plans to take Clare; Daisy would never put her at risk."

I hear Stuart growl from the driver's seat.

"She's safe; he won't get the chance to get to her," Desmond whispers to the youngest member of my team.

I wish Daisy were as safe as Clare is now. What I would give to know she was out of harm's way.

"We get her out, then what? You take her from me again?" I ask, still not trusting the guy not to double cross us.

"No, I've learnt my lesson. You win; you can protect her better than me." I look at him through the screen and blink a few times.

"What? That easy? You're just going to walk away?" I ask, not believing him. Kellan looks at me, confused.

"What part of this has been easy, Michael? I've watched over her for years. I finally get close to her, and you fucking show up and steal her away. I even tried to kill you twice, but Daisy nearly died instead. She is part of me, but she chooses you; it will always be you, so I have to walk away again. I'll make sure she is safe and then leave. But I'm telling you now, you fuck up, and I'll make sure you pay," he warns.

Suddenly Kellan's head snaps back as if he's been hit. All I can do is stare at the screen as his nose starts bleeding, and his lip splits as if he'd been punched.

"What the fuck?" Jon yells as he drops the tablet, I can't see what's happening, but I hear Kellan gasp five words that cause my insides to drop.

"We're running out of time."

Chapter Fifty-Eight

Daisy

"Grab her!"

I jump from the bed where I'm sleeping as four guys hurtle towards me. I'm dizzy, weak, and in no shape to fight them all. I somehow manage to land a few punches and maybe a kick, but before I even know what's happening, I'm pinned to the floor, all four men holding me down as I shout and fight against them.

"What the fuck?!" I yell as I try again to get loose but to no avail.

"Just stop before you hurt yourself." Jackson laughs as he squats down by my head. Someone grabs a handful of my hair and forces my head to the side and against the floor, so I'm looking in Jackson's direction.

He still has a black eye, and the swelling is still visible around his broken nose; I can't help but laugh.

"What's the matter? Realised you'll only get what you want if I'm held down or unconscious?"

"I don't want what you think. There's plenty of time for that, sweetheart," he replies as he smirks at me. He looks at the guys who are holding me down and nods. They pick me up, and I fight them again, but their hold's too tight. There's no opening for me to get free now.

As they lift me, I see two other guys bring in a chair. I'm quickly forced into it and held as my limbs are tied with cable ties to the arms and legs.

"You know what you need to do to get out of this. It will hurt, but you can do it." I hear Marcus's voice. Three times he tied me up just like this, and twice I managed to get free.

I watch Jackson as he seems to be examining my face.

"It's a little late to be looking for flaws, Jackass. Any scars are from the last time you kept me tied up." I huff as I sit back and try to look bored. Trying hard not to show that this is the first time I've been terrified.

"I'm just checking for any new cuts or bruises," Jackson says as he pulls the collar of my t-shirt from my neck.

"Well, if I have any, it's your thugs that put them there." I snap as I pull away from him as much as I can.

"No new aches or pains then?" he asks.

"No, why should I … Kellan's escaped, hasn't he?!" I laugh, which gets cut off as Jackson backhands me across the face. Fuck, that hurt like a bitch. "You caught me in the eye, you fuckwit!" I shout seconds before he punches me in the jaw. I turn and spit out the blood that gushes into my mouth.

"Where has Kellan gone?" he asks as he leans towards me; I look up at him frowning.

"Why should I know where he is?"

"Because that prick will do anything to protect you," Jackson growls.

"He's done fuck all to protect me. Why should I give a shit about where he's gone? He won't go anywhere near my pack; he can't fucking risk it." I point out, praying that he has gone to get help. I'm starting to think he's as much of a prisoner here as me.

"Do you expect me to believe he hasn't confided in you? Everything that idiot's done in the last three years has been about you. Why would he stop caring now?" Jackson growls as he hits me again. I'm sure he has busted my nose this time. I can feel the blood running down into my mouth.

"I've known the dick for less than a year. I don't know how you think we know each other, but he was just a kid from my class," I shout. Jackson turns and stares at me for a moment, and then he starts laughing. Not just a chuckle but that deep evil laugh he does when he thinks he has one over you.

"He knows something we don't." My wolf whispers. No fucking shit and I don't like it.

"You don't know, do you?" He laughs.

"Are you deaf or just thick? I already told you I don't know where he is." I snap, rolling my eyes.

"You don't know who Kellan is, you smart-mouthed bitch." He smirks at me; I stare at him and wait for him to tell me more. The longer he takes, the higher I feel my brows getting.

"Well, go on then, enlighten me. Who is he?" I finally demand, realising he's waiting for me to ask.

"Oh, I'm not going to tell you. If he hasn't bothered, then why should I? He can tell you himself when we find him and bring him back. That's if lover boy doesn't find him and kill him first. Cause let's face it, it's a real possibility." Jackson steps closer before leaning toward me until he is inches from my face, and I can smell his rancid breath. "And what happens if he kills him, Daisy?" he asks.

"I get away from you, and you die when Michael finds out what you did," I reply, smirking.

"Or the guilt of what he's done kills him first," Jackson says, grinning at me as my insides freeze. "Imagine how he will feel when he realises that by killing Kellan, he killed you too. What will that do to him? Will Michael Adams, the big tough protector, be able to live with himself?" Jackson asks, gloating as if he has already won.

I know Jackson can see I'm worried for Michael. The smug look on his face says it all.

"But if I die, who do you have to breed your pups from? You've hunted me for three years for a reason, Jackson; you won't just let me die now that you finally have me." I point out, hoping I am right.

"I will. You see, whilst you've been here, I've done a little more research into your little coven sister Clare, and I think she will be the perfect replacement. She may not have as much strength magically as you, and she may not have the fight I love in you. But she'll make a good substitute, don't you think? She's certainly pretty enough."

"Don't fucking touch her!" I snarl as I pull against the restraints. I can feel the cable ties cutting into my skin, but I don't care.

"If you die or don't start behaving yourself soon, you'll leave me with no choice, won't you?" Jackson growls back at me before standing tall. "So what's it going to be, sweetheart? Are you going to start behaving, or do I grab your coven sister and use her instead?"

My anger explodes, I feel my body tense, and all four cable

ties snap as I scream. I can hear the gasps of the men around me as they realise what I've done. I launch myself at Jackson, but he's waiting for me and kicks me straight in the stomach, not holding anything back. I feel my ribs crack under the pressure of his boot as I sail across the room and hit the wall with a head-splitting crack. I look up as he stands over me, smirking as I gasp for breath, winded from the impact. I've bitten my lip as I hit the wall. With a mouth full of blood, I turn and spit it on the floor. It takes all my willpower not to spit it in his face.

"The more you piss me off, sweetheart, the more likely I am to kill you and go after Clare. So think about it, what would you prefer? To agree to be my Luna and help me build this pack into the unbeatable force, it could be? We could have the strongest wolves in existence.

"Or, will you keep fighting me until I decide I'm bored and kill you? Then, all I have to do is go after Clare and use her instead." Jackson grabs my hair at the back of my head and yanks it hard, so I have no choice but to look up at him.

"Think about it. You have tonight to choose, whilst I arrange for us to move to our next property. When I return in the morning, I expect you to have made the right decision." He leans down and crushes his lips into mine; I want to fight him, but I know that's what he wants; he's looking for a reason to hurt me further. Jackson's tongue forces its way into my mouth as I sit and pray that's as far as he'll take it this time.

It's luckily only seconds later when he pulls away from me and grins down at me.

"That's more like it. I'll give you until morning as promised. After that, I'll come down here to get what I'm owed for being so patient with you." He uses his hold on my hair to force me to the ground; I hit my head against the concrete floor and can't stop the hiss that escapes my lips.

"The clock is ticking, sweetheart," he says as he and the guys all head out of the room, leaving me lying on the floor.

I attempt to stand, but the pain in my stomach and side is too much; I feel myself crumbling back to the floor.

"You keep fighting, and you don't give up." Marcus had

drilled it into me repeatedly as I punched the sparring pads. I can hear him now, telling me I'm stronger than I seem and braver than I believe. Quoting fucking Winnie the Pooh at me over and over again.

I pull myself up into a sitting position and lean against the wall as I wrap an arm around my side and press my hand to my ribs. I know they must be broken from the pain that shoots through my whole body. At least they haven't punctured a lung; breathing hurts but not that much. Jackson's done that before. The pain was so bad I passed out for a couple of days. When I woke up, they'd healed. It was one of the only times I was glad to be a wolf back then.

I sit and take a few shallow breaths as I try to think. My mind's fogged with the pain that's radiating through my body. I want to lower my defences around the bond and hear Michael's voice. I need to hear him and ask him what I should do. But he would feel this pain and panic, and it would kill him to know I'm so injured. He'd blame himself. Even though I would give anything to hear his voice, I can't add to the stress I know he will be under trying to find me.

"But you have to warn him not to kill Kellan. If he kills him, he kills us." My wolf whines. I don't think Michael would kill him straight away, he would beat him within an inch of his life, but he will keep him alive in the hope that he will tell them where I am. I have to hope Marcus is with him to help control Michael.

I lean against the wall and close my eyes. I picture the woods at the back of our house, in the small clearing where Marcus and I would train. I remember our conversation after one session where I'd pushed myself to the point of being physically sick.

I was leaning against a huge tree trunk like I am now against this wall, and I'd turned to see Marcus with his eyes closed as he basked in the sunlight shining through the leaves above us.

"What do I do if I can't fight him?" I ask; Marcus turns and looks at me, frowning.

"Why do you think you won't be able to fight him? You are

getting stronger every week."

"But I know him, Marcus. Jackson used my family against me last time. What if he finds a way to use all of you against me again?"

"Do you believe we would let anything happen to your family?" Marcus asked with an arched brow. I sigh and shake my head as I look ahead of us.

"It's not that simple when it comes to him. He doesn't care if I'm conscious or not. He doesn't care if he has to tie me up so I can't move." I feel bile burn my throat, and I quickly swallow it down. Marcus takes my hand and squeezes it.

"If the only way to stay alive is to let him, then you do," Marcus says softly as he places a hooked finger under my chin and turns my head so I'm looking at him. "If it's the only way, you stop fighting him physically and let him. The more you fight, the more it will hurt you." He whispers. I nod as I know; I learned that when Jackson held me captive the first time.

"Mikey will never look at me the same way again," I whisper, finally admitting the fear eating me up from inside.

"Michael loves you more than life itself. He will destroy the prick who hurt you, who raped you. But he will never stop loving or seeing you as what you are. A fighter."

"But if I give in." I start, but Marcus shakes his head at me.

"You will still be a fighter. We have to learn which battles we fight with our fists and which we fight up here." Marcus says tapping his head. "IF you have to stop fighting physically and let Jackson do THAT to you, you start fighting with your mind. You shut it off and remind yourself that Michael loves you; he will fight heaven and hell to find you and bring you home. He will still love you and worship the very ground you walk on, even if you have had to save yourself by allowing Jackson to rape you." Marcus says quietly but firmly. I feel him wiping away the tears that have run down my cheek.

"No matter what you have to do, Daisy, you do it, and you survive long enough for us to find you. Do you understand me? You fight. You fight to get back to Michael like he will fight to find you. Like I will fight to find you." I take a deep breath, look into Marcus's brown eyes and nod once, letting him see I *understand.*

I look up at the white ceiling of this cell and try to take another deep breath. I know what I need to do. I don't want to do it. I don't. It goes against everything that's screaming inside me. But I will protect Clare, my oldest friend. I'll never let Jackson hurt her as he has me. I won't let her get dragged away from her mate as I have. I smile, remembering that Clare has a mate and that Stuart will spoil her, protect her, and love her with everything he has. She can have the best life with him by her side. They are perfect for each other. I have to let them have that. I have to protect them from going through what Michael and I are.

I slowly use the wall to pull myself up from the floor until I stand on my two shaky legs. One step at a time, I make my way to the bed. I lower myself down until I'm lying in the most comfortable position I can find.

I feel a warmth on my side and feel the pain ease slightly. Not entirely, just enough to make breathing a little easier. I almost smile, realising that Kellan must have healed us enough so Jackson wouldn't know. I close my eyes and take a slightly deeper breath than I've been able to in the last twenty minutes. *"If Michael is going to find us, now would be a perfect time for him to do so,"* my wolf whispers; she sounds as deflated as I feel.

Trust me, I know.

Chapter Fifty-Nine

Michael

This is the longest drive of my life. The mood has been sombre since we watched Kellan's injuries appear, all knowing that Daisy was taking a beating and there was nothing we could do to prevent it.

"What do we know about this place?" I ask as I look up at Marcus sitting on the bench opposite me. He's tapping away on his laptop. Will's communicating with him from the other van through the tablet as they discuss access routes and hiding spots for us all.

"It's a sixteen-bedroom manor house in the middle of freaking nowhere. No nearby houses, which means fewer witnesses. How Jackson found it is beyond me. I think our best bet will be getting Natalie to go in first and assess the access from inside the building."

"Nat's not in the best mood, so she'll be able to handle herself. God help any wolf that pisses her off when we get there." Will sighs.

"I heard that, Matthews." Natalie snaps in the background.

"Not helping the situation dickhead." Jon adds, which is quickly followed by a growl from Natalie.

"Adams, I know you hate me, but sticking me in with these two is just uncalled for," Kellan sighs.

"Shut up!" Natalie and Jon snap together.

"Michael, we have everything we need to separate Daisy and Kellan. I will perform the spell when we get to the outskirts of the manor. They will be separated, and you can kill him if you want." I hear Alex add.

"We need him to get Daisy," I point out.

"We made a deal, Adams. I get you, Daisy, and you'll never need to worry about me again," Kellan says as the screen turns to him.

"What about Daisy's magic? Will you give her back full

control?" Alex asks.

"Yes. As soon as I know she's safe, I swear she will have full control of it; I'll also remove the tracking and blocking spells from the ring," Kellan answers.

"Why should we believe you?" I hear Natalie ask.

"Because, believe it or not, I want what's best for Daisy. The difference in her from the first time my brother took her is huge, and there's no denying Michael's right for her. I kept her hidden, but he made her stronger. Not just emotionally but physically as well. I watched her take out three of Jackson's men in less than thirty seconds. She fought like a machine."

I look at Marcus, who is grinning as he continues tapping away on his laptop.

"What the hell have you been teaching her?" I ask. Marcus shrugs before he looks at me, his face lit up with pure pride.

"Nothing I wouldn't teach this lot."

"Whatever it was, thank you," I say, meaning every word. Marcus looks across at me.

"He's right, Mikey; you made her stronger. Without the confidence and emotional strength she has gained since you two mated, she would have never been able to fight as hard as she has. She's fighting to get back to you. It's always been about getting you back together where you both belong." Marcus explains as I look away to compose myself.

"Well, I hope it's enough as she's taken a beating tonight, and I just pray we can get to her before he breaks her," Will's voice calls through the tablet.

"Daisy knows what she needs to do. She knows when to fight with her fists and when to fight with her mind," Marcus replies as he goes back to working on his laptop.

"We must get her out as soon as possible as Jackson isn't messing about. He's won in his eyes; every time he hurts her, he chips away at her strength and knows it. I'm healing us, little by little, so he doesn't notice, but I can't risk healing us completely," Kellan says. I hate to admit it, but I'm grateful for the bastard at that moment for taking away some of her pain when I can't.

"Is there any way you can get word to her that we are on

the way?" I hear Jon ask.

"No, I risked trying to access her dreams, but she's awake or shut off completely. Whatever she's doing to shut down this bond of yours, Michael, she's shutting everything off." I hear Kellan say.

"Why would she shut it down so tightly?" Will asks; I look out the front window as the dim view flies past.

"Because when Jon and I crashed and fought Jackson's men, she felt everything; it nearly destroyed her. She doesn't want to risk me feeling any of what she is going through," I reply quietly. "If I could get her to open it for just a moment, then I could tell her everything will be okay. That we're on our way, and it will all be over soon." I don't know if I'm trying to reassure my team or myself.

"Daisy knows how much you love her and how hard it will be for you that she's there. She won't want you to feel everything that is happening as well. You wouldn't handle it; I know you wouldn't," Marcus says as he looks over at me.

"What happens if you fail, Michael? Do you think you'll be able to get her out of there?" I hear Kellan ask.

"I will die trying if I have to," I answer. I look at Marcus and Stuart and think of Will, Jonathan, and Natalie. "My team know that if they have to leave me, they do. Their priority is getting Daisy out of there and to safety. The rest we'll deal with as it happens. But no matter what, we go in and get her out."

"What about Jackson's men?" Natalie asks.

"If we can keep them alive, we do; if we have to kill them, we kill them. They had no idea what they were getting into when they agreed to join the bastard," I state.

"Yes, they did. They knew what would happen when Jackson got Daisy; they were trained to turn a blind eye to her pain," Kellan says.

"If that's the case, I say we kill them all," Natalie declares. But I shake my head.

"No, we give them a chance first. If we can save some of them, then we do." I reply. I look over at the Alpha, who nods in agreement.

"You're a better man than me, Adams," Kellan says.

"We know that," Jonathan snaps.

"We're about a half-hour from the address. What's the plan?" Stuart calls from the driver's seat.

"We pull over in a lay-by half a mile from the manor. We unlink Kellan and Daisy. After that, we all get out and get into positions. You've all been given a spot. If you see any guards, disarm them and knock them unconscious. Kellan has told us where they are stationed, but things could have changed in the time since he left. They may have upped security; now they know he's missing," Marcus says from his seat. "Kellan can take down the wards, and we can fight our way in to get Daisy," He adds, looking at the team through the tablet. I hear Alex relaying the plans to the coven in the cars behind their van. Jon is talking into a phone to a third van behind the coven, where members of our pack who have offered to fight with us are travelling. There are fifteen in that van.

Altogether, thirty-five of us are on our way to rescue Daisy. This includes her coven, excluding Sara, Mary and Clare, who stayed behind to ensure Jackson couldn't find Clare. From the call I heard between her and Stuart earlier, she wasn't happy, but Stuart let her yell and curse at him and then told her they would talk about it when he got back and hung up. I think he'll be fine handling her after the experience he gained from dealing with Daisy for nearly six months.

"Kellan, you're to stick close to me. You disappear, and I'll take it as if you've double-crossed us. We are going in, and you'll take me to Daisy's cell. Once I have her, you teleport us out and to the van. After that, you're free to go and do your own thing," I say as I pick up the tablet and look at the screen.

"You make it sound easy. Like I can just forget about her." He sighs, rolling his eyes.

"Well, I could always kill you if it's easier." I hear Natalie offer.

"Sorry scary lady, I didn't live to be two hundred and fifty-seven years old to be killed by you. No offence," Kellan states.

"Just when I think I can't hate you anymore, you open your mouth, and it's like 'nope, I hate you more.' How can you look that young at that age?!" Natalie sighs

"Is there anyone you don't hate, Nat?" I hear Will ask, chuckling.

"Mikey and Mama B. Oh, and Daisy, I like her," Natalie replies. I can hear the smile in her voice. "I guess Marcus and you, Will. Oh, and Stu, he's alright. I'll also add the Alpha and Luna to people I like." Natalie states as everyone, smirks.

"Thanks, Natalie. I feel privileged." The Alpha calls, looking over his shoulder from his seat next to Stuart.

"Just leaves me on the hate list, then." I hear Jon sigh; no one says anything, as we can all sense the tension between my old second and brother.

"You're an arsehole, so, yep," Natalie snaps.

"All joking aside, does everyone know where they need to be and who they will have with them? I don't want any fuck ups once we get there," I call out for all to hear.

I hear a chorus of 'yes' and 'no problems here'. I take a deep breath and sit back in my seat. I try to open the link between Daisy and me one last time before we get to her.

"I'm coming, darling; keep strong. We'll be together again soon, I promise."

Chapter Sixty

Daisy

I sit with my back against the wall and try to think. I need a way out of here. I'm too weak to fight, as I haven't eaten in days. Maybe if I could get a little food, it would help.

"Any idea how long I have to wait to get something to eat in this place?" I call out to whoever is now guarding the door. I've only had a few slices of toast since I arrived. I'm starving. As usual, there's no reply. I roll my eyes and push myself to my feet before walking to the door; every part of me aches.

"You know, it's rude to ignore someone when they're speaking to you," I call out as I lean against the door. I can hear activity outside of it; the hatch at the bottom opens, and a bag of crisps gets thrown in. "oh, har har, like that will even make a dent in how hungry I am." I moan as I reach down and pick up the packet.

"Maybe if you did as you were told, the Alpha would feed you," the voice outside my door mumbles.

"Really? Why hadn't I thought of that? Maybe because your alpha is a prick." I snap back.

"Don't speak ill of our alpha." He roars, and I smile, knowing I've pissed him off.

"That prick is not my alpha; my alpha is a real man who doesn't need to kidnap and abuse women to feel powerful. *My* alpha doesn't treat those in his pack with such disrespect." I state, waiting to see how mad I can make him.

"Alpha Jackson *is* your alpha, and you are his luna. It's time you learned to accept it." The guy outside shouts.

"What's your name?" I ask, only to be ignored. "Surely, if I'm his luna, that makes me yours, so you have to answer me when I ask you a simple question. Let's try again. What's your name?" I demand.

"Tom." The guy mumbles back.

"Well, Tom, how about this? You come in here and let him rape you, and I'll stand outside the door and pretend it's a perfectly acceptable thing to do." I'm met with silence. I smirk as I walk away. "I thought as much," I state as I head back to the bed and sit down to eat my crisps. Uhh, ready salted. Who even likes ready bloody salted? Mindless half-wits called Tom, that's who.

Suddenly there's a commotion outside, and I look up as the door flies open and Kellan slides across the floor and lands by the bed.

"You found him then?" I ask, looking down at Kellan. I realise that he's badly beaten, yet I felt nothing. I quickly feel my face and realise it doesn't feel half as bad as his looks.

"Someone removed the link between you," Jackson snaps. I look at Kellan again and shrug.

"Did me a favour then." I pick up my discarded crisps.

"Aren't you even curious as to who removed it?" Jackson asks, crossing his arms over his chest. I look at him and shake my head whilst pouting.

"Not really; whoever it was will let me know when I get out of here," I reply as I pop a crisp into my mouth.

"Still so sure that you'll be getting out, sweetheart?"

"Oh, I know I will. I just need to decide how many of your men I kill as I leave," I reply, adding a smile for good measure. Jackson laughs as he walks toward me. I want to move out of his reach, but I refuse to back down; I won't let him see I'm scared. The beating earlier has really dented my confidence, but I refuse to let him see that.

"We'll be moving out in half an hour. When we get to our new premises, you will never see the light of day again. You've had luxuries of space and freedom here. The chains are already installed; I have a muzzle with your name on it, so even shifting won't save you." He snarls through gritted teeth, his face mere centimetres from mine. I grin and move a little closer to him.

"Michael will still find me, and he will still kill you. There's nowhere on this earth you could hide me from him. It's just a matter of time," I say, grinning before leaning back against the wall.

"Oh, he'll never find you where we are going, sweetheart. If he does, my men will be told to shoot on sight. He won't even make it onto my territory." Jackson steps back and walks over to the door. Just as he opens it, he stops and turns around.

"Oh, I almost forgot; what should I do with this one?" he asks, pointing to Kellan, who has managed to prop himself up.

"I don't know why you act like you aren't about to kill me. We both know you want to use me as an example of what will happen to her if she doesn't do as she is told." Kellan groans as he sits up and leans against the bed.

"Maybe that old friendship you two built whilst in class is still there, and she will do anything to stop me from killing you?" Jackson smirks vindictively.

"You need to get some new threats, Jackson; these are getting old." I groan as I pop a crisp into my mouth. Jacksons shrugs.

"True." I watch in shock as a guard steps out behind him, pointing a gun towards the bed. I scream as the sound of a shot echoes through the room. I look down at Kellan sitting there, eyes wide with shock as he looks from me down at his chest, his t-shirt becoming darker as blood seeps from his body.

"Fuck." Kellan whispers as he slumps to the side; I dive down to the floor and lower him, resting his head on my knees. I might have despised him at times, but no one deserves to die like this.

"I'll leave you to say your goodbyes. I'll return for you as soon as the van is ready." Jackson walks through the door and slams it shut behind him. I pull the bottom of Kellan's t-shirt up and hold it over the gunshot wound; he hisses as I apply pressure.

"We don't have long," Kellan whispers; I shake my head as the tears start rolling down my cheek.

"Don't talk; you'll be okay; give me some energy, and I'll heal you." I sob, but Kellan shakes his head before placing a hand over mine.

"Don't; I need you to listen. He's here, Michael has the full team and more here. They have the place surrounded. But for you to get out, you need all your power," Kellan says quietly. I shake my head.

"I can't let you die," I whisper. Kellan looks up at me and

moves his hand to my cheek.

"When I die, you will have all your power back; I've been using it since the day he first took you three years ago; I had to use it to heal you and keep you safe when you couldn't," Kellan explains.

"You were there?" I ask, shocked. Kellan nods, then cringes in pain. I notice how much blood has pooled underneath him as it seeps into my clothes and onto my skin.

"I've never left your side; I used your magic to keep us hidden." Kellan starts coughing. I use part of my top to wipe the blood away from his mouth. It's getting harder for him to breathe as the colour drains from his skin.

"Why did you do all that?" I ask as I run my hand over his brown hair.

"Because you are destined to do great things, Daisy. I thought I would be there to see you achieve things others have only ever dreamt of. I've loved you since the first time I saw you, and I wanted to protect you from everything the fates threw at you. But I was too weak to protect you from him. So I swore I would get stronger, and we would get away together." Kellan gasps for breath and starts coughing again; there's so much blood now, I know there's no way to save him.

"I don't know what to say. I'm so sorry for all the things I said to you." I sob as I start to shake. Kellan takes my hand, which is pressed to his chest and lifts it to his mouth to kiss it.

"I deserved it; I really should have gone about things differently. I should have been honest from the start." Kellan coughs a few times as blood runs from his mouth again.

"Look, you have to concentrate. When I die, you will get all your power back; you are much stronger than you were, so use it. Get out to Michael and kill Jackson. He's a weak alpha; none of these men truly submit to him; they follow him blindly, make them yours. Use them and turn them against him. Kill anyone who stands in your way." As Kellan speaks, his voice becomes weaker and starts to shake. I can't hold in the sob that escapes me as I lift his head from my knee and move to lie down next to him. I curl up, so my head is on his shoulder as I start to cry. Kellan turns his head and plants a kiss on my forehead.

"Do me one favour, Daisy," Kellan whispers. I turn and look at him.

"Anything."

"Live a full and happy life with Michael. Get married, travel the world, have kids, and do those things happy people do. He loves you so much; I never understood the mate bond until I saw what you being taken did to him. He has fought tirelessly to get to you, as you have to get back to him. Don't let it be in vain." Kellan's voice is now less than a whisper, and his breath shallower. I know he's only got moments left.

"I promise." I lay there with him silently, watching his chest rise and fall until it falls that last time. I wait and watch for it to move again, praying that he is just holding his breath, but nothing happens. My own chest tightens as I try and bring myself to look up at his face, knowing what I will find.

"Kellan?" I whisper; I slowly lift myself and look down at him on the floor; blood pooled underneath us, his eyes staring up at the wall behind me, and the colour drained from his bruised face. I feel a bubble in my chest, getting bigger as the pressure builds; I gasp for breath as I realise he's gone.

"I'm so sorry." I manage to whisper before a heart-broken scream escapes as the grief and power hit me.

Chapter Sixty-One

Michael

Fuck, this isn't going to plan. The second we separated Kellan from Daisy, the bastard disappeared, promising to get Daisy out. Do I believe him? Not in the slightest! But there's not much I can do about it; one of Jackson's men has a gun to my head as he leads me to the house the rest of the team has surrounded. Hopefully, they'll all stick to the plan and keep hidden. They're under strict instructions to get Daisy out of there, no matter what happens to me.

It's pitch black, the only light coming from the half-moon and the few lights lit in the house. It's three in the morning. Hopefully, half of Jackson's men will be asleep and unaware of what's happening out here.

We stop outside the building as somebody kicks the back of my knees, forcing me to kneel. I somehow manage to keep my hands behind my head whilst stopping myself from faceplanting the ground.

"Ever heard of asking?" I sigh, rolling my eyes.

"Shut up and stay there." One of the guys snaps. Just as I'm about to reply, a gunshot quickly followed by a piercing scream sound from inside the house.

"Daisy!" I roar as I jump to my feet; I spin to face the guy with the gun to my head, grabbing his arm and snapping it before elbowing him in the face breaking his nose and knocking him out. As the gun drops from his hand, I grab it and point it at his accomplice, who now has his gun trained on me. The guy starts shaking, staring at the gun barrel in his face.

"If you drop the gun and walk away, you'll be spared," I say as I ready my finger on the trigger. The guy looks at me as he drops his gun.

Before it reaches the ground, another shot sounds out; I spin around to see Jackson standing in the doorway of the house holding out a gun; I aim mine at him as the guy standing next to me drops to the ground, dead.

"I have no space for cowards in my pack," Jackson says casually as he looks at his fallen pack members.

"Who was shot?" I call out. Jackson grins at me; Daisy's right; his grin is pure evil.

"Wouldn't you like to know?" He asks as he steps forward; I do the same, keeping my gun trained on him.

"Well, I'm asking, so I guess that's a giveaway," I reply, casually shrugging. Jackson raises his eyebrows at me before rolling his eyes.

"I see now where Daisy has got her mouth from. She used to be so well behaved before she met you. Now she has an answer for everything."

"She's always had an answer for everything. It's her that's rubbed off on me," I call back, my heart aching to hear her sassy comebacks just once more.

"Either way, she has put up more of a fight this time. It makes it much more fun, that's for sure." I feel my finger twitching on the trigger; I want nothing more than to end him, but I also know killing him could seal Daisy's fate.

"Where is she?" I growl through my teeth.

"She's spending some time with an old friend. It's okay; they should be parted soon enough." He looks at me and tips his head to one side, taking another step forward. "I thought you would be more of a challenge Michael. I expected more of a fight. Maybe the rumours about you are just that; rumours. Maybe the big bad wolf isn't so bad after all."

I grin at him and stand up tall, "put the gun down and face me like a wolf and we'll see how strong I really am." I taunt him, longing for the chance to punch that smug look from his face.

Jackson pretends to think about it and shakes his head.

"Or I could kill your whole team and watch you crumble as I walk away with Daisy." He's about to say more when a scream sounds from the house again, and magic fills the air as the ground shakes. Daisy's screams cause my wolf to rush forward, begging to take control.

"What are you doing to her?" I howl as I run towards Jackson. But he doesn't move, he smirks at me as he whistles, and I see Marcus and Jon walk into view, their hands behind their heads, both have guns pressed into their backs. I stop at the sight of the two of them. Fuck could this mission get any worse? The whole plan has gone to shit, and I don't know what to do!

"This is between me and you, Jackson. Let them go." I growl as I turn back to face him.

"What? Are you not going to try and save your brothers? It Seems we do have more than just Daisy in common. Judging by the scream, I'm betting that my dear little brother has departed this world and is back with our mother. Oh, and your sister." He grins at me as I step toward him. My wolf is ready to rip him to ribbons.

"Just kill him, Mikey, save Daisy," Jon calls. I turn just in time to see him get punched in the gut. I can feel the magic building in the air, and I know the coven must be working on something if I can bide them some time. Jackson looks at Marcus and sniffs the air as the breeze picks up.

"You must have been the boyfriend? I could smell your scent all over my mate." Jackson growls, turning his nose up at Marcus.

"I can see why she rejected you, you psycho piece of shit," Marcus growls as he steps toward Jackson.

"Maybe it was me who rejected her. After you had ruined her." Jackson snarls, grinning, "Do you want to know what her last words were as my hands tightened around that pretty little neck?" He asks, grinning at Marcus as he takes a step forward. "Michelle called out to you, and you weren't there. You let her down when she needed you most." Jackson almost purrs as he watches Marcus's form bulk up, his wolf racing to the front.

"If she had chosen me, I wouldn't have let her down; I would have been able to protect her," he adds as Marcus roars and goes to rush towards him, only to be frozen to the spot as he screams in pain. I see Jackson holding his hand towards Marcus, using those powers Kellan warned us about.

"STOP!" I yell from my spot; I need to distract him quickly before he kills Marcus. Jackson turns to me as Marcus stops screaming.

"Let my team and Daisy go, and I'll stay and help you build your pack," I announce as I lower my gun.

"No!" Jon and Marcus shout together. I don't turn to face them. I stay looking at Jackson.

"I can turn them; I can train them. You will have the strongest pack in the UK; you won't have to breed them, so you won't need Daisy. Let her go with my brothers, and I will stay," I add as I hold my hands up.

"Now, there's a thought, but how do I know you won't just kill me?" Jackson says as he tips his head to the side, smiling.

"We'll make a pact, a blood oath I'll serve you and only you, as long as you forget Daisy ever existed, and she gets to live in peace," I call out. I'm talking out of my ass, of course, because as soon as I get a chance, I'm killing the bastard or distracting him enough for the guys to get free and get to Daisy.

"That sounds like a fair deal," Jackson says; I take a step forward to get closer, knowing that there is a real chance I will never see Daisy again, but at least this way, she can live her life and do all the things we had planned, just without me.

I have almost reached him when the whole ground shakes and what could be thunder sounds around us.

"You take one step closer, Adams and I'll kick your ass myself." My head snaps up to find Daisy standing in the doorway; Jackson spins around to face her, and his jaw drops open. I stand frozen to the spot as I finally lay my eyes on the woman I love after the longest six days.

"How the fuck did you get out?" Jackson growls as Daisy grins at him before casually strolling out of the house and towards him like she hasn't been held hostage or beaten tonight; she is oozing with confidence and power, and I could not be prouder if I tried.

"There's a hole where my door used to be," Daisy answers with a shrug. "Oh, and I have something for you." With a flick of her wrist, every window at the front of the house smashes as bodies fly out of them. Landing in a pile in the middle of the lawn. I can see they are all dead. She looks up at the men standing around Marcus and Jon. A look flicks over her face I've never seen before.

"The answer to my question earlier was eight. I killed eight of your men on my way out." Daisy shrugs as she steps closer to Jackson before turning back to his men standing behind our brothers.

"Unless you want to join that lot, I suggest you drop those guns and step away from my family NOW!" The sound of guns hitting the ground fills the silence. I realise then Daisy is taking control of Jackson's pack. She's the stronger alpha, and by projecting her alpha magic and power, she's become their leader. Jackson looks around as he realises what she's doing; he lifts his gun back up, pointing it at me.

"Take another step, or try and control my men again and I will blow lover boys head off," he growls out. Daisy looks at me, and I see something in her eyes; for a second, it's fear, but it's quickly replaced with a new level of anger that scares even me. I watch as she walks up to Jackson and looks him straight in the eye. She's face to face with her abuser and doesn't show an ounce of fear.

"You wanted a powerful luna? Well, you got one. The problem is I'm more powerful than you will ever be." Daisy warns as she leans toward him before standing tall and addressing him again. "Now, unless you want to see just how powerful I've become, I suggest you stop pointing a gun at my mate's head. Because if you so much as think about pulling the trigger, I will destroy you from the inside out; you will suffer the most painfully slow death that you'll beg me to end you." She warns, and I can see that she means every word.

"You don't scare me," Jackson says as he pulls the trigger, I hear my brother scream as the gun sounds. I look at Daisy, wanting her to be the last thing I see. But she just smiles at me.

"Not today, sorry handsome. I have plans for us, and I need you alive to see them through." I turn slowly and see the bullet spinning in mid-air, inches from my face, before dropping to the ground. Daisy turns to Jackson as he crumbles to the floor, clutching his head and screaming in pain. She stands over him and growls.

"I warned you. No one threatens my mate."

Chapter Sixty-Two

Daisy

I knew Michael was safe; the bullet wouldn't get through the protective shield I had around him, Jon and Marcus. I look at Jackson and can smell the fear in him; I increase the pressure building in his head with the slightest flick of my wrist as he withers on the floor in pain.

"Mikey, can you come and collect his gun, please? The coward won't need it now," I call out as I keep watching Jackson. I hear the slightest stammer in Michael's voice as he answers.

"Of course, darling." I sense Michael's approach and turn to face him, overcome with the need to be in his arms.

"Hey, you," I whisper as I take a step forward, grab his shirt, and pull him towards me so that his lips crash into mine; he instantly wraps an arm around my waist and tugs me against him as he deepens the kiss further.

"Uh guys, now may not be the time for that," Jon calls out. I reluctantly pull away from Michael and smile.

"I know he's right, but I'm picking up from that point once this is all over," I whisper as I take a step back.

"I am so up for that," Michael answers grinning. I watch as he looks down at my body, and his eyes darken. "Is any of that yours?" he asks in a low growl. I glance down and see Kellan's blood all down my side, where I had laid next to him. I can feel the panic building in my chest, but I quickly breathe through it. I will deal with that after. I turn back to face Jackson before answering.

"No, it's Kellan's," I answer as I flick my wrist, freezing Jackson to the spot and watch as he starts sweating, his moans getting louder as I cause his body temperature to rise, slowly cooking him from the inside. I wait until I know all his men can hear his cries before speaking aloud to them all.

"You all wanted a Luna, but you got an Alpha instead. I know everyone who stood guard outside that room, knowing what was attempted inside; you can't hide, and you will pay for your ignorance. I suggest you all lay down your weapons and let my family go. As your true Alpha, I command all from the Luna Dais pack to step forward and await your fate." I watch as fifteen males walk into view and stop in the large green at the front of the house. I look up at Mikey and finally open up the bond between us. The love and support that floods through it from my mate is almost enough to bring me to my knees.

"Can you get the team to gather them? If you have other options than killing them, then do it. I've killed the most dangerous ones," I tell Michael down the bond.

"Whatever you need, darling. We are at your disposal." Michael answers as he walks away but stops and looks at me over his shoulder. *"I'm so unbelievably proud of you."* He says before calling out to the team.

"Team, you know what to do. Their alpha wants them gathered up, so let's help her."

"Any chance you have your phone so I can call OUR alpha? I need his help." I ask Michael; he turns around again, grinning.

"Just shout; he'll hear you. I don't think you realise how many people are here." Michael replies before bringing his fingers to his mouth and letting out a loud whistle. I watch in amazement as over thirty bodies walk out of the trees.

"You are more loved than you will ever know. Every pack member who could fight is here. Most of your coven as well." I see them now, my uncle, Alex and the coven, Will, Stuart, Desmond, and Natalie; when my eyes fall on Richard, Carl and Tony, I nearly break down in tears. They all came here, for me.

"Stay strong, darling; remember what Desmond told you when dealing with the demon. When all this is over, lean on me as much as you need to, but right now, remember you have taken control of this pack and need to remain in control for as long as possible," Michael whispers down our bond. I nod once and take a deep breath.

"Alpha Desmond Gibbs, can I have a word, please?" I call out; I watch as my alpha walks towards me. "Coven leader Nigel Evans and his second Alex Rogers, can you join us also?"

I call out. My legs nearly give way as I see them both walk toward me.

"You've got this, darling," Michael says before turning back to the team, and I hear him barking out orders.

As the three men reach me, it takes all my willpower not to fall into my uncle's arms.

"Is that yours?" he asks, looking pale as he nods at my clothes; I shake my head and see all three visibly relax.

"What do you need?" Desmond asks. I look around and try to take everything in.

"I don't want any of this; how do I dissolve the pack?" Desmond places a reassuring hand on my shoulder.

"Are you sure that's what you want? You and Michael could turn this into a great pack." I shake my head,

"We are blood moon wolves; that is our pack, our family." I look at Jackson's guys on their knees with Michael and the team standing by, guarding them. The contrast between the males of the two packs is obvious. Michael and the guys have collected all the guns and discarded them, not needing them over their physical strength and self-control.

"This isn't a pack; this is a group of thugs who were given a gift in the hope of causing pain with it. They were willing to stand outside that room and let me get beaten and raped. Some even attempted to hold me down. I want nothing to do with them." I add as I look at Michael, who smiles at me from across the field.

"Then you can refuse all claims on the pack, and the connection to them will be dissolved, the pack will no longer exist, and all who were members of it become rogues," Desmond explains.

"The hell you're dissolving my pack!" I turn and face Jackson trying to pull himself to his feet, using his magic to fight my own. "This is my fucking pack, not yours!" Jackson jumps up and attempts to grab my uncle, but Desmond gets there a second quicker and pulls him out of the way. Jackson turns to face me, I can see the murderous look in his eye as he advances towards me, but a dark brown wolf barges into him, knocking him away from us, and onto the grass. Jackson shifts and jumps to his feet, facing Michael.

"Fuck." I curse as I watch them start circling, teeth bared, ears standing to attention. Everything in me tells me to shift and go to Michael, but I know he needs this. This man took his twin from him and made the last few months a living hell for us. Michael has more rights than anyone to be the one to take him down.

For a moment, it's hard to see who's getting the upper hand as they move so fast; all I can see is the blur of black and brown fur, claws and teeth. They are moving closer and closer to where I am standing; I'm just about to move when Michael gets Jackson pinned on his back. Michael bares his teeth and is just about to rip through Jackson's throat; when a gunshot rings through the air. I spin around just in time to see one of Jackson's guys have his neck snapped by Marcus. I spin back, knowing already what I'll see.

Time slows as I watch Michael fall to the floor as Jackson jumps to his feet and moves toward him; I pull out of my Alpha's grip as I scream and rush towards them. I shift mid-air, and land perfectly in front of Michael, and face off to Jackson's black wolf growling.

"NO!" I hear Michael shout down the pack bond.

"Stay down!" I snap back as I jump at Jackson, guiding him away from Michael.

The last time I fought him as a wolf, I was inexperienced and had to let my wolf take over. This time I'm going to kill the bastard, ending this nightmare once and for all.

Jackson moves to go around me, but I dive for him and force him further away from Michael. I flashback to the night I escaped him the first time. Except for this time, I'm fighting to get him away from my mate rather than my auntie and uncle, I jump at him and show him I am not backing down, and neither is my wolf.

I can tell Jackson is already tiring after fighting Michael; I push until he's panting, and I'm still fighting strong, all feeling of tiredness and weakness from lack of food forgotten. My wolf wants revenge for what he has put us, our mate, and our families through. I won't let him win.

Every time Jackson advances on me, I dodge and attack him. I feel my teeth scrape his skin a few times, but I can never get enough of an advantage to do real damage. I can hear Michael and Marcus in my head as I realise Marcus has shifted as Michael begs him to help me.

"Trust her, Mikey."

Hearing Marcus's belief in me gives us the boost we need. My wolf and I somehow get the advantage and sink our teeth into Jackson's front leg, causing him to howl in pain. I keep hold of it and pull with all my might. I feel my teeth slice through the fur, flesh and muscle as he howls louder. His blood fills my mouth as I pull the leg from underneath him. But I can't do enough damage like this, and I stupidly release him. He takes my release of his leg as the opportunity he needs and clamps his jaw down on my shoulder. I try to stop the howl from escaping me, but I can't, as I fall to the floor.

Michael

"Get up now!" I scream through the pack bond as Daisy drops to her side; I can hear her crying in pain, even from the other side of the field. I try to get up, but two pairs of hands hold me down.

"Michael, stay still; the team are going now." I look just in time to see them all, old and new, rush across the field, shifting as they go; there must be at least ten of them. I need to go, too; I need to know she's okay. I try to listen to her through the bond, but I can't pick out her voice.

Suddenly a howl fills the air, and I know it's her, I try to see what's happening, but Desmond and Alex are trying to stop me. Her howl sounds again, and I don't hold back anymore; I jump to my feet, sending them flying; they hit the ground as I take off towards Daisy.

I skid to a stop when I hit a wall of wolves, which Marcus and the rest have formed around Daisy.

"MOVE!" I yell, and they part instantly. On the floor are Daisy and Jackson, lying on their sides, only inches apart. I stand in front of Daisy protectively as I turn to face Jackson; his

throat's been ripped out. He's dead; I spin around to see Daisy breathing heavily; she lifts her head to look at me, with her beautiful green eyes, before it flops back down to the ground, exhausted.

Daisy is covered in blood; I don't know how much of it is hers and how much is his. I lie beside her, so our heads are against each other.

"Is he dead?" I nod as I watch her eyes close, and she takes a deep breath.

"Is it finally over?" she asks.

"It's over darling," I reply as I start licking at her shoulder, where she's bleeding. She nudges me away and stands up, her legs shaking, before turning to Marcus.

"The rest?" she asks as she takes a shaky step forward.

"Dead. They all started to fight back when Jackson did; we had no choice," Marcus answers. Daisy nods and looks at me.

"Mikey, can we go home now?" I stand beside her, so I'm there for her to lean against.

"Absolutely, darling."

I watch in awe as Daisy starts walking towards the wall of wolves, which parts for her. She stops and turns back to me, waiting, her body showing no sign of her pain; her eyes, however, show me how close she is to breaking. I hobble to her side, my leg hurting from the gunshot wound, but I ignore it to give Daisy the support she needs.

"I'm right here," I whisper as we walk back towards our friends and family. As soon as we are clear of the team, I hear an almighty roar of applause and cheering, Daisy automatically jumps, and I can feel the panic radiating from her. *"It's okay; they're cheering for you,"* I whisper. Daisy starts looking around, faced with her friends and family clapping, and cheering for her. I can feel it's becoming too much. After everything she's been through, her emotions are finally surfacing.

I quickly shift back and kneel beside her as Daisy stays in wolf form. Pain radiates down my left arm as the bullet dislodges itself from where it hit and falls to the ground.

"Guys!" I call out, and everyone becomes quiet. Daisy lies

down and puts her head on my lap; I can feel her shaking as the adrenaline wears off and shock kicks in. "I need a couple of blankets and the van now," I shout; within seconds, I can see Tony and a coven member rushing forward with blankets. Daisy stays where she is; as I run my fingers through her thick golden bronze fur. I look up as they reach us; Tony places a blanket over Daisy as a woman wraps one around my shoulders.

"Is she okay?" Tony asks; I look down at Daisy, who's wiped out physically and mentally.

"She's holding strong." I look up as the Alpha, Nigel and Alex reach us. "I don't know how much longer she can hold it together," I explain.

"Get her in the van and take her home. We'll stage the scene. Make it look like a drug den or something before setting it alight," Desmond explains; I feel Daisy shift before jumping to her feet.

"No! You can't burn it, not yet. He's still in there; you have to get him out; he isn't one of them. He needs to get out." She spins around and stares at me with pleading eyes. "Get him out; please get him out first." I wrap the blanket around her as she falls against me.

"Who? Get who out, darling?" I ask carefully.

"Kellan! You have to get him out, don't burn him, please." Her whole body starts shaking violently.

"He's alive?" I hear Alex ask. Daisy shakes her head. The tears start to flow then, and the last piece of control she holds on to gets closer to snapping. I lower her to the floor as she crumbles, and the tears flow. I look up at Desmond, who squats down and reaches over to cup her cheek with his hand.

"We will get him out and bring him back to our land and bury him there," he promises her as he leans over and plants a kiss on her forehead. Daisy nods as I pull her against me and help her onto her feet to steer her towards the van Lawrence drives down to us.

"I need to get her out of here," I whisper; looking around, everyone nods in agreement. Marcus and Jon are both standing naked at the back of the van holding the doors open.

"Marcus, you stay and take control here; Jon and Desmond come back with us; Stuart can drive." I turn to Nigel. "You lot head back to ours; we'll meet you there; I'll contact the healer when we are on our way," I explain, holding Daisy to my side as she looks up at the house behind us. Marcus steps forward and puts a hand on my shoulder.

"Concentrate on Daisy; I will sort everything else." I watch as he looks down at Daisy and kisses her on the top of the head. "You were fucking amazing," He whispers. She looks up at him and stares at him for the briefest moments before throwing her arms around his neck; Marcus takes a deep breath and pulls her into his arms, his relief at having her back alive is unmissable.

"Mikey get in; I'll help her," Jon whispers next to me. I look at my brother and nod as he pulls Daisy from Marcus's arms and lifts her into his own.

"And you say I'm the one always causing trouble. You topped me here, witchy," he whispers as he looks down at Daisy in his arms.

"Somebody had to show you how it's done properly, wolf boy." She replies quietly. She turns and looks at Marcus again.

"Did you see his black eye?" she asks. Marcus nods whilst smiling. "I did that when he took me. He only just regained his sight in it." Marcus laughs and holds out his fist; she bumps her own against it.

"I'll make a protector out of you yet." Marcus chuckles as he ruffles her hair.

"No thanks, I'm never leaving the house again," Daisy replies shaking her head and leaning into Jon's chest.

"I'll second that," I add, looking at her from the back of the van. Jon follows me and places Daisy on to my knee. I hold her tight as she rests her head on my chest, instantly lifting her hand to rest over my heart. Jon takes a seat opposite us, and Marcus goes to close the door.

"I'll see you in a bit." He says as he looks at Daisy and smiles softly at her. "We will get Kellan, I promise." Daisy whispers the quietest 'thank you' as Marcus closes the van doors and Stuart starts the engine.

We travel in silence for a few minutes before I lean down and press my lips to Daisy's ear.

"We're away from there now, darling. You're safe. It's over." I feel her whole body shake violently as she bursts into tears. Her emotions finally burst to the surface. I wrap the blanket around her and hold her tightly whilst rocking her as the stress, shock, and pain take over. The sound of her breaking is too much, and I feel my eyes well up; I look up at my brother sitting across from me and can see he can no longer hold it together. He moves to sit beside us before reaching over and taking her hand, squeezing it as I continue to hold her against me.

"I knew you would find me," Daisy sobs into my chest.

"I will always find you, baby. I wouldn't have stopped until I had." I reply as I place my finger under her chin, lifting her head so I can look into her eyes. "I'm so proud of you, darling."

"He couldn't touch me, not like that, he tried, but I fought him; I fought him with everything I had." I hold her as the tears continue to flow from all of us.

"You are incredible, do you know that?" I whisper.

"He kept saying you had given up on me and weren't even looking for me. I just laughed in his face, which he hated. He couldn't break me like last time."

Chapter Sixty-Three

Michael

Daisy cries in my arms quietly for an hour. I don't know what to do other than hold her and run my hand over her head, whispering the occasional word of encouragement through the bond. She feels so much lighter than she did six days ago. Now I can look at her properly; I realise how sunken her face looks and how exhausted her mind and body are. Jackson may not have been able to touch her sexually, but he harmed her in a whole different way. I have no idea how she fought him with such furiousness when she was so starved.

I keep my head pressed to hers, inhaling her scent even though it's all wrong. I can smell the bastard on her, as well as Kellan. She's still covered in their blood which taints her sweet floral scent. But I don't care; she's in my arms and alive. I'd been terrified I would never get to hold her again, but she's here. When I get her home, I'm never letting her out of my sight. I don't care how much she kicks and screams about it. I never want to be that close to losing her again.

I expect Daisy to sleep at some point, but she doesn't. She sits silently in my arms, leaning against my chest. She only moves when we had to stop for half an hour, and I help her put on some clothes we'd brought for her. Jon also ensures my arm is bandaged and Daisy's leg and shoulder. As soon as he's happy for us to continue on our way, Daisy climbs back onto my lap and stays there silently, holding her hand against my chest over my heart.

"I have something for you," I whisper into her hair. Daisy lifts her head from my shoulder and looks at me. I reach over to the bag I had brought and pull out her necklace.

"I thought you might want this back," I say as I hold it out for her. Daisy nods and pulls her tangled hair to one side as she turns so I can put it around her neck.

"Why did he take it?" Daisy asks as I fasten the clasp.

"Because he had somehow worked out Alex had placed a

spell on it so it would act as a beacon," I answer. Daisy turns back to look at me, frowning.

"When? I haven't taken it off since you gave it to me."

I nod as I respond. "I know; he did it that morning after the BBQ when I went to train the Cornwall pack. I met up with him and gave him the necklace before I went to the pack. We met up after, and he gave it back to me. I would have been able to find you a lot quicker if you had it on. We don't know how Jackson knew. I'm sorry I didn't tell you; I just -" Daisy stops me by placing a finger over my lips.

"None of that matters now. I'm just glad I have it back," she whispers before going back to resting against my chest. I tighten my arms around her and let out a deep sigh.

There are so many things I want to say to her; I want to tell her how proud I am of her and how strong she is. But I can't find the words. She's been through so much. Just when I thought she was about to break, she somehow held it together. I know under the surface of her composed exterior is a breakdown waiting to happen. It'll be tough when she finally breaks, but I'm ready for it. Now I have her with me, I know I can give her anything she needs.

Since we left the scene, only a handful of words have left her lips. It's been so quiet as we all process what happened in such a short time. Jon has been uncharacteristically quiet. He has stayed beside Daisy and me for most of the journey, holding her hand and occasionally asking if she needed anything. Jon seems as lost and relieved as I feel. He has accepted her as his baby sister and loves her like family. I have seen how much her being taken has affected him, which is why I wanted him to travel back with us.

"We are nearly there. Do you want us to call ahead?" Desmond asks from the front, breaking the silence.

"Please, Des," I answer. Daisy looks up at me and then to the front seat as if remembering someone is there.

"Mama and Edward will be there when we get back. I want Edward to check you over. We were with Kellan this evening when you were hurt," I whisper. I hear Daisy's breath catch with the mention of Kellan, and I want to ask what happened between him disappearing and her escaping her holding cell. But I know she will tell me when she's ready.

"Can Edward wait?" Daisy whispers. I look down at her and nod.

"Whatever you need, darling," I answer, kissing her head as she goes back to leaning against my chest.

"We are here," Desmond says quietly from the front ten minutes later. I feel Daisy tense in my arms.

"Where's here?" She asks, looking around, scared; I can hear her heart racing.

"Home, darling," I whisper as I run my hand down her back, feeling each vertebra.

"Are we really home?" I can see the tears welling up in her eyes; her lip quivers as I nod.

"We are." I look at Jon, who's still next to us, "Can you get Mum out of the way, please? I'm taking Daisy straight to our room and will let Edward in when she's ready. The coven and the rest of the team won't be far behind; I want everyone kept out of the way. I'll communicate with you, and you only." Jon nods and jumps straight out of the van and holds the door open for me as I lift Daisy into my arms and make our way out of the back.

As soon as we are through the open doors, I hear Mum gasp from the front of the house; Jon quickly rushes over to her.

"Mama, you need to go inside. Daisy's safe but very overwhelmed," Jon whispers. I feel Daisy hiding her face in my chest, and I know she isn't ready to see people yet. I watch Jon and Mum disappear into the house before making my way in with Daisy in my arms.

The first time I brought her home, I carried her as we entered. We'd been so happy and excited about our first night together. It was the night we had made love for the first time and marked each other. It feels so long ago now. So much has happened and changed for us. But I'm determined to make this the safe place my mate deserves.

I carry the much lighter Daisy over the threshold and straight up the stairs to our room. On the bed are Daisy's dressing gown and fresh PJs; I notice that the bedding has also been changed. I hear the sound of two other vehicles arriving outside, quickly followed by doors opening and slamming. Each loud noise makes Daisy jump and her heart race harder. Jon and Stuart rush out to let everyone know that they are to be as quiet as possible and that Daisy is not up to seeing anyone just yet. I sit on the edge of the bed and hold her to me; she shakes as her body reacts to all it's been through. I hold her and rub my hands up and down her back to soothe her.

"What do you need, darling?" I ask as I look down at her in my arms. Daisy looks up at me, lost.

"I don't know." She whispers as a few stray tears leave her eyes.

"Shall we start with a shower?" I ask. I want to get the blood off her. Slowly Daisy nods, and I stand with her in my arms before carrying her into the bathroom attached to our bedroom. I place her on a stool keeping the blanket around her, before walking over to the shower and starting the water. I want to get her clean so that I can assess her injuries. I'll relax when I know whether she needs any treatment.

I walk back over and help to take the clothes off her. There's still so much blood on her skin. I try not to think about how she looked when she appeared in that doorway. She had said it was all Kellan's, but I am sure some would have been hers after what I witnessed through Kellan this evening.

Her body is covered in bruises at various stages of healing; there are marks on her wrists and ankles where she was tied up and must have fought against the restraints. Her body is so malnourished that her shifter healing abilities have been suppressed. I run my finger over one of her wrists, where there are obvious signs of restraints.

"He had his men tie me to a chair using cable ties," Daisy whispers as she looks down at her wrists. "I broke through all four when he threatened to come after Clare." As if summoned, a car pulls up, followed quickly by the sound of the front door opening,

"Is she here?" Clare's desperate voice sounds through the

silence.

"She is, but you can't see her yet," Stuart answers. Daisy looks up at me, and I see relief in her eyes.

"She's safe now," Daisy states quietly. I look at her and nod.

"You both are, thanks to you." I point out as I place a soft kiss on her sore wrist.

I lead her to the shower and help her slowly step under the warm water. Daisy stands under the stream and closes her eyes, letting the warm water wash over her; she looks down to get her soap but freezes. As her skin gets wet, the water turns red around her from the blood, and I realise the huge mistake I've made.

I watch the second the final strand of strength snaps, and a sound escapes her lips like none I have heard before as she screams at the top of her lungs before looking at me with eyes that will haunt me for the rest of my days.

"Get it off! Get it off! Please get it off! Mikey, get it off!" Her screams become hysterical as she fights to escape the blood on her body and in the water. I grab her and pull her into my arms as I get into the shower with her; as she starts scrubbing at her body hysterically, screaming the whole time.

"Get it off me! Get it off!" Daisy screams over and over again. I grab her face in my hands and force her to look me in the eye and away from the blood.

"Darling, I have you. Look at me and nowhere else." I whisper as she stands with me in the shower, shaking and crying. I reach above us and take the showerhead from the holder. Keeping eye contact with her as she cries, I use the water to wash off the blood. At one point, Daisy's eyes wander down, and she sees the blood again, which causes the screaming to restart. But I quickly get her attention back on me, and I carry on washing her.

"I've got you, darling; it's almost off, I promise. Keep looking at me." I repeatedly whisper, only glancing down quickly every few seconds to check I'm getting all the blood off. As soon as I see the water running clear, I look Daisy in the eye and place the showerhead above us again.

"It's off, darling. It's all off." I catch her just in time as her legs go from underneath her. I lower us both to the floor, sitting under the flowing water, holding her as she cries into my wet chest.

"You are safe, darling. It's over."

Chapter Sixty-Four

Jon

The whole room freezes when we hear the first ear-piercing scream come from the room above. Daisy's pain radiates through us all as our hearts bleed for the woman upstairs.

"Mikey has her; he will look after her." I hear Stuart whisper; I turn to see him holding Clare as she cries into his chest. Her whole body ridged as she hears her coven sister and best friend's hysterical screams above. I look around and realise I'm not the only one struggling. Marcus is holding Mum as she cries into his chest. Alex and his wife Sara are huddled together, crying for their goddaughter, and Daisy's auntie and uncle look like they are fighting every maternal instinct to run up the stairs to their niece as she falls apart.

I hear someone let out a quiet sob next to me and find Natalie with a hand over her mouth, tears streaking down her face. I don't stop to think before I pull her to me; she shakes in my arms as she cries quietly, resting her head against my shoulder. As I lean my head against hers, I try my hardest but fail to stop the tears as I listen to my baby sister's heart-breaking, knowing how hard this will be for my brother too.

Slowly the screams die down, and all we can hear are the soft tones of Michael's voice as he reassures her and the sound of the shower running. Natalie straightens in my arms; for the briefest moment, we stare into each other's eyes before she turns and walks out of the room. I hear the front door open and close as she leaves. I let out a sigh and turn to find Mum looking at me. Her eyes are red from crying.

"Give her time." Mum whispers. I nod as I know she's right.

I look around and see everyone whispering in little groups. Marcus is still talking to Will and the Alpha at Mum's side. Stuart's whispering to Clare, who's still in his arms, as he comforts her. Nigel, Mary, Alex, and Sara are all whispering together. No one knows what to do with themselves. No one knows if we should stay or leave. One thing's for sure we are all exhausted and emotionally drained. It was a night I never wish to repeat.

I feel my phone vibrate in my pocket. I quickly pull it out and look down at the screen.

Mikey: Can you send Edward up? I want Daisy's injuries looked at.

Jon: Will do; how is she?

Mikey: Come up with Edward.

I walk over to the healer, who's talking to the Alpha.

"Mikey, just text, Can you come up with me to check Daisy's injuries?" Edward nods. As we turn to leave, someone touches my arm; I look down to see Mary standing beside me.

"How injured is she? Did he …?" I know what she's asking and shake my head.

"She told us in the van she fought him every time he tried," I reply as I place a hand on her arm and see Mary visibly relax. I give her arm a slight squeeze and force a one-sided smile. "I'm going up with Edward so Mikey can tell me the plan. He won't let anyone near her until he knows she can handle it. He'll put her before any of us right now."

"I know, and I understand. It's just… that scream." Mary whispers as her lip quivers. I nod as I felt it too, deep in my heart. I turn and walk away from her and lead Edward up the stairs to the bedroom.

We find Michael sitting on the edge of the bed; Daisy is lying down, curled up, holding on to her childhood teddy as she rests her head on his lap. Michael brushes his hand across her head repeatedly as Daisy cries silently, her whole body visibly shaking. Now she is clean, and in shorts and a vest top, I can see how bruised and hurt she is. I have to swallow down a growl which threatens to escape. I feel my hands ball up into fists as I wish the prick wasn't dead so I could kill him myself for what he has done to my baby sister.

Michael's voice brings me out of my thoughts and back into the room.

"Edward, can you check the cut on Daisy's right leg and shoulder, please? I want to get her settled into bed as soon as possible," Michael asks.

"Of course. Don't move. I can assess both while you lie like this," Edward whispers. I watch as the healer walks over to the chair they keep in their room and starts rummaging in his bag. I take the opportunity to squat in front of my sister and press my lips to her head.

"How you doing?" I whisper. Daisy shakes her head and looks at me; her usually bright eyes that shine through the darkest of nights are dull and bloodshot. I hadn't noticed before how broken she truly looks.

"She isn't great; she needs time. Please let everyone know that Daisy isn't up to visitors just yet. If they want to stay here, make them comfortable, but no one is coming into this room," Michael says, not taking his eyes off Daisy.

"I'll offer your aunt and uncle my bed; that way, they are close by if you need them. Mama will be in her usual room. The rest, I will try and get them to go home. But I can't promise anything." I look at my brother and realise his clothes are soaking wet from obviously holding Daisy in the shower. "Mikey, get changed. I'll stay with Daisy whilst Edward checks her out." But Michael shakes his head.

"I'm fine."

"No, you aren't. You're soaking wet. It will take five minutes tops. Go and get changed." I reply sternly. Daisy sits up and looks at Michael, who shakes his head. They're communicating through their bond, which usually drives me mad, but if it's the only way she's able to talk to someone, then so be it. I know she wins when Michael sighs and leans over to kiss her on the top of her head.

"I'll be two minutes." He whispers as he stands and walks to the chest of drawers; he grabs some sweatpants and a t-shirt before heading into the bathroom, glancing at Daisy one last time before closing the door.

Michael

I lean against the closed bathroom door and take a deep breath. I held it together as Daisy fell apart, even if only barely. I washed her until there was no trace of blood and held her until her screams subsided. My poor Daisy is broken, and I have no idea how she will come back from this.

I open my eyes and look at the bathroom around me. There are still signs of blood in the shower, on the clothes I had removed from her, and on the floor where some of the blood and water had escaped. Using the towels, I quickly mop the floor before cleaning everything to help remove the copper smell of blood. I gather the clothes I took off Daisy and the towels now covered in blood and water before chucking them all in the laundry basket and adding my clothes to the pile. I'll ask Jon to take them downstairs so Daisy doesn't see them again. He can burn them for all I care; I never want to see any of them again.

I quickly wash and pull on my clothes before glancing around the bathroom to check if there's anything that will upset Daisy further. When I'm sure all is cleared away, I compose myself before walking back into the bedroom.

Daisy's sitting on the edge of the bed as Edward bandages her leg; Jon's sitting beside her with his arm around her shoulder as she leans against him. I can see he is whispering to Daisy, but she isn't responding with more than a nod or a head shake. Since she stopped screaming, the only way she's communicated with me is through our bond. Jon looks up as I close the bathroom door.

"While Edward's here, let him check your arm," he says softly. I shake my head as I take Jon's place next to Daisy.

"Get your arm checked," Daisy whispers through the bond as she leans against me, resting her head on my shoulder. I look at her and wipe some fresh tears from her face. They haven't stopped since the screaming started.

"It's fine. I've checked it," I lie.

"Please, Mikey." she pleads.

"If it will put you at ease," I whisper as I kiss the top of her head for what feels like the millionth time.

Daisy closes her eyes as she tries again to compose herself.

"I'll go down and speak to the others. Anything you want people to know?" Jon asks us as he squats in front of Daisy again. I hear Daisy answer through the bond.

"Daisy wants her family and coven to know she loves them but just needs a little time," I whisper as fresh tears escape her eyes. I wipe them away and turn to face my brother. "Can you tell Marcus he's in charge until further notice. Things should be quiet now anyway."

"I think he already planned on it. No one wants you two to do anything but focus on yourselves," Jon says as he looks between us.

"When did you last eat something?" I ask Daisy gently.

"I haven't, really. I didn't drink much because I was worried it was drugged," She whispers.

"Edward. Daisy wasn't fed or given a lot of fluids. What's the best option?" Without looking at the healer, I ask, unable to take my eyes off Daisy. Looking at her is the only thing stopping me from losing control as the extent of the abuse she suffered comes to light.

"Water and toast to start with, slowly increasing meal and fluid sizes," Edward whispers. I nod and look back at Jon.

"I'll sort it. What about you?" Jon asks quietly.

"I won't eat if you don't." I hear Daisy add. I look back at my brother.

"Do me the same, please." I turn and look at Edward, who is now examining my arm.

"Michael, this already shows signs of infection; I need to reopen and clean it properly," Edward whispers next to me. I look at my arm and can see it's red where it has already started healing.

"Not now. I'll deal with it later." I reply, shaking my head. An infected arm is the least of my worries right now. I feel Daisy move beside me as she reaches over and places a hand on the wound. A warming sensation passes through the whole arm and a slight sting as pieces of debris dislodged from the skin. As the sensation passes, Daisy pulls her hand away, and I see that the bullet wound is completely healed; I open Daisy's hand to find three tiny pieces of metal.

"What have I told you about healing me. You can't afford to," I point out, frowning at her.

"I think you'll find she can now," Edward says next to me. I look at her, suddenly remembering all she did with her magic outside the manor and how she wasn't drained from it.

"You got all your power back?" I ask; Daisy looks at me and nods as fresh tears escape her eyes.

"It was one of two last gifts from Kellan," she whispers.

"What was the second?" I ask carefully.

"A future with you," she replies as she starts crying again. I grab her and pull her onto my lap as her whole body shakes with each gasp for breath. I bury my face into her hair and feel my own tears fall.

Since the day I met Kellan Cole, I despised him. I hated how he looked at Daisy and the arrogance he displayed whilst strutting around campus. But now I wish the guy wasn't dead. I wish I had the chance to thank him for what he tried to do for her. For bringing her back to me and giving us the chance to have a life together, free of any more pain and suffering. For that, I'll be forever grateful.

Chapter Sixty-Five

Jon

Edward and I quietly leave the room and stand on the landing, leaving Michael and Daisy alone with their shared pain.

"She's going to need a lot of time to recover from this, isn't she?" I ask him; Edward looks back at the bedroom door and nods. We make our way downstairs to where everyone is waiting for an update.

As soon as we walk into the lounge, everybody stops and looks at us, waiting for any news on Daisy. Edward is the first to speak.

"Physically, Daisy's okay; she has a deep gash on her right leg and shoulder and quite a few bruises and healing wounds. Her ability to heal has been dampened as she is malnourished and has lost a lot of weight due to having very little to eat or drink.

"Psychologically, there's a lot of damage there that will take a substantial amount of love, support, and time to recover from," Edward says before looking at me for me to continue.

"Daisy will only communicate with Mikey through their bond. He's relaying messages for her." I turn and find her auntie and uncle together with Alex and Sara; Clare stands beside her parents, leaning against Stuart, who has his arm around her waist.

"Daisy wants you and the coven to know she loves you, but she needs a little time before seeing anyone." I look directly at Nigel and Mary before continuing. "I've said you can have my room, so you are close by should she need you." I turn to face the rest of the room.

"Mikey has said everyone is free to stay, and we'll make room for you all. But no one but me is to take anything up to them." I turn and face Marcus. "He says you're in charge until further notice." Marcus looks at me with a raised brow. "I know; I told him you already planned on it. Don't look at me like that."

"Does she need anything?" I hear Mary ask as she steps out of her husband's arms. I look at her and nod. "Daisy needs to eat, so Edward said she should start with some toast and water and slowly increase it. Mikey asked that I take some upstairs for both of them." I watch as Mum walks up to Mary and takes her arm.

"Come on; I'll show you where everything is. I'm going to make this lot some food anyway." Mary looks at Mum and nods before following her to the kitchen.

"I don't think anyone wants to leave right now, and Mikey's happy for us to stay, but we need to keep the noise to a minimum as Daisy is still on edge. The next few days will be rough for them. But from what I've just seen, Mikey will get her through this, and she'll be okay in time." I explain before turning to speak to the Alpha, as I know he wants to get off to check on the Luna. I'm just saying goodbye to him when I see Nigel approaching me.

"Thank you, Jon," he says as he shakes my hand.

"There's no need to thank me. That's my brother and sister upstairs. They are family, and we look after our own."

"That we do," Mum says from behind me. I turn to find her standing beside Mary. They're holding a large plate of toast and a jug of water with two glasses. "Take these up to them and give them our love," Mary says as she hands me the plate. I thank her as Mum nods towards the stairs. I know she will follow me with the jug and glasses.

As we get to the top of the stairs, Mum leans up and places a kiss on my cheek.

"You're the best brother to those two, and I couldn't be prouder of all my children." She whispers before handing me the jug and walking away. I watch as she heads back downstairs and out of view, before I turn in the direction of Michael and Daisy's room and giving the door a quick knock.

"It's me."

I hear movement inside, and Michael opens the door. "I bring toast and water. Do you need anything else?" I ask as I walk in.

Daisy's now sitting in the middle of the bed, her teddy still in her arms, as she leans against the headboard with a blanket over her legs.

I place the plate and jug on the bedside cabinet. "Make sure you eat some of this, please. Both of you." I look directly at my brother, who rolls his eyes at me. Michael takes a glass and fills it before handing it to Daisy. She takes a few sips before giving it back to Michael, who swaps it for a small plate of toast. She pulls a face before taking a bite. Michael chuckles from his spot on the edge of the bed.

"If she manages to eat all this, she can have chocolate spread or peanut butter on the next round" he says, not looking away from Daisy, who almost smiles at him.

For the briefest moment, I watch my baby sister and realise her spark is still there even after all she's been through. I leave the room quickly, telling them to text if they need anything else; I need to get out before they see me break.

I walk out the door and take a deep breath; I make it to the top of the stairs before sitting down and placing my head in my hands. My breathing becomes rapid as the emotions I've been bottling up escape.

Since we got out of the vans when we reached the manor where Daisy was being held, I've shut off all my emotions as I do on any mission. But this one was different. We were going in for one of our own, and we had no idea if we were all going to make it out alive. I knew failure wasn't an option; we had to save Daisy and bring her home, even if that meant leaving Michael behind as he made me swear to protect Daisy over anyone else, including himself.

I wasn't worried when Marcus and I were held at gunpoint, I was willing to die if it gave the others time to save Daisy, but I've never known fear like when I witnessed two of the most important people in my life fight for their lives, and all I could do was watch from the side-lines.

Seeing Michael face-off with the arsehole who killed our sister was pure hell. I wanted nothing more than to jump in and kill the bastard, but Michael and Marcus have always drilled into us about fair fights. But just before Michael was shot, all hell broke loose as Jackson's men started to fight back. I hadn't realised Daisy had shifted until I heard Marcus curse. I tried to get to her, but Marcus stopped me, telling me to wait before he shifted himself. But everything changed when we heard her howl in pain and saw her fall to the ground.

Every wolf ran to her aid, but as we got there, we realised she'd been faking to get Jackson close enough to her. As soon as Jackson leaned over, ready to rip her throat out, she sprang into action and knocked him onto his back, sinking her teeth into his throat and ripping it out before he knew what was happening. The howl that left her when she realised she had finally beaten the male that had caused her so much pain was empowering. I've never felt pride as I did at that moment.

"Jonny?" I look up from my hands to the sound of her voice and see Natalie standing at the bottom of the stairs.

"Even after everything he did to her, the cheeky, mischievous little witch is still in there trying to fight her way back to us," I whisper as I fall apart. I place my head back in my hands and don't even attempt to stop the tears. I smell her sweet rose and honey scent getting stronger as Natalie sits beside me before holding me as I cry.

"From what I've heard about Daisy, I know she's far stronger than I'd ever be after going through what she has. She also has Mikey, you, Mama B, and everyone in that lounge to help her. Whether wolves, witches, sorcerers or demons, everyone is here because they love her and are all on hand to help her and Mikey in whatever they need," Natalie says quietly as she holds me.

I nod as I know she's right. I wipe my face and try to stop the rest of the tears whilst trying to compose myself. I look at Natalie and smile softly.

"Thanks, Nat." For a moment, our eyes lock again, and I feel my chest tightening. Natalie's the first to look away.

"No worries." She smiles as she stands up and walks away from me, again. I watch as she walks down the stairs and back into the lounge, where the others are whispering amongst themselves.

I stand and take a few deep breaths before following her

down; everyone turns in my direction as I walk into the room. I can't help but smile slightly as I whisper, "she wants chocolate spread on the next round."

Chapter Sixty-Six

Michael

I open my eyes, and the first thing I see is the top of Daisy's head. We'd curled up not long after finishing our toast and fallen asleep. I have no idea what time it is, but I feel like I've slept for hours. I glance down at my mate, who's in the same position she was when I closed my eyes. She's curled up on her right with her head resting on my chest. In her left arm is the teddy her father gave her before he was killed. She always clings to it when she's upset or anxious. She once told me it's like her father is hugging her back.

I slowly slide from underneath Daisy, quickly placing a pillow under her head. She murmurs my name in her sleep; I lean over and kiss her gently on the top of the head before stroking her hair until I know she's settled back down. Slowly and quietly, I make my way out of the bedroom and onto the landing, planning to use the main bathroom so as not to wake her.

I stand on the landing and notice how quiet it is. I can hear Mum's steady breathing coming from her room and Nigel and Mary's from Jon's. I reach the bathroom and use it as quickly and quietly as possible, hoping not to wake anyone.

As I leave the bathroom, I realise Marcus is sleeping in my study. It's not the first time he's slept in there this week. I should have known he wouldn't be far away.

Quietly I walk down the stairs and stop in my tracks when I glance into the lounge. The coffee table has been pushed against the far patio doors. On the floor under blankets are Tony, Richard, and Carl. Will and Stuart are asleep, sitting on opposite ends of one of the sofas with Clare sleeping between them. She's resting her head on Stuart's lap and her feet on Will's. Sara's fast asleep on the other sofa. I enter the kitchen to find Alex at the breakfast bar, nursing a glass of my bourbon.

"Any left for me?"

Alex spins around, cursing, "Fuck, Michael, I didn't hear

you come down." He gasps, placing a hand on his chest. I place a hand on his shoulder and squeeze it before heading to the cupboard to get a glass. I pick up the bottle and realise only a tiny amount remains.

"Sorry, I'll replace it tomorrow; we all needed a drink after last night," Alex says sheepishly. I can't help but chuckle slightly.

"Tell me about it." I look up at the kitchen clock and blink twice when I see the time. It's eight at night. We fell asleep around eleven this morning.

"How is she?" Alex asks quietly. I take a deep breath and sip my drink before looking at him. "That bad?" Alex adds; I nod as I close my eyes.

"She won't speak aloud. I don't think a word has passed her lips since she broke down in the shower." I sigh, knowing even without the wolf hearing, he would have heard everything.

"Fuck," Alex curses. I watch as he necks the last of his drink and picks up the bottle, only to realise it's now empty. I turn and reach up into one of the top cupboards. I pull out a fresh bottle and hand it to him.

"You didn't see that. It's my stash Jon, Stuart and Daisy don't know about." I whisper as Alex pours a drink and hands me the bottle so I can pour myself another.

"She told us everything last time. She would talk about what had happened. For her not to talk at all is worrying," Alex says as he takes a sip.

"It's different this time," I whisper. Alex looks up at me, confused; I know he can't imagine that being possible.

"Jon said he couldn't get to her this time. That he didn't ...."

I shake my head at him. "He didn't rape her. She fought with everything she had. She may have only been there for six days this time, but it was worse."

"How?" he asks.

I take a sip of my drink and consider whether to tell Alex the rest.

"Last night, when he beat her, he gave Daisy an ultimatum.

She stopped fighting him and accepted that she was his luna and would breed his pups. Or." The words get stuck in my throat, Alex looks up at me, and I realise he knows what I'm going to say; Kellan had said it was a possibility, but to hear it was true is a whole different matter.

"Or he would kill Daisy and take Clare instead. Daisy was tied to a chair by four cable ties at the time and tore through all of them in anger. He beat her and left her to consider which option she would choose." I run my fingers through my hair as I try and stay calm. Whenever I think about the emotional abuse he inflicted on her, I want to punch something.

"Daisy would have protected Clare no matter what," Alex says, looking to the room where his daughter's sleeping soundly.

"Daisy had accepted she would have to sleep with him to keep him from chasing after Clare. Clare's safety and future were more important to her than her own," I whisper, thinking of the sacrifice Daisy was willing to make.

"Daisy's always been protective of Clare. They we eight months old when they met. Daisy is only older because she was two months premature. They loved each other instantly. Even when Daisy's world was turned upside down by the death of her parents, she was more worried about how Clare was handling everything. They are more than best friends; they're sisters in their own unique way," Alex whispers as he takes a deep breath and knocks back the rest of his drink.

"Well, Daisy's world has been turned upside down again. You must remember that she killed nine people last night, Alex. She has never killed before, even though she knows they'd have killed her or us. That's a big deal. After my first kill, it took days for me to recover. I couldn't eat without throwing up and I was trained for it. She killed nine with no training at all. It will take a lot of time to recover from."

"Shit, I hadn't even thought about that." I watch as he pinches the bridge of his nose, "she got her magic back at least." He sighs, desperately looking for a silver lining.

"Yeah, she isn't coping with that either. She got it back when Kellan died in her arms after one of Jackson's men shot him in front of her," I explain, bowing my head.

"Fuck." I look at Alex and see him struggling to take it all in.

"She blames herself. She said she was taunting Jackson at the time; next thing she knew, a guy stepped around him with a gun in his hand, and Kellan slumped to the floor with a gunshot wound in the middle of his chest." I explain quietly.

We stay silent for a moment, trying to find the words and the reasoning behind it all. But there's none.

"How do you come back from that, Michael?" Alex asks, his voice breaking the silence around us. I shake my head before finishing my drink.

"I don't know. I don't know how she will recover from it all. It's going to take a lot of time." I look up at the ceiling as I hear a sound come from our bedroom and dash for the door. "Fuck."

I'm already halfway up the stairs taking them three at a time when an ear-piercing scream fills the silent house. As I reach the landing, all the doors open. I don't stop; I throw open our bedroom door to find Daisy screaming in the middle of our bed. I pull her onto my lap as she screams and cries into my chest, clutching at my T-shirt desperately.

"I'm so sorry, darling. I've got you. Shh, baby, I'm right here." I whisper into her ear as she screams into my chest, her whole body shaking. I rock her as I sit on the edge of the bed, continuously whispering words of encouragement into her ear; soon, the screaming stops, but she's still crying hard, struggling to catch her breath. I pick her up and carry her out of the room, knowing what she needs to get out of the panic attack.

"Michael?" I see Nigel, Mary, Marcus, and my mum standing outside our room on the landing.

"She's having a panic attack," I say as I look at Marcus. "I need to get her into the woods, get the doors and keep everyone inside." He nods as he rushes in front of me down the stairs barking at everyone to stay in the lounge and out of the way. Holding a still hyperventilating Daisy tightly to my chest, I walk down to the dining room and see Marcus standing holding the patio doors open for us with a blanket in his hand.

"Shout when you are ready, I'll keep everyone out the way," he whispers as we reach him.

"Thank you," I reply as I let Marcus place the blanket over Daisy, as she gasps for breath. He walks back through the doors, closing them behind him.

I can feel everyone watching from various windows in the house, but I don't care. I need to get her into the open. I walk us into the woods behind the house and head straight to the area I slept in. I sit down and place her between my legs so her back is pressed against my chest; I wrap the blanket and my arms tightly around her.

"Five things you can smell, darling," I whisper through the bond. She shakes her head, crying as she tries to get back on my lap, but I hold her in place. I thread my fingers of one hand into hers and start running my other hand over her head. Keeping it lifted and against my chest.

"Come on, baby; you can do this. Five things you can smell."

"Blood," she gasps as a fresh wave of panic builds, but I squeeze her hand.

"There's no blood, darling."

"There is; I can smell his and Kellan's blood." Daisy gasps and cries hysterically, her heartbeat getting faster; I'm terrified that her fragile body won't handle the stress.

"Darling, I swear there's no blood; I would smell it. Focus on another scent." I almost beg her.

"It's too strong." She gasps as her body starts shaking violently. I flashback to the night I watched her wolf lose control after Kellan drugged her, I thought I felt helpless then, but now it's even worse. *"Shift; I'll help settle her wolf again,"* my wolf says. I let go of her hands and move away from her.

"Mikey, don't go," she begs as she reaches for me. I tug off my sweatpants.

"I'm not going anywhere. I'm never leaving your side again," I say before I shift and lie down around Daisy, who instantly curls against me. I position myself so one of my front legs is under her head and another around her, tucking her against my chest. I feel her fingers thread into my fur as she runs them through it.

"What do you smell now?" I ask

"You, only you." I give her a few seconds to catch her breath before nudging her with my nose.

"Pick out another scent." It takes a few more seconds before Daisy replies quietly.

"Dirt."

"Good, now four more."

"Pine trees."

"Another?"

"Lavender."

"Two more, darling," I coach.

"Mikey, I can't." She sobs, nestling further into my chest, trying to hide.

"Yes, you can, baby, two more." I encourage her whilst nudging her with my nose again.

"Grass." Daisy answers after a moment.

"Good, last one."

"Jonny." I frown down at her and sniff the air. My brother's scent fills my nose instantly. I should have known he wouldn't be far.

"Do you want to see him?" I ask as I press my nose to her wet and salty cheek. Daisy nods into my chest.

"It's okay, Jonny, you can come out," I call as I use my nose to wipe away Daisy's tears. I look up as Jon's wolf walks into the clearing.

"Sorry, I was out for a run when I heard Daisy crying."

"It's okay; Daisy's having a panic attack." I watch as Jon shifts back and quickly tugs on my sweatpants before sitting down beside Daisy. He runs a hand over her head, and she curls further into me.

"Dais, tell me what you need, and I'll get it for you," Jon whispers. Daisy shakes her head and leans further into me. I look up at Jon and shake my head; he nods in understanding.

"Okay, Dais, I'll leave you and Mikey alone. Get him to call me if you want anything." Jon goes to stand, but Daisy grabs hold of his hand.

"Stay." She whispers aloud for the first time as she looks at my brother. I watch as tears fill his eyes, and he quickly blinks them back.

"Okay, Dais. If you want me to stay, I'm not going anywhere." I watch as he reaches over, pulls the blanket from behind him, and places it over Daisy as she settles back into me, her fingers running through my fur as she cries quietly before drifting off into an exhausted sleep.

"She needs to spend more time outside; after being inside for so long, her wolf must be going insane," Jon whispers as soon as Daisy's breathing signals that she's asleep. I look up at him and nod.

"The poor woman's exhausted; you both are. Take this time to rest; I'll keep an ear out for anyone," Jon says as he runs a hand over Daisy's head again and tucks the blanket around her tighter. I huff through my nose before lowering my head, so it's resting above Daisy's as I close my eyes, grateful for my brother's endless love and support.

Chapter Sixty-Seven

Daisy

I wake up back in our bed, with Michael nowhere to be seen. I frantically sit up and jump as a hand lands on my shoulder.

"Shh, Daisy, it's okay." I turn to find my Auntie Mary sitting beside the bed. She gently rubs my shoulder. "Michael's gone for a shower; he'll be back in a moment." I open my mouth to speak but can't find the words. So I nod as I sit up so my back is against the headboard. Auntie Mary moves so she is sitting closer to me.

I watch as her eyes fill with tears. I want to tell her I'm going to be okay. That Jackson's gone, and he can't hurt anyone ever again. But I can't because I don't think I will be. Even though he's dead, he's still hurting people, as we remember what he did. Mama, Michael, Jon, and Marcus will forever grieve for Michelle. Auntie Mary and Uncle Nigel had to miss out on so much as they hid from him to protect me. Every time I close my eyes, I see Kellan fall, the blood seeping through the fabric of his top, his eyes as his life drains from him.

I can feel my eyes filling up with tears, and I quickly try to blink them back before my auntie notices them. But I'm not quick enough.

"Don't do that, Daisy. Don't hide your pain from me, I know you better than anyone on this earth, and I can feel it when you're hurting." She reaches over and places a hand on my cheek.

"I know you can't talk out loud at the moment, and that's fine, dear. If talking to Michael through your bond is easier for now, then you do that. You do what you need to do to recover. But know that me and Uncle Nigel are always here for you and love you so much." I can feel the tears escaping as they run down my face. Auntie Mary pulls me into a hug and holds me tightly. I hug her back and cry into her shoulder.

I don't deserve this woman; I don't deserve the love she and my uncle constantly show me. Not after everything I've done. Not after everything I've put them through. They deserve a niece who's as sweet and kind as they are. Not a murderer.

I hear the bedroom door open, and Michael's scent fills the room.

"Sorry. I'll come back." I take his entry as an excuse to pull away from Auntie Mary and wipe my face. I look up at him and see him looking at me with worry in his eyes; he can feel my emotions through the bond.

"Please get her out of here. Gently." I beg him.

"Whatever you need, darling." He smiles as he turns to Auntie Mary. "Daisy's wondering if there's any chance of your famous chocolate chip cookies. It seems it's all she has been thinking about." I watch as her face lights up as she looks at me. I try to force a smile. It's a weak one, but her eyes shine anyway.

"Of course, I'll get your uncle to take me to the shop to get everything I need. I'll make as many as you want." She leans over and kisses me on the cheek before standing up and leaving the room. She gives Michael's arm a quick squeeze as she passes him.

As soon as she's out of the door, I grab my teddy to the side of me and lie back down on the bed. As the tears start to fall again, I quickly roll, so my back is to the door and the rest of the world. Michael creeps to his side of the bed and lies down, facing me. He gently runs a hand over my head and tucks some stray strands of hair behind my ear.

"Talk to me, darling." I hear his voice as he whispers through the bond; I don't know what to say, so I shake my head.

"Baby, please. I can't help you if you don't let me in."

There is a bang as the front door closes, and I jump. Michael curses out loud as he gets to his feet. I turn to watch him as he storms to the bedroom door but stops in his tracks as he throws it open.

"Breathe Mikey, then tell me what you need." I hear

Marcus whisper. I watch Michael take a deep breath as he tries to control his temper, but he's still on edge.

"Let him in," I whisper. Michael steps back from the door and waves Marcus in. Marcus enters the room and walks over to the bed before sitting down on the edge of it facing me.

"Good to see you awake."

I offer a half-hearted smile before nodding at Michael as he stands by the now-closed door, running his fingers through his hair.

"Mikey, talk to me," Marcus says. Michael shakes his head.

"I'm fine," Michael lies. Marcus looks at him with a raised brow. "Fine, you want to know what's wrong other than the obvious? There are too many people here, Marcus; every little noise has Daisy jumping, don't you think she's been through enough? It's near impossible to think straight as all I want to do is focus on her, yet as soon as I step foot out of this room, someone is there asking how she is. They need to go and stay in their own homes or the pack houses, and I will call them if and when she's ready to see them all," Michael blurts out. Marcus looks at him and nods.

"I was coming up to tell you we've already started getting people to leave. Tony, Richard, and Carl have just gone. Stuart and Jon are going to stay at Will's as it's closer. Alex, Sara and Clare are already back in the pack house, and I will head home in a bit after I've taken Mama B home. That will leave Daisy's aunt and uncle, who may take a little more persuading, which you will need to do," Marcus explains calmly.

"Oh," is all Michael says as he looks at his pack brother, embarrassed by his outburst.

"Mikey, everyone stayed as we crashed out after Daisy's rescue. As they've woken up and realised that she needs more time before seeing them, they realised the best thing they can do is go home and leave you both in peace," Marcus explains before turning to face me.

"Message me when you are ready to talk to people, and I'll run interference. If you want to talk about other stuff but aren't ready to speak aloud, then text me, and I'll text you back, and we can communicate that way. Whatever you need, you know I'm here for you and this stroppy bastard."

"Hey!" Michael protests as Marcus winks at me, grinning. I feel a small genuine smile appear on my face for the first time since I got home. Marcus smiles as he leans over and presses a kiss to my forehead.

"I've missed you, you little witch. Text if you need a break from him, and I'll pop round and drag him out." Marcus stands up and looks at Michael.

"If you need anything, message one of the team; we are at your disposal. But I must warn you that the Alpha is on his way and wants to see Daisy. I suggest letting him see her. I think it may help." Marcus walks out of the room as I stare at Michael. I can feel my chest getting tighter as what Marcus said sinks in.

"Darling, breathe," Michael whispers as he sits where Marcus was just sitting. I shake my head as I can't. "Darling, if you don't calm down, you'll pass out. You know what to do when a panic attack starts. Slowly breathe in with me." I look into Michael's eyes as I slowly breathe in, copying him. I take three breaths to his one, the same when we exhale. But as we breathe in again, I only need to take two breaths to his one. After a couple of minutes, I can breathe in and out simultaneously with him.

"That's my girl. Now tell me what started it," Michael asks as he tucks my hair behind my ear.

"The Alpha is coming round," I reply, not trusting myself to speak out loud.

"I was expecting him to. He will want to see for himself that you are okay," Michael answers.

"Why?"

"Because you're a member of his pack, and he's been worried sick about you; the whole pack has."

"He's not going to kick me out, is he?" I ask as the tears fall again.

"Why on earth would he kick you out?" Michael asks, frowning at me.

"Because I don't deserve to be a blood moon wolf," I admit as I go to turn away, but Michael grabs my shoulders and forces me to look at him.

"Darling, please speak to me; tell me what you mean." I try to look away again, but Michael isn't letting me. "Baby, look at me." I look Michael in the eye as the tears start again.

"Daisy Andrews, you will listen to me. You deserve to be a member of this pack as much as anyone else. Nothing that happened was your fault," Michael snaps.

"Yes, it was," I reply, wishing he'd drop it.

"No, it wasn't, darling." Michael insists again.

"YES, IT WAS!" I scream aloud. Michael stares at me in shock, but the ball's now rolling. "How many people are dead because of me? How many families will never know what happened to their loved ones because of me? If I kept my mouth shut instead of trying to piss Jackson off, Kellan would still be alive. So yes, Michael, it's *my fault!* It's *all* my fault!" It's like a floodgate opens, and once I start talking, I can't shut up. Everything I've bottled up since fighting Jackson flows out of me.

"You want to know why I can't even face my friends and family? Because I don't deserve them; I don't deserve their kindness or comfort. My auntie sat there telling me she loves me, but how could she? How can she love someone who killed eight people in seconds? I didn't even stop to think, I recognised their scents from when they held me down or came in with him, and I killed them. I killed them where they stood, not giving them the chance to redeem themselves. All I could think was that you and the guys were outside and could be killed any second. I didn't think about whether those I killed had people who cared about them, all I could think was I wanted revenge, and I needed to protect you and kill Jackson." I look at Michael through my tears and see a tear fall from his own blue eyes.

"How can you love me when you know I killed them without a second thought? How can I deserve your love? Because right now, I don't feel like I do. I'm terrified you'll walk out that door and never return because you'll realise you're mated to a murderer." I sit and expect Michael to walk away, say that I finally realised what he's been thinking and that he's going.

Instead, Michael takes my hand and entwines our fingers together.

"Do you remember the day in the forest when I told you about the team? I told you I had killed a rogue who was wanted for a string of sexual assaults. Do you remember what you said?" I look at him and nod.

"You said 'okay'. Nothing more, just 'okay'. I remember sitting there and thinking, 'why isn't she running? Why isn't she rejecting me? But then you told me that males like that don't get better, they get worse, and you told me you were glad I'd killed him. Every time you tell me you love me after I have been on a mission, I think, 'how can you when I just killed someone?'"

"Mikey, it's different. You have to kill them to protect your pack and others." I sigh.

"Why is that any different from what you did, darling?"

"Because it is." I sob, wishing he would just see that it is different; it's completely different.

"It's not. Those men were willing to ignore that you were being held against your will, and some were even willing to hold you down as you were raped. Are you telling me they would have gone on to live quiet lives and would have never assaulted anyone again? I'm sorry, darling, they wouldn't have. Jackson picked those men for a reason, because they had the same views as him, that women are there to satisfy a man's needs, whether consensual or not."

"You don't know that," I whisper. Michael shakes his head.

"Marcus can you bring up the file on Jackson's men," Michael calls, knowing his second will hear him. Almost instantly, I can hear two sets of footsteps on the stairs, and I freeze. The bedroom door opens, and Marcus and the Alpha walk in. I go to jump from the bed to bow, but Michael places a hand on my shoulder to stop me.

"Stay there, Daisy. It's fine," The Alpha says as Michael holds his hand out. Marcus places a file in his hand.

"This is all the information we could find on the people we knew about before we left to go to that address in Exeter, which was a stupid move, I should add." He looks up at the

Alpha, who holds his hands up.

"You have made your views on that decision perfectly clear," the Alpha points out. I watch as Michael opens the file and pulls out a piece of paper.

"Simon Bolt, two arrests for sexual assault on women he lured into his car pretending to be a taxi driver." He pulls out a second piece of paper. "William Greenwood, too many convictions to list on one piece of paper. A lot of sexual assaults, rapes and kidnapping. How he was out of prison, I will never know." Michael pulls out a stack of papers and puts them in front of me.

"There are ten men in that pile, every single one has a history of attempted sexual assault, or they succeeded. The police have never caught some; they were free to do it again and again. This is just what we found on the ones we knew about. They also had a history of violence towards men and women. The families were all glad to get away from them." Michael places a finger under my chin and lifts my face so that I'm looking at him.

"Now sit there and tell me that what you did is any different from what me, Marcus and even the others have done." I can't speak. I just look at Michael as the tears roll down my face.

"Daisy, if you hadn't killed those men, I would have ordered the team to anyway. As soon as you said you wanted to dissolve the pack, and what they had been willing to do, I knew I'd have to give the order," I hear the Alpha say as he steps next to Michael. "Wolves like that cannot be allowed to live. You wouldn't have been the last to be hurt by Jackson if they had. As his men would have carried on where he left off," he adds, moving to kneel in front of me; he takes my free hand and holds it between his.

"I wanted to come and check on you today to make sure you know that I have *never* been prouder of a member of my pack as I am of you. When we got to that house, I was sure we would find you broken. But instead, you walked out of that building with your head held high and confronted the bastard who had held you prisoner, for six days. You looked him straight in the eye and showed him not one ounce of fear. I heard from Kellan that you never once backed down or let Jackson see you as anything other than the strong female you are.

"The whole time you were there, you protected yourself and your mate by closing down your bond even though I know there would have been times when you wanted to hear Michael's voice, but you never let that wall down."

"I couldn't let him feel my pain or fear," I whisper. I look up at Michael. "I felt everything that day with the crash. I couldn't let you feel that." Michael lifts my hand to his mouth and kisses the back of it.

"Michael thought that was why you had done it," the Alpha says as he glances at Michael before looking back at me. "I *never* want to hear you say that you don't deserve to be in my pack. You said it yourself yesterday outside that house. You are a Blood Moon wolf and deserve to be in this pack as much as any other member." The Alpha lets go of my hand as he stands up and turns to Michael.

"Did Daisy tell you what she declared to Jackson when he tried to tell her he was her alpha and her mate?" the Alpha asks. I freeze, wondering how he heard about that. Kellan wasn't even there. Michael shakes his head as he looks at me. The Alpha turns and smiles at me. "How did it go? 'You are not my alpha! My alpha is Desmond Gibbs, who is a million times the man you claim to be. I will *never* abandon my pack, as they will never abandon me.' Apparently, Jackson didn't take it too well. Do you remember what you said when he lost his temper and tried to scare you into submission?" I look at the Alpha and nod.

"I am the mate of Michael Adams, a member of the Blood Moon pack, and I bow to no one but *my* alpha." I turn and look at Michael; as soon as our eyes meet, they lock. I can't see anything but those blue eyes—my safe haven.

"We'll leave you alone for a moment," the Alpha says as I hear the door open and then quickly close. I don't see if they've left, as I can't look anywhere but Michael's eyes, which are as full of tears as my own. I open my mouth to say something, but

Michael cuts me off as he launches himself at me and kisses me with such passion that it knocks the breath right out of me. I throw my arms around his neck and kiss him back as I wanted to the whole time we were apart.

Too soon, Michael pulls away and looks me in the eye as we both try and catch our breath.

"You truly are amazing. Whenever I think you've made me the proudest wolf alive, you do something that makes me even prouder. Never doubt that I love you or believe in you completely, because I do. How you survived this last week shows how unbelievably strong you are, and I know you will only get stronger. I am privileged to be the one who stands beside you, holding your hand as your mate and watching you concur with every challenge that passes your way." Michael moves so he is kneeling in front of me. "I want to watch you grow and become everything I know you can be and more. Not only as your mate but as your husband." My heart stops as my hand flies up to my mouth. "Daisy Angela Andrews, will you do me the greatest honour of agreeing to be my wife?" I nod before throwing my arms around Michael's neck as I cry into his shoulder. "I think you may need to answer aloud for the wolves eavesdropping downstairs," Michael chuckles.

"What did she say?" We hear Jon call out.

"Yes!" I answer back loud enough for the wolves to hear at least and start smiling as everyone cheers down below.

"I love you, Mikey."

"Not as much as I love you, darling."

Chapter Sixty-Eight

Michael

I carry Daisy downstairs a few minutes later to see our friends and family. As happy as Daisy is, I can still tell there's a lot of pain for her to work through. When I try to place her on the sofa, she looks up at me and begs me through the bond not to leave her, so I place her on my knee instead. I hold her tightly and act like I can't bring myself to let go of my new fiancée. In reality, I'm monitoring everything, from Daisy's facial expressions to her heart rate. When this becomes too much, I'll whisk her out into the woods, where she can sit in the sun and breathe.

Thankfully everyone seems aware that Daisy is still overwhelmed, and they don't all rush to congratulate us at once.

The first person to us is Mary, with Nigel by her side. Mary pulls Daisy into a hug and then places a kiss on my cheek. Tears stream down her face as she smiles at her niece.

"I'm so happy for you both." Mary croaks as she smiles through her tears.

"We both are," Nigel adds as he kisses Daisy on the cheek and shakes my hand.

"Thank you," Daisy whispers. Smiling at them both. Her uncle winks at her for encouragement before pulling Mary to one side and letting my beaming mum get to us.

"No one deserves this more than you two. I'm so happy for you both," She whispers as she pulls us into a hug before kissing each of us.

"Thank you, Mama," I whisper as I kiss her on the cheek. Mum cups my face in her hand, and I can see there's so much more she wants to say, but now isn't the time. She looks at Daisy, and I know one day Mum and her will have a long, painful chat about what happened; it's something they both need to do. But neither is ready for that yet, now is a celebration.

"Mind if I cut in Mama B?" We both look up at the Alpha, who instantly holds his hand out to stop us from getting up.

Desmond kneels before us, so he's at eye level with Daisy again.

"I'm so happy for you both. I know you will achieve great things together, and nothing will stand in your way or get between you," he says, smiling at us.

"Thank you, Des," I reply, holding out my hand to my alpha and friend. I turn and catch Daisy's eyes opening wide.

"How's the Luna, Alpha?" she asks. Desmond turns and looks at her, smiling.

"She and baby are doing just fine; thank you, Daisy."

"She's had the baby?" we both ask together.

"Yep. A beautiful little girl, she was born last night. She already has her big brother, and I wrapped around her little finger," Desmond replies, beaming with pride.

"What are you doing here? You should be with them!" Daisy exclaims; Desmond looks at her with a severe face.

"Daisy, Jayne was adamant I came to check on you and speak to you myself. She wants to know that you're okay," he says as he looks at me. I know that Jayne wanted him to check on us both.

"What have you called her?" I ask.

"Sophie Michelle Gibbs." My heart nearly bursts. I knew Jayne wanted to honour her best friend, but hearing my sister's name makes me prouder than I ever thought it would.

"Beautiful name," Daisy whispers as she smiles at the Alpha, then at me as she picks up on my feelings as always.

"Thank you, Daisy," he replies, still smiling.

"Make sure you go straight home to them, Alpha. That's an order." Daisy replies as she leans into me; I can't help but chuckle as I hold her tightly against me.

"I will now I know you are on the right track, Daisy. Jayne will want to know all about you two," Desmond says as he stands up. I look up as he winks at me before stepping away.

Daisy and I look up to the back of the room where my team are gathered. I feel Daisy shift on my lap as she attempts to stand up. I move my arm under her legs to lift her, but she looks at me and shakes her head. Slowly Daisy stands up for the first time in days. I stand next to her and offer her my arm, Daisy takes it, and we walk over to the team.

Marcus, Jon, Stuart and Will all stand together, smiling at Daisy as she slowly makes her way to them. We stand together in front of four of the most influential people in our lives. I look at each of my brothers and see them all smiling.

Daisy's focus is purely on Marcus.

"I never got the chance to thank you," Daisy whispers as she looks up at him. Marcus looks down, smiling. "I wouldn't have been as strong without you. What you taught me saved my life," Daisy whispers. But Marcus looks down at her and shakes his head.

"You were already strong; I just showed you how to use that strength. As for saving you, you saved yourself. No one helped with that; it was all you," he whispers. I feel Daisy step away from me as she drops my hand; I reach out for her instinctively but stop when I see her throw her arms around Marcus. Marcus chuckles as he hugs her back.

"The best gift I could have asked for today was seeing you safe and back home," Marcus whispers. Daisy pulls away from him with her eyes wide.

"Shit, Marc, it's your birthday!" I exclaim. "Man, I'm so sorry I lost track of time." Marcus laughs as he raises his eyebrows at me.

"I think you've had more important things on your mind."

"It's a good job I'm organised then." Daisy chimes in, grinning. "Mikey, there's a box in the bottom of that cabinet," Daisy says as she points to the sideboard. I frown at her as I walk over and open the doors. Inside is a gift box with a bow on the top.

"When did you organise this?" I ask, lifting it out.

"A few weeks ago." She winks at me as I hand her the box. She holds it out to Marcus.

"It's from Mikey and me, but mainly me." She chuckles. Her eyes are sparkling for the first time since she walked out of that building. Marcus notices as he smiles at her, lifts the lid off the box, and pulls out a ...

"Winnie the pooh?" Jon and I ask together as Marcus looks at it and roars laughing. In his hand is a teddy of Winnie the Pooh with something around his neck,

"Read the heart." Daisy chuckles.

"You are braver than you believe, stronger than you seem and smarter than you think." Marcus reads it out loud and looks at Daisy, laughing.

"I told you, he said it first," Daisy says as she smiles up at Marcus, who rolls his eyes.

"You couldn't let me have that one, could you?" he replies, smiling down at her.

"Nope," Daisy says, shaking her head.

Marcus looks at the teddy in his hand and then at Daisy, and his face changes into the softest smile I've seen on his face in five years.

"Thank you, Daisy. I love it," Marcus says as he leans down and kisses her on the cheek.

"Happy birthday Marcus," Daisy whispers as he steps back, still holding his teddy.

"Welcome back, little witch," Marcus replies.

"Now the birthday boy has his gift. Can I get a hug from my baby sister?" Jon declares as he steps forward and pulls Daisy into his arms. Daisy squeezes him back.

"I am so glad you are back, and even gladder, you said yes to this one," Jon says as he steps back from Daisy and pulls me into a hug.

"Congratulations, little bro." Jon grins at me.

"Four months, Jon." I sigh before hugging him back. "Thanks, big brother," I whisper back so only he can hear. Jon pats me on the back as he stands tall again. I turn just in time to see Stuart hugging Daisy.

"Is Clare okay?" she asks, looking concerned.

"She's better now you're home. She'll be livid when she hears she missed Mikey proposing," he replies, smiling as he steps back. Daisy looks up at Will.

"Do I want to ask how you took that news, Will?" She asks him. He pulls her into a gentle hug as he chuckles.

"Better than Alex did," I add as Daisy breathes in through

her teeth before looking back towards Stuart.

"Good luck with the new father-in-law." She smiles.

"Thanks, I'm going to need it. He isn't going to let this be easy, that's for sure. But Clare feels it too, and I'm willing to wait as long as he makes us," Stuart replies, rolling his eyes.

"Clare's his little girl. I'm sure my dad would have been the same with Mikey." Daisy says in the hope of reassuring him.

"Nah, I would have had him eating out the palm of my hand like I did Alex and Nigel," I reply, kissing the top of her head as I place an arm around her waist and hold her against me. Giving her the physical support I can see she's starting to need.

"That can change, Adams."

We both turn to see Alex stride into the room with an excited Clare and Sara behind him.

"Nah, you love me; just admit it," I reply, grinning at Alex, who stops in front of us and looks at me with arched brows. He then looks down at his goddaughter, and his whole face changes.

"Hey, Daisy-do," Alex whispers.

I watch tears fill Daisy's eyes as she whispers, "Hey, Papa Bear." He pulls her into a hug and holds her so tightly I'm worried he will hurt her. Alex buries his face into Daisy's hair, and I see his shoulders shake. I hear them whispering and turn to see Sara looking between the two with tears in her eyes. She quickly blinks them back and looks at me with a smile.

"Congratulations, Michael. We knew it wouldn't be long," Sara says as she pulls me into a hug. I kiss her on the cheek as I hug her back.

"Thank you, Sara."

"Dad, get off her so I can see the ring!" Clare sighs next to her dad, who pulls away from Daisy.

"Clare, there's no ring. I don't think Mikey had planned on proposing at that moment." Daisy says as she smiles at me. I feel Jon nudge me from behind.

"No, I hadn't planned to do it then. But I do have this." I pull my hand from behind my back and produce a ring box. Daisy looks at me wide-eyed.

"When did you get that?" she asks, her hand on her chest. I step towards her as Stuart pulls Clare away from Daisy, smiling.

"I promised you a holiday, no pack, no dramas, just you and me for a month after everything was sorted. I *had* planned on asking for your hand when we were in Paris or Rome. But when I heard how you declared yourself as mine, I couldn't help myself." I open the box and produce a white gold ring with an amethyst stone between two smaller diamonds.

"That's ..." Daisy starts as her eyes widen.

"Your mother's ring, I asked your Auntie Mary for advice on what you would like, and she suggested you might like another of your mum's; as soon I saw it, I knew it was the one. Jon's been looking after it since we all went down to Cornwall." I lift it out of the box and take Daisy's left hand before sliding the ring onto her finger and kissing it.

"Mikey, it's perfect." Daisy sobs as she looks at the ring now on her finger.

"It's just like you then," I whisper as I pull her into my arms and hold her against me.

"Cheese ball," Daisy whispers as she smiles up at me.

"I'm your cheese ball, though," I whisper back as I press my lips to hers lightly.

"Yes, you are."

Chapter Sixty-Nine

Michael

I'm putting away the last of the shopping when I hear Marcus's car pull up outside. I rush to open the front door before he barges in. As Marcus walks down the garden path, I quickly place a finger on my lips before signalling for him to follow me. Once we're in the kitchen, I close the door.

"Is Daisy sleeping?" Marcus asks quietly. I nod and go back to sorting the fridge.

"Yeah, she had a rough night. She woke three times from nightmares." I shake my head to clear the image of my fiancée crying into my chest.

"Not the best time to discuss why I'm here then," Marcus sighs as he rubs the back of his neck.

"What's happened?" I ask as I turn and face him, holding out a beer. Marcus takes it and twists off the top.

"We need to do something with Kellan. He's still in the cold unit. The Alpha wants him buried as soon as possible, ideally today."

"Fuck. I forgot you'd promised to bring him back." I sigh as I twist off the top of my beer.

"Yeah, well, you've had your hands full here. I hear her auntie and uncle have moved back to the pack house," Marcus points out.

"Yeah, I said I wanted everything as normal as possible for Daisy, including Jon being here. They didn't argue; I think they plan on going back to Exeter in a day or two anyway because Nigel's needed for some coven business. Alex, Sara, and Clare are staying here to help Daisy with her powers for a while." I sigh, running my fingers through my hair.

"Do you think Daisy will be up to discussing Kellan, or shall I bury him and take her to the grave when she's ready?" he asks as I lean against the fridge and sip my beer.

"I don't know. His death was hard on her; I don't know whether her being there will be the closure she needs or make things worse?" I take another sip of my beer. "Whatever she decides, I want to be the one to bury him. I owe him that much." I look towards the lounge, where I know Daisy is sleeping. "Fuck." I sigh as I put the bottle on the side and head out of the kitchen with Marcus on my heels.

I walk into the lounge and look to the sofa where Daisy is still sleeping, her white teddy bear lying on the floor where it must have fallen whilst she slept. She hasn't been anywhere without it since returning.

"You sure you want to wake her?" Marcus whispers. I shake my head.

"I don't want to, but she'll struggle tonight if she sleeps too long. Plus, she needs to eat." I sigh as I walk over to the sofa and kneel on the floor.

"Darling, time to wake up," I whisper as I run a hand over her head. Daisy moans as she opens her eyes and blinks at me.

"What time is it?" she croaks as she looks around.

"Just after twelve," I whisper as Daisy sees Marcus by the door,

"What's happened?" she asks, sitting up. I sit next to her as Marcus sits on the coffee table in front of us.

"We need to talk to you about something," I say carefully as I put an arm around her. She looks from Marcus to me, frowning. I open my mouth to speak but don't know what to say or how to say it. Thankfully Marcus does.

"We need to know what you want to do about Kellan." He says as he reaches over and takes Daisy's hand. "We brought him back with us as we promised, and he's been in the cold unit. But we can't leave him in there any longer. It's been four days; we need to bury him," Marcus explains. I can see the tears welling up in Daisy's eyes again as she nods.

"Where will you bury him?" she asks. I reach up and tuck a stray section of hair behind her ear.

"We have a patch of land for people who can't be laid to rest in traditional graveyards, people who have died in wolf form or if their deaths will raise too many questions," I explain.

"Where you bury the rogues?" Daisy asks as she looks at me.

"Yes," I nod.

"Actually, no," Marcus answers; I turn to him, frowning. But he's looking solely at Daisy. "He will go somewhere else. This is usually only for pack members, but the Alpha will allow Kellan to be buried there," Marcus says. I hadn't expected that. I don't think there's ever been a non-pack member buried on our land. "The Alpha's making the exception after Kellan's efforts to help you." he adds before squeezing Daisy's hand. She looks up at him as a tear slips down her cheek.

"When?" she asks.

"Today," Marcus answers softly.

"You don't have to do anything if you don't want to, darling. I'll be there when he's buried, and I can take you at a later date," I whisper.

"No. I want to be there. He did so much for me." Her voice starts to break, and I can't stop myself from scooping her up and placing her on my lap. She buries her face into my chest as she cries silently.

"Do you want me to contact anyone to let them know?" I ask quietly. Daisy nods against me as she pulls away from me whilst wiping her face.

"Tony might want to know. As well as Richard and Carl," she whispers. I kiss the top of her head.

"I'll call them; maybe Tony can come and sit with you at Mum's until we are ready," I suggest.

"Will you be digging the grave?" Daisy asks.

"I owe it to him," I reply as Daisy nods before standing up from my lap and looking at me.

"Can you please call them while I have a shower? Tell them that it's fine if they don't want to come. I understand." I stand up and take her hand.

"Of course, I will. Go and shower, and I'll make you a sandwich for when you get out."

"I'm not hungry," Daisy murmurs, looking away.

"I know, but if you eat at least half, Mama won't try and force-feed you when you get there," I add with a small smile. Daisy nods and walks off towards the hallway. I wait until I hear her heading up the stairs before sitting back down and placing my head in my hands.

"She's lost so much weight," Marcus whispers. I look at him and nod.

"She hardly eats or sleeps. She wakes up from nightmares that make her sick when she does."

"At least she's talking now," Marcus points out, but I shrug.

"Not all the time. Sometimes she'll only communicate with me via the bond." I look up at the ceiling and hear the shower running above us. "I hate seeing her like this," I sigh. "I don't know what to do for the best; I'm winging it," I admit as I lift my head to look at Marcus.

"You're giving her everything she needs, Mikey. She just needs a little time and a lot of love. Today may give her the closure she needs to accept it's finally over," Marcus adds.

"I haven't risked checking the news; anything on the manor house?" I ask; Marcus shrugs at me.

"Police are saying it was a house full of squatters. They couldn't identify anyone due to them being too burnt. It helped that we knocked out their teeth and ensured there was no way of identifying the bodies."

"How many times did Will puke?" I ask, trying to lighten the mood. Marcus chuckles from his spot on the coffee table.

"Natalie will tell you, as she made sure she kept count." Marcus looks up at the ceiling before looking back at me. "Have you thought about asking Nat to speak to her? Remember how she was after her first mission? Speaking to a woman who has been there and experienced something similar might help," Marcus suggests.

"I'll speak to Nat later and see if she can talk to her before heading home," I reply, leaning back into the sofa.

"She's not staying then?" Marcus asks. I shake my head.

"No, she has a whole new life away from here now. New job, new friends."

"New fella?" Marcus enquires; I nod my head. "How did that go down with you know who?"

"Think he'd already guessed. He's spent a lot of time moping in his room or with Daisy. He's been great with her when I've got to get bits done."

"You know we are all on hand to run errands for you. All you have to do is shout. Even if it's just getting the shopping," Marcus points out.

"I know, Marc, and I appreciate it. But I think the tiny bit of normality I can get is all that's keeping me sane at the moment. Just getting out for some shopping helped today, whilst Jon sat with Daisy."

"Has she been out at all?" Marcus asks.

"Only for short walks in the woods out back. Today will be the furthest she has been since we brought her home."

"Hopefully, it'll be a step in the right direction." Marcus sighs, giving me a half-smile.

"I hope so." I look up as I hear the shower turn off and sigh. "I need to get this call over with, and then we can make a move to Mum's." I stand up and retrieve my phone from my pocket.

"Want me to give everyone a shout. Let them know what's happening?" Marcus offers; I nod at him.

"That would be great; thanks Marcus."

"No worries, pal. I'll do it when I go and get everything sorted. I'll meet you at Mama B's, and we can go from there." I shake Marcus's hand and walk him to the door. As soon as he leaves, I dial Tony's number, dreading this call.

Chapter Seventy

Daisy

"You don't have to do this. You know he would understand if you want to go to the grave later," Tony says softly as he glances at me in his rear-view mirror as we drive to the pack graveyard. Mama is in the front passenger seat so she can give Tony directions.

I hadn't expected either of them to come; I know people struggle to understand anything Kellan did. But they weren't there. They don't know the Kellan I saw in those last few days. The one who stood between Jackson and me and tried to keep me safe. He risked our lives to get me out of there and back to Michael, and I'll never be able to thank him for that. If being there when he's buried is the only way to say thank you, then I will be there.

This afternoon, I researched some of Kellan's family history and found that honeysuckle is his fae family's house flower. There is a large bush of it in the woods at the back of Mama's garden. I took some cuttings so they can be added to his body when he's buried. The fae believe that if they are buried with their family flower, they will be reunited with their ancestors in the afterlife, or Summer Lands as they refer to it. I like to think Kellan will be back with his family, and Jackson won't be there as he wasn't buried with honeysuckle. Kellan had been as much of a prisoner as me, but at least now he's free.

"Daisy, we're nearly there. Mikey's going to meet us at the entrance, okay?" I lift my head to the sound of Mama's voice and nod. I don't trust myself to speak right now. Sometimes I struggle to find the words to express how I am feeling. Sometimes just the thought of communicating at all brings tears to my eyes and an aching panic to my heart.

We pull off the road and stop in a tiny lay-by. I look out the window, and all I can see is a wall of trees. I look around for a clearing, but I can't see one. I'm about to ask if we're in the right place when Michael walks out of the trees and heads straight to us. As soon as he's beside the car, his mum gets out and pulls him into a hug. I know she's whispering in his ear as Michael nods and whispers something before opening my door. As soon as I have my legs out of the car, Michael kneels in front of me and places his hands on my knees, preventing me from getting out.

"You don't have to do this, darling. Tony can take you home or anywhere you want to go." I look at him and shake my head.

"*I want to do this,*" I reply through the bond; Michael nods. He takes my left hand and kisses where my engagement ring now sits.

"*Then lean on me; I won't leave your side,*" he whispers back. I lean forward and rest my forehead against his. I close my eyes and inhale his woodsy scent to calm my racing heart. Michael gives me a moment before helping me out of the car.

We walk up to where Tony and Mama are standing together. Tony takes my other hand and squeezes it before letting go and offering his arm to Mama. Together the four of us walk through the trees and deeper into the woods silently.

We walk into a clearing, and I stop in my tracks. I was expecting it to be just the four of us and maybe Marcus here, but I see instead a group of people, each holding a piece of honeysuckle in their hands and a single rose.

"When word got out what we were doing today, everybody wanted to come and pay their respects and support you," Michael says quietly next to me. "After you told me about the honeysuckle, I chose to bury him here as he will be next to a large bush of it. We've all taken a cutting, and the red roses are our pack's tradition. All blood moon wolves are buried with a red rose from each wolf present at their burial," Michael explains as he leads me to the group of our friends and family.

My Auntie Mary and Uncle Nigel step forward to greet me. My auntie passes me a single rose with honeysuckle wrapped around the stem before kissing me on the cheek.

"Whatever you need, we are here," My uncle whispers as

he kisses my cheek and pulls me into a hug.

As they step away from me, I see Alex, Sara and Clare standing together, Stuart standing close by with the team plus Richard, Carl and Natalie. Mama joins them as Tony stays with me. I look to where there's a mound of earth; next to it, I can see a body wrapped in a white sheet. Vines of honeysuckle are crisscrossing around the body. I notice someone has made up a willow wreath with honeysuckle and roses interlaced into it. It lays on his chest, and I know once he is buried, it will be placed on the burial site as in witch's and sorcerer's tradition. Several candles around the site will stay lit for the service, as another magical rite. Seeing three different species' traditions present at one burial makes it even more unique, and I know Kellan would have appreciated each one.

Standing next to Kellan's grave is the Alpha, who smiles at me reassuringly.

"The Alpha wants to say a few words, and then Marcus and Alex will place Kellan into the ground. If you want to say anything at any point or if you want to leave, just let me know. No one will think less of you if you can't stay, darling," Michael whispers through the bond.

I lean into him as he places a supportive arm around my shoulders and holds me close. We move to stand on the opposite side of the grave to the Alpha as he looks at Michael, who nods to signal it's okay to start.

My eyes start to burn as the tears threaten to fall. I look at Kellan's remains, and I'm grateful they didn't ignore my wishes and brought him back, so he wasn't burned in the building with the others. He deserved better.

I hear the Alpha clear his throat and force myself to look away from Kellan.

"We are all here today to pay our respects to Kellan, a member of the fae Mournmoon bloodline. He has also been named an honouree member of the Blood Moon pack for the care he showed your future, Luna, Daisy. He sacrificed his life to ensure her safe return to us, and we will *all* be forever grateful."

As the Alpha speaks, I try my hardest not to think of those

last moments with Kellan, how I felt his heartbeat against my cheek slow until it stopped, how I held his hand until his grip loosened on my own. I take a deep breath and realise I could smell a hint of honeysuckle in those last few moments. The copper smell of his blood overpowered it, but it was there. I look at his body now and realise in those last few minutes with Kellan, I finally smelt his scent as he died. It was the sweet citrus scent of honeysuckle and orange.

Instantly hundreds of little memories flood my mind, all of Kellan. But they aren't recent memories of the last six months. There are some from down in Cornwall and before that, in Exeter long before Jackson abducted me.

I pick out one, I was four years old, and I'd fallen whilst playing in a park. A young lad was there, and he told me I was going to be okay and helped me walk to my mum. The young lad was Kellan.

Another memory flashes in front of my eyes, and I stagger back as I gasp; my knees buckle from underneath me as Michael grabs me, his panic radiating through the bond.

"Darling?" Michael says, the worry evident in his voice as his eyes widen. I turn from him and look at my uncle.

"I was in the car with Mum when she crashed." The words spill from my lips before I can stop them as I look at him. Auntie Mary's hand shoots to her mouth as the colour drains from my uncle's face.

"You remember?" he whispers.

"I was dragged from the car," I add as I nod.

"No. You got yourself out; no one knows how but you got out of the car before it filled with smoke," My uncle explains as he steps forward. I shake my head.

"No, I couldn't undo the buckles on my seat; someone helped me and carried me from the car." I point at Kellan. "I remember now; it was him. He pulled me from the car."

"Daisy, you never mentioned anyone helping you before; are you sure?" Nigel asks, but I nod my head.

"His scent is of honeysuckle and oranges. Now I can smell it; I remember it all. Every time he has been there. I fell in a park; he took me to Mum. He spoke to me outside the garden after Dad's memorial. He told me that ...."

" 'The people who love us never truly leave.' He gave you a white teddy and told you that every time you hugged it, it would be like David was hugging you back," Clare says from her spot as she grabs Stuart's hand for support as he steps up next to her, looking concerned. Alex looks between Clare and me, obviously confused. Clare notices and looks at her dad as she explains.

"We were in the garden; Daisy was upset, and there were so many people, so we hid away from everyone." She says before looking back at me. "I knew he looked familiar. I thought it must have been from a photo you sent when in uni or something. But he was there in the garden; I remember it now." I look at her, glad I'm not the only one remembering him.

"The teddy you've had with you all week?" Michael asks me. I nod. I've clung to it more than usual this week, and I couldn't work out why. But now it makes sense; it wasn't my dad who gave it to me; it was Kellan.

"Kellan did more than protect me from Jackson; he sat with me for three days whilst I completed the change. He tried to stop Jackson from beating me a few times and would heal me when he failed. I remember hearing Jackson beating him too. I even witnessed it a few times." I look up at Michael as the tears flow and all the memories return to me.

"But he drugged you?" Tony points out next to me.

"He never meant for me to wander off. He said I would have been safe with him. I think he thought I would have fallen for him if he had separated me from Michael; maybe he was just sick of being on the outskirts? I don't know, but I have many memories of him helping me, saving me." I turn and look at Alex.

"You found me on a clifftop after Jackson took me the first time." Alex nods as a tear rolls down his cheek.

"You'd left a note saying you couldn't live with what he had done to you. I found you sitting in a daze at the top of the cliff, away from the edge. But you had no intention of jumping by the time I found you. It was like you had forgotten why or even how you got there; I put it down to the stress and depression," Alex explains quietly.

"Kellan talked me down," I whisper as I lean into Michael's side. I look at Kellan's body and smile as my own tears flow. "He said that one day I would learn to love my wolf, that one day someone would show me what it's like to be loved for who and what I am, not what they can use me for." I lift my head so that I can see Michael.

"He wasn't wrong, as someone did teach me to love my wolf, and I'm loved for who I am. He just got the person wrong. He thought it would be him, but it was you. It was always going to be you," I whisper as I look into my fiancé's tear-filled eyes.

"You never told me you were that bad," Michael whispers.

"I didn't remember. It's like every memory of him was hidden. But they all returned when I realised I smelt his scent in those last moments," I explain as I look at Kellan's body again.

"That must be why his scent was always hidden," Marcus says from his spot. I look at him as he smiles. "He knew that when you smelt it, you would remember everything. He wanted to protect you from the pain of your past and the memories," He adds. I nod and lean back into Michael.

"Well, now I feel bad for all the shit I gave him." Natalie sighs from her spot; I feel a giggle escape me.

"Tell me about it; I spoke to him like shit the whole time I was there." The tears fill my eyes again.

"Are you okay, darling?" I hear Michael ask as I turn and place my face into his chest, needing to smell him and only him. I nod as he holds me tight and runs his hand over my head until I compose myself.

"Sorry," I whisper as I look at the Alpha.

"Daisy, I think what you've just shared is far better than anything I could have said. Is there anything else anyone else would like to say?" the Alpha asks as he looks around.

"Yes, I would like to say something." I hear Michael announce. I look up at him as he looks down at me.

"It's common knowledge that Kellan and I didn't get along for obvious reasons. But when he came forward and told us where you were and took us to get you, I realised that he did care for you, and everything he did was his way of keeping you safe. He hated it when you were in pain, and he promised that when he knew you would be free, he would give you back your magic, and we'd never hear from him again. I realise now that he knew he would die in that house. He died so I could get you back, and for that, I'm forever grateful for everything he did to make sure that you got to this point, where you are here with me, your family, and your friends. So, I want to promise Kellan today that I will carry on where he left off, and I swear I will protect you with my life. No matter what happens, I'll be here by your side, and we will face everything together. I may be unable to fix every problem we face, but I'll support you as we work through them." Michael leans down and kisses me gently before he steps out of my arms and shakes his head at Marcus, signalling he will help Alex place Kellan into the ground.

Tony stands beside me as Michael and Alex walk over to Kellan's body and lift ropes I hadn't noticed before. They lift his body using the ropes and slowly lower him into the ground. I link my arm through Tony's and lean my head on his shoulder.

"He wasn't a complete wanker then," Tony whispers; I chuckle and shake my head.

"No turns out he wasn't."

"You going to be okay, Dais?" Tony asks. I lift my head from his shoulder and turn to face him, and feel a slight smile on my lips.

"I think I will be, Tony."

Chapter Seventy-One

Michael

It's been four weeks since Kellan's funeral, and nearly everything is back to normal. Only four days after, Daisy told me she wanted to return to uni and has been going from strength to strength since. The funeral was the closure she needed to realise that she was safe and finally free from Jackson forever.

There are still times she struggles with what happened. Usually, in the middle of the night, when the nightmares wake her, she rarely screams anymore though. Instead, she curls up in my arms and cries silently into my chest until she falls back asleep as I play with her hair. It will be a long time until she is truly free from the abuse she suffered from him, but in true Daisy style, she refuses to let it ruin her life anymore.

I got Daisy an extension on her essays, which had been due, by explaining she'd come to me and told me of an ex who trapped her in his home and refused to let her leave. We wanted to be as honest as possible, as Daisy's panic attacks can be triggered easily, and she was still showing physical signs of the abuse for a while. Her bruises took a lot longer to fade as she was so malnourished. But her appetite improved almost instantly after the funeral as she asked me to make her pizza that night and has been eating full meals since.

One of my pack brothers is a police officer and managed to forge an investigation report to help us out. Although I'm not sure why we bothered, as Daisy, as always, was more prepared than I gave her credit for, and she hit every single deadline and sat every exam on time. As usual, she didn't need my help after all.

Today Daisy sat her last exam, and other than two classes on Monday, she has finished her first year. So tonight, we are sitting down and enjoying her favourite meal with a couple of bottles of wine to celebrate. Jon is staying out tonight, so we have the whole house to ourselves for the first time in a while.

"Mikey, I think this may be the best steak you've ever cooked me," Daisy says from her chair to my right. I look over at her and laugh.

"Did that even touch the sides? I gave you the biggest steak, and you still finished before me." I chuckle, shaking my head.

"That just shows how good it was." Daisy answers shrugging. I chuckle as I lean over and kiss her gently on the lips.

"I'm glad you enjoyed it. So, what do you want to do tonight to celebrate?" I ask as I go back to finishing my food.

"I can think of a few ways I'd like to celebrate," Daisy replies seductively. I put down my knife and fork as she stands; I push my chair back to make room for her as she straddles my lap and wraps her arms around my neck.

"Oh, really, and what do they entail," I ask, grinning as I look into her once again bright green eyes. Daisy lowers her head and kisses my neck; I lean my head back, moaning, to give her better access.

"You and me," she whispers as her lips brush my neck; her hands slide over my shoulders and to the front of my shirt, where she starts to undo the buttons.

"Naked." Her lips move further down my neck as she slowly slides my shirt off my shoulders.

"On this table." She adds as her lips brush over her mark on my shoulder, sending shockwaves of pleasure through my whole body.

"Fuck." I hiss as I nearly lose all control.

I'm just reaching around her to push my plate out of the way when a loud knocking comes from the front door. We both look at the door frowning.

"Who the hell's that? No one ever knocks," Daisy asks; I look at her and smile. She's right; everyone has a key and lets themselves in whenever they feel like it.

"You move the plates; I'll check it out," I answer as whoever knocks again. I stand up and quickly reposition my raging hard-on causing Daisy to chuckle. I lean over and place a kiss on her lips.

"Whoever it is won't be staying," I whisper as I slap her ass, causing her to squeal as I head to the door; whoever is on the other side knocks again.

"Alright, I'm coming," I call as I quickly button my shirt up and open the door, only to stop in my tracks.

"Hey, sorry, am I interrupting something?"

"Steph, what are you doing here?" I answer a little louder, knowing Daisy will hear.

"I'm hiding in the dining room." she quickly says through the bond.

"I need to talk to you about something, and I would rather do it in person and away from work. Can I come in?" Steph answers, looking up at me nervously.

"Uh yeah, sure, come on in," I answer, still shocked that she's here. I open the door wider and let her come in. My heart racing as I step out of her way, subtly blocking her view of a picture of Daisy and me, which we have in the entrance hall. "Come through to the lounge?" I say as I show her in. Instantly spotting another picture of us on the fireplace. Shit. I signal for Steph to take a seat on one of the sofas as I position myself in front of the fireplace and the photograph.

"You have a lovely place Michael, very cosy," Steph says, smiling at me.

"Thanks, I like it," I answer, keeping the worry from my voice. "What's going on, Steph?" I ask.

"I'll be honest with you, Michael; I have heard a few students commenting in class, and rumours are starting to spread. At first, I thought it was just typical student gossip. You know what they can be like. But the more I thought about it, the more I realised they might not be wrong. So I wanted to come and ask you myself, and I want a straight, honest answer."

"Okay," I answer as my mouth becomes dry, and I can feel Daisy starting to panic through the bond.

"Is there something going on between you and Daisy Andrews?" I feel my stomach drop. Fuck.

I open my mouth to tell her no, but Steph puts up her hand to stop me.

"Before you answer, I saw you dropping her off at her house this morning; I've noticed she visits your office more than any other student, and you both seem to be ill or have family emergencies at the same time. I know something's going on. I know she has a difficult past and doesn't always feel safe after the horrendous incident last month, but I think you are more than just someone she speaks to. I think she's the reason you applied for the psychology department job." Steph stops and looks at me. "I'm right, aren't I?"

I stare at Steph for a moment and take a deep breath before answering.

"Yes, Daisy and I are in a relationship."

"Is it serious?" I nod, unable to reply aloud. "How long has it been going on?" Steph asks.

"Six months", I answer. Steph looks at me wide-eyed.

"That long?" I nod again, not sure what to say. "Christ, Michael." I walk to the other sofa and sit down before leaning forward and putting my head in my hands.

"You have no idea how hard I've been trying to leave my post at work, Steph. I've tried to transfer to a different department, and I've tried to leave, but Martin wouldn't accept my resignation, Daisy has offered to transfer or quit, but I won't let her. I've not told the university the truth because they'll force her to leave, and I won't do that to her. You know how hard she has worked on hitting every deadline over the last few weeks."

"You are serious about this relationship, then? It's not just a fling?" Steph asks. Fuck it, in for a penny in for a pound, as Mum always says.

"She is my whole world," I reply as I look Steph in the eye and can't stop the smile on my face.

"How the hell have you kept this quiet? How many people know?" she asks, the shock evident on her face and in her tone.

"At the uni? Only Tony and Beth. You know how close the three of them are." I answer as I run my fingers through my hair.

"I know this sounds strange, but I'd like to talk to you and Daisy about this. Could you call her, please?" I can't help the chuckle that escapes my lips as I stand up and walk to the lounge door.

"Come on in," I say as I open it knowing Daisy's in the hallway. She walks in and looks at Steph sheepishly.

"Hey," Daisy says as I stand beside her and place a hand against her lower back in the hope of calming her racing heart.

"Of course, you're here," Steph says, rolling her eyes and shaking her head. "How often do you stay?" she asks. Daisy and I share a quick look before she answers.

"I live here," Daisy answers quietly as she starts rubbing her hands together, which is the first sign she is starting to feel anxious.

"Daisy moved in a couple of months after we started dating," I lie, as it was actually a couple of weeks. With my hand on Daisy's back, I guide her to the sofa, and we sit down.

"Was all that stuff with your ex true?" Steph asks. Daisy looks at the floor and nods as I feel my temper rise.

"I get that we've been sneaking around, it's not like work gave us much choice, but we certainly didn't make all that stuff up to skive off. Daisy went through hell, Steph, and questioning if it happened is an insult to her ordeal," I snap. Daisy reaches over and takes my hand. I look at her as she smiles softly.

"It's fine, Mikey; I understand why she asked."

"I'm sorry, I didn't mean it to sound like I was doubting her; I'm just trying to get my head around everything," Steph says. I nod and squeeze Daisy's hand.

"Yes, it all happened; it's been tough on both of us. Mikey can sometimes be a little overprotective of me," Daisy says, smiling at Steph.

"I can see that. So I take it your families know about the two of you?" Steph asks. Daisy and I both nod. "How did that go down? If you don't mind me asking," she adds quickly. Daisy looks up at me and smiles.

"My family love him, and we have their full blessing," she answers.

"My family loves her more than they love me and have said they'll choose her over me if we ever separate," I reply, smiling down at Daisy.

"That's because I'm great," Daisy says, winking at me; I laugh as I put an arm around her back and pull her against me so I can kiss the top of her head.

"Yes, you are, darling," I reply, smiling.

"Okay, you two are too cute." We both turn and look at Steph. "I can see you are both very happy."

"You have no idea. I'd leave everything for this woman. She just won't let me," I say as I tighten my hold on Daisy again. Steph nods to show she understands as she stands up from her chair, and we quickly follow suit.

"Are you going to report us, Steph?" Daisy asks; I look over at her nervously and relax as she shakes her head.

"No, I'm not. I think you've been through enough and don't need the added drama." Daisy steps away from me and hugs Steph, who chuckles as she hugs her back.

"Thank you, Steph," Daisy whispers before stepping back beside me.

"I'll leave you both to whatever you were up to when I interrupted." She smiles.

"Stay here, darling." I quickly say through the bond as I step away from her.

"I'll see you out, Steph," I say as I hold my arm towards the door. Steph and Daisy say a quick goodbye before Steph follows me into the hallway.

"I'm happy for you both, but remember, if I can work it out, so can others, be careful, and I hope you find a way for everything to work out for you both," Steph says as I open the front door for her.

"Thank you for being so understanding; I know this puts you in an awkward position," I reply, feeling guilty.

"I think the uni is outdated regarding things like this. You are both grown adults, who care very much about each other, why shouldn't you be together? I will help any way I can." Steph turns to leave but stops and looks back to face me. "I hope you can help her recover from everything she's been through. I've seen how on edge she is. So if I can do anything to help, please don't hesitate to ask."

"Thank you, Steph, that means a lot," I reply as Steph

smiles at me one last time before walking to her car.

Chapter Seventy-Two

Daisy

"Well, I wasn't expecting that tonight." I sigh as I lean against the lounge doorframe. Michael turns to me and chuckles whilst running his fingers through his hair.

"You're not the only one," he replies as he steps forward and places a hand on my cheek. "Are you okay?" he asks gently. I look up at him and smile.

"Surprisingly, yes. I feel better knowing that someone else knows about us." I place my hand on Michael's chest to feel his heart beating. "How about you?" I ask.

"Same. What do we do now?" Michael asks. I look at him through my lashes as I slide my hand across his chest and undo his buttons again.

"First, I think we should continue from where we left off in the dining room." I don't get any further as Michael quickly lifts me so I can wrap my legs around his waist. He strides into the dining room and places me on the table before kissing me with such passion I can't breathe.

"Hey, where are you?" Marcus calls out as the front door opens.

"I'm changing the locks," Michael growls under his breath as he leans his head on my shoulder. I burst out laughing, nodding in agreement.

"Do I even want to ask what you are doing on that table?" I hear Jon ask.

"And kicking his ass out," Michael adds before pulling me off the table and placing me back onto my feet next to him as we turn to face Marcus and Jon.

"I thought you were out for the night?" I ask, looking at Jon.

"I am, but we need to talk to you about something," Jon says as he looks at me. I feel my insides freeze.

"Why, what's happened?" I ask; I feel Michael's arm around my shoulders, pulling me closer to him.

"Come into the lounge, and we'll explain everything," Marcus says as he nods to the room behind him. I look up at Michael and see him frowning at the guys. He has no idea what this is about, either.

Michael guides me into the lounge as we sit back on the sofa. Jon takes his usual seat while Marcus sits on the coffee table, just like he did before Kellan's funeral.

"What the hell is going on?" Michael demands as his arm tightens around me protectively. Marcus takes a deep breath and looks at me.

"When Kellan came to the Alphas office to tell us where you were, he left me with some instructions if he didn't return."

"What?" Michael and I ask together.

"Why am I only now hearing about this?" Michael demands, looking at his second.

"Because I wasn't going to do anything about them," Marcus says, looking at Michael before turning back to me. "But after you remembered everything at his burial, I decided to do as he asked. He had asked me to contact someone if he didn't make it out of the house, he explains.

"Who was it?" Michael asks. Marcus doesn't take his eyes off me.

"It was a solicitor," he answers.

"Why did he want you to contact a solicitor?" I ask as I can feel my anxiety starting to build.

"This solicitor is also fae and has dealt with Kellan for a long time. He knew about you and how Kellan has kept tabs on you for nearly twenty years. I contacted the guy, and he wanted to speak to you or at least your solicitor." Marcus explains as I try to keep up, my mind still focusing on Kellan being sensible enough to have a solicitor. It goes to show I didn't know the guy at all.

"That's where I come in," Jon says from his sofa. I look at him as he offers me a soft smile.

"Daisy, I know how much you've been struggling, and with your exams and end-of-year deadlines, I decided to handle everything for you," Jon explains.

"I'm her legal representative," Michael growls beside me. Jon looks at his brother, shaking his head.

"He knows you're her mate and told Marcus it had to be someone else; he was even reluctant for it to be me as he knows I'm your brother. He only agreed after we explained what had happened last month and how Daisy was dealing with it," Jon says as he looks at his brother.

"What did he say?" I ask as I place my hand on Michael's knee, hoping it will calm him down as I can see his whole body is tense; he hates things being hidden from him, especially when it comes to me.

"Kellan had named you the sole beneficiary of his estate," Jon explains.

"What?" I exclaim. I feel Michael place a hand over mine.

"It means you get everything he owned," he explains next to me. I look up at him and nod.

"I know that, but why me? Plus, surely he didn't have anything left to leave?" I say, looking back at Jon, who's smiling at me.

"Actually, you've been left four houses which have been paid off, so no mortgages, everything in them and a substantial sum of money. Enough that you will be set for life, and so will your children and possibly your children's children." Jon opens the briefcase I only now realise is next to him and pulls out an envelope.

"Everything is explained here. I haven't read it; it wasn't my place." I watch as Jon passes a white envelope to Marcus, who holds it out to me. I take it from him nervously.

It feels like a brick in my hand; I look down at the envelope and see my name in Kellan's flawless handwriting on the front.

"When did you get this?" Michael asks next to me as I lean further into him, needing any contact I can get as I attempt to process everything.

"It was all handed over to us an hour ago," Jon answers. I can hear them talking, but I'm not listening. I'm too busy looking at the envelope in my hand. Suddenly everything feels too much, and I need to get out into the open; I need air and space.

"I need a minute," I whisper as I stand up from the sofa, Michael instantly jumps to his feet too, but I shake my head at him. "I mean alone," I whisper. Michael takes my left hand and kisses my engagement ring.

"Okay, darling. Just call if you need me," he whispers. I nod, head to the back of the room, and straight out the patio doors.

I walk through the garden into the woods behind our house; I've been coming out here more frequently since I escaped the manor; it's always calming and peaceful. I stop in my favourite spot, where Michael and I have often sat in silence, listening to the wildlife around us. I sit down on the ground and lean against a tree. I close my eyes and take a deep breath as I attempt to calm my racing heart.

Slowly I open my eyes and look down at the envelope; I'm unsure if I can bring myself to read it. Scared of what it will say inside. *"Kellan would have written it for a reason,"* My wolf whispers. I nod as I know she's right. I turn the envelope around and carefully open it.

Inside are two pieces of letter paper, his scent fills the air around me, and I can't help but wonder if he were hoping I'd remember everything he did for me if I hadn't already. I unfold the paper and read the first line as my hands start to shake and tears fill my eyes.

Dearest Daisy,

If you are reading this, then I'm probably dead. My lawyer will have made contact if I haven't been in touch with him for six months or if I somehow managed to get a message to him. If I am dead, I want you to know that everything I have ever owned now belongs to you.

I don't know if I ever got the chance to tell you who I am or why you are so important to me, so I will try and explain all in this letter.

I've wanted to tell you all this for so long, and there is so much to tell; I guess it's better to start at the beginning. As you've probably guessed, I'm not human; I am fae and over two hundred fifty years old.

My mother and father were both pureblood faes. We fled our realm when I was a child. My mother was next in line to the throne, and one of her brothers chased her from the realm to ensure she would never claim her rightful place. My mother knew one of her other brothers had been banished to the human realm many years before and came in search of him to see if he could help us build a life here.

Not long after we arrived, we all fell sick as many faes do in your polluted realm; my father and sister succumbed to the disease, but my mother's brother found us in time to cure my mother, myself, and my older brother. My mother never recovered from losing her daughter, and 'true other', or mate as shifters refer to them. She withdrew into herself. My uncle became a replacement father for my sibling and me; we did everything with him. He taught me the ways of your realm and educated us so we would not stand out. We continued to live close to each other for over one hundred and fifty years. Now and again, I would travel and experience the different cultures of this realm, but my brother always stayed close to our uncle.

But then, one day, he stopped coming around as much; he would miss dinners and stay away from us for months on end. We discovered that he had met someone and fallen in love; she was a witch with no fae blood. He kept her away from us as he believed his sister would be ashamed that he was with a human. However, my mother supported him completely; it was my brother who caused an issue.

If you do not know by now, my older brother is Jackson.

Jackson loved our father, and his loss caused him great pain; when our uncle stepped up, Jackson formed an attachment to him. But when our uncle chose to spend time with a human witch over his own flesh and blood, Jackson decided he would return to the fae realm and find an uncle who would show him our true ways and help him take his rightful place in the fae courts. He was met with hatred and banished from the courts because the human realm had influenced him. Something changed in him that day, which caused the hateful and evil Jackson you came to know.

I returned home one evening to find our mother lying in a pool of her own blood. It turns out Jackson had told the courts where she was; her brother, the one who we had fled from, organised her assassination. I held her and went to heal her, but she begged me not to; she asked me to let her die so she could be with my father and sister again. She also made me promise on a blood oath that I would always protect my brother, forgive him, and bring him back from the darkness that was consuming him. I promised her as she lay in my arms and passed on to the Summer Lands, where I knew my father and sweet little sister would be waiting to greet her.

That night I contacted my uncle, who helped me bury her. As we returned from her small burial, Jackson arrived drunk and showed no signs of grief when I informed him of mother's passing. I will never know how I didn't break my oath that night, as the grief was unbearable, and the need to avenge my mother was overpowering. I wish now, more than anything, that I had killed him there and then; you would have never fallen into his hands and had your life changed the way you did.

I left that night and swore I would keep tabs on my brother from a distance, and I did for about a decade. Even after he was bitten and turned, I cleaned up his messes without him ever knowing, and I kept myself to myself until one day, my uncle contacted me and asked me to meet with him.

It turned out my uncle's now wife bore him a son, and Jackson had found out; my uncle asked me to help him find a safe place for his wife and child to hide. Together we came up with a plan. It was a plan that killed my uncle internally as he wiped their memory of him and anything regarding the fae world. He then walked away, as the pain was too hard to bare. He asked me to watch over them and keep them safe. So, I did. I watched as my cousin grew up and developed his magic. Having forgotten he was half-fae, his mother believed him to be a powerful sorcerer; the magical council never questioned it. My aunt and cousin were happy and remained off Jackson's radar, so once my cousin was in his teens, I left for a while, thinking he was safe.

When I returned to check on him several years later, I discovered his mother had died, and he had moved to Exeter. On my first day in the area, I felt strong fae magic for the first time in many years. I located the source and was surprised to find a tiny four-year-old with my mother's bright green eyes; if I hadn't known better, I would have believed I was looking at my little sister again.

I saw you in that park and knew instantly who and what you were. Because you, Daisy Andrews, are no ordinary human. It's not just the witch blood and now shifter genes that flow through you. You are part fae. I knew you were part of my fae family the moment I saw you. I watched you for five minutes as you made flowers bloom with your magic until a lady came running over and gently pointed out you weren't to use your powers in public. I watched as you nodded and ran into the bushes to hide and continue using your magic. But whilst you were there, you tripped and scrapped your knee; you were so upset that I couldn't leave you, so I took your hand and walked you over to the lady watching you. I realised then that you were my cousin's daughter, the cousin I'd been asked to watch over.

I promised myself that day I would watch over you as I had my cousin. I am so glad I did, as if there is danger within a hundred-mile radius; you, Daisy, will find it.

Just days after our initial meeting, I witnessed you and your mother in the car crash that took her life; I ran to the car and knew your mother could not be saved, but you were crying in the back seat, calling out to her. I got you out before the car filled with smoke and stayed until the emergency services arrived, then disappeared, taking your memory of myself and the crash with me.

From that day, wherever you went, I went. I spoke to you several times but always ensured you wouldn't remember. I gave you a teddy when David died less than a year later. You were sitting in the garden with a girl you introduced as your friend. I gave you the bear and told you that every time you hugged it, it would be like David was hugging you back. I was amazed when I saw it on your bed in your dorm room. I can't believe you have kept it all this time.

But my protectiveness of you caught my brother's attention, and he looked into you himself; that was when he realised how powerful you are, and he wanted to make you his. He mistook the feeling of the family connection for the wolf mate bond. This is why he was sure you were his second chance mate. I'm sorry my protectiveness was what drew him to you.

When he abducted you, I tried to free you many times, but I was weak and scared of him, but slowly as you became stronger, so did I and that night you escaped, it was I who left the door open, knowing it was the best time for you to run.

I went back to watching from a distance, but I was more powerful as I tapped into your powers and used the mixture of our magic to keep us hidden. I was there when you wanted to kill yourself, and I was there when you realised you could be stronger. I watched you grow and bloom into the strong, independent, beautiful woman you are.

When you moved to North Wales, I saw my chance to get close to you and finally play a role in your life and maybe introduce you to your fae heritage. But then you met Michael, and I'd seen what becoming a wolf has done to my brother and was sure Michael would be a danger to you, especially as he's a powerful alpha.

I had also heard rumours that my brother's pack was looking for us. I had to keep us moving to hide us, so I scared you away and staged my house to look like I'm obsessed with you so that my brother would think that's why I'm protecting you. The last thing I want is for him to realise that you are not only part fae but part of our bloodline too. I hated setting up that room, but I had to do it after my failed attempt to run with you on your birthday. That was why I drugged you; I thought I could hide you away and keep you safe from not only Jackson but Michael too.

The night I attacked you in The Crow, I did it because I thought one of my brother's men was there. I wanted them to report that I'm possessive and will fight for you. I felt sick when I left, knowing I had hurt and almost drained you while blocking the others from coming close. I'm so sorry.

I now realise I made a terrible mistake and, as usual, my plan to protect you went wrong because you did the opposite of what I expected. I've been kept prisoner by Jackson for weeks, if not months, and I'm risking everything to get this letter to my solicitor as I feel there will be no way to escape this time. Not now he has you.

I helped him to take you as I believed I was strong enough to help us escape him again, and this time I would keep you close to me. But you are as determined to get back to Michael as he is to find you. I admit I was wrong about him, and he loves you, and I see you love him too. Maybe that is enough for you both to have the future you deserve.

I'm sending this letter as you are in the cell downstairs. I'm building a plan to get us out; if that goes wrong, I will find a way to get word to Michael of where you are, and I pray he finds you before Jackson breaks you. I can't see a way for us both to survive this, but I'm happy to die so you can live.

I'm sorry I've failed to keep you safe. But know that everything I did, was of pure intentions. Somewhere out there is your grandfather, who loved your grandmother and father so much that he sacrificed his happiness to protect them. If you ever get the chance to find him, the last name I knew him to be using was Regan Holdsworth.

As for everything that has been left for you, please use it.

Tell Michael to leave his job and be the couple you want to be, get married, have kids and live your life the way your family would have wanted you to.

You are so loved, Daisy, and I am honoured to be your kin.

All my love, Kellan xxx

Chapter Seventy-Three

Michael

"Well, you two morons couldn't have timed that any better if you fucking tried!" I growl at my brothers as I watch Daisy walk into the woods, holding the letter to her chest. I sit back down and run my fingers through my hair.

"We didn't know the extent of everything until the meeting this evening. Neither of us expected her to inherit as much as she did. If we had, we would've told her sooner," Jon says from his seat.

"You still should have told *me* what was going on so I could have prepared her. It's been one fucking shock after another tonight, and it could knock her back." I growl as my jaw clenches.

"Why? What else has happened?" Marcus asks from his spot on the coffee table. I look at him and unclench my jaw as I take a deep breath.

"One of my colleagues turned up at the front door." I sigh as I lean back into the sofa; Marcus and Jon curse together.

"Did they see Daisy?" Jon asks.

"Not initially, but they came to call me out on our relationship, so it seemed pointless hiding her any longer," I answer.

"So, what's going to happen now? They going to report you?" Marcus asks; I shake my head.

"No, but Daisy and I will have to think carefully about what happens next; she could lose everything she's worked so hard to achieve the last couple of weeks," I point out.

"Does she need to finish her studies? I mean, she's extremely wealthy now. Neither of you needs to work," Jon points out. I arch an eyebrow as I look over at him.

"Neither of us needed to work anyway. I, unlike some, have never touched my inheritance from Dad or our grandparents."

"So what's the big deal if she doesn't finish her studies?"

Jon asks, frowning.

"It would be something else that someone took away from her." Marcus sighs; I turn to him and nod.

"If Daisy decides to drop out, then fine, although I would prefer for her to complete her studies, she's too clever not to make something of herself. She would make a fantastic lawyer and could run her own firm one day. Tony and her had so many plans before we mated, I'd like to think they'd still go through with them. I don't want everything to change for her because of me or because she now has money," I explain.

"Ah, I see," Jon sighs. I look through the patio doors out towards the woods. I can feel Daisy through the bond and can sense her sadness. I want to rush to her side but know that she'll call me if she needs me. I've had to learn the last four weeks to give her space at times, to let her work through her emotions independently.

"What's left for Daisy to do regarding this inheritance from Kellan?" I ask; Jon reaches into his briefcase and pulls out a thick A4 envelope,

"All the documents are in there; Kellan had already set up a bank account for her and organised everything. She didn't have to sign any papers, as the less paperwork, the better. Her new bank card and the keys to the properties are in there. Everything is ready to go."

"When did he organise all of this?" I ask as I reach for the envelope Jon hands over.

"He opened the account when she was four," Marcus answers. I look at my brothers, amazed.

"Daisy's first memory of him was when she was four; why would he go through all this trouble for a child he didn't even know?"

"Who knows, but all the answers are apparently in that letter he has written her," Marcus says from his spot.

"That will depend on when he last updated the letter," I point out, but Jon reaches into his briefcase again.

"He sent a new letter five weeks ago. So it will be up to date," Jon explains as he pulls out a bundle of what looks like letters all tied together. "These are all the ones he has sent over the years. He would update them yearly or if something major happened."

"Five weeks ago, they were both being held by Jackson. How did he get a letter out?" I answer.

"I asked the same thing; the lawyer just said they had a way," Jon replies, shrugging. I turn and look at Marcus.

"When he was at the Alphas, did he ever say why he stalked her the way he did?" I ask; Marcus nods.

"I asked him about the room in his place, and he said it was all staged. He did it, so if his brother ever found them, he would think Kellan was obsessed with her."

"Well, he was. You didn't see him the night he attacked her in the bar. He was screaming that she belonged to him and no one else. He was like a madman," Jon says, the anger shining in his brown eyes.

"Mikey?" I hear Daisy through the bond.

"Are you okay, darling?" I ask softly.

"Yes and no," even through the bond, I can tell she's crying.

"Want me to come and sit with you, baby?"

"Please."

"On my way." I stand up and look at my brothers.

"Daisy's upset; I'm going to her. Mind not being here when we get back? I want to give her my full attention." Both of them nod as I walk toward the patio doors.

As soon as I close the doors behind me, I take off running, knowing where Daisy will be; I find her in a couple of minutes, leaning against a tree.

"Hey," I say gently as I approach her. As I thought, she's crying. I drop down next to her and pull her into my arms. Daisy starts sobbing the second her face hits my chest. She moves her hand to rest over my heart as she always does when anxious.

"Darling, I'm so sorry they blindsided you like that. If I had known, I would have told you." I whisper into her hair a little while later when she's all cried out.

"That's not what upset me," she whispers into my chest. Daisy pulls away from me and picks up the letter from beside her. She holds it out towards me.

"You don't have to share this, darling. It's between you and Kellan," I whisper as I tip my head to look at her properly, but Daisy shakes her head.

"I want you to," she whispers. I kiss her head before taking the letter from her hand. She moves so she's sitting across my lap, leaning against my chest as I lean back against the tree and start reading.

By the time I reach the end of the letter, I'm lost for words. Reading everything in black and white like this, it all makes sense why he's always looked after her the way he did, the change in character, the house and all the pictures, plus his attitude towards me.

"Shit, darling. That's a lot to take in. How do you feel?" I ask as I wrap my arms around her.

"I don't even know how to process some of that. Like the fact that my dad was half-fae. Or that Kellan has left me all this money and property. What the hell do I do with it all?" I can feel the panic within her as I start stroking her hair to calm her down.

"Darling, you don't have to do anything right now. We can deal with it all at a later date. Take your time to process everything and face it one day at a time. Just know I'm here for you, whatever you decide to do." I reassure her as I press my lips to her head.

"At least if they fire you, we don't have to worry about money." Daisy chuckles into my chest. I laugh with her.

"I quite like the idea of being a kept man," I joke.

"You can be my trophy husband," Daisy giggles in my arms, which quickly turns into a squeal as I start tickling her until we both end up lying on the ground laughing hysterically. I roll onto my side and prop my head upon my hand as I place my other hand on her stomach.

"No matter what happens, we face it together," I whisper, smiling at my gorgeous mate. Daisy holds on to her necklace and looks at the engraving on the back.

"Always," she whispers as she rolls over and kisses me, and I lose myself in her touch.

Chapter Seventy-Four

Michael

I wake up to the sound of my phone ringing. I look at the clock. It's six a.m. Monday morning; who the hell is calling me now?

"Tell them to go away," Daisy moans as she moves off my chest and rolls to face away from me. I grab my phone and see the name on the screen. I quickly kiss Daisy's head before climbing out of bed as I connect the call.

"Hang on, two secs," I whisper as I rush out of the bedroom, grabbing my sweatpants.

"The fact you're phoning me at this time of the morning can't be good," I sigh as I pull on my sweats and head down the stairs.

"Sorry, Michael. I wanted to give you a heads up that I've been called into the principal's office this morning to discuss your relationship with Daisy." Steph says down the phone; I stop in my tracks.

"They found out?" I ask.

"I swear it wasn't from me. The pupils gossiping in front of me apparently did the same thing in front of Martin." I find myself laughing out loud.

"It was going to happen eventually," I reply.

"What do you want me to tell them?" Steph asks.

"Tell them the truth. Don't lie for us. It's not worth your job if they find out. I'm sorry you've been dragged into this," I answer honestly.

"I'm sorry you two are going through this. You love each other, and Daisy doesn't need assistance with her work or the added stress after everything she's been through." Steph sighs down the phone.

"No, she doesn't. She's smarter than any student I've ever taught. I hope they see that. I don't care what happens to me. I have another job waiting in my brother's firm. But Daisy's worked too hard to lose everything now." I take a deep breath and lean back against the kitchen counter. "Thanks for the heads up Steph. Again, sorry you've been involved in it all." I sigh as I pour the coffee blend into the machine.

"I hope everything works out for you both, Michael, and I hope this doesn't cause issues in your relationship."

"No matter what, Daisy and I will be fine. We have each other, and that's all that matters." I answer with a smile, knowing it's true. Nothing can come between us.

"Good luck, Michael." I hear Steph say.

"Thanks, Steph," I answer before hanging up and taking a deep breath.

I always knew this could happen; I'm only worried about Daisy, we discussed a few plans over the weekend, but we have been so busy we haven't made any concrete ones. I quickly make two mugs of coffee before returning upstairs to tell her the news.

I find Daisy sitting in bed, looking pale with her phone in her hand.

"I've had an email from Martin. I need to go in and speak to him and the principal at nine a.m." I hand her a mug and sit on the edge of the bed.

"That was Steph on the phone. She's been called in as they want to discuss our relationship after some students were heard gossiping about us," I explain. Daisy laughs out loud.

"Oh, I know who that would have been. Rosie and Samantha are the biggest gossips in the class," she says as she rolls her eyes. "Plus, they *really* fancy you and would be jealous as hell," she replies, smirking.

I laugh before leaning in and kissing her quickly.

"Well, if they think they can take me from you, they will be very disappointed." I sit back and take her hand. "Whatever happens, darling, we face it together as we agreed."

Daisy looks up at me. "Do you ever regret it?"

"Regret what, darling?" I ask, frowning.

"Me coming here? Me being in your class? Us?" I take the mug from Daisy's hand and place it on the bedside cabinet before climbing onto the bed next to her. I sit up against the headboard and pull her into my arms. I take her chin between my thumb and forefinger and turn her head to look her straight in those beautiful green eyes as I answer.

"I don't know how many times I have to say this, but finding you in my class was the best thing to ever happen to me. Even when we have kids, I'll remember that day as the best day of my life because nothing would have been possible without it. You make me happy in so many ways. Nothing, and I mean nothing, could ever make me regret us. I'd face all the shit thrown at us and more if it meant spending another minute with you by my side." I use my thumb to wipe a stray tear from Daisy's cheek before gently pressing my lips to hers.

"If I go in there today and they fire me, I don't care, but I will fight for you to complete your studies. I won't be why you must walk away from another thing you want."

"Mikey, I don't care about the studies. I don't care if they kick me out. It's just a degree; it's a piece of paper I'm not sure I even want anymore. But I don't want you to lose your job over me." I look deep into Daisy's eyes and wonder how she's always so selfless. Even after everything she's been through, she has put others before herself.

"I don't give a shit about the job, darling. I don't need it; I never really needed it. Plus, I'm so busy with the team that I don't have time to work anyway," I answer.

"You were only busy because of Jackson and me. What about now that's over?" Daisy asks.

"If I get bored and need something to fill in the gaps between spending time with you and being a protector, I'll go to work with Jonny. He's been bugging me long enough to join his firm, or I could be a bouncer for Will's company; there are plenty of things I could do. Plus, it'd get me out of the classroom and away from the student drama." I add with a grin.

"Hey, I'm one of those students!" Daisy laughs as she slaps my chest. I smile as I hold her tightly against me so she can't hit me again.

"And don't I know it." I chuckle. I kiss the top of her head and smile into her hair. "No matter what happens, it will all be worth it to continue calling you mine. At least if they fire me, I

can put a second ring on your finger quicker than we planned."
I chuckle as I hear my phone signal an email. I sigh as I pick it
up, already guessing what it will be.

>   To: Michael Adams
>   From: Angharad Jones
>   Subject: Important meeting.
>
>   Mr M. G. Adams
>   Please attend a meeting at ten a.m. this morning
>   (Monday 24th July) to discuss a matter brought to our
>   attention over the past weekend.
>   We have received word that you are abusing your
>   position as a lecturer in the Law Department to form
>   relationships with the students. The student who has been
>   named has been contacted and also asked to attend a
>   separate meeting. If we feel that the student has been
>   coerced to protect yourself, the police will be contacted.
>   You are welcome; if not advised to bring council to the
>   meeting, a union rep will be offered if requested.
>   I hope this is all a misunderstanding that can be put to
>   rest by the end of the university's investigations. If you have
>   been abusing your post, your employment contract will be
>   terminated.
>   Until your meeting, please do not attend any classes or
>   approach the student in question or any staff member. Please
>   remain off the premises until your designated appointment.
>
>   I appreciate your cooperation in this matter.
>
>   Principal Angharad Jones

I put my phone down and look at Daisy with a smile.
"Apparently, I'm not allowed to see or speak to you before
the meeting." Daisy looks up at me with a glint in her eye as
she lifts herself onto her knees before straddling my lap. She
gently runs her fingertips over my eyes to encourage me to

close them.

"You better keep your eyes closed then," she whispers. I do as I'm told, smiling as I feel her lips lightly brush over each eyelid before feeling her lips against mine. "I can think of other uses for your mouth too," she adds before I grab her and throw her onto her back, so I can show her just how many ways I can use my mouth on her without saying a word.

Chapter Seventy-Five

Daisy

"Thanks for staying with me, Tony." I lean against my best friend as we stand outside the principal's office. My email said I could bring someone to support me. I thought about asking one of the guys, but I know Tony will have my back. So now I'm anxiously waiting to see what the university will say about Michael and me.

"Bitch please, did you really think I would miss all this drama? Hell no!" he answers, grinning as I roll my eyes. "But on a serious note, how honest will you be?" Tony asks as he takes my hand and gives it a quick squeeze.

"As honest as I can be without giving away what we are. Mikey and I will tell the truth; we're not ashamed of our relationship and are consenting adults." I'm cut off when the door opens, and I see Steph standing in the doorway. She takes one look at me and gives me a sympathetic smile. As soon as she notices Tony next to me, her smile changes, and she has to stop herself from chuckling.

"Of course, you're with her." Steph chuckles as she opens the door for us.

"At least you know why we aren't dating now." Tony chuckles as he walks into the room. I close my eyes and take a deep breath before opening them again and walking into the room with my head held high.

"No matter what happens, I love you." I quickly send down the bond to Michael.

"I love you too, darling." He instantly replies, making me feel a little braver.

The first thing I see as I walk into the room is Martin and the principal sitting at a table facing two chairs. Tony's already sitting in one with his ankles crossed in front of him like he's about to relax in front of the TV, not watch me getting my ass grilled.

"Glad to see you're nice and chilled." I sigh as I take a seat next to him. He winks at me whilst grinning like Jonathan in a whiskey bar.

"It's not me in the shit for a change," he replies.

I shake my head, smiling at him. This is why I wanted him here rather than Beth. He's excellent at keeping me calm.

"I don't think you two realise how serious this meeting is." I hear the principal say from the front of the room. I turn to face her and notice the stern look on her face.

"Oh, we do; we just think it's ridiculous." Tony sighs next to me; I slam a hand over my mouth to stop myself from laughing.

"Tony Simons, just for once, can you try to take something seriously." Martin sighs from his seat next to the principal.

"I guess I could try." Tony sighs as he slumps into his seat further. Gods, I'm so grateful for this giant dickhead right now.

"Daisy?" I turn and look at Martin as he addresses me. "Do you understand why you've been asked to come here today?" he asks.

"I do," I reply, keeping a straight face.

"And you understand that whatever you say in this room is completely confidential unless needed in a further investigation by the police," he continues.

"I understand," I answer.

"Are you sure you don't want to have an adult present to represent you? I know your family are quite far away, but Steph is here if you need her. I can ask a counselling team member to attend if you wish," the principal offers. I again shake my head as I start rubbing my hands together on my lap.

"I don't need a counsellor," I answer. As my heart starts racing, I hear Tony snort next to me. "Yeah, you do, but not over this."

I flip him off without looking at him. I make a mental note to beat his demon ass later.

"Tony Simons, I will remove you if you carry on," the principal warns. Tony makes a show of zipping his lips, locking them and throwing away the key. I can hear Steph trying not to laugh to the left of me. I have to stop myself from looking at her knowing I'll start laughing too.

"Thank you," the principal sighs. "Daisy, we've asked you to come here today to discuss some information we've received. It implies that a member of our faculty team has been using his position to coerce you into having a sexual relationship with him, and we wanted to give you the chance to tell us what's happening from your point of view. You're not in any trouble; you are the victim here, which I understand is not the first time. I believe the lecturer in question has used your traumatic past to manipulate and groom you. The university will do all it can to protect you, offer you any support you need, and ensure that Michael Adams can never get near you or any vulnerable individual again," the principal states.

I sit staring at her as the room becomes silent, I try to open my mouth to say something, but I've been rendered speechless.

"What the fuck?!" Tony exclaims next to me. I point at him and look at the principal.

"What he said," I answer. The principal looks at me, confused.

"Daisy, we'd like to hear your side of the story," Martin says. I turn and look at him shaking my head in disbelief.

"You think I'm a victim? You think Michael has groomed me?" I ask, confused; if they knew Michael, they'd know he doesn't have a manipulative bone in his body.

"Yes, Daisy, that's what we believe. Mr. Adams may have told you many things, but they'll all be lies. He's manipulated you, Daisy, and used your fragile mind to control you. This isn't a healthy relationship that you find yourself in," the principal explains. I look at Martin, who's frowning at the Principal; when I look at Steph, she looks just as confused as the rest of us, plus a little angry.

"With all due respect Principal Jones that contradicts everything I've told you regarding what I've witnessed between the two of them," Steph says as she sits up tall. I look over at Tony, feeling sick to my stomach. He looks as shocked as me as he glances over. As soon as I see he's worried, I start to feel the panic building. This is not going how I expected.

"I wonder what Michael would say to all of this," he

whispers as quietly as possible as he taps his head. Shit, he wants me to tell Michael what's happening.

"Mikey?" I call nervously down through the bond.

"Baby? Are you okay? What's the matter?" I can tell by his voice he has picked up on my anxiety. Shit, is that a good thing or not?

"The principal is acting like you're some kind of sexual predator. I don't like it, and neither does Steph or Tony."

"Fuck, I'm coming." I look at Tony and nod before turning to the principal as the connection goes quiet.

"Michael hasn't lied to me about how he feels," I state, trying to keep the anxiousness out of my voice.

"Do you believe an adult could care for a child, Miss Andrews?" the principal asks, with her brow raised.

"I'm twenty-three; in what world does that make me a child? There is only a five-year age difference between us. Michael is not a predator or a threat to me. He would never hurt me," I declare, trying to get her to see sense.

"But he is hurting you by lying to you," the principal says; I stand up and shake my head.

"He's not lying to me," I answer as I step away from my chair and towards the door. I can feel a panic attack taking over, and this would be the worse time to have one.

"Miss Andrews, please sit down. This is a safe place. We're trying to get you to see that this relationship is wrong," the principal says firmly as she stands up and leans on the desk. "Mr. Adams has abused his position and made you the victim of his lies," she says as her voice becomes raised; Tony is watching me with a concerned look on his face. I glance at Steph and realise she knows I'm close to a full panic attack as the walls start to close around me.

"Stop calling me a victim," I whisper, hearing the anxiety in my voice.

"That is what you are, Miss Andrews, you were a victim in your previous relationship, and you are a victim now," the principal snaps.

"I am not a victim!" I shout as my chest tightens, and I can't breathe. The walls close in completely; there's no air in the room. Why is there no air? My sight becomes blurred around the edges, and I feel my legs go from underneath me as I gasp for breath.

"Daisy!" I hear Tony shout as he rushes to me. Tony wraps me in his arms and holds me as I grab hold of his top; Steph drops to her knees beside me.

"Mike.." I gasp, begging them to get him in here. I need him here now. The panic has taken over, and all I want is Michael.

"Get Michael," Tony growls, looking behind him.

"Mr. Adams will not come into this room; this is his fault." I hear the principal declare; I glance at Steph, kneeling beside me and grab her hand.

"Get Michael in here now!" Tony and Steph scream together. The door flies open behind me, and I feel Michael charging in, quickly followed by Jon's scent.

Michael's beside me in a heartbeat.

"It's okay, darling. I've got you. Just breathe," Michael says gently to me as I grab hold of his shirt; my throat is raw and dry, my whole body shaking. Michael pulls me against him, and his scent flows through me, along with the love and support I feel through the bond.

"Mr. Adams, you are not included in this meeting," the principal shouts. The more she shouts, the harder I shake. Michael picks up on it instantly.

"Somebody shut her up," he growls, not taking his eyes off mine.

"Get back there and give my clients some space," Jon snaps; I see a glimmer of a smile on Michael's face that helps me take the tiniest breath.

"Darling, look into my eyes; nowhere else, I have you. I'm right here." Michael whispers as he runs a hand over my head; I lift my shaking hand, which he takes and places over his heart.

"Count them." He whispers, knowing what I need like he always does. I close my eyes and try to distance myself from everything else in this room. I start counting aloud through the bond, focusing purely on Michael's touch and counting his heartbeats.

"Michael Adams, I demand that you leave," the principal shouts behind him, but I focus on Michael as my breathing starts to calm, and the walls start to move back as the shaking eases.

"Principal Jones, I think you need to open your goddamn eyes and see that Michael is helping her!" Steph snaps. A slight smirk appears on Michael's face as I open my eyes and offer him a small smile in return.

"That's my girl," Michael whispers as he leans over and kisses the top of my head. I take one last deep breath and look into Michael's eyes.

"I'm okay," I whisper. Michael uses his thumb to wipe away the tears on my cheek.

"Are you sure?" Michael asks. I nod as I look up at him.

"I'm sure."

"Right, now Miss Andrews is fine; you can leave." Principal Jones snaps; I see Michael's eyes darken as his wolf comes to the surface. He stands up and looks at Tony.

"Stay with her," he whispers, his jaw clenched. Tony nods and sits beside me; even he can see how pissed off Michael is.

Michael turns around to face the principal as Jon steps beside him. Both of them have their hands clenched at their side.

"I was told Daisy was being called in for a meeting. This isn't a meeting. It's a witch hunt. How dare you upset her to the point she has a full panic attack. I want to know what you said to her to make her so upset," Michael demands as he stands to his full height in front of me, protecting me as he always does.

"I will not allow you to continue making a victim of this young girl; you will leave this instant," The principal shouts.

"Daisy is not a victim; she is a survivor and a fighter. To call her anything else is an insult to her and the traumatic events she has *survived*. As for her being a young girl, I think you need to check your records; Daisy Andrews is twenty-three years old and an adult capable of making her own decisions. If you were to ask your staff or anyone who actually knows her, you would learn that no one, myself included, can control her. Daisy knows her own mind; she can and does make her own decisions," Michael snaps.

"Mr. Adams, I suggest you watch your tone and leave now," Principal Jones declares.

"No!" I shout as I stand up; Michael rushes to my side to help me. I take his hand but shake my head when he tries to put an arm around me; I want to stand tall on my own.

"No?" the principal asks, frowning at me.

"No, Michael won't leave. You said I could have an adult present, as apparently, I'm not one. Well, I choose Michael and his council to be here," I declare.

"I strongly advise against this, Daisy," the principal warns.

"I strongly advise that you let my clients speak," Jon snaps from the other side of me. I have to stop myself from glancing over and smiling at him. He's gone into big brother mode, and he is not happy.

"Very well. Daisy, please tell me what Mr. Adams has promised you will get from this fling," the principal asks as she crosses her arms over her chest. I feel Michael's grip tighten on my hand as his temper rises.

"Michael hasn't promised me anything other than to love and support me in our *relationship.* Michael has never abused his position or tried to make my studies easier for me; if anything, they are harder as he doesn't help me at all. Even when I'm stuck, I speak to Steph or Martin, and if I can't ask them, I go to the library," I point out.

"And what would your family say if they were aware of this *relationship*? Do you think they would approve?" the principal asks, raising her eyebrows at me. Tony and I both laugh as I hold out my hand to Michael.

"Can I have your phone, please, Mikey?" Michael looks at me, smiling.

"Of course." He places it in my hand, and I quickly pull up a number.

"Hello?"

"Hey, Uncle Nigel, what would you say if I said I was dating my lecturer, Michael Adams?" I hear my uncle laugh down the line.

"I would say what I've said to him repeatedly, which is usually along the lines of good luck; you will need it, as well as no returns or refunds."

"Thanks for that," I reply sarcastically as my uncle chuckles. "By the way, you're on speakerphone, and I'm in the meeting with my department head and university principal, being asked how Michael has manipulated me and groomed me," I explain as my uncle burst out laughing.

"They do realise you make that man's life hell, don't they? If anything, it's the other way round; he can't do enough for you. If I'm on speakerphone, I would like to point out that I have brought Daisy up since she was about six years old and love her as my own daughter. Her Auntie Mary and I could not be happier that Daisy and Michael have found each other. Given Daisy's past, we're glad she has someone who understands and looks after her like Michael. Their relationship has our full support, and anyone who sees them together will wholeheartedly agree that Michael Adams loves Daisy with all his heart and soul. We are honoured to have him join our family."

"Bravo, well said," Tony calls as he starts clapping; I hear my uncle chuckle down the phone.

"Should've known you'd be close by, Tony," he calls as the principal glares at Tony.

"Thank you, Nigel, that means a lot," Michael adds, smiling at the phone.

"I've told you before that you deserve a medal if you can deal with Daisy and her mood swings; you're a braver man than me."

"Hey! I'm a freaking saint!" I protest as I hear my uncle, Michael, Jon and Tony all laugh before continuing.

"Now I've said my piece. Do you need to hear from her Auntie as well?" The principal looks at the phone before clearing her throat.

"I think we have heard all we need to thank you, Mr. ...."

"Evans," my uncle replies.

"Mr. Evans. Thank you for your contribution." The principal says through gritted teeth.

"Well, if you need me to say anything else about Daisy and Michael's relationship, please don't hesitate to call. Daisy, please call your auntie later. She will want to know what's going on."

"Will do, Uncle Nigel. Thank you," I reply, smiling.

"Any time, Daisy. Speak to you both later." Uncle Nigel calls as I hang up the phone and look at the principal as she walks back behind the desk.

"That's what my family would say of our relationship. I know if I call my godparents, they will also show the same level of support."

"As would my family," Michael says next to me as he places a hand on my lower back.

"I know our relationship doesn't fit your ideal little world here. As you know, I've requested to transfer to another department on more than one occasion. I've even tried to leave, but you refused my resignation. The only reason I didn't come clean was that I was worried for Daisy as her ex was sniffing around, and if you had banned me from campus, I couldn't protect her," Michael admits honestly.

"And now we know the truth. What would you say if we gave you the ultimatum of your position here or Miss Andrews?" the principal asks, looking sure of herself.

"I would choose Daisy every single time. Nothing will ever come between us, not this job, not her ex, nothing," Michael states. "In fact," he adds as he reaches around me; I see Jon hand him a white envelope. Michael winks at me before walking toward the desk and placing the envelope on it.

"Here is my letter of resignation. I'm happy to take a leave of absence until my leaving date. But I do demand that Daisy is allowed to continue her studies and that there's no fallout because of our relationship," Michael states, not taking his eyes off the principal. If she were a male, I know he would have punched him by now. Fuck, I'm still considering it.

"So you admit that this relationship is wrong, and you have abused your position?" the principal states as she clutches at straws. Michael frowns at her.

"I'm not admitting that at all. Our relationship is not

wrong, nor have I abused my position. Please tell me, Principal, how did you meet your husband?" Michael turns and looks at Martin. "Martin, you told me you and your wife met in college and have been together ever since. The only difference between your story and ours is that I'm a lecturer, and Daisy's my student. If we were both lecturers, you wouldn't feel it necessary to hold this meeting," Michael points out. "And I certainly don't understand where the idea that I am some kind of sexual predator has come from, as it is so far from the truth it's laughable," He adds, shaking his head.

"Principal, I think you can see that Michael and Daisy are serious about this relationship, like I said. Daisy hasn't been victimised or coerced in any way. She's happy; they both are. I think enough has been said on the subject," Steph says as she steps forward from behind me, giving me a supportive smile as she does.

"I believe we have as much information as we're going to gather today," the principal says as she places her hands on her desk before continuing. "Is it worth me saying that you two are not to see or speak to each other until we decide whether to accept Michael's resignation?" I look at Michael, smirking.

"You don't have a choice whether you accept my resignation. I quit." Michael states as he smiles at me.

"It may be impossible not to see or speak to each other either, sorry," I reply.

"Are you really saying you can't go twenty-four hours without seeing each other?" she sighs as she drinks from the glass of water on the desk.

"Yes, as we live together," I state. Tony laughs as the principal chokes on the water.

"Steph, take Daisy and Tony to class. We'll continue to discuss this with Michael now. I suggest you keep this from your classmates until a decision has been made," Martin pipes in from his chair. He's been so quiet I had almost forgotten he was there.

"That might not be possible," Tony says from where he's standing; we all turn and look at him. He holds up his phone. "It seems there's a rumour in the class that Daisy and Michael are in a relationship."

"Tony, I swear if you...." Michael growls as he faces my best friend, who throws his hands up in defence.

"It wasn't me. It's the same people gossiping to anyone who will listen." I turn to Michael, who sighs and shakes his head before running his fingers through his hair.

"Daisy, stay out of class for now. Michael, Martin and I will discuss Michael's options, and then Michael will address the rumours. Steph, act as if you know nothing," the principal says as she rubs her eyes and sits down in her chair.

Michael turns to me and takes my hands.

"Everything will be fine. I'll let you know what's happening. Just be careful and don't go to class until I say." I nod as Michael pulls me against him and holds me in his arms. I feel him plant a kiss on my head before stepping back.

"Marcus is in the carpark; get him to take you off campus," he whispers. I nod before grabbing Tony's hand and leaving the room.

"Come on, Marcus is waiting for me; you coming for a drive?" I ask as I pull him down the corridor.

"Might as well; where are we going?" Tony asks as I pull out my phone.

"Come with me, and all will be revealed," I reply, winking as we rush off to the car park.

Chapter Seventy-Six

Michael

I watch Daisy walk out the door and listen until her footsteps vanish before I turn around and face the principal.

"Okay, you've had your say. Now it is my turn." I stand tall with my hands fisted to the side of me, Jon to my left.

"How dare you upset Daisy like that? It was not only unprofessional, but it was downright bullying. She's done nothing wrong here; she just fell in love with her lecturer, who loves her too. Bullying her into saying she's a victim is wrong on many levels," I growl.

"I would watch your tone, Mr. Adams." the principal starts, but I walk to the table and slam my hands down on it.

"No, you will watch yours! Do you know how to handle a person who has been through a traumatic event like Daisy? I'll take how you handled her this morning as a no. You *never* call a survivor a victim. They are called survivors for a reason, and to call them anything else is downgrading the hell they've been through. I expect you to contact Daisy as soon as possible to issue a formal apology. In future, if you're unsure how to deal with someone who's a survivor respectfully, I suggest contacting the university counsellor and asking them to be present to ensure you don't cause any more damage than you did today," I add.

"Have you quite finished, Mr. Adams?" the principal asks through gritted teeth.

"No, I have not. This meeting was handled poorly and caused unnecessary stress and upset to Daisy. I will not stand by and see that happen again. You have my resignation there on the table; I will not be returning to this university after today. However, If I find out you've continued to treat Daisy or any other student in the way I have just witnessed, I can promise you that I'll be back as a legal representative. I will drag you through the courts so fast that you won't know what hit you, is that understood?" I demand as I glare at the principal.

"I think you've made your feelings abundantly clear. Now would you like to sit down, and we will discuss you leaving."

))●((

An hour later, I walk out of the principal's office and head straight to my own. As soon as we walk in, Jon sits in the chair in front of my desk.

"Well, that could have gone better." Jon sighs as I collapse into my chair, rubbing the bridge of my nose. This whole mess has given me a headache.

"At least they gave me until the end of the day to get my shit sorted and ensure the other staff know what's been covered." I sigh as I lean back into my chair.

"How do you think Daisy's going to take you leaving? I know you had hoped it would happen, but she likes having you close, especially with her anxiety being like it is at the moment," Jon asks.

"She'll be fine. We spoke about it this morning. At least we don't have to hide anymore. After today we can go out in public and not worry about who sees us," I point out, unable to stop the smile from spreading across my face. I've already booked a table in a restaurant for tomorrow night and Friday. Daisy and I have five and a half months of dates to catch up on, and I can't wait to take her wherever she wants to go.

"There is that." Jon chuckles; he looks down at his phone. "Marcus messaged to say he has taken Daisy and Tony off-campus as she was worked up after the meeting," He adds as he types on his phone.

"I knew she would be. I could have killed the principal when I walked into that room; Daisy was in such a state," I reply through gritted teeth. It's been two weeks since Daisy's anxiety has been that severe.

"I don't know how you didn't; I was ready to do it for you," Jon replies, shaking his head.

"It's been a shit few days. I'm looking forward to a drink tonight with dinner." I sigh as I pick up my phone and look at the time. Daisy's second class will be starting with Steph at any moment. Maybe it'll be best to address everything whilst Daisy isn't here. I say as much to Jon, who agrees.

Jon and I part ways outside the building before I head off to Daisy's class. I notice more heads turn my way than usual this morning. Gods, the rumours about Daisy and me have travelled fast. Not that it surprises me; rumours always spread quickly in universities.

I approach the classroom door and take a deep breath before knocking. I stick my head in and see Steph standing in the front of the class; all the students turn and stare at me.

"Is this a good time to chat with everyone?" I ask; Steph nods and smiles at me softly. I walk into the class and close the door before heading to the front of the room.

Everyone's whispering amongst themselves. Thanks to my wolf hearing, I can hear every word.

"I bet he's going to come clean about him and Daisy."

"No, I bet he's going to tell everyone off for spreading lies."

"Why is he here now?"

"Where are Daisy and Tony?"

I look over at Steph and smile at her.

"How long?" she asks.

"Until the end of the day. But I'm relieved, no more hiding; that's why I'm here now," I whisper back.

"How's Daisy?" Steph asks, looking concerned.

"I had a mutual friend take her off-campus; she was upset, to say the least." I sigh, rubbing the back of my neck.

"I wish I could have done more to protect her in there. To protect both of you," Steph says, but I place a hand on her arm.

"You did more than enough; neither of us could have lived with ourselves if you had lost your job over us. So, thank you." I take a deep breath and smile at Steph. "Time to face the music."

"Good luck," Steph says as she steps back, and I turn to face the class. I lean against the front of the desk, with my legs stretched out in front of me and my arms crossed over my chest, and I wait for everyone to stop talking and give me their full attention.

"I know you have all heard the rumours circulating

campus," I say once I have nearly everyone's attention.

"I'm well aware that someone has been telling everyone who'll listen that Daisy Andrews and myself are having 'a fling,' as I've heard it referred to, and I wanted to come in front of you all and say, yes, we are in a relationship. Before you all start talking at once, can I ask for you to take it in turns and raise your hand if you have a sensible question."

"How long have you been sleeping together?" Samantha asks from her spot at the back of the class. I open my mouth to correct her when the door flies open and Tony rushes in with Daisy on his tail.

"As if you started the party without us!" he calls as he winks at me and heads over to a spare seat next to Beth.

"It wasn't my fault neither of you could make it to class on time." I chuckle, shaking my head. Daisy looks at me and places her hands on her hips whilst gasping for breath like she's running a marathon.

"Adams, you're not even meant to be here, so shut up." She turns to Steph and smiles at her sweetly. "Sorry we're late; somebody tried to keep me away so he could discuss our relationship without me being present." Daisy turns back to me. "How did that work out for you?" she asks, staring at me with 'the look'.

"Why do I have a feeling I will find out later," I reply, smirking. Daisy walks over to me, turns to face the class and lifts herself onto the desk, so she's sitting on it with her legs crossed; I glance over at her with an arched eyebrow.

"Are you comfortable, darling? Can we continue now?"

Daisy

I throw my hand out, signalling for him to carry on. Michael turns back to Samantha and smiles.

"What did you ask, sorry?"

"How long have you been sleeping together?" Samantha repeats, smirking. I never did like that bitch.

"Sam shut the fuck up; we're in a *committed relationship*; not everyone's a slut like you." I sigh as the whole class bursts out laughing, Michael turns and stares at me, but I just shrug.

"What? We both know it was her who started all this shit," I point out.

"There's a time and a place for name-calling, darling," Michael replies, trying to stop himself from smiling. On the other hand, I have no fucks left to give and shrug as I turn back to face the class again.

"We have been in a relationship for nearly six months," Michael answers next to me.

"Is it true you're going to be moving in together?" Rosie asks; I smile and turn to Michael.

"Can I move in?" I ask, fluttering my eyelashes at him.

"You are loving this, aren't you?!" Michael sighs as my smile gets bigger.

"A little bit." As I turn and face Rosie, I admit, "we've been living together for a while now."

"Is it serious?" someone asks from the back of the room. I look at Michael and smile, as he smiles at me.

"Yes, it is," he answers. I look back, and there are about six hands in the air.

"Will you be leaving now everyone knows?" Beth asks next to Tony, who's grinning at me.

"Yes." Michael and I answer together; Michael turns to me with raised eyebrows.

"I hope you're just answering for me?" He asks, but I shake my head and smile at him before turning to face the class.

"I'll be leaving to work with a friend of ours. We're going to be starting a new charity project together for people escaping abusive relationships. The Michelle Adams Project will have safe houses all over the country and will be able to house males and females and their children who need somewhere safe to hide. Counselling and aftercare will be offered as well as training so the individual can find work and take care of themselves and their families." I look at Michael, staring at me with his mouth hanging open and tears in his eyes.

"They will also be trained in self-defence so that if they ever find themselves in danger again, they know how to defend themselves," I add, not taking my eyes off Michael.

"How have you set this up?" Steph asks behind us as she walks to the front of the class.

"I recently came into some inheritance, and I think the person who left it to me would want me to use it to help others," I explain.

"Why the name?" Ellis asks. I look at Michael and smile.

"Michelle Adams was my twin who was murdered by someone who should have looked after her and protected her," he answered, unable to take his eyes off me. "Why am I only now hearing about this?" he adds.

"Because I wanted to be sure everything would go ahead before I told you." I turn and face the class.

"Our good friend Jayne and I have been playing with the idea for a while, but Jayne gave birth to a beautiful baby girl a little over four weeks ago, and she's been a little preoccupied. When we went to see her and baby Sophie this weekend, I mentioned that I had the funds and properties to start putting our plan together, and she was all up for getting involved. We already have four safe houses scattered around England and Wales, and I just paid the deposit on our fifth. We also have two friends, female and male, who have agreed to help with the self-defence training." I look at Michael before adding, "no family should lose a loved one to the hands of an abuser, whether temporarily or for good. No family should go through what ours has with Michelle and me," I add quietly.

With no warning, Michael grabs my face and kisses me with such force I have to grab the table to stop myself from falling off before throwing my arms around his neck.

"As if it's not bad enough when you're at home, now you're making out in class!" Tony groans. I chuckle as Michael steps back, grinning at me before flipping Tony off behind his back.

"Hey! You can't do that to me here!" Tony protests. Michael turns around and laughs at him.

"What are they going to do, Tony? Fire me? I've already handed in my notice; I leave at the end of the day."

"You don't have to quit if Daisy is leaving," someone calls

from the class, but Michael grins as he turns to face me.

"I do, as I've just been offered a new role myself."

"What?" I ask, jumping down from the desk.

"Yep, another friend of ours has asked me to be their second in command of their organisation."

"Desmond?" I ask aloud. *"You're going to be Beta?"* I add through the bond, staring at Michael, who grins at me as he nods.

"He messaged me just before your meeting. We're going there for tea tonight to finalise the details. It gives me time to quiz Jayne about you two being sneaky."

I squeal and launch myself at him wrapping my arms around his neck. Michael catches me laughing, as he lifts me off my feet.

"I told you everything would work out," Michael whispers.

"Anyone else get the sneaky suspicion he'll be proposing soon?" Ruth laughs from the back of the class. I grin at Michael as I lift my left hand.

"He already did," I declare as the whole class gasps, and the room erupts with laughter and people shouting congratulations. But I don't pay any attention to it. All I can see and hear is my amazing fiancé, my mate.

"No more hiding," I whisper as I stare into his bright blue eyes.

"No more secrets," He replies, grinning before his lips crash into mine again.

Epilogue

Stuart

It's been four weeks since we brought Daisy home. It's been tough on everyone seeing her trying to recover from everything she went through; she has good and bad days, which can only be expected. Clare and her parents have been there every day with her. They've been helping her learn how to control her new powers as they are stronger than anyone expected. The team and I have been doing as much as possible for Michael so he can concentrate on helping Daisy heal.

Every day Clare and I try to spend a little time together. We haven't discussed the bigger picture yet; I've told her I want us to spend time getting to know each other and for her to decide if I'm who she wants to spend the rest of her life with. Because for me, there will never be another; Clare's intelligent, funny, strong and beautiful, she is everything I could ever ask for in a mate, and I know that if she agrees to be mated to me, then I'll happily spend the rest of my life doing whatever makes her happy, whether it be here or in Exeter. Clare has hinted that she wants to move here, but I've told her not to rush into any decisions.

The biggest problem we have is her dad, Alex. He still doesn't like the idea of his little girl growing up or being mated to a wolf. I don't think he would have a problem if it were anyone else. I think his problem is with me in general.

It's Sunday evening, and I've just arrived at Daisy and Michaels to pick Clare up as she wants to have dinner in town. As soon as I walk through the front door, Michael's there.

"Hey, Stu, can you come into the dining room for a second," he asks; I follow him and notice Alex sitting at the table. Shit.

"Don't panic. He won't kill you," Michael says, smiling at me as he points towards a chair as he takes his usual seat at the head of the table.

"What's going on?" I ask as I look from Michael to Alex.

"I'm taking Clare home tomorrow," Alex says bluntly. I feel my breath catch in my throat, I knew they were going to be heading back soon, but I'm not ready for her to go yet. But I also know there's nothing I can do about it.

"Okay," I manage to croak; I turn to Michael, hoping he'll have some words of advice here as I want to tell Alex no, he can't take her, but I also know he's looking for any reason to prevent us from mating. "When will I be able to see Clare next?" I ask, dreading the answer.

"I want you to stay away for two weeks. If she wants to see you after that time, you can visit for a weekend." Alex says as he leans on the table. "I wanted it to be four, but Michael has argued in your favour," he adds, not even trying to hide his distaste for me.

"You're hoping she'll decide she doesn't want me," I reply.

"I'm not going to lie, yes. I think she's too young to be mated or settled down for life," Alex says.

"And if she does want me?" I ask, trying to stay calm.

"Then you still have a long way to go to prove to me you are right for my daughter. I won't just let you take her away from me and her coven."

"I would never take her away. My brother moved away to be with his mate, and I would do the same for Clare," I answer, not taking my eyes off her father. Refusing to let him think he intimidates me, even though I know the fate of mine, and Clare's future rests in his hands.

"But would you, Stuart? Would you leave the team and your pack brothers in the lurch like that?" Alex asks with an arched brow.

"With all due respect, no matter what I answer, you will take it as I'm unworthy of your daughter. Would I leave the team and my family for your daughter? Yes, absolutely, I would. Would I ask Clare to move here to be with me? No, her place is with her coven and family. *But* if she wanted to move here to be closer to her best friend, and wanted to start a life here with me, I wouldn't stop her. Clare can make her own decisions and is more clued up than you are giving her credit for," I answer.

"She is still a child," Alex starts.

"Clare is *your* child and always will be. But she isn't one. She's twenty-three; how old were you when Clare was born?" I ask, knowing he was younger than Clare is now.

"That's completely different. Clare's too young to be a mother," Alex snaps.

"I don't think that is what Stuart meant by that," Michael says from his seat.

"Hell no, I'm too young to be a father. Kids are a long way away; I'm just trying to prove that Clare is an adult and can make her own decisions," I add quickly.

"As I explained to you, Alex, Daisy was only twenty-three when we mated; yes, she's a little more mature than Clare, but that's because she had to be. Daisy was forced to grow up quickly when Jackson turned her. But forcing Clare and Stuart to be apart will only hurt them. Even though they are not mated yet, Clare may feel the discomfort of the distance; I know Stuart will," Michael says from his seat as he looks at Alex.

"My pain doesn't bother me, but if it hurts Clare for us to be apart, I can't just ignore it," I say, looking at Alex. "To be clear, I have no intention of Clare EVER becoming a wolf. I'm not that arsehole, Jackson; I don't care if she's a wolf or not. Clare matters to me, not her species," I say as I look at Alex, who visibly relaxes a little.

I'm just about to say more when the door flies open, and Clare storms into the room.

"Did you even plan on telling me that we are leaving tomorrow? Or was the plan to drag me away?" she shouts at her dad, who raises an eyebrow at her.

"I was going to tell you later," he states.

"What if I don't want to go?" She asks as she stands next to my chair. I stand up, place a finger under her chin, and turn her head, so she's looking at me.

"We discussed this. We both agreed that you would go home with your parents, and we would see each other at weekends for the time being." I cup her cheek and smile at her, "You can still call me or text me whenever you want."

"So, you will come and see me next weekend?" Clare asks. I can see the hope in her eyes, and I hate that I will disappoint her immediately.

"Not next weekend, baby girl. Your dad wants us to spend two weeks apart first. If you want me to come and see you after that, I'll be there in a flash; nothing will stop me. I'm sure Michael will give me the time off."

"Stu will have every other weekend off duty, Clare. On the weekends, he is on duty; you're welcome to come and stay here and see him during his quiet times," Michael says, smiling. "I'm sure you and Daisy can find ways to keep yourselves and the regulars in the bar entertained," he adds with a chuckle.

"What if I want to stay here with you?" she asks as a tear slides down her cheek. I swipe the tear away with my thumb and smile at her.

"That's a conversation you, me and your parents will have at a later date. We don't need to decide where we will live or what we will do. We have the rest of our lives for all that," I whisper as Clare starts to cry. I pull her into my arms and feel her crying into my chest. It's so hard to keep my cool with her dad when he is the one causing her so much pain.

"Two weeks will fly by, baby. Anyway, next weekend you have your friend's birthday. You've been planning it for ages," I point out in an attempt to lighten her mood.

"Plus, Stuart's busy next weekend as the team are all going out to celebrate us both finding our mates. It's our first chance since Daisy and I got together," Michael says as he winks at me. I pull back slightly and look down into Clare's tear-filled blue eyes.

"See, and if you want me to come down the Friday after, I'll be there in a heartbeat."

"Promise?" Clare asks; I lean down and gently kiss her lips.

"I promise."

"Okay, can we go now?" Clare asks. I smile down at her and nod.

"Of course, get your bag, and I'll meet you by the car," I reply, kissing her again. I love how her face lights up as she rushes out of the room. As soon as she is out of sight, I turn to her dad and lean on the table before addressing him.

"I will play by your rules; I'll stay away for two weeks. But if it's too much for Clare, and she is in any pain, I won't stand by and watch her suffer to prove a point to you." I stand up and walk out of the room before Alex has a chance to respond.

)) ● ((

A few hours later, Clare and I walk through the forest where Daisy and Michael sometimes run. It's nine o'clock, and I know we'll need to head back soon.

"I don't want to go back tomorrow. Can't I stay here with you?" Clare sighs. I stop walking and get her to sit on an overturned tree before squatting in front of her.

"I wish you could stay too, but we have to do things your dad's way for a while. But I won't let him keep us apart for long. I will move up there if he plays games or if this causes you any pain," I say as I place a hand on her cheek. "Anyway, you may go home and realise you don't want to be with me," I joke, smiling. Clare looks at me, frowning.

"Or you may find some hot wolf to be with instead." She sighs, smiling playfully. I look at her, smirking.

"Nah, I'm more into witches these days," I reply before kissing her cheek.

"I'm glad to hear it. Because this witch is really into you." Clare replies with a smile as she wraps her arms around my neck before kissing me softly pulling away.

"Will we be okay?" She asks as her eyes meet mine. I smile at her and nod. I remove her arms from around my neck and take hold of her hands.

"We will be everything you want us to be. Whatever you decide whether you want to be mated to me or not, I will always be here for you," I whisper as I kiss her hand.

"Two weeks apart isn't going to stop me from wanting to be with you," Clare whispers, smiling.

"Good, because it certainly won't make me want you any less," I reply. "I think I'll want you even more," I add with a grin as I lean in to kiss her again.

Suddenly I'm hit from the side and sent flying across the

grass. I hear Clare scream as I roll over to find a giant brown wolf grinning at me. I look to see Clare with an orb in her hand, about to throw it.

"It's Michael!" I shout, holding my hand up to stop her before the sound of laughter fills the air.

"Mikey, I warned you she would blast your ass." Daisy laughs as she walks out of the trees.

"Daisy, you're naked!" Clare shouts as she covers her eyes causing Daisy to laugh harder.

"You'll need to get used to it, Clare Bear. All modesty goes out the window if you move to pack territory." Daisy calls, winking at me as Michael walks back over to her, as she places a hand on his head. "You however, Adams, can stay in wolf form. You don't want to make Stuart look inferior before they do the deed." Daisy smiles whilst looking down at Michael, who nudges her playfully.

"You scared the crap out of me, Michael!" Clare shouts as I walk over to her and put an arm around her shoulders, laughing.

"Who else was it going to be? We don't have wolves in the UK, Clare. Plus, rogues wouldn't dare come this far into pack territory." Daisy giggles as she climbs a tree and pulls out a bag hidden in the branches. Daisy stops in her tracks and turns to look at Clare.

"Hang on, haven't you seen Stu in wolf form yet?" she asks; Clare shakes her head. I look at Daisy and shrug casually.

"Been too busy doing human stuff, plus Alex hid her away when it was the full moon in case I got any stupid ideas of changing her," I answer, grinning. Daisy shakes her head as she jumps down from the tree.

"Well, that needs to be rectified. Strip Stu!" she calls as she grins at Clare. I turn and look at Clare, who's grinning at me.

"You heard the girl, strip," she says, wiggling her eyebrows at me.

"Baby girl, if you wanted me naked, all you had to do was ask," I reply with a wink as I grab the bottom of my top and pull it off, not taking my eyes off Clare, who is looking a little flushed as she takes in my washboard abs. I instantly pick up on the change in her scent and grin at her as I wrap an arm around her waist and tug her to me so her body is pressed tightly against mine. I lower my head so my lips brush against her ear.

"Judging by your scent, I would say you like what you see," I whisper as Clare giggles in my ear as I kiss her neck.

"Stu, stop teasing the poor girl," Daisy calls out; I step away from Clare, chuckling as I quickly pull down my shorts and boxers.

"I see why you said once you go wolf, you don't go back, Dais," Clare calls as she looks me up and down whilst biting her bottom lip. I quickly wink at her and drop to the floor, landing in my blonde wolf.

"You were loving that, you fucking tease." Michael laughs through the pack link. I quickly turn and throw myself at him taking him down. Michael and I are soon wrestling each other playfully. I look up to find Clare watching us whilst sitting on the fallen tree next to a now fully dressed Daisy, both laughing.

"It's an amazing feeling, isn't it," Michael asks next to me. I turn and nod at him. *"Are you going to be okay when she goes back?"* he asks.

"No. But what choice do I have." I reply honestly.

"I will help you as much as I can, Stu, but you have to prove your worth to Alex yourself," Michael explains as we walk back over to our mates.

"I will do whatever it takes to keep her in my life," I reply as I rest my head on Clare's lap, she instantly runs her hand over my head and threads her fingers through my fur. I look up at her and know at that moment I will fight through heaven and hell and sacrifice *anything* for a lifetime with her by my side.

THANK YOU SO MUCH FOR READING!

FOR MORE ADVENTURES WITH THE BLOOD MOON GANG, PLEASE FOLLOW MY PAGES ON SOCIAL MEDIA FOR FUTURE RELEASE DATES, GIVE AWAYS AND EXTRA CONTENT.

@debartleywriter

CAN BE FOUND ON,

FACEBOOK

INSTAGRAM

TIK TOK

Playlist

Jealous – Labrinth

You Are The Reason – Calum Scott

Trying Not To Love You – Nickelback

Unstoppable – Sia

Fight Song – Rachel Platten

Here Without You – 3 Doors Down

Call Me Fighter – Matt Beilis

Amen – John Adams

Born Ready – Zayde Wolf

Dusk Till Dawn – Zayn

I'm Not Okay – Citizen Soldier

THE PLAYLIST CAN BE FOUND ON SPOTIFY

Acknowledgements.

I don't even know where to begin with the acknowledgements, but I will give it a try.

Rogue exceeded all my expectations, as I never dreamt it would be as popular as it was and still is. So thank you to every person who picked up my book and read it and hopefully enjoyed it enough to read **Her Protector**.

Daisy and Michael's story has a very special place in my heart as I have spent years playing with it. I started it before my eldest was even born; he is sixteen this year! Knowing so many people enjoyed it as well makes my heart burst. So thank you.

I couldn't have written any of my books without the constant support and encouragement from my fantastic husband and children. They never moan when I sit at the computer to work, well, to me anyway, lol. So to them, thank you will never seem like enough.

To all my friends and family who have had me sign their copies of my books or shown so much love and encouragement, thank you so much; I love you all.

I can't miss my fantastic work friends who constantly remind me that I should be home writing and not working nights, you are all amazing, and I love you all, even my bald-headed "Tony" George, well, I tolerate you ;).

Thanks to my fantastic friend, beta and proof-reader, Karen. Your continuous support and encouragement has gotten me through some tough days when I doubted my ability to put words to paper. Thank you will never be enough for what you do for me. But thank you, thank you, thank you!

All that's left for me to say is I hope you enjoy

Her Protector as much as I have writing it and continue to follow Michael, Daisy and the gang's stories in the books to follow.

Thank you all; I love you xx

ABOUT THE AUTHOR

D. E. Bartley lives in Wales, UK, with her husband, three feral boys, guinea pig and a budgie. To say her home is a madhouse would be an understatement, but she wouldn't have it any other way.

When Bartley isn't working nights, running around after her tribe or driving her husband up the wall, she can be found reading and hoarding books like a magpie hoards shiny things. Other than her writing, her biggest dream is to achieve her black belt in Tae Kwon Do. She might get her ass handed to her by twelve-year-old's regularly, but at least she is trying, and not just her instructor's patience.

Nothing is as important to Bartley as time with her family, and she loves her trips home to Cornwall with them more than anything else in the world. What could possibly compare to sitting on a Cornish beach, with a glass of Cornish gin in one hand and an authentic Cornish pasty in the other, whilst the monsters, I mean children, play and bodyboard in the sea. Absolutely nothing.

Printed in Great Britain
by Amazon